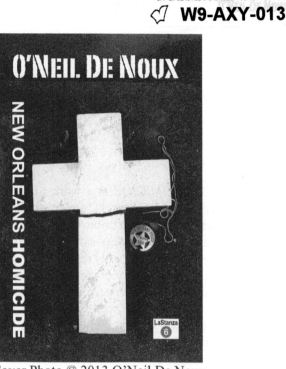

Cover Photo © 2013 O'Neil De Noux

NEW ORLEANS HOMICIDE

O'NEIL DE NOUX

For Bob Garner
sometimes a hero lives up to it

Author Web Site: http://www.oneildenoux.net
Twitter: ONeilDeNoux

BIG Kiss

Published by
Big Kiss Productions
New Orleans

First Printing 2013

THIS IS NEW ORLEANS
1986

Monday, April 21, 1986

8:01 a.m. – The Rigolets

"I think we have to talk, ma'am."

"Looks like a bullet hole to me." LaStanza pointed to the neat, round hole in the back of the skull, partially buried in the ditch. "But what the fuck do I know? I'm just a detective."

Homicide Detective Dino LaStanza: five feet – six inches tall, weighing one forty-five with thick, dark brown hair and a full moustache, stood and stretched. Shading his eyes, hand over brow, he watched a crime lab technician named Perkins gently remove the skull from its shallow grave in the wide, dry ditch next to Highway 90. Slipping extra-dark, mirrored sunglasses – gangster glasses, over his eyes, LaStanza still had to squint in the brilliant New Orleans spring sunshine.

"Jesus, it's fuckin' hot," the crime lab tech said, wiping his brow with his wrist. His light blue NOPD uniform shirt was streaked with perspiration. Sam Perkins: six feet even, weighing two-twenty, balding, laid the skull atop a brown paper bag on the hood of his crime lab SUV and went back to fetch the rest of the bones. He'd already photographed the scene, triangulated measurements from the burial site to the two telephone poles alongside Highway 90 and one across the road.

LaStanza turned to his partner and nodded. "Jacket."

Jodie Kintyre handed him her portable radio, better known as an LFR or *little fuckin' radio,* and took off her beige jacket. LaStanza exchanged radio for jacket and took off his navy blue suit coat as he moved back to their gray, unmarked Ford parked ten feet beyond the last police car lining the road.

Turning back to Jodie, he watched her shift her weight from one leg to the other, as she stood on the blacktop next to the ditch,

3

in the heat without a hint of perspiration on her powder blue blouse. Jodie Kintyre: five-seven, one hundred ten pounds, yellow blonde hair freshly cut into her usual page boy, tapped her sunglasses down and gleeked LaStanza, peering over the top of her glasses with those cat-like, hazel eyes.

"Don't look now, but Country-Ass just pulled up." She rolled her eyes.

LaStanza tapped his glasses down and focused his light green Sicilian eyes on his partner's face.

"You never sweat." He shook his head. She was twenty-seven but looked twenty-one most days, even after working eighteen hours. LaStanza was feeling his thirty-five years that morning, even after a good night's sleep.

"Don't fuckin' tell me," announced a deep voice, dragging out each syllable with a country twang. "Y'all got *bones*."

Paul Snowood: six feet tall, two hundred ten pounds, thirty-eight years old with thinning brown hair, wore a yellow cowboy shirt with gold fringe, double row of gold buttons down the front, dark brown jeans, snakeskin cowboy boots, a ten-gallon white Stetson on his head and gangster sunglasses identical to LaStanza's. Stepping around the crime lab SUV, Snowood glanced at the skull and pointed to LaStanza. "You up, ain't ya'?"

LaStanza nodded, acknowledging this was his case.

Snowood pulled off his Stetson and started dancing in place and singing, "Dere goes yoar perfect record. Dere goes yoar perfect record. The Wop ain't perfect no more!"

LaStanza looked around, in case anyone had come out of the two camps nearby, both wooden structures elevated on creosote pilings. The cops were still alone. The crime scene, along the narrow strip of land between Lake Pontchartrain and Lake St. Catherine, was about a mile from the old Civil War fortress, Fort Pike, along blacktopped Highway 90, a marshy area with the occasional cypress tree. The area smelled of decaying wood and stale water.

Leaning his hand on his partner's shoulder, LaStanza started chuckling as Snowood waved his hat around.

"Notice anything different about him?"

Jodie shook her head.

"He's got a fuckin' six gun, now."

Sure enough, Detective Paul Snowood sported a nickel-plated six shooter in a cowboy rig on his right side, hanging low as if he were a gunslinger.

"What happened to your Glock?" Jodie called out. She wore her Beretta .9mm in a shoulder rig, extra clip on the other side to balance the rig.

Snowood stopped dancing and turned his right hip toward them. "This here's a genuine replica Colt forty-five, 1872 model, with ivory grips. Since we got the OK to up the caliber of our firepower, I figured I'll go all out."

"Look at this," Perkins called out.

LaStanza stepped over as Perkins gently rolled the skull and there in the dirt packed inside the skull, partially protruding from the right eye socket was the brass jacketing of a medium-caliber bullet.

"Looks in pretty good shape."

"Good," LaStanza agreed, able to see the lands and grooves on the bullet necessary to identify the weapon, if they ever found it.

"How long you think this has been in the ground?"

"Couple years at the most," Perkins said. "But what the fuck do I know? I'm just a lab tech." He laughed as LaStanza nodded the return of his smart-assed remark.

"I think I got an entire skeleton here." Perkins waved to the paper bags he'd stacked next to the ditch. He grabbed his camera and took more pictures. "I'll use the metal detector. Make sure we got no more bullets around here."

LaStanza readjusted the new canvas holster riding on his right hip with his stainless-steel Smith and Wesson .357 magnum tucked inside. It was actually lighter than his old leather holster. On his left side, he carried another canvas pouch with two speed-loaders filled with semi-jacketed hollow point ammunition, 125 grain magnums. Handcuffs, as usual, were tucked into his suit pants, at the small of his back, one of the cuffs dangling outside.

Snowood hovered over the skull and said, "We gotta call this case *Dem Bones*. The Wop was beaten by *Dem Bones*. You ain't ever gonna solve this one."

LaStanza slipped his LFR into his back pocket and pointed to the nearest camp, telling his partner he'd take that one. She started moving automatically to the other as the excess police cars drove away. Walking up the long, oyster-shell drive, LaStanza examined the camp as he neared it. The unpainted wooden structure looked silver, bleached by the strong sun and salt air. He had to maneuver around half-broken steps up to the gallery, surrounding the place, which smelled of tar. The pilings supporting camps outside the hurricane protection levee system were coated with creosote that never dried.

"This a fishing camp or does someone actually live here?" Snowood had followed, waiting at the bottom of the steps with his Stetson nice and low on his head. He stood with his legs spread, in case a straggler from the James-Younger Gang was inside the camp.

LaStanza stepped over a black extension cord draped a foot from the front door. He saw it led up over the roof. He knocked on the rickety door and it rattled. He spotted two more extension cords jerry-rigged on the front porch, each disappearing into windows that were shut tight.

"The air-conditioner over here's running." LaStanza followed Snowood's voice and found the cowpoke alongside the camp pointing up at a small window AC unit that hummed.

LaStanza went back and knocked on the door again, standing to the side in usual precaution, his voice rising. "Police! Open the door."

He heard a sound behind the door and the lock click and a withered face peeked out at him. What hair remained on her head was white and fell loosely around her narrow face.

LaStanza pointed to his gold detective's star-and-crescent badge, clipped to the front left side of his belt. "I'm Detective LaStanza, ma'am. New Orleans Police. What's your name?"

Her eyes became wide as she dropped her hand from the door and it opened slowly as if drawn by gravity. LaStanza realized he was standing at a tilt, his legs spread slightly.

"Are you alone, ma'am?"

The old woman nodded, took in a breath and said, "My name is Hilda Johnson and I'm a widow-woman with no kin. I live off my social security." Her hazel eyes became narrow and she looked as if she was about to cry.

"Sorry to bother you ma'am but we found something in the ditch out front of your house." LaStanza stepped aside and pointed to the crime lab SUV.

Hilda Johnson craned her neck forward but didn't move. She was a tiny woman, not quite five-feet, nowhere near a hundred pounds. She wore a long dark blue dress with a high collar.

LaStanza watched her carefully as he said, "We found a body in the ditch, ma'am. A human body."

Her knees buckled and he reached for her, but she backed away and didn't fall. She held on to the door frame.

"You all right?"

"Yes." Hilda looked down at her shoes, black high-top Keds tennis shoes. They looked comfortable, at least. A fresh wave of creosote stink wafted up on a gust of hot air.

Hilda stepped aside and opened the door wider. She slowly walked to a carved wooden rocking chair and sat. The house was surprisingly clean inside and neat to the point of surreal, out here among the camps. There was beige sofa-set, end table, nice lamps, overheard ceiling fans. The small air conditioner had the room a lot cooler. LaStanza closed the door and stood next to it, notebook in hand now.

She'd called herself a widow-woman.

"How long ago did your husband die ma'am?"

"A year ago." Hilda stared at the wood floor. The heavy wax on it gave it a slight sheen. "I buried him in Greenwood Cemetery on Canal Street. You want to see his death certificate?"

"Sure." *Why not,* LaStanza thought. *Make sure it isn't the old guy out in the ditch.*

Hilda moved into a back room and returned momentarily with a gray metal box. She pulled out a Louisiana death certificate and handed it to LaStanza without looking up.

Joel Barlow Johnson died of cardiac arrest a little over a year earlier. The manner of death was listed as natural.

Unlike the body in the ditch – LaStanza thought.

"He died in his sleep at Charity Hospital," Hilda said, looking at a side window now. "Died peacefully."

"Unlike the body in the ditch," LaStanza said and watched the old woman wring her hands as she stared at the window.

"There's a cowboy lookin' in at me." Hilda's voice quivered.

Snowood had his face just outside the window, eyes wide as he stared in at them.

"It's OK. He's with me."

Hilda looked at the floor next to LaStanza's shoes. "Y'all have cowboy police?"

"He just thinks he's a cowboy." He waited for her to look up and when she did, her gaze rising as far as his chest, he asked, "Do you know anything about that body in the ditch, ma'am?"

"No, sir." Hilda sat up straighter and stuck her chin out.

Several unproductive question later, LaStanza left a card on the small table next to the front door. Snowood was already back by the crime lab SUV, along with Jodie. As LaStanza arrived, Perkins slipped a human femur into a large brown paper bag.

"I think I got all the bones," Perkins said. Atop the hood of the SUV were more paper bags, all stacked in a neat line, a separate bone in each.

"Who found Dem Bones?" Snowood asked.

LaStanza – "Ditch man."

"What ditch man?"

Jodie – "We interviewed him and he left like you should."

"Whaddya mean, ditch man?"

LaStanza thought – *for someone who's not interested, he sure is interested.* Pointing to the little red flags in line next to the ditch he said, "He's a spotter for the electric company. New poles coming."

Snowood took off his Stetson again and fanned his face. "Must have been a shallow grave."

"Why don't you just get lost?" Jodie said, stepping around to LaStanza and pointing to the other camp. "No body there."

"It's a trick," said Snowood. "I know. We ain't in the city no more. You gonna weasel out from under this one. You sure we're still in the city?"

LaStanza pointed to the bridge over the narrow waterway separating Lake St. Catherine and Lake Pontchartrain. "That's

Chef Pass and The Rigolets beyond. This is Orleans Parish. Across is St. Tammany. Orleans is ours, you dumb country-assed fuck."

Perkins said, "I'm tired of waiting for the coroner's office. I'm taking the bones to the lab."

"I need that pellet examined right away," LaStanza said.

Perkins nodded as he started stacking the bags into the back of the SUV.

"I'm hungry," announced Snowood. "I got a hankerin' for some sowbelly and grits. Y'all comin'?" He moved toward his car.

LaStanza waved him off and nodded to Jodie that they should wait.

As Snowood pulled away, he called out, "It's yoar loss."

LaStanza looked back at the Johnson camp as a snowy egret glided past and landed next to the ditch a good thirty yards away.

"No water here," he told the bird, remembering it hadn't rained that much lately. Strange for New Orleans. LaStanza looked down, running the sole of his penny loafer through the grass next to the dry ditch.

"You got something?" – Jodie.

He shrugged.

"Gut feeling?"

"After I pointed to the crime scene, she never looked me in the eye again."

He started back to the camp with Jodie, their shoes crunching on the oyster shells drive. When Hilda answered her door, LaStanza looked her in the eye and said, "I think we have to talk, ma'am."

She looked at Jodie and tears welled in her eyes.

Hilda Johnson, sitting in her rocking chair, LaStanza sitting on the beige sofa, Jodie standing with her back against the closed door. Hilda said, "He was a drifter. Middle aged. Stopped in for a drink of water. Joel pulled up in his pick-up, came in and found us sitting at the kitchen table. I shoulda seen it, the way he looked at us. He was mad."

Hilda stared at the floor as she took in a deep breath.

"I watched Joel walk the drifter back to the highway. Seen him take out his pistol and deliberately shoot him in the back of the head. Then Joel come back and got two shovels and we buried him right there in the ditch."

In the ensuing quiet only the sounds were the hum of the AC and the ceiling fan clicking.

"We never talked about it again and my Joel died."

More quiet, broken by LaStanza. "When did the, um, shooting happen?"

"Two summers ago." Hilda looked up at Jodie and wiped her eyes with her hand. "You want me to get the gun?"

It was a Webley Mark IV .38 caliber revolver. British. Hidden beneath a stack of Sears & Roebuck catalogs in a back bedroom. LaStanza called Perkins on his LFR to come photograph and secure the weapon, dust it for prints.

While they waited for Perkins, Hilda told Jodie what it was like living on Lake Catherine. *Lake Catherine,* LaStanza thought, *another way we natives identify each other.* New Orleanians always called Lake St. Catherine – Lake Catherine. Same way natives mispronounce certain street names like Burgundy, Orleans Avenue as Awleens and Bordeaux as Burdeaux.

Hilda took a wrap with her, a lime green knitted thing she draped over her shoulder before she locked up her place and followed Perkins, LaStanza and Jodie out to their car. The egret was gone but a red-tail hawk was perched atop one of the telephone poles. It watched them as they passed.

"Got lots of rabbit here," Hilda said without prodding. "Field mice too."

A breath of salty air washed over LaStanza as he unlocked the car. The air smelled like rain, wet and almost cool.

"Does the ditch ever fill up?" – LaStanza.

"When it floods," – Hilda.

11:45 a.m. – Detective Bureau

"The hedgehog sure runs straight when the coyote moon is high."

LaStanza slipped the cassette tape of Hilda Johnson's formal statement, implicating her husband in the murder of the unknown subject (UNSUB) found buried in the ditch alongside Highway 90, one-point-two miles from the Rigolets bridge in New Orleans East, into the envelope for the stenographer to transcribe. He sat at his gray metal government-issue desk and reminded Hilda she'd have to sign the statement once it was typed out.

Hilda nodded. She sat in the uncomfortable, gray-metal folding chair next to LaStanza's desk, hands in her lap. Sunlight streaming though the wall of windows across the room cast her sallow face with shadows. The green tint, painted on the outside of the windows had peeled in places, giving the windows the look of leprosy, giving the room, even with bright fluorescents on, a dappled look as if the sun beamed through the leaves of a giant tree.

Sitting at her desk, which abutted LaStanza's, Jodie put the finishing touches on the daily report on the case. Suddenly Hilda broke down. LaStanza reached into his left desk drawer for a box of Kleenex and handed it to her.

Hilda looked at him. "Are you arresting me?"

"No, ma'am." Technically, burying a body was against the law. No way LaStanza was booking a seventy-three year old widow with that. "You're not in any trouble."

"You're not going to take my husband's body out of Greenwood Cemetery for this?"

Where did that come from?

LaStanza – "No."

"You're not going to take Joel's bones away too?"

"No." An another thought. "Did he kill anyone else?"

"No," Hilda said, wiping her eyes with the Kleenex. "Just the one."

LaStanza was thinking he still needed to try and identify the body, checking missing persons. That was a long shot. He sat back in his gray metal desk chair and stretched as Hilda composed herself and Jodie finished the daily.

She slid it over and LaStanza thanked her.

"Are you ready to go?" he asked Hilda, who stood up quickly. Like most civilians, Hilda was eager to leave.

LaStanza's phone rang. It was the firearms examiner.

"Good," LaStanza said. "Thanks for rushing it." Hanging up he nodded to Jodie and said, "It's a match. One empty casing in the Webley and it's the gun."

Hilda was walking away and didn't seem to pay attention. LaStanza almost smiled because it was over already. The Webley was the murder weapon. He could take his time identifying the body, if ever. There wouldn't even be a trial.

As soon as they stepped back into the hallway and the POLICE ONLY elevator opened, LaStanza did smile. Snowood stepped out swinging his Stetson in his left hand.

"Hey," LaStanza called out. "Want you to meet Mrs. Hilda Johnson."

Snowood stopped and bowed slightly.

"This is the man who was peeking in your window."

Hilda nodded. "The one thinks he's a cowpoke."

Snowood chuckled as he started around them. Jodie stepped in his way and told him they'd just solved the case.

"What case?" Snowood tried to squeeze past, then his eyes shot open. "Not Dem Bones!"

LaStanza wished he had a camera. Jodie took Hilda's elbow and guided her into the elevator to leave LaStanza to drive it home.

"Happened two summers ago." LaStanza took his time as the elevator door closed, telling about the drifter, the jealous husband, the Webley Mark IV, the statement from the eye-witness.

Snowood leaned back against the wall. "You're makin' this up."

LaStanza pushed the elevator button and pointed over his shoulder, "There's a daily on my desk."

Stepping into the small elevator, he grinned at his old partner. Snowood slapped the Stetson against his leg and said, "I don't fuckin' believe it!" As the door slowly closed, he added, "The hedgehog sure runs straight when the coyote moon is high."

Whatever the fuck that meant.

2:05 p.m. – Detective Bureau

"I have a teletype for you."

Getting off the POLICE ONLY elevator, LaStanza said, "She was so relieved to get back home."

"You hungry yet?" Jodie.

"Det. LaStanza?" a light feminine voice called out. An intern leaned through the glass in the reception area. A dark brown face, hair in corn rows, eager eyes and a shy smile. He stepped over and she said, "I have a teletype for you."

He nodded and thanked her when she passed it to him.

Jodie went into the squad room as LaStanza opened the yellow police teletype, which stopped him in his tracks. He couldn't breathe for an instant and then slowly, he moved to the orange plastic chairs against the wall in the waiting area and sat, reading the teletype again and then closing his eyes. He leaned back, head against the wall.

He took in a deep breath and thought of his wife. A sad smile crept across his face. She would be happy when he showed her the teletype from the Superintendent of Police. She would be very happy. He took in another breath, read the teletype again and closed his eyes.

He thought back to his first murder scene in Homicide. The Slasher Case, Dauphine Street, but that wasn't the scene that flashed in his mind. It was another scene, the low-point, back when everything was falling apart, when he'd almost destroyed his marriage, when he and his partners were up against it, big time, when there was nothing before them except blood, so much blood.

He saw the Good Friday murder scene on Claiborne Avenue and remembered how it started that evening –

Good Friday, March 28, 1986

8:01 p.m. – Detective Bureau

"I think Snowood just nailed another one."

When Detective Paul Snowood announced he was bored, LaStanza stopped typing and looked at the clock above the unofficial logo of the Homicide Division, a vulture perched above a gold NOPD star-and-crescent badge. A minute after eight and LaStanza felt the acid in his stomach.

He looked across his desk at his partner, who had also stopped typing and sat glaring at Snowood. Jodie Kintyre picked up her stapler and threw it at Snowood's snake-skin cowboy boots, propped up on his desk. It careered off Snowood's empty desk and crashed to the floor. Snowood didn't even look up from under his black Stetson, which covered his eyes.

LaStanza grabbed his stapler and drew back but held up as Sergeant Mark Land stepped out of his tiny office and bellowed, "Are you fuckin' insane?" He stomped over to Snowood, yanked the Stetson off his head and sailed it across the squad room.

"Say it again and I'll yank your head off!" Mark: six-feet, two hundred seventy-five pounds, unruly dark brown hair and a Viva Zapata moustache, leaned over Snowood and gave his patented impersonation of a grizzly bear, baring teeth and snarling.

Snowood opened his left eye and grinned, showing tobacco-laced teeth. He picked up the Styrofoam cup next to his right hand and spit brown saliva into it.

LaStanza put his stapler down, stood and stretched. LaStanza, with the same unruly dark brown hair as Mark Land, only wavy, patted down his own thick moustache with his thumb and index finger as he walked over and picked up the Stetson. He tossed it even further away. As it landed, the telephone rang. LaStanza froze. Jodie pulled her blonde hair over her eyes and slowly sank back in her chair. Mark backed away from Snowood's phone as if it was contagious. Snowood put his hands behind his head and waited for someone else to pick up the phone.

14

After the ninth ring, LaStanza snatched up the nearest receiver and punched the blinking light of line one.

"Homicide, LaStanza," he snarled.

"Hey, Babe." It was Lizette.

He let out a sigh, waving to Mark as he leaned against the nearest desk and told his wife hello.

"You're still coming home right after work?" she said, hopefully.

"Snowood just said he was bored. Out loud."

"No!"

The phone rang again and LaStanza saw line two blinking.

Mark snapped up Snowood's receiver and answered. His shoulders slumped immediately and LaStanza told his wife they just got nailed.

"Are you kidding?"

"Fuckin' Country-Ass jinxed us."

Snowood took that moment to stand and stretch. Jodie beamed him with her *Far Side* desktop calendar, bouncing it off his pointed head.

"Hey!" Snowood complained, patting down his thinning hair. "That hurt."

Mark hung up and looked at the ceiling and announced, in a load, deep voice. "Country-Ass just killed someone!"

"But – but," Lizette stammered. There went her carefully planned Easter weekend. "You should have taken vacation time!"

"Just hold on," LaStanza. "We all won't have to go. Unless it's a mass murder." He kept his voice calm. He could hear her breathing heavily on the other end.

"Fuckin' barroom on Chef. Shitloada witnesses." Mark's voice rose again as he headed for his office. "I'll go with Country-Ass, since he ain't got a fuckin' partner tonight. But I'm taking my own car 'cause I ain't staying!"

Snowood packed up his briefcase and moseyed over to pick up his hat.

LaStanza to Lizette, "How's it going so far?"

"Everyone's here, except you." Her voice was softening, but only slightly. He could picture their house full of people, the mansion her father had given them as a wedding gift with its wide gallery outside, cut-glass front door, huge spiral staircase rising from the red marble foyer, long cherry wood dining table beneath the ornate crystal chandelier.

"How's the Prof doing?"

"Fine. Can't wait for you to meet him." Someone said something to Lizette in the background and she told him to check in the kitchen.

LaStanza watched Mark and Snowood cross the squad room and the phone rang again. Jodie snatched up her receiver. Her chin sank immediately.

"I think Snowood just nailed another one."

"You up?" Lizette asked if he was up for the next murder.

"No, Jodie's up," which meant him too, because she was his partner and Lizette knew what that meant.

"What about Fel?"

LaStanza grimaced. "He's off."

"He took off and *you* didn't?" She stammered. "See you when I see you." Lizette hung up without waiting for a reply.

He went back to his desk and stuffed his notebook into the thin, tan leather briefcase Lizette had given him from his birthday. He picked up his dark green suit coat, so dark it was nearly black, another gift from his rich wife; and slipped a fresh spiral notebook and his Colibri ball-point pen with the extra-fine pale-blue ink refill into his inside left coat pocket. He watched Jodie slowly pack her black Samsonite briefcase and waited for her to tell him.

She slipped on the light gray jacket of her skirt-suit, covering her shoulder rig. Finally she met his eyes and said, "30, 29-S. First Street."

They walked out, the incessant chatter on the LFRs bouncing off the hard walls and floor. 30, 29-S – a murder, suicide. First Street was familiar to LaStanza, in the Sixth Police District, where he'd worked as a patrolman. The Garden District, upper class whites. Someone let temporary depression push him, or her, over the edge, convincing them to take a loved one with them, probably a mate. Same old, same old. It was a paperwork case.

"I'll drive," Jodie said as they stepped into the police garage along the first floor of headquarters.

"It's in the Sixth. You know how to get there?"

She didn't even smile.

Before they got a block away, Headquarters called Mark Land on the radio.

"3122, go ahead." Mark sounded weary.

"Second District has a Signal 30 working, Claiborne and Carrollton. Called for Homicide and the coroner."

LaStanza felt his heartbeat. He was up for the next murder. Mark didn't have to call, but he did.

"3122 – 3124, you got that?"

"10-4. I'll drop my partner on First Street."

The acid in his stomach churned. He hadn't eaten since lunch, looking forward to the banquet at home and now he'd pay for it. He didn't look at Jodie until she pulled up on First Street, next to a marked police car in front of a three story Georgian townhouse. On the front porch stood two bored-looking uniformed cops in their sky blue shirts and dark blue pants.

"See ya'," she said, climbing from the car, leaving it running. He went around and climbed behind the steering wheel. Jodie was still next to the front fender, jotting in her notes, getting the script of the house down.

"Hey," he called out. "Know what you need?"

"Shut the fuck up." She moved away from the fender.

He almost smiled. "I was gonna say lunch." And pulled away.

8:32 p.m. – Claiborne Avenue

" – killer of Mafia hit-men and anyone else who pisses him off."

LaStanza parked the unmarked Ford in the empty taxi stand next to Palmer Park, directly across Claiborne Avenue from the crime scene, and spent the next four minutes looking around before getting out.

The crime scene was behind the K&B Drug Store, corner of Claiborne and Carrollton Avenues, uptown-lake side of the wide intersection. Three marked NOPD cars were parked along the avenue, next to the scene, their blue lights flashing. One had its headlights on, trying to illuminate the scene.

He counted four uniforms, four civilians standing beyond the cars, next to the busy avenue. Three middle-aged black men watched from the edge of Palmer Park. He spotted more people at the bus stop at the corner and even more across Carrollton at the end of the streetcar line.

LaStanza left his suit coat in the car, taking his pen and notebook, tucking his LFR into his left rear pocket. He tugged up on his belt as he crossed Claiborne. Weighted down by his .357 magnum, speed loaders, cuffs and now the weight of his LFR, it was a wonder his pants stayed up. A quick breeze felt cool on his face although the air smelled of exhaust fumes from the cars zipping by. It had cooled nicely from the high eighties of the afternoon.

A tall officer turned to him and he recognized John Raven Beau of the Second District. Beau: twenty-four, six-two, one ninety pounds, with straight dark brown hair, nearly black.

"Det. LaStanza," Beau said, stepping aside to let LaStanza see the body.

Next to an up-ended aluminum walker lay the small body of an elderly man, feet pointing toward the avenue, head in a huge pool of reddish-black blood.

"I found him," Beau said. "I'm working a 64 around the corner at the Shoe Town. Robbers ran this way."

Carefully inching forward, LaStanza noted the cuffs on the old man's pants, navy blue gabardine. He wore black suspenders and a black belt. A careful man. Black shoes with laces, soles worn thin.

"How many?" – LaStanza.

"Two perpetrators. Black. Late twenties. Took the security guard's gun."

The old man wore a white dress shirt, long sleeved with silver cuff links.

"Ran this way, right?" LaStanza said. "Know what we say about coincidences?"

"No such thing in police work."

"Fuckin' A. We'll use your item number. One investigation. Make sure I get all your reports."

"Right."

The old man's arms were spread, pallid white fingers curled as if he was still gripping his walker.

LaStanza remembered Beau was half-Cajun, half-Sioux, remembered him from the murder of the tall officer's girlfriend a year ago around St. Patrick's Day. Another cop killed her. A real whodunit. Interesting case. Beau took it hard, however.

LaStanza eased to his left to see the old man's face, only it wasn't there. A wisp of white hair crowned the old man's head, small eye-brows beneath, the rest caved in a pool of blood. He caught a whiff of it, that sickening coppery scent of blood.

"Hey, hey. Candy-Ass!" A familiar voice boomed behind LaStanza, who didn't turn. He slowly backed away and felt a hand slap his shoulder.

"Y'all know who this is?" the same voice bellowed. "This is *the* detective. He's short, but he's the *shit!*"

LaStanza looked back at the man who was his first partner, Sergeant Stan-the-Man Smith: six-two, blond and blue-eyed. He blinked at the numeral "2" on the collar of Stan's police uniform shirt, which was tailored to show off his chest and biceps.

"You transferred to the Second?" LaStanza knew better than to talk with Stan, but couldn't help it.

"Temporary assignment, Candy-Ass. They needed my expertise, my good-looks, my debonair –"

LaStanza spotted a woman with a notebook and pen standing behind Stan. He was about to run her up the street when he saw the silver star-and-crescent badge hanging from her notebook. She was tall, blonde, dressed in a slinky silver evening gown.

"I'm absconding Beau and the other three men here," LaStanza told Stan.

"No problemo." Stan grinned and stepped aside. "I have the pleasure of introducing Public Information Officer Alice Walker. No relation to the writer."

Officer Walker gave Stan a prissy look.

"This here's the *infamous* Det. LaStanza, killer of Mafia hit-men and anyone else who pisses him off."

Alice Walker stepped around LaStanza, stopping when she saw the body.

"She's got a hot date," Stan said, pointing to Alice Walker's rear end.

She retched, wheeled and hurried back toward the neutral ground.

LaStanza tapped Beau's shoulder. "Go tell her what she needs to know. Then come back to me."

Waving the other three patrolmen forward, LaStanza pointed to each with his instructions. To the youngest, most eager looking – "Write down the license plate numbers of every car parked in a three block radius. Three blocks in *every* direction, even on the other side of Palmer Park." LaStanza pointed over his shoulder. "Start with all the cars in the parking lot behind K&B." The drugstore faced Carrollton so the parking lot ran along Claiborne. Building was two stories, blond-brick, solid wall along Claiborne, no windows except in front, rear wall solid except one metal door and a loading bay with its metal awning down.

"You want scripts of the cars?"

"No. Just get the numbers right. Find any blood, call me over."

To the other two, one black, one white – "Get the names and addresses of everyone out here on the street. Go to those men next to Palmer Park first, then to the bus stop and streetcar stop. Get the information from their driver's licenses, including DL numbers. Then ask them if they saw anything. Anyone refuse to give you their DL, hold them for me. They don't like it, fuck 'em. This is a crime scene and they leave when we say they can leave."

The older of the two, the white cop, said, "I got better things to do."

"So did he." LaStanza pointed to the body.

Another patrolman hustled up, curiosity drawing him like a moth to a porch light. LaStanza pointed to him – "Go into K&B and around the corner to the fire house." LaStanza remembered a fire station around the corner. He told the new patrolman the routine. Get driver's license information from everyone.

"Ask the firemen nicely," He added as the new patrol officer started away. "They might want to lend a hand." Under his breath, LaStanza added, "They got nothing better to fuckin' do."

Beau stepped back up. "She's in a hurry. Late for a date." He nodded at the shapely ass of Officer Walker as she slinked toward a group of reporters, including a TV van with a cameraman just setting up.

Crime Lab Technician Perkins arrived with his camera case and evidence case. LaStanza pulled Beau aside as Perkins started processing the scene.

Back to Beau – "Check for surveillance cameras in these stores, especially Shoe Town. Then come right back." Beau turned to leave. "Keep the witnesses inside Shoe Town until we can get statements."

Backpedaling, Beau held up a set of keys. "Soon as I found the body, I locked them inside. I'll stroke them when I check for cameras."

He had the makings of a good Homicide man, the poor bastard.

The TV lights came on and a black reporter began interviewing Officer Walker. LaStanza recognized him. Good, local reporter who'd gone to St. Augustine High School. Knew his shit, unlike many who had trouble pronouncing Chartres Street, Carondelet, calling Lake Pontchartrain – Pontchartrain Lake, like calling Lake Superior – Superior Lake.

Perkins started with photos from the neutral ground in the center of Claiborne, quartering his shots as he moved closer, getting the entire area, his strobe light popping. LaStanza got out of the way, watching Perkins close in for more photos, took a close-up of the victim's face, then put his camera away and took out his measuring tape. LaStanza went to hold the other end, so they could triangulate the measurements from the body to fixed positions, like the streetlights, telephone poles and the rear edge of the K&B building.

"3122 – 3124."

LaStanza pulled out his LFR. Mark was calling. "Go ahead."

"What's your situation?"

Keeping his voice in the standard monotone of homicide detectives, LaStanza explained in as few words as possible.

"I'm in route," Mark said. "This is one big C.F. over here."

C.F. – Cluster Fuck. Good. Snowood started all this, saying he was bored. Serves him right.

As Perkins started dusting the walker, Beau stepped back with two video cassettes in hand.

"From inside Shoe Town and K&B. They might have gone in the drug store first. Pretty sure we got the perps on the Shoe Town tape."

"Hope fuckin' so."

"No cameras outside any of these places." Beau again.

LaStanza tried not to show surprise on his face, a patrol officer thinking like a detective. Beau had potential, all right.

"No cameras at all in the Skate Town."

"The what?"

Beau pointed back toward the corner. "Above Shoe Town there's a Skate Town. Roller rink. There's a Good Friday Skate-a-thon. That's why all the cars are out here."

"Lord!"

"Exactly. Only five people there now. Left Sider to get their names."

It took LaStanza a moment. "Did you say 'Left Sider'?"

"Yeah. I left Jimmy Sider, the eager rookie who came late."

Left Sider? Ha. LaStanza had that familiar feeling, as if he had one foot in the Twilight Zone.

Perkins lifted three prints from the walker, complaining they were probably from the victim. LaStanza told him Beau would take him around the corner to the Shoe Town for more dusting.

"Shoe Town?"

LaStanza told him about the armed robbery.

"Jesus Huckleberry Christ. When it rains it fuckin' pours."

LaStanza to Beau, "On your way you can tell him about Left Sider."

"Sure, why not?"

"What was that?" Perkins said, following Beau.

As soon as Beau returned, LaStanza asked, "How'd the 64 go down?"

Beau ran his fingers through his hair. "The two went in together. Big one pulled out a chrome revolver and took a blue steel Smith-and-Wesson, model unknown, from the sixty-six year old security guard. Smaller one jumped the counter, rifled the cash registers. Big one put a gun to the head of the woman night manager and she opened the safe. Got about six hundred bucks.

"Scripts – big one was about six-two, skinny, in blue tee-shirt and jeans. Smaller one was five-seven, heavy-set, dark shirt, jeans. Both dark complected. Left on foot, moving fast, but not running, toward the K&B.

"Manager peeked out and saw them round the corner this way." Beau nodded to the body.

"Hey, Mister Detective!" The older, white cop who had better things to do waved at LaStanza from the K&B parking lot. He had a heavy-set white man in a red shirt with him.

"This is a relative. Of the victim!"

LaStanza started that way, nodding for Beau to come along when another voice yelled from the neutral ground.

"Hey! Hey! Hold up." It was a uniformed lieutenant, balding with a paunch belly. He let a car go by and trotted over. LaStanza waited, not wanting this in front of the victim's relative.

"You got all my men tied up here. I got calls backin' up all over the District!" The lieutenant's name plate read Jones. LaStanza never heard of him. He looked around wondering where the hell Stan-the-Man had gone.

"Hey. Look at me when I talk to you. I got calls up the ass!"

Yeah, LaStanza thought, *bullshit burglar alarms, drunk in public calls, neighbors pissed off at each other calls. I got a fuckin' murder here.*

LaStanza gave him the Sicilian stare, letting his unblinking light green eyes bore all the way through the man's eyes to the back of his skull.

"You can't tie me up like this!"

LaStanza kept his voice low, "The fuck I can't."

A car's brakes squealed and Mark Land got out before his car was completely stopped. LaStanza backed away from the angry lieutenant, pointing to him with an index finger, then nodded to his sergeant. Let the Homicide watch commander handle this.

The big man in the red shirt blinked tears from his eyes as LaStanza stepped up.

"That's my father," his voice rasped. His chin quivered and the big man leaned back against the trunk of a yellow Olds. He was middle-aged but solidly built, looked all muscle.

LaStanza took out his ID folder and showed his credentials to the man. "I'm Det. LaStanza. Homicide."

The word had the usual effect. The man stiffened, a confirmation hitting him between the eyes. LaStanza leaned closer and in a low voice asked, "What was your father doing out here?"

Hands behind his back, the man held on to the trunk as he explained how his father walked from his house every evening, around the corner to the K&B to get his newspaper. The old man, ninety-one last month, insisted on going alone, even when he had to use a walker. It was a ritual.

"Everybody at K&B knows him. Everybody in the neighborhood knows him. He's been living in the same house for seventy years." He stood up straight and said, "I want to go see him."

"No you don't." LaStanza stared into the big man's eyes, remembering the old man's caved-in face.

"I wanna see his face." He gasped. "Close his eyes."

LaStanza grabbed the man's shoulder. "He died instantly. You'll see him after they clean him up." He took his hand away and pulled out his notebook. The man bolted around him and ran to the body.

Beau started after him but LaStanza put his arm out and shook his head. The man stopped ten feet from the body, legs locked as if frozen for two long seconds, then he wavered and stumbled back toward them. Beau helped him to the trunk of the Olds, where the man leaned away from them and puked.

When he finished, LaStanza took him around to the front of the Olds.

"What's your father's name?"

"Huh?" Glassy eyes blinked at LaStanza, who looked down at his notes.

"Your father's name?"

The man had a tough time catching his breath. "Grosetto Venetta. Everyone called him Senoré." He spelled it out but

LaStanza already had it correct in his notes. "He was ninety-one." The big man looked over his shoulder and pushed off the car.

"My mother."

"Where?"

"She's still inside the house. I have to go to her."

LaStanza raised a hand and asked his name.

"Paolo Venetta. Pauli." He pointed to the row of houses beyond the K&B parking lot and gave LaStanza his mother's address.

"Let me see your driver's license."

"Huh?"

"I'll bring it over to your mom's house."

Pauli dug out his wallet and handed LaStanza his driver's license, then hurried away. LaStanza stepped back toward the streetlights and wrote down Paolo 'Pauli' Venetta's vitals, noting the big man was fifty-five and lived next door to his parents.

Mark Land stood over the body now, hands hanging at his sides.

"Jesus," he mumbled as LaStanza and Beau arrived. He glanced at them. "Never seen anything like this. Bones must have been like egg shell."

LaStanza, "He was barely five feet tall. A real fuckin' menace to some tough-guy robbers."

A white, coroner's office van eased up along the avenue and stopped in front of Mark's car.

LaStanza asked Beau for the Shoe Town keys. Mark's eyebrows rose.

"He's got our witnesses locked inside." LaStanza passed the keys to Mark. "Can you start their statements?"

"Fuckin A." Mark winked at Beau. "Locked 'em in, huh? Where'd you learn that?"

"I hate disappearing witnesses." Beau to LaStanza – "Want me to go with him?"

"No. Stay here and learn something. You know how to take a statement."

Mark moved away as a portly coroner's investigator stepped up to examine the body. LaStanza watched carefully, Beau at his side, as the investigator pulled on a pair of rubber gloves and checked out the body, going through the old man's pockets, bringing out a set of keys, a pocket watch with a long brass chain, seven dollars in ones, ninety cents in change and a black wallet, which he passed to LaStanza who passed it to Beau as he continued taking notes.

Beau pulled out Grosetto Venetta's driver's license, State-Farm car insurance card, AARP card and several pale green business cards for Venetta's Men Store on Magazine Street.

The coroner's man lifted the head carefully and felt beneath it. "No exit wound." He gently placed the head back down, pulled off his bloody gloves and dropped them in a paper bag provided by Perkins. Two coroner's assistants stepped forward with a gurney and a black plastic body bag, while LaStanza secured the investigator's name for his report.

As the body was rolled away, a marked police car pulled up and Jodie Kintyre climbed out, thanking the driver and heading for LaStanza and Beau. Her eyes brightened slightly as she recognized Beau.

"How ya' doing?" – Jodie to Beau.

"OK. Considering."

When she looked at LaStanza, he said, "Finished already?"

She gave him a pained look. "Just paperwork. This one bad?"

He gave her the gist as they moved through the K&B lot to the one-way street directly behind the lot and the Venetta residence across the street. A long black cat crossed Dublin Street in front of the three.

Jodie shook her head.

LaStanza, "That's good luck for me. Everything that's bad luck for anyone else is good luck for me. The mobile over my crib was a vulture, which has followed me ever since."

That brought a slight smile to Jodie's lips, at least.

10:16 p.m. – Claiborne Avenue

"I always get them. *Always.*"

The Venetta house was a brick double, two stories with ten concrete steps up to a front porch shared by two addresses. The door on the left side was open. LaStanza tapped on the screen door.

Pauli Venetta's face appeared beyond the screen before he unlatched it. LaStanza handed him his driver's license, then followed him into a living room that smelled of furniture polish. A brown-haired woman in her mid-thirties sat on a dark green sofa next to a tiny woman with snow-white hair, both staring up with red eyes. Both wore dark dresses, the younger woman in high heels, the older wore the same style of thick black shoes the nuns used to wear when LaStanza was in elementary school, Our Lady of the Holy Rosary.

Pauli leaned on the end of the sofa and introduced his wife, Gail and his mother, Calli Venetta, eighty-five years old.

"Her English isn't that good," Pauli said as Jodie moved to the opposite end of the sofa, Beau remaining by the door, LaStanza commanding the room's center, introducing himself to his victim's wife.

Calli Venetta blinked at him, her small lips shaking as she raised a fist and said, "Basta. Basta!" Tears rolled from her eyes as Gail and then Pauli wrapped arms around her, lifting her, half-carrying her into the back of the house. The acid in LaStanza's stomach bubbled.

Beau caught LaStanza eye and asked, "What's *basta?*"

"It means *stop it*. Italian."

Jodie pointed to the family portrait behind the sofa, a large framed picture of Mr. and Mrs. Venetta sitting on a small love-seat, Pauli and Gail standing left of them, a younger woman with strawberry-blonde hair standing to the right. There were more pictures around the room, mostly of the younger woman, some looked like professional model photos of her in designer clothes, bathing suits.

LaStanza noticed the room was immaculate, more like a display in a furniture store, the hardwood floor covered in oriental rugs, the matching lamps on either side of the sofa had pale green shades, the coffee table shined as if covered with glass. The room beyond the living room held a dining room table, small but as elegant as the long cherry wood table in LaStanza's mansion.

He felt something else inside now, felt the leopard starting to prowl back and forth. His eyes automatically narrowed and he felt his pulse increase. He was heading for that higher level of awareness, felt his senses increase where he could hear better, smell better, see better. He felt the predator within and wanted those claws bared, feeling the thrill of the hunt.

"Basta," she'd said. Didn't even want to meet the man who would track down her husband's killers, didn't want to hear a fuckin' word from him and he didn't blame her.

Jodie pointed to a leggy picture of the strawberry-blonde. "This was a pantyhose ad. Haynes or Leggs. Must be a professional model."

Beau inched around for a better look just as the screen door opened and the strawberry-blonde woman stepped in, looking right at LaStanza with large, dark brown eyes. She was tall and looked young, early twenties maybe, her gaze lingering on LaStanza as if her eyes were trying to glean something from his. She wore a red skirt-suit and looked – elegant.

The stare continued until Pauli Venetta moved back through the dining room with a black suit on a hanger in his hands. He went to the woman, engulfing her in his arms.

"This is my daughter Lori."

She almost broke down but continued to stare at LaStanza who kept his face expressionless. No way to rush this, although he itched to be outside working the case. LaStanza smoothed down his moustache with his thumb and index finger.

Pauli held up the suit and said, "This is what my father did better than anyone I've ever known. He was a tailor, made handmade suits. One at a time in the back of the house. You can go look at his workshop if you want."

Gail came back in and Lori joined her on the sofa. LaStanza couldn't help notice the women looked nothing alike as Pauli went on to tell his father's story, born in Sicily, immigrating to New Orleans as a child to live with relatives after his parents died in a train wreck.

Lori's large brown eyes continued staring at LaStanza's eyes, still pulling at him. When Pauli paused for a breath, LaStanza asked if there was anyone suspicious in the neighborhood, anyone who didn't get along with the Senoré.

"No," Pauli said. "He was a gentle man. Truly gentle."

Lori started making signals with her hands, sign language. Pauli interpreted, "You think it was premeditated?"

LaStanza faced Lori so she could read his lips. "We don't think anything right now. We're just gathering facts." He spoke slower. "It looks like he was in the wrong place at the wrong time. Two men robbed Shoe Town and ran around the corner right into him."

"My daughter is mute but she can hear."

LaStanza closed his eyes, hoping his face didn't show how foolish he felt.

Pauli started up about how his father worked his way through school. Nodding, LaStanza eased toward Jodie and asked if she could take over here. No need for both of them and Beau. Jodie nodded, knowing the routine, already jotting notes, getting the deep background information about the victim.

When Pauli paused again for a breath, LaStanza told them his partner would take it all down. He started toward Beau and the door. He spotted Lori making signs again and stopped, watching those eyes reach for him. Her eyes were wet now.

Pauli interpreted again. "She asks what are the chances you'll catch them?"

"A hundred percent," LaStanza said flatly. "Y'all take care of each other, mourn together and I'll take care of the bastards to who did this."

He took two business cards out of his ID folder, passed one to Pauli and one to Lori, who stood and grabbed his hand, her eyes reaching into his again. Returning Lori's stare, he told the Venettas, "You don't know me, but I never give up. I always get them. *Always.*"

As Lori let go of his hand, he glanced back at Jodie whose cat eyes were wide now and she bit her lower and nodded almost imperceptibly.

On the way back down the stairs Beau said, "You gave me a chill back there, man."

"It's fuckin' true. I always get 'em."

They crossed Dublin Street for the other patrol officers LaStanza had absconded, now assembled back at the crime scene, each with sheets of paper in their hands, including the cop who had better things to do that night and the eager Officer Sider, who'd be known as Left Sider, probably for the rest of his career, at least to the Homicide Division.

10:58 p.m. – Dublin Street

" – my partner's Sicilian. So Sicilian it hurts."

Jodie Kintyre watched LaStanza and Beau leave, then turned her attention to Pauli Venetta.

"Your father worked out of this house?"

"We have a store on Magazine and he worked there too, but mostly here."

Lori made more hand signals and Pauli said, "Good idea."

Gail rose and started back through the dining room.

"My wife's making coffee. Why don't we talk around the table?" Pauli went over and flipped on the lights in the dining room, pulling a chair for Jodie as Lori waited for her to sit.

Jodie put her notebook on the table and sat, feeling the tiredness in her legs.

Lori pulled out her own notebook from her purse and wrote quickly, printing in all caps, easy to read: *What your partner said sent shivers through me.*

"He does it to me, sometimes, along my spine. But it's the truth. He's the only one of us, only detective, with a perfect solution record. He always catches them."

Pauli, sitting across from Jodie now, laid his large hands flat on the table. "Gail'll sit with my mother."

Jodie to Lori – "Like y'all, my partner's Sicilian, so Sicilian it hurts."

Lori wrote again and showed it to Jodie: *I'm only half-Sicilian. My mother was Irish. Died in car wreck when I was twenty.*

So Gail's her step-mother. Jodie jotted that in her notes, asking everyone their age, surprised to find Lori was thirty. She looked younger.

In a low voice, Pauli Venetta explained how his parents met. Lori rose slowly and went into the kitchen. As the big man spoke, Jodie couldn't help her mind returning to her scene on First Street, the two bodies on the king-sized bed in the master bedroom, .38 pistol between them, detailed suicide note confession on the nightstand. Paperwork. The wife was dying of cancer, husband a dentist, a deadly combination. Dentists still had the highest suicide rate.

Cops would, Jodie thought, *but sometimes we get to take out our frustrations, shooting the occasional criminal, striking back at others stupid enough to fight with the police.*

When Lori returned with a tray with three coffees, Jodie eased Pauli back to the present, fishing for a name, anyone who would have recognized the Senoré, someone around here who'd decided to rob the Shoe Town and knew the old man would ID him.

The coffee was strong, coffee-and-chicory that pepped Jodie up immediately, even with two sugars and a heavy slurp of evaporated milk. When it was clear Jodie wasn't getting any more from the Venettas, she passed out her business card, reminding them her partner was in charge of the investigation.

"But you can call either of us." She stood. "If you think of anything else or hear anything from your neighbors. Sometimes neighbors will tell the family things they don't want to tell us, or aren't sure of. OK?"

Lori nodded and Pauli thanked her. The big man looked smaller as she walked away. Lori followed her to the door, jotting on her notebook again, showing it to Jodie: *So Sicilian it hurts?*

"My partner's been in – several shootouts with criminals and is a pretty good shot. After he killed a particularly bad character, his father, a retired cop, started calling him *mio leopardo piccolo.*" Jodie could see Lori didn't understand Italian that well. Eye to eye Jodie noticed Lori was slightly taller in the high heels she wore, probably and even five-seven, like Jodie.

"It means *my little leopard.* You see, pound for pound, the leopard is nature's most efficient killing machine. It was a compliment, of sorts."

Lori's eyes seemed to glisten and she patted Jodie on the shoulder on her way out.

11:57 p.m. – Detective Bureau

"You know what Venetta means in Italian?"

The best witness from Shoe Town sat at the desk next to LaStanza's as she went through the final mug book of men arrested for armed robbery the last ten years. Evangelista Luz: twenty-six, five-five, one thirty-five with short straight black hair and brown eyes as bouncy as an owl's. Born in El Paso of a Mexican father and an 'Anglo' mother, Evangelista was eager to help police catch the man who shoved a pistol against her temple.

"Maybe some of these men have changed since they were arrested?" she asked.

LaStanza, putting the finishing touches to his daily report on the Senoré murder, nodded wearily to Evangelista. She was sharp, all right. He took a sip of his sixth coffee-and-chicory that evening. "Most of the pictures are a few years old. Some older."

"I'm glad they weren't Anglo. You Anglos all look alike to me." She shot LaStanza a teasing smile.

"I'm not Anglo."

She tilted her head to the side.

"I'm more Latin than you. Hundred per-cent Sicilian-American. I don't have a drop of Anglo-Saxon in me." He pointed to Jodie, "She's Anglo."

Jodie rolled her eyes. She sat at her desk next to the second-best witness, Shoe Town clerk Andy Pitney, as he went through the mug book Evangelista finished a few minutes earlier. Pitney: a pasty-skinned white boy of twenty, frizzy red hair, five-nine, one-forty. He also had better things to do to, until LaStanza told him, "Not tonight."

The sixty-six year old security guard, Thomas Eustis, a dour man with splotchy dark brown skin, sat squirming at Snowood's empty desk. His bloodshot eyes had that far-away alcoholic's glaze to them. Dying for a fuckin' drink, the man could barely describe the robbers, except they were black, he thought. LaStanza jotted a note to himself to check out Eustis carefully, check associates, where he lives, the works. He mumbled under his breath, "Because you never know."

Of the three Shoe Town witnesses, Eustis was the only one with a criminal record. Three arrests for Disturbing the Peace by Drunk in Public and one DWI arrest.

"Anglo means white people," Evangesita said in a hushed voice.

"I'm not white," LaStanza said, not looking up from his typewriter. "Sicilians are a mixed race." He closed his eyes and ran through the speech his wife, the history grad student, had given him, again and again. "Founded by the Phoenicians, Sicily was conquered by the Greeks, Carthaginians, Romans, Saracens, Moors, Spanish, French, Neapolitans. Only blood we don't have is Scandinavian." He winked at Evangelista. "And Anglo-Saxon." He took a hit of coffee and returned his best witness's smile.

When he found the bastards, she would identify them. He could see it in her eyes.

"Damn!" LaStanza reached for the liquid paper.

Jodie shook her head. "You should bring in the computer Lizette wants to get you. You can make corrections on the screen, even check your spelling, then you push a button and it prints out your daily."

LaStanza took one more hit of coffee while the white shit dried on his daily. Evangelista pointed to the printing on his coffee mug and her owly eyes became even wider. Alongside the black mug was printed, in neat red letters: *I'm one of those bad things that happens to good people.*

"My wife gave it to me."

Evangelista ducked back to the mug book. LaStanza leaned back in his chair, hands behind the head and closed his weary eyes for a moment. They burned for a second but that went away.

"We don't spot them," Pitney finally spoke, "that means they've never been arrested?"

"No," Jodie sounded fatigued. "It means they haven't been arrested for armed robbery in Orleans Parish in the last ten years. They could be from Jefferson."

"Or they coulda changed." Evangelista said she'd recognized a man in one of the earlier books, he's dead now, her neighbor. Saw a picture of him when he was younger, barely recognized him.

"How'd he die?"

She was surprised. "You guys shot him last year."

LaStanza opens his eyes. "Not this Wop."

He sat up and finished his coffee. He glanced through his notes. The canvass had listed fifty-six license plate numbers from cars parked around his scene and thirty-two names, addresses and phone numbers of people stopped and interviewed on the street, including the men next to Palmer Park, people who saw nothing, not a fuckin' thing except all the cops.

LaStanza jotted reminders to himself to run all of the names, especially the names from the car registrations for criminal records. Contact the cab companies, in case a cabbie dropped off or picked up two dudes at the cab stand along Palmer Park before LaStanza pulled up, because you never knew until you asked.

Jodie said, "Always wondered if dying on Good Friday's better than dying on a regular day, dying on the same day as Christ."

She was alive all right, needling him now. Evangelista made the sign of the cross.

LaStanza came back with, "There's not a goddamn thing good about Good Friday. And don't give me all that bullshit about Jesus dying to save us. He was a murder victim."

Jodie to Evangelista – "He's just venting. He knows I'm not Catholic."

Evangelista closed her mug book. "Any more pictures?"

"That's all."

Snowood picked that moment to mosey into the squad room, Stetson in his right hand, briefcase in his left hand. He waved the Stetson in a wide arch and said, "Heidi. Heidi y'all doin'?"

Evangelista turned to LaStanza. "Heidi?"

He hated having to interpret Country-Ass. "He means *howdy.*"

Snowood shooed the bleary-eyed security guard away from his desk and dropped his briefcase on it. "Y'all go park it over there, pardner." Waving toward the empty desks closer to the wall of windows.

Snowood said, "Y'all shoulda seen ma' crime scene. Fulla ignerts. All ignert. Shoulda node, barroom on the Chef." He pulled a tin of smokeless tobacco from his briefcase then reached into a desk drawer for a white Styrofoam cup.

Evangelista tapped LaStanza's arm.

"Last time I interpreting him." LaStanza stood and stretched. "Ignert means ignorant. Node is past tense of I know and the Chef is Chef Menteur Highway and it's time for us to pack up."

Jodie pulled her daily out of her typewriter and picked up LaStanza's to drop both in their sergeant's IN basket. Passing Snowood, she said, "If he were any more stupid, you'd have to water him twice a week."

Grinning tobbacoed-teeth at Evangelista, Snowood said, "I still can't understand why sheep don't shrink when it rains on 'em."

LaStanza led the way out. At the elevator, Evangelista asked, "What happened to that good looking cop? The tall one."

LaStanza fought back a chuckle at the exhausted look on Jodie's face.

LaStanza – "Officer John Raven Beau had to go back on the street. He doesn't work up here."

"He's dreamy," Evangelista said, which brought a moan from Andy Pitney.

"I'll tell him," LaStanza.

The door opened. "You're not so bad yourself," Evangelista added. "For an older man."

The laughter started deep in his belly and rose quickly and wouldn't let go. He'd never been called that before. Even Jodie smiled, mainly at him holding the elevator door open and almost falling down.

"What's so funny?" Evangelista.

They waited for LaStanza to recover before going down. As they stepped out, Evangelista asked, "So you think you'll catch 'em?"

"Absolutely." LaStanza looked at Jodie, said, "You know what Venetta means in Italian?"

"Our victim's last name?"

"Venetta means *Revenge*."

Saturday, March 29, 1986

2:07 a.m. – Exposition Boulevard

"Do I make you uneasy being nude?"

LaStanza climbed out of the LTD and stretched the kinks in his back before reaching in for his coat, briefcase and LFR, asking Jodie, "You sure you don't wanna come in and eat? There was a goddamn feast."

She shooed him away, telling him she'd see him at the post-mortems, looking at her watch, "In less than five hours."

LaStanza watched her pull off before walking over to the double-wide sidewalk known as Exposition Boulevard, which ran along the park from St. Charles Avenue all the way down to Magazine Street. He freed his right hand, slipping his radio in the back pocket of his pants.

He stopped and looked out at the dark expanse of the park. The breeze had picked up, coming from the river now a little over a mile away, rustling the leaves of the old oaks. Sounding like waves rolling to shore, the wind was almost cool, smelling of rain, lifting the Spanish moss beards, like ghostly curtains.

Turning to his right, he looked up Exposition, remembering another night, looking toward the spot where the Twenty-Two Killer took a pot shot at LaStanza. Turning to his left he looked down the dark avenue where he'd chased the bastard in a long, running gun battle past Magazine all the way to the zoo where he splattered the bastard's brains against the base of a magnolia tree.

Reaching around, he ran his fingers across the scar on his neck where the Twenty-Two Killer's last bullet grazed him. Lizette touched it enough for the both of them, frightened by his brush with death, fearing the next sound of gunfire.

Through the wrought iron fence of their small front yard, LaStanza crossed the manicured lawn of fine china grass up to the steps to the wide gallery running around the first floor of their newly re-painted white mansion. He punched the alarm code into the keypad outside the cut glass front door and it popped open.

36

Behind him, he heard a roll of thunder in the distance as the door automatically shut.

Through the foyer, to the right through the long dining room LaStanza could find no evidence of a party. The place even smelled lemon clean. He found a note taped to the kitchen counter in Aunt Brulie's spindly handwriting:

Wop,

Food in fridge. Put plate in micro. Three mins. Take off foil first.

The old black woman who'd raised Lizette was taking care of the man she considered a gigolo. He smiled, as if he didn't know to the take off the foil.

He plopped his briefcase and coat on the counter and noticed they forgot to turn off the lights in the back yard. He turned back to the refrigerator and pulled out an oversized plate, removing the foil before slipping into the microwave. Roast pork, mashed potatoes, corn and cornbread.

He heard the French doors behind him opening and spun reaching for his .357 magnum, leaving it half-raised as a naked lady stepped in from the deck just outside the kitchen. Towel on her head, she was still damp from the Jazucci.

Smiling as she approached, she spoke in a heavy French accent, "You must be Dino."

Holstering his magnum, he nodded slowly, trying not to check out her body parts, the round breasts and light brown aureoles around brown nipples, at the contours of her flat belly and the dark brown triangle of hair between her slim legs.

Valerie LeGris. Lizette had described the French professor's Caribbean-born wife, but not like this. "Yeah. Uh, I'm Dino, all right."

"I couldn't sleep," she said, "could not get in the hot tub earlier. Too many people in it."

Jesus. Some fuckin' party I missed. For a moment, he wondered what Jodie would have said if she'd come in for a late night bite. He tried not to stare at Valerie, but it was very difficult with her standing here, hands on hips with that smooth tanned skin, perfectly round breasts and dark bush. His dick, which always had a mind of its own, was as hard as nails already.

37

"Do I make you uneasy being nude?"

He was too tired to look away. "Not if you don't mind me looking." He felt his dick throb.

"Oh, look all your want." She did a slow turn, pointing her butt at him and bending over slightly, rolling her fine ass.

What the fuck is this?

Turning back, she moved up, pressed her breasts against LaStanza's arm and kissed him on the mouth, her tongue gently working against his. His dick a diamond-cutter now, he tired not to kiss her back, but his mouth was as Italian as his dick and didn't obey.

Pulling her mouth away to catch her breath, keeping her boobs pressed against him, she said, "That was very nice."

She looked down at her breasts and said, "Not bad for a woman over thirty, no?"

LaStanza caught a movement behind her and saw his wife standing in the doorway by the back stairs leading from the bedrooms. Hair in a pony-tail, Lizette was in one of his white undershirts and white panties, her breasts bulging through the thin undershirt.

He let out a high pitched, "Ha" as the microwave pinged.

The sight of her husband French kissing a naked woman in her kitchen, sent a jolt through Lizette's heart. Knowing the predatory nature of Valerie LeGris and the fact her husband looked dog-tired eased the shock somewhat, but only a little.

"Oh," Valerie backed away when she realized who was behind her. "I was just going up." She smiled at Lizette as she tip-toed away, leaving Dino standing there with a goofy look on his face.

"So," LaStanza said as Lizette came over. "How was *your* evening?"

"Get your food." Lizette sat up on a stool. He took the plate from the microwave, then reached back into the refrigerator, passing over the St. Pauli Girl beer for a bottle of Abita Springs water before sitting next to Lizette.

"I forgot to warn you about Valerie. She's a bit forward."

"Her tongue was probing for my tonsils."

"You lost your tonsils when you were two."

"She found that out on her own."

Lizette reached over and ran her fingers along LaStanza's scar. "So, tell me about it."

Eating slowly, he told her about the old man and the walker, about the two bad asses with their guns, the victim's son and his mute daughter, the night manager who thought Beau was beautiful, Jodie's suicide-murder, Snowood's cluster fuck.

Brulie's food was delicious, as usual, and LaStanza had to force himself to slow down.

"Fel's off," he concluded, "because he's got Saturday duty. Jodie's got Easter Sunday."

That's right, she remembered snapping at him, asking why Felicity Jones was off that night. Lightning flashed outside, followed by an immediate crack of thunder. The rain rolled in a moment later.

"Who's Beau?"

LaStanza finished chewing and explained about the tall second district patrolman, who'd probably make a good homicide man. "He's the one whose girlfriend was murdered by the cop last year. Remember?"

She nodded just as Professor LeGris came in wearing black pajamas with red hearts on them. He introduced himself to LaStanza, shaking hands. Well over six feet tall, LeGris was silver-haired with a lean, chiseled face, a trim man with lively green eyes.

Lizette climbed off her stool and asked if LeGris would like some wine.

"Actually, I came for that opened bottle of Bordeaux. My wife and I need something to aid us to sleep." He turned to LaStanza. "I must apologize for my wife. She's what we call, a free spirit. A wild woman to be blunt."

LaStanza nodded, taking a bite of cornbread and thought how a heavy French accent, so alluring in a woman's voice, could be so obnoxious in a man's.

Lizette climbed off the stool and moved to the refrigerator, bending over to reach in for a bottle. LaStanza stared at his wife's ass through her sheer white panties. His dick throbbed again and he caught LeGris staring too.

Lizette passed the wine and two wine glasses to LeGris, who thanked them and went up the back stairs just as a wall of rain began peppering the windows.

When wearing make-up, Lizette was as beautiful as any model, yet he loved her this way too, with no make-up, fresh faced, those topaz eyes, brown with flecks of gold shimmering at him as she stood next to him. She looked more like a high-schooler than a twenty-four year old woman.

"So remind me what's on tap for tomorrow." LaStanza voice came out scratchy and Lizette sighed.

"Dinner party at the Estate at seven. That's it. You can sleep all day."

She saw it in his eyes. No, he had to go to the autopsy in the morning, Saturday or not.

"Tomorrow? More formal than the thing tonight?" He finished the bottle of water, went and got another.

Lizette rubbed her temples, her eyes closed now. "It's white tie. I have your new tux upstairs. The French Counsel will be there, the presidents and heads of the history departments of Loyola, Tulane, Xavier, U.N.O., S.U.N.O., even L.S.U. Not to mention the mayor, both of our senators and the French Ambassador to the U.S."

"No governor?"

She put her elbows up on the counter, chin cupped in the palm of her hands as she said, "I'm wearing a new silver dress. Halter top cut down to my navel and slit up front, almost to my crotch."

"You're not wearing it for me," he teased. "You're not even wearing it for the other men. You're wearing it to piss off your mother."

A little of all that – Lizette thought.

"She'd have seen quite a sight tonight," Lizette said.

"Hey, I was just minding my own business in my own kitchen –"

"I don't mean you. We had at least a dozen naked people in and out of the Jacuzzi."

"You played naked host?"

She shook her head. "No time to get naked. I just played host." Her chin rose and she squinted her eyes at him. "You know it's only fun getting naked if you're around to watch."

"Yeah. Right."

She ran her hand along the back of his neck as he took another drink of water.

"Valerie asked me to find her a black man to screw her."

LaStanza coughed up a mouthful, sat back and coughed again. Lizette kept patting the back of his neck.

When he recovered, he managed to say, "You won't believe what I thought you said."

"Valerie wants me to find a black man to screw her. The professor wants to borrow our video camera and tape it."

For the second time that evening, he had the feeling he was slipping into *The Twilight Zone*.

"Time for bed," he said. "Before Rod Serling steps in to explain all this."

2:22 a.m. – Milan Street

"Y'all just stay home and get yoar beauty rest, Lil' Filly."

Jodie Kintyre parked the LTD in her driveway behind her blue Saturn. Climbing out, she walked around her new car, checking it out. She had to duck under the air-conditioner sticking out of her bedroom window on her way back to the LTD. The narrow driveway barely had room on either side to pass with the wooden shotgun houses so close together in this quiet uptown neighborhood.

Walking around to the front of her house, she looked up Milan then down at busy Magazine Street, which was rarely quiet, only a block away. Passing through the front gate of the double house she shared with her parents, them on the left, her on the right, she thought of the Venetta's and their double house irrevocably shattered tonight. She climbed the four steps up to the wooden gallery with its gingerbread overhang above, neat yellow bug lights brightly illuminating the porch, lights her father put up, back when they'd rented out Jodie's half of the double. An orange face worked its way through the closed Venetian blinds of her living room window before Jodie punched in the alarm code and stuck her key in the dead-bolt lock.

Jodie smiled at Cody as she unlocked the door, flipped on the living room light to her cat's high-pitched chatter, "Yow, Yow, Yow!" Cody's big brother, Shane, came stalking in from the back of the house, head lowered, ears up, looking like a miniature lion with his long strides.

She locked the door, re-arming the alarm, and put her briefcase and LFR on the small desk, flipping off the radio, draping her coat over the back of the desk chair as Cody jumped up on the desk for his pets.

More "Yows" from Cody as she ran her hand from the top of his head along his back to his tail which rose, then curled under in pleasure. Cody was shorter than his brother, looked more like a jaguar, stockier, heavier. Litter mates, she'd gotten them as kittens a year ago. Plain old orange tabbies, the ad described them in the paper. There was nothing plain about these boys.

They followed her through the dining room into her bedroom where two messages waited for her on her answering machine. Sitting on her queen-sized bed, she pulled off her shoes and punched the replay button.

The first message was from Andy Gee, the unrelenting Dr. Gee, trying to act casual, asking how she was, when he could see her again, how he was thinking about her. She pulled off her shoulder rig, laying it on the nightstand next to the answering machine as the next message started and she cringed.

"Heidi, Lil' Filly. I'll take your autopsies in the morning." Snowood's voice sank after the initial *Heidi,* pronouncing the words more slowly with only a hint of country accent. "No reason you need to get up. Shit, I'm the one who killed all those people. I'd call the Wop but his ain't no paperwork case like yours." He actually sounded remorseful. "Y'all just stay home and get yoar beauty rest, Lil' Filly."

He had to add that!

He wasn't finished. "That was pretty funny, 'bout waterin' me. Took me a while to get it but it was funny."

Jodie almost smiled as she pushed the erase button and began stripping down to bra and panties. She went into the bathroom, the cats following. Shane adding his "Yows" to the continuing conversation. He had such a tiny voice for such a big cat. Jodie blamed herself, getting them fixed when they were too young, not knowing how old they were because the man who sold them to her lied to get rid of the kitties, adding weeks to their date of birth. But they turned out fine, except for the tiny voices.

As she removed her make-up, Shane jumped up on the sink and she had to use one hand to pet him, one to remove her eyeliner. Cody joined in too, back feet atop the closed lid of the commode, front paws up on the sink. She shooed them away and brushed her teeth, then went out to pour fresh food into their cat dish and fresh bottled water in their water dish before going back into the bathroom.

Washing her face, Jodie wiped it and stared at herself in the bright bathroom mirror. Her partner said she had cat-eyes and he was right, long slit eyes, hazel eyes most men found mysterious. Her nose was a little too round and little too large, but not enough to do anything about.

Many women would kill for her natural yellow-blonde hair and high cheekbones. She patted her chin but there wasn't a hint of sag there, like her mother.

Jodie dropped her bra and panties into the dirty clothes hamper and went back into the bedroom. Catching a glimpse of herself in the full-length mirror in the corner, she stopped and examined herself. Her breasts were heavier with age, fuller actually, her nipples thankfully pointing high, giving her breasts a more round look than when she was a teen.

Her bush, a shade darker yellow-blonde, was a perfect triangle between her long, thin legs. She turned around and look at her ass, still round and smooth without a hint of droop.

"Nice body," she told herself, knowing it, having men leer at her since she was thirteen, before she even developed. Blonde hair and a pretty face will do that.

A snapshot of Lori Venetta flashed in her mind, long legs and long strawberry-blonde hair streaming in the breeze, red lips pursed. She sure didn't look thirty. And for an instant Jodie felt something else, a warning in the way that woman had looked at her partner. He didn't see it, obviously. He was in leopard-mode, but if Lori shot those looks at him later, he'd see it all right. So Sicilian it hurts, LaStanza was the most heterosexual man she knew. Yet, not pushy with women.

As aggressive as he was in pursuing criminals, he was the opposite with the opposite sex, never aggressive with women. Sure, he was married to the rich and gorgeous Lizette, but all men were attracted to other women, Jodie's father no exception. If this Lori was the clingy, aggressive type and made the first move –

Jodie slipped beneath the sheet and flipped off the light as the cats settled at the foot of her bed. She closed her eyes but couldn't turn off her mind. Hell, if she and LaStanza's weren't so close, like lovers who'll never touch, they would have had an affair years ago. In a way they were having an affair, a shared affection for a partner that would be ruined if they became physical. By not, they remained close. If she ever tried to explain it, no one would understand.

Except Lizette. She knew from the start, had always seen it and let herself become the sister Jodie never had. Affection there too. Strange, but it worked and Jodie would keep an eye on that Lori and her piercing stares, red lips, long legs and flowing strawberry-blonde hair.

For a moment, she thought of the dark, good-looking John Raven Beau, with his lean face and square jaw, those hooded, light brown eyes. He had the look of the hawk about him. Probably his Sioux blood. She could picture him on a horse, naked chest dark brown from the unrelenting Dakota sun.

Too bad he's so young.

Jesus, I'll never get to sleep like this.

She turned on the light on the nightstand and reached into the top drawer for a book she'd picked up at a bookstore in the Quarter. The lady behind the counter said it was written by a New Orleans writer, an historical novel, *Red Hawk* by John Edward Ames. It was a love story. A blonde settler woman and a Sioux warrior, according to the sales lady.

The warrior on the cover had long dark hair and hooded eyebrows, a square jaw and the look of the hawk about him. The book opened with a buffalo hunt along the high plains, warriors on ponies running down the huge beasts, slaying them with bow and arrow, the women and children following behind on foot to skin the buffalo and carve up the beasts, using every part of the buffalo.

Red Hawk was twenty years old as the book began, a warrior in the Wolf Clan of the Oglala. They were the Lakota. Cousins of the Cheyenne. Enemy of the Arapaho and Crow. Their enemies, including the white eyes, called them Sioux –

6:45 a.m. – Orleans Parish Coroner's Office

"Wouldn't have thought it possible."

LaStanza found the body bag containing the cadaver of Grosetto Venetta on a gurney in the narrow hall outside the autopsy room, pushed the gurney into the room and asked the two coroner's assistants if his body could go first. The two men, both huge, with blue-black skin, could pass for twins, with their shaved heads and dull eyes. The closest nodded and LaStanza pushed the gurney next to one of the two stainless steel autopsy tables, then backed away and waited for the pathologist, trying his best to ignore the smells he could never identify. The strongest was an acidic, eye-watering stench. Probably formaldehyde mixed with the nasty-sweet smell of human flesh slowly decaying.

He turned to the sound of footsteps and Snowood walked in without his Stetson, a large white Styrofoam cup in each hand, notebook tucked under his left arm.

"Shoulda knowed you'd beat me," he passed one of the cups to LaStanza.

Both detectives wore tee-shirts and jeans, Snowood's with *Tombstone* across the chest, LaStanza's a red Archbishop Rummel High shirt. At least the coffee was hot and strong with cream and two Equals, the way LaStanza liked it. Then again, Snowood was his old partner.

Suffering from a lack-of-sleep headache, LaStanza was thankful for the coffee.

"Jodie's not coming," Snowood said when he came back after lining up his body and her two bodies to be next in line. "I'm takin' her's."

LaStanza waited, knowing he would continue.

"Hell, I'm the one who started all this shit with ma' big mouth. I was just jokin'."

LaStanza gave him the Sicilian stare.

"I hate that look," Snowood turned away. "And I got you coffee."

They each took a hit of coffee.

"She ain't goin' to court on hers, not like you-n-me, pardner."

Unless the Senoré's murderers managed to get killed together, in a car wreck or shot by police, LaStanza knew he'd be in court.

Dr. McNeese came in, as usual, in a rush. McNeese: six feet, sixty years old, medium build with close-cropped salt-and-pepper hair and a narrow face, slipped on a white smock and safety glasses and nodded to the attendants who pulled the Senoré's body bag up on the first table.

A bald crime lab tech LaStanza had never seen before, short and stout with thick glasses, carrying a camera case and evidence case, plopped on a stainless steel stool and said, "Didn't want to be late."

LaStanza pulled out his notepad. "What's your name?"

"Gershwin. George Gershwin."

LaStanza looked up.

"Seriously. And I got a brother named Ira. My mother still thinks it's funny."

As the body bag was opened, even Dr. McNeese was taken aback by the damage to the Senoré's face. Gershwin added, "What happened to him?"

McNeese looked down at Gerschwin's bald head. "He fuckin' died."

Caught Snowood with a mouthful of coffee, started him coughing and spilling coffee all over his Tombstone tee-shirt.

"Son-of-a-bitch. Motha fuck. Goddammit!" Snowood hurried to find something to clean off his shirt.

As soon as Gershwin was finished taking close-up photos, McNeese used a portable X-Ray machine to see if there was a bullet anywhere in the Senoré's head. He shook his head and pulled the machine away, yanked on a pair of rubber gloves and began fishing through the bloody goo that was once a face.

An eye-ball was pulled aside, the second floated in the mass of blood as LaStanza backed away, feeling the coffee trying to crawl up his esophagus for a moment. Thankfully, it settled as McNeese declared, "I'll be darned."

He pointed to the bridge of the Senoré's shattered nose. "Looks like a blow against the nose. Caved in the entire face."

LaStanza, "Wouldn't have thought it possible."

McNeese waved him forward. "What does that look like to you?"

LaStanza stepped up to see the indention on skin of the nose, an impression made by a blunt instrument, checkered marking.

"Like the trigger hammer of a revolver." LaStanza turned his right hip around and pointed to the trigger hammer of his .357 magnum Smith and Wesson, stainless steel hammer, checkered so the thumb wouldn't slip when cocking the hammer for single action firing.

Gershwin took close-up pictures before McNeese sliced around the wound, pulling the flesh away, dropping it in a vial of clear liquid.

LaStanza learned long ago there was no dignity in death and the body of the victim was the most important piece of evidence in any murder case. This particular piece of the Senoré's body could be scientifically matched to the hammer of the murder weapon, if found.

McNeese picked up part of the Senoré's cheekbone and showed it to LaStanza. "Look how thin the bones are. See how the shoulders are hunched over. He had osteoporosis. It's not just for women, you know. Very brittle bones. One blow of great force shattered the entire face. What was he, ninety?"

"Ninety-one, last month."

McNeese picked up a scalpel and laid the body cavity open with precise slices from the tips of the each shoulder, over to the breastbone and then straight down to the crotch. LaStanza backed away from the stale smell within the body, the gases that filled the small autopsy room.

LaStanza remained through the entire autopsy, making sure there were no surprises, taking this quiet time to link with his victim. LaStanza was, after all, the most important witness to all this, the one who'll explain to the jury, in layman's language, the old man's vivisection, the final indignity performed on this gentle man.

He had to link with his victim.

Venetta.

After all, he was all the victim had left – revenge-wise.

1:07 p.m. – Exposition Boulevard

"Poor man shot in the face."

When LaStanza walked into the kitchen with a newspaper under his arm, Lizette looked at the clock and said, "That was the longest autopsy."

She was on a stool at the counter, cup of coffee in front of her. Her hair was still damp from her shower and a towel lay across her shoulders. She wore a yellow tee-shirt and blue running shorts.

"You won't get much of a nap."

LaStanza put his paper and notes on the counter and looked around the kitchen, then peered through the French doors at the deck and Jacuzzi.

"She's upstairs getting ready, which is what I'm about to start doing." Lizette took a sip of her coffee. "I have to go by the Estate."

Check on things, he was sure. Leaning around his wife, he kissed the side of her neck, then lifted her hair and kissed the nape of her neck. She bent her head forward and he continuing kissing her.

"I did a canvass of my victim's neighbors," he said between kisses. "Got a paper at the K&B, where the Senoré bought his paper every evening, even when he had to use a walker."

When he stopped the kisses, Lizette told him to go up and take a nap. "I'll be back to wake you in plenty of time."

He yawned and stretched and opened the paper. Page one headline was another spread on the South Louisiana Sniper. No matter how bad his case was, at least LaStanza wasn't part of that circle-jerk investigation. Fuckin' FBI-led task force trying to locate the man with a hunting rifle who'd shot three political figures in two months. The vaunted FBI profile narrowed it down to a white male in his mid to late twenties, affluent and a loner. How they came up with that was a mystery in itself.

The case exploded a week ago when the third victim was gunned down, a state representative from Gonzales outside the man's home. One shot through the heart. All of the victims were shot in the chest or head with a high-powered rifle, probably a Mauser, according to the firearms examiners. High-powered hunting rifles in "Sportsman's Paradise" Louisiana was a common as mosquitoes. All of the victims were political figures, the first an assistant state treasurer then a justice of the peace.

"Your case is in the paper," Lizette told him, pointing to their newspaper spread out on the kitchen table. "Page one of the Metro Section. Poor man shot in the face."

Shot?

LaStanza stepped over to read the typically inaccurate newspaper account of the Senoré's murder. He could almost hear Public Information Officer Alice Walker, no relation to the writer, as she hurriedly told the press what happened, assuming the old man was shot in the face.

Grosetto Venetta's name was horribly misspelled, but LaStanza's name was spelled correctly as the case officer. They had his name down pat, used to writing about him, mostly when he was brought in front of another Grand Jury for shooting someone.

He'd have to warn Pauli to keep quiet, not to go correcting the paper. The family would learn the truth from the coroner's office and may tell neighbors the old man wasn't shot and that LaStanza did not want. Right now only the police, the pathologist and the killers knew the truth. Sometimes, the truth brought the police and the killers together.

He remembered cases, many cases where killers corrected news reports, telling friends and neighbors, "She wasn't shot. She was stabbed." Proclaiming, "They didn't break in through the window. The back door was unlocked."

"Have you eaten?" Lizette climbed off the stool.

He shook his head and yawned again.

"Well, eat something. You'll sleep better." She went up the back stairs.

He went to the refrigerator and pulled out leftovers. The smell of roast pork turned his stomach, so he put the platter back, reached for a carton of milk and went for the Grape Nuts in the cupboard.

He used four packs of Equal to sweeten the cereal, pinching himself along the side where the love handles, as Lizette called them, were sprouting. As he ate at the counter, he reminded himself, again, to set up a schedule and start running again.

Hell, he had an entire fuckin' urban park for a front yard.

6:16 p.m. – Uptown Square

"Since Det. Sgt. Jones seems to prefer working Homicide ..."

Detective Felicity Jones parked his dark blue unmarked unit against the chain-link hurricane fence of the rear parking lot of Uptown Square Shopping Center, turned off the engine and examined the crime scene for a few minutes. Three uniformed officers stood aside from the victim's body as she lay next to the open trunk of a new, shiny red 1986 Nissan Stanza. Two emergency medical technicians stood next to their ambulance, red lights still flashing atop.

Uptown Square wasn't a mall, but a series of buildings, three-story, some two-story, some stucco, some brick, most with corrugated tin roofs painted brown. Linked by covered walkways, the buildings were set in a labyrinth, so shoppers had a hard time not running into more shops on their way in or out of the shopping center.

Climbing from his car, Fel slipped his LFR into the back pocket of his tan suit pants. He pulled out his notepad and pen, leaving his suit coat inside and glanced behind his car at the rear fence of the shopping center. A row of trees lined the fence and a street dead-ended against the fence, a yellow car with its hood up parked there, pieces of motor littering the ground. The houses along the street were small, middle class wooden one-story.

Jesus, I need to get over there. If I had a partner –

Fel Jones: 5'8", 165 pounds, with short-cropped black hair, brown eyes had blue-black skin and a ready smile, except on evenings like this. Newly re-assigned to the Homicide Division, he hadn't been assigned a partner yet because he was a detective-sergeant with no command responsibility. He'd worked Homicide before, but had the good sense to return to the Intelligence Division when he got his stripes. That was before his old patrol partner LaStanza dragged him into a racial-murder on Pleasant Street. A couple weeks after Fel and LaStanza shot the racist-murderer Kaiser Billyday, to death, the Chief of Police transferred Fel back to Homicide. In the official teletype, the Chief had stated, "Since Det. Sgt. Jones seems to prefer working Homicide, we shall oblige him."

Everyone, including Fel, was waiting for the Chief to find a way to get rid of LaStanza completely, a man the Chief described as "unstable with an unacceptable penchant for violence." They figured the chief was taking so long to make LaStanza sweat. Obviously, he didn't know LaStanza at all.

Fel approached the body carefully, avoiding two cigarette butts and an empty Coke can. Before the EMTees got away, he got their names and discovered they'd found no vital signs on the body.

Stepping close to the body, Fel stopped and took a deep breath, moved to the side to get a good look at the woman's face. If he hadn't just left his girlfriend, he'd have thought – *Jesus.* She looked so much like Wanda, Fel had to rub the goose bumps from his arms. Even the reddish-tint of her hair was like Wanda's.

She was in her twenties with light brown skin, full lips, a sculptured nose and soft, round chin. She was beautiful. Lying on her right side in a form-fitting red dress, her legs crossed, her left high heel stood next to her foot, as if she'd been shot from it. She was thin, a model's figure. He studied the large wound at the back of her head, the exit wound through her left eye, her long hair matted in blood.

Next to her head lay two plastic shopping bags, one with green lettering "Uptown Square Book Shop" with two paperbacks protruding, *The Last of the Mohicans* and *A Confederacy of Dunces.* The other bag was white with a shoe box inside.

Fel went down on his haunches next to her, touched her arm. It was already cool to the touch.

"You guys see a purse?" he asked the patrolmen.

"No."

Fel looked under the car, stood and looked in the open trunk. No purse.

"We'd like to stay," the white patrol officer said. "But our lieutenant wants us back on the street."

"Who was here first?" Fel stepped toward them and the young black cop raised his hand. His name tag read: Anthony.

"You gotta stay, my man."

Another patrol car came skidding up and out popped Stan-the-Man Smith in his tailored uniform. He pointed to the white cop who was about to get in his car and snapped, "Where you goin'?"

"Back on the street."

"Nope. You're staying with me." Stan moved up to Fel and patted his old buddy on the shoulder. "He's gonna need all the help he can get."

Fel thanked him as the crime lab van arrived, then asked if Stan and the cop so eager to leave could start canvassing the shopping center. As they left, Fel asked Anthony to go around getting the license plate numbers from all the cars in the area.

As the tech began taking pictures of the body, Fel spotted several people peeking out of their houses from beyond the fence. He pulled out his LFR and called headquarters, asking them to start with Sergeant Land and then go down the list of detectives on his squad.

He needed assistance.

6:05 p.m. – Exposition Boulevard

"I can adjust those for you."

LaStanza slipped his .357 magnum into a canvas holster that clipped to the rear of his tuxedo pants at the small of his back, gun-butt pointing to his right so he could reach back with his right hand

and pull it out quickly, in case some maniac went after the mayor tonight, or, more likely someone might go after Lizette's mother, who needed her own bodyguard she pissed off so many people.

The tux was black, with a white vest and bow tie, which Lizette had to tie for him because no one wore a clip-on tie to an uptown event. Without the coat on, he looked like a fuckin' waiter. With the coat he looked like a butler in an old British flick.

He watched his wife sitting at her vanity table as she put on her make up. Naked, she applied a light coat of silver-blue eyeshadow above her eyes, those pouty lips pursed in concentration. At five-two and a half inches, Lizette weighed all of ninety pounds. A slim body with nice round hips, she was top-heavy, with oversized breasts, coral-colored aureoles and small nipples.

LaStanza sat on the edge of the bed and put on the new supershiny black shoes Lizette bought for him. She said they weren't patent leather although that's what they looked like. They fit perfectly, just like the tux, just like all the expensive clothes Lizette loved to buy for him.

"Don't look so hang-dog," she said.

"You know how much I *love* hanging with the rich folk."

"You are a rich folk and I've been one as long as you've known me, Mister Middle-Class Italiano." She gave him a haughty look over her shoulder. *Good*, LaStanza thought, *she's feeling a little better.*

"We're not like them," he teased back.

Lying back on the bed, feet still touching the floor, he cupped his hands behind his head and closed his eyes and remembered last month's long weekend on Guadeloupe, where they'd spent their honeymoon three years earlier. He remembered that first afternoon on that black pebble beach under an overcast sky, as he rubbed sunblock on those breasts beneath the peering eyes of other couples on the beach and passers-by. He kneaded those breasts and felt his heart leap when Lizette rolled over and slipped off the bottom of her bikini to lay naked with him.

He remembered rubbing sunblock on her ass and the wide eyes of the passersby, especially one particular tall man with chocolate skin who stepped up to admire her, saying how beautiful she was in a thick Caribbean-British accent. Lizette thanked him and rolled on her back to lay there, face up, full frontal nudity. LaStanza's dick became a diamond-cutter and he again recognized his long-suppressed voyeuristic tendencies matched his wife's exhibitionism.

There were two pictures he'd taken right after, Lizette standing with the man with chocolate skin on that beach. With an arm around each other's waist, stood naked Lizette, smiling at the camera. In the first shot the man was smiling at the camera. In the second he was looking down at her body.

Later, in the heat of their hotel room, as they fucked, he looked down into those gold-brown eyes as she gasped, "You liked him watching, didn't you?"

LaStanza wouldn't admit it, but she knew. Her beautiful face seemed to glow as they made love as they moved against each other, his dick working within the hot folds of her wet pussy.

"I like showing my body to strangers," she admitted.

LaStanza's eyes snapped open and he sat up with difficulty. He had another raging hard-on.

Lizette moved from her make-up vanity to the bed to pull on her sheer pantyhose. Naked, she wore nothing under the pantyhose and would go braless beneath the silver halter-gown. Her breasts rose as she pulled up the hose, smoothing it along her sleek leg, lifting the leg. She pulled up the second leg, stood and tugged the pantyhose up to her waist.

She climbed into the dress, buttoning the halter top, reaching inside to adjust those full breasts within the halter, which covered most of her breasts but not all, leaving a slice of cleavage in front and the sides of her breasts exposed.

"I can adjust those for you." He smiled.

"We'll be late if you did." She rolled her hips at him on her way to the walk-in closet.

She came out with a pair of silver high-heels, sat back at the vanity and pulled them on, then checked her face in the mirror.

LaStanza grabbed his coat, slipping a thin notepad into a coat pocket, along with the fat Colibri ball-point pen, because a good homicide man never went anywhere without something to write on. He clipped on his beeper and carried his LFR in his left hand.

Waiting in the kitchen, Professor LeGris wore a similar tux as LaStanza. Valerie LeGris, a few inches taller than LaStanza in her gold high-heels, wore a white halter dress with a chocker collar and a small, gold lamé jacket, her long hair lying straight down her back. She took LaStanza's arm as they moved out to the black limo Lizette had engaged to drive them to her family's house both she and her husband called The Estate.

6:35 p.m. – Rosa Park

"You busy?"

Only eight blocks from the Exposition Boulevard mansion Lizette's family had given their daughter as a wedding gift, The Estate sat at the corner of St. Charles Avenue and a private street called Rosa Park.

An immaculate, three story, florescent white, Greek revival, the Louvier Family Estate faced St. Charles with a dozen large Ionic columns running along the front and uptown side of the gallery, six smaller columns along the second story verandah. Its cut-glass front door faced the avenue and sparkled with light glimmering from inside. Along the Rosa Park side of the house was a sheltered driveway that always reminded LaStanza of a funeral parlor. The limo parked there and they climbed out, LaStanza leaving his LFR with the driver, who turned out to be a retired NOPD sergeant.

"Watch this for me?"

"Sure."

"I'll send some food down to you."

"It's a deal." The retired sergeant winked as Lizette shot her husband a long stare, looking as if she just realized he's brought the radio.

"I'm leaving it in the car."

"You have a beeper."

"Yes." He reached around her waist, fingers brushing the side of her right breast. "But if I get beeped, I'll have to talk to them."

Lizette continued the long stare, trying her best to do what LaStanza did so well – keep her face expressionless.

She's getting good at it, he thought as she took his hand and led the way around to the front of the Estate where twenty wide marble steps led up from the manicured lawn to the cut glass door where a prim waiter stood in an all-white tux, which contrasted nicely with his dark brown skin. The waiter opened the door for them. LaStanza thanked him as they stepped into the Italian marble foyer where Lizette's parents waited to greet everyone.

Descended from the Valois Kings of France, Lizette's family had been confidants of Henri of Navarre and later, Robespierre during the French Revolution, covering all bases. Both sides of Lizette's family, the Louviers and her mother's family, the Raveneauxs were descended from French royalty. LaStanza only recently learned from Lizette how a Louvier and a Raveneaux had fought at the Battle of New Orleans. 1815.

The only famous battles the LaStanzas fought were losing skirmishes with the Mafia back on the sandy isle just off the boot of Italy. Before they escaped to America.

Lizette's mother, Donna Raveneaux Louvier, dark brown hair piled atop her head, wore a beige evening gown. A lovely woman with high cheekbones, she would still be considered quite beautiful if she ever smiled.

As Lizette introduced the prof and his wife, LaStanza caught her father's eye and Alexandre Louvier II nodded his approval of Valerie LeGris to LaStanza, following it with a strong handshake. Still a young man in his mid-forties, Alexandre was Louisiana's most successful banker, member of the most exclusive club in New Orleans, the Boston Club, member of the oldest Mardi Gras club, the Mystick Krewe of Comus. Very little disturbed Alexandre, even his wife's constant disapproval of what their daughter wore and even stronger disapproval of LaStanza.

The only anguish LaStanza witnessed, had visited the Louviers the night Lizette's twin died with such violence LaStanza thought the family would never recover. Lizette certainly hadn't recovered and probably never would and looking around at the lace curtains and fine furniture, at the veneer of wealth, LaStanza knew, deep inside, the family was far from recovered. Like new paint on a wrecked car. It was a façade, a mask they all wore in public. Sudden violence does that to families. They try to get back to normal but it's always there, that ghost. They were the family of a murder victim.

Mrs. Louvier bumped cheeks with Lizette, each kissing the air. In a low voice she said, "You're falling out of your top."

"I know," Lizette said, leaning over to kiss her father. "Wait 'til Valerie takes off her jacket."

Which Valerie LeGris did a moment later, passing it to another waiter as she stood among the crowd in her gown with its diaphanous halter-top, those round breasts clearly visible, pointed nipples and all. Lizette's father tried to hide his smile, but his wife caught him and her eyes became hardened.

LaStanza leaned close to his wife's ear. "Where's your brother? He'll enjoy this."

"He's not old enough to attend these things." She waved to a tall couple. "He's probably playing Nintendo at a friends."

The people Lizette were waving at came up and she introduced her husband and the LeGris to a woman named Lilli and her husband Hans who dutifully tried not to look at Valerie's or Lizette's breasts. Lilli stood around six feet and Hans was even taller, both with white-blonde hair and pale complexions.

LaStanza excused himself and went to get drinks for everyone from one of the bars. Standing in line, he watched the people watching the two most beautiful women in the place, Lizette and Valerie, noting the pissed disapproval of some of the females and the sneaky peeks from most of the men.

LaStanza always felt out of place among the rich, especially Louisiana's Reagan Republicans who brought their snooty condemnation to the Estate because nothing ticked off these new Republicans more than rich Democrats who refused to join their elitist club, like Alexander Louvier II and his daughter. The Louviers, especially Lizette, were ardent Democrats who continually dotted their lawns with election signs for Democratic candidates, like the black mayor of New Orleans.

Reagan, with his state's rights platform, the veiled hint to southern whites to vote for him, he's not one of those northern liberals, he'll keep America strong and white and who gives a damn about the economy anyway. Just face down the Russians and those damn labor unions like the air-traffic controllers. Go out on strike, you're fired. Gone. Finito.

Lizette had once told LaStanza he had the making of a good southern liberal Democrat. Maybe she was right.

A tall woman wearing a khaki tent-looking dress stood in the corner with a violin, accompanied by a man in a black tux playing the grand piano. Their chamber music echoed in the background as the woman's head twisted spasmodically from side to side as she played. They were very good actually. LaStanza planned to ask if they knew any Led Zeppelin.

As LaStanza was returning with the drinks, the mayor arrived and seemed to spot Valerie LeGris right away, smiling that warm candidate-smile of his and eased his entourage in her direction.

LaStanza handed his wife her Sazerac, LeGris and Valerie their champagnes, managing to not spill any of his club soda along the way.

"You're not drinking?" Lizette asked as she took a hit of her strong liquor.

"More fun watching these people while sober."

The lead bodyguards of the mayor arrived, two huge robbery detectives who looked like professional wrestlers, trying to look officious as they checked out Lizette and Valerie's tits.

"Hey," LaStanza whispered to his wife, "let's introduce Valerie's breasts to the mayor."

The beeper startled LaStanza. Lizette closed her eyes and took in a deep breath. Stepping away, LaStanza looked at the small screen atop the pager and saw "30. 108. 10-18. 3128."

Jesus. Another fuckin' murder. Officer needs assistance on follow-up. 3128 was Felicity Jones who had Saturday duty.

"I'll just call on the radio," LaStanza told his wife, avoiding the introductions with the mayor as he slipped around the group. He finished his club soda on the way to the bar and grabbed a Coke. At the front door, he stopped a waiter with a tray of coconut shrimp, and pulled out a twenty.

"You the son-in-law, ain't ya?" the waiter said.

"Yeah."

"I seen you around." The waiter was young with skin almost as dark as Fel Jones's blue-black complexion.

"Good," LaStanza said, slipping him the twenty and taking the platter and the Coke out to the limo for the driver who said, "Hey. Hey. Thanks man."

LaStanza turned on his LFR and called Fel, "3124 – 3128. What'd you have?"

"Shopping Center fulla witnesses. Can't find anyone else. You busy?"

A mischievous smirk came to LaStanza's lips as he looked down at his monkey suit. "Negative. Not at all."

"Can you 10-19?"

"10-4. On my way."

7:35 p.m. – Uptown Square

"Another Bad Night In The Old Town Tonight."

"Just let me out here," LaStanza told the chauffer as the limo pulled up in front of Fel Jones' unmarked unit.

"You want me to wait?"

"If you want to. Enjoy the shrimp."

LaStanza took his notepad and pen from the tux coat, leaving the coat in the limo. Stepping away, he keyed the mike of his LFR to advise headquarters, "3124, 10-97 Uptown Square."

"10-4."

He slipped the LFR into the rear right pocket of his tux pants and clipped his gold star-and-crescent badge to his vest as he approached the crime scene in a roundabout route, watching the crime lab tech take close-up photos of the victim's head. He waited for the tech to step back and moved closer. *Damn.* She looked just like –

Fel Jones came around from the front of the red Nissan and froze. As LaStanza stepped up, Fel spread his arms and said, "What the fuck?"

"Damn, man." LaStanza pointed at the body. "For a second I thought it was –"

Fel thumped LaStanza's bow tie with a finger, spreading his hands again.

"Oh." LaStanza shrugged. "I was at a thing."

Fel's eyes became wide. "Not one of them Estate things?"

LaStanza nodded. "What you got here?"

"*Jesus.* Lizette's gonna kick my ass. Don't tell me you left her at a white-tie gig."

"She's with her parents and a lady with a see-through top."

"What?" Fel's eyes became squinty.

LaStanza leaned close and spoke as if talking to a child. "What – the fuck – do you – need me – to do?"

Fel pointed to the back street, to the yellow car with the hood up. "Canvass the neighbors. OK?"

"Sure."

LaStanza took another moment to look at the body. "Fuckin' shame."

Fel let out a long sigh and said, "A.B.N.I.T.O.T.T."

Since coming back to Homicide, Fel had picked up the annoying trait of initializing sayings. It drove Mark crazy, exasperated Jodie and befuddled Snowood. LaStanza was getting used to it and started trying to figure them out.

"A.B.N.I.T.O.T.T.? A Bellydancer Nightly Is The Only Thing Tonight?"

"You got *Tonight* right. But it's Another Bad Night In The Old Town Tonight."

"Oh." LaStanza walked away, having to round the rear fence and walk through Carver Playground, talking to three children sitting on a small merry-go-round. They saw nothing.

The first lady he spoke with, at a small wooden house painted dark green at the corner of Prytania and Leake Avenue eyed him up and down and went, "Woo, you look good, Baby. What kinda police are you?"

"Homicide. We're trying for a more formal look."

She'd seen nothing, as did everyone along Prytania, including the men in the Sports Bar, a shoddy place with bad lighting. It was fully dark by the time he found the owner of the yellow car under repair along the rear fence of the square, dead end of Lowerline Street.

He called Fel on the radio, "Got an eye-witness over here."

"I'll be right over."

The eye-witness, one Shelton Turner, III, was fifty and looked so much like Danny Glover, LaStanza couldn't stop staring. A night of look-alikes. Weird.

"You the most formal lookin' cop I ever saw," Shelton said as they waited for Fel. The big man was nervous, shook from seeing what he'd seen.

"What year's your car?"

"Sixty-six Pontiac Le Mans GTO with a rockin' V-8, 7456 ccs, hardtop coupe. You ever drive a GTO?"

"Nope." LaStanza busied himself writing down Turner's vital information from the man's driver's license, handing the license to Fel when he arrived, standing aside for Turner to repeat his story.

Turner had just pulled out from under his car when he spotted the victim. He never missed a pretty woman and was hawking her as she went to her car, opened the trunk and bent over. It was then he saw a white male jog up, point a gun at the woman and grab her purse.

"She seemed to panic. Tried to pull away and turned away and he shot her in the head. Just like that. And took off with her purse. I ran to the fence and saw she wasn't moving and then saw the man jump into a dark blue car with another man driving, looked like a black man, and they drove off down Leake Avenue."

"What kind of car?"

"I've been trying to visualize it. It's an American car, but they all look alike these days. GM car. Olds or Pontiac or maybe a Chevy."

"Did you get a good look at the shooter's face?"

Turner shook his head. "Too far away. But he was white. In his twenties. 'Bout five-nine or ten. Light brown hair."

As Fel jotted down the killer's description, LaStanza caught a movement on the other side of the fence and saw Jodie approach. In a maroon blouse and black slacks, shoulder rig with her semi-automatic dangling beneath her left arm, badge clipped to her belt, she leered at LaStanza and snapped, "Get the hell over here."

He grinned at his junior partner but could see she wanted none of that, so he waited until she came around through the park and up the street, watching her stomp her way to him. Many of the people

LaStanza had interviewed on his way down Lowerline were peeking out at her as she passed.

As soon as she arrived, Jodie grabbed his arm and pulled him to the other side of the GTO.

"Are you insane?"

"Some of the time."

"You get your Guinea ass back to wherever you left your wife. I'll help out here and Mark's on the way."

"Yes, mother."

"Don't start with me." Jodie poked him in the chest with a knuckle. "You won't win."

LaStanza passed Fel his notes and started away.

"T.F.C.," Fel said.

T.F.C.? LaStanza pointed toward Jodie. "The Fine Chick?"

Fel almost smiled. "Thanks For Coming." He shrugged at Jodie and said, "A.B.F.N."

Jodie closed her eyes and sighed wearily.

"A Bad Fuckin' Night?" LaStanza said.

"*Another* Bad Fuckin' Night." Fel corrected him then said, "A.B.F.N.I.T.S.D."

"Wait," LaStanza said. "You went too fast."

"Another Bad Fuckin' Night In The Sixth District. And we ain't even in the Sixth."

"Stop!" Jodie knuckled Fel in the chest this time.

LaStanza started away, turned back and told Fel, "This is the Second District."

Fel looked around and said, "Yeah. That's why I said we ain't even in the Sixth."

Jodie stood between them, right in Fel's face with her hands on her hips.

LaStanza walked back around Palmer Park to the parking lot and the limo. Before climbing in, he looked at the victim's car, sitting alone in the center of the lot with a bored patrol officer standing next to the still-open trunk and the stain of blood on the pavement. He felt a sinking in his chest.

How'd the man put it? "He shot her in the head. Just like that." That quickly a woman's life-blood lay on the cement beneath the parking lot's yellow lights. *Jesus*. It just kept happening over and over –

He climbed into the limo and left for the party back at the Estate, those short miles away, where they were laughing and drinking and flirting and doing what people did, passing a good time. And the blood on the cement looked black, like oil.

Fel watched the limo pull away and turned back to Jodie just as she said, "I'll take this guy's statement, then meet you back at the scene." She nodded toward Uptown Square.

"Thanks," Fel said, slipping his notebook into his rear pocket.

Shelton Turner III offered Jodie iced tea as he led her toward his house, slyly checking her out. The man did say he never missed a pretty woman.

The crime lab tech had located the bullet about fifty feet beyond the body. It was a large caliber, probably a .38 and looked in fairly good shape. Felicity Jones discovered, from the assistant manager of Uptown Square, a jittery man sporting Ben Franklin half-glasses, that there were sixty-six retail outlets in the shopping center and twenty-one business offices, mostly along the third floor. There were no exterior video surveillance cameras at Uptown Square, although they were being discussed.

The evening manager at Uptown Square Book Shop was Sophie Dunn: white, forty-four, with bright orange hair. She remembered the "attractive" young woman who bought the two paperbacks. The bookstore, little more than a over-sized, round kiosk, was filled to the ceiling with books and surrounded by windows facing the interior of the square and the parking area along Leake Avenue.

"Is there a surveillance camera in here?"

"No. I never liked Confederacy," Sophie said. "Of Dunces, that is. The first part was funny enough, but it dragged in the middle –"

Oh yeah, Fel thought. One of the books his victim bought. "Was she alone?"

"Huh?" Sophie batted her eyes at Fel.

"Was the woman alone, when she shopped?"

"Yes."

"Was there anyone else here when she was inside the store?"

"Nope. It's been a slow night. Is she a friend of yours?"

Fel shook his head. "Did you see anyone outside when she left?"

"No." Sophie's voice deepened.

Fel pointed over his shoulder at the parking area. "Did you see a dark blue car this evening?" He described the white male with the gun.

"No. Can you tell me what's going on, officer?"

Fel tapped his badge, clipped to the front of his belt. "I introduced myself as a homicide detective," he reminded her. "The woman who bought the books was murdered shortly after leaving here."

Sophie covered her mouth. "Tonight?"

"Yes, ma'am."

He thought she was going to collapse, but she only leaned back against a bookshelf. When Sophie recovered she was kind enough to retrieve the credit card receipt the woman used to buy the books. The name on the slip was Monique Williams, the same name from the registration of the shiny red 1986 Nissan Stanza.

"Are you going to be all right, ma'am?" Fel paused before leaving the book store.

Sophie took in a deep breath and asked him to wait a minute. She turned off the cash register, grabbed her purse and flipped off the lights before following Fel out. She locked the deadbolt and asked if Fel could walk her to her car.

"Sure," he followed her out to a tan Toyota where he gave her a business card and asked her to call if she remembered anything he forgot to ask or heard anything from any of the other retailers. She drove away leaning forward, her chin nearly touching the steering wheel.

Monique Williams bought a pair of navy blue high heels at Capo's Shoes shortly before her stop at the book store. The bag was in the truck. The woman who waited on Monique said she was alone. No one was around at the time – slow night – and no surveillance camera in Capo's. Monique paid forty-two dollars and seventy cents for a pair of shoes she'd never wear.

Fel Jones stepped out of Capo's and decided the take all the stores along the ground level of the shopping center one after the other. Passing a pay phone, he stopped and called Wanda.

"You OK?" she asked.

"Yeah. I'm fine. I'm gonna be a while though, so don't wait up."

"OK, Baby."

"I love you," he said.

She told him she loved him too and he could tell she was going to worry although there was nothing to worry about. It was all over, except the leg work. He told her that often. They're dead by the time we arrive.

That was before he and LaStanza got in a shootout with Kaiser Billyday.

9:05 p.m. – Rosa Park

"He says he went to a murder."

The mayor just finished an impromptu speech as LaStanza eased his way back into the Estate. He slipped through the crowd. A hand grabbed his arm and Hans called out to Lizette, "Look what I found!"

Lizette was twenty people away, standing with Valerie LeGris and several male admirers, middle-aged men mostly with smiling faces. Catching LaStanza's eyes, his wife nodded and started his way.

"So where you'd disappear to?" Hans said. Lilli took LaStanza's free arm and sort of hugged it, pulling it between her breasts. LaStanza looked up into her blue eyes that seemed shiny. Too much vino.

"Can't believe you left your beautiful wife with us wolves," Hans said and Lilli giggled. She hiccupped and asked, "Where did you go?"

"A murder."

Hans laughed. "Funny man."

Lizette eased up and took LaStanza's free hand. She looked as if she'd had too many Sazeracs, which meant she was pissed to the max or mellow as hell, depending on LaStanza's luck, which wasn't that good lately.

"He says he went to a murder," Hans said, patting LaStanza's shoulder. "Didn't know he was so funny."

"He's not," Lizette said. "He's a homicide detective." She wasn't pissed and wasn't mellow. She'd said it sharply with almost a touch of pride.

"Like Rockford," Lilli said, pulling on his arm.

"Or Magnum," her husband added. "You drive a Ferrari?"

LaStanza shook his head. "Maserati."

Lilli and Hans laughed, sounding like geese honking.

11:40 p.m. - Exposition Boulevard

"Does that make you think you're in charge?"

The new 1986 Maseratis were in the garage along the Garfield side of the mansion, Lizette's sea-foam green Biturbo 425I and LaStanza's darker British racing green 450I with its tan interior. When Lizette bought LaStanza's first Maserati, the one stolen by street thugs back when he was working the Batture Murders, she'd said he looked as if he belonged behind the wheel of an Italian sports car.

He'd only put twenty-two miles on this new '86 model. Parking a Maserati in the neighborhoods he frequented was like waving a red flag at a fuckin' bull. Hey, over here – steal me. New Orleans wasn't only known of its high murder rate. It was number one in stolen cars in America.

"You'd think we'd have a pro-active auto theft division," he told his wife as she picked out the new Maseratis at a boutique auto dealer on the first floor of an office building in the central business district on Baronne Street.

"Hell no. They recover cars and only when the insurance company calls and says that hulk parked next to the Desire Projects was stolen from Canal Street a month ago."

The Maserati salesman, who couldn't have been twenty-one, with a blond crew-cut, offered them espressos in demitasse cups and smiled. "That's why God invented insurance," he'd said and LaStanza had to agree. Only reason God woulda fuckin' bothered.

As the group from the party piled out of the limo, Valerie grabbed LaStanza's arm to keep from falling down the five slate steps leading into the kitchen from the side door along the Garfield Street side of the mansion. Hans and Lilli were along and stood awkwardly in the brightly lit kitchen as Lizette went outside to fire up the Jacuzzi and Valerie explained, in her seductive French accent, everyone went naked.

LaStanza opened two bottles of wine, a bottle of white from the fridge and some Valpolicella from the pantry as LeGris climbed out of his tux and Valerie dropped her dress in one motion to stand naked facing a giggling Lilli and a stunned Hans.

Lizette came in and helped with the wine. LaStanza dug towels out of the pantry putting them on the small kitchen table next to the open French doors leading to the deck and hot tub.

The two naked LeGris went out as Lizette stepped up to her husband and unfastened his tie.

"It'll relax you," she said softly, a wicked look in her golden eyes. She knew a hard-on didn't relax LaStanza and that's what was stirring inside his jockeys, especially as his wife stepped back, kicked off her heels and climbed out of her dress, then wiggled out of her pantyhose. She made a point to turn back for the wine to give Hans a good look before taking the wine out to the hot tub.

LaStanza felt that rush again, that excitement knowing another man was looking at his naked wife. He'd been resisting it, trying to get himself angry over it, only he couldn't. It turned him on and there was no getting around it. Lizette the little exhibitionist and her husband a voyeur. *Jesus.*

"Get the glasses, Honey." Lizette called back to him as he climbed out of his jockeys and grabbed the wine glasses.

Valerie was sitting up in the Jacuzzi, her wet breasts shimmering in the golden light. Lizette was up to her neck in the bubbling water. LaStanza climbed in next to her, glad his dick was only a blue-veiner and not sticking straight up like a fuckin' flag pole, yet.

Hans came out and climbed in on the other side of Lizette and Lilli finally tip-toed out, chirping, "Don't look! Don't look! Don't look!"

"Don't say it," Lizette warned her husband.

Jesus fuckin' Christ.

Lizette grabbed his dick and snuggled next to him and LaStanza had a diamond cutter now. His wife smiled and he closed his eyes, letting the hot gurgling water flow over him, letting his mind float away until he saw blood on the cement, black like oil and blinked open his eyes.

Later they made love in their king-sized bed, not saying a word, French kissing deeply, grinding their hips together, reaching for it, watching his gorgeous wife's face glow with the pleasure. She never looked lovelier than when making love.

Later still, watching her sleeping, her face nuzzled against his shoulder, LaStanza realized she looked just as lovely that way. Lizette fell asleep quickly but he couldn't. He tried deep breathing, tried letting his mind drift, careful not to let it envision blood and the carnage of his life's work. But sleep wouldn't come.

Lying safely in their beautiful mansion, behind dead-bolted doors and a state-of-art alarm system, .357 magnum atop the nightstand, LaStanza still couldn't let it rest, knowing another family wasn't sleeping tonight.

He saw her again, lying on the cement at Uptown Square. Her family's world was forever shattered tonight, with malice and for no good fuckin' reason except the meanness in the world had engulfed that lovely young woman, just as it took away the Senoré and so many victims, too many victims.

LaStanza felt the leopard pacing within is chest, back and forth, head lowered, eyes glimmering in anticipation of the hunt. He knew the steps he would take to run down his prey, to weave his way through the city streets, following their scent until he identified them, as he knew he would. It was what he did best.

And lying awake was part of it. Letting the leopard have its way, allowing the feline killer instinct to sharpen him, pulling him toward his prey. So he daydreamed himself to sleep, letting his imagination take him back to Claiborne Avenue.

LaStanza saw himself there, wearing all black, his stainless steel .357 magnum in hand as he stood around the corner from K & B as Senoré Venetta slowly approached with his walker. LaStanza cocked his weapon and approached the old man and the Senoré smiled at him. LaStanza nodded and turned as two men rounded the corner, the first raising a pistol high as he neared the old man, about to smash the man's face. LaStanza raised his weapon with the standard two-fisted police stance, bending his knees slightly, aimed at the would-be killer's face and squeezed the trigger. The gun erupted, red flame shooting from the muzzle as the semi-jacketed hollow point magnum round struck the would-be killer in the forehead, snapping the head back, sending a cloud of bloody brain matter into the air.

The other armed robber fired at LaStanza who calmly sent two rounds into the man, sending him tumbling to the cement. He wasn't dead. As LaStanza approached, the robber raised his pistol and LaStanza squeezed off another round, right through the man's left eye.

Quickly reloading with a speed loader, LaStanza stepped over to reassure the old man that everything was all right.

"Police," he said, showing his gold star-and-crescent badge.

And then he was at Uptown Square, approaching the red Nissan as the woman who looked like Wanda neared her car. They made eye contact momentarily and LaStanza smiled and turned to the dark blue car, which stopped fifty feet away. The woman opened her trunk as her would-be killer jumped from the blue car and jogged toward her. As he pulled out his gun, LaStanza went through the same routine – two-fisted stance, squeezing the trigger as he aimed at the jogger, revolver erupting. The man staggered from a round striking his chest and tried to shoot LaStanza, who fired again, catching the man in the throat, sending him to the cement.

The blue car suddenly accelerated and attempted to turn away as LaStanza fired again, blowing out the right front tire, sending the car into a light post. LaStanza carefully approached the car. The driver climbed out and stood away from the car, a blue-steel revolver in his right hand. His feet were apart as he raised his gun. LaStanza raised his weapon and they fire simultaneously.

LaStanza felt the bullet pass his face, felt its heat, sounding like an angry hornet. The man went to his knees with a gaping wound in his chest. He raised his gun again and LaStanza shot him in the forehead.

Suddenly Jodie was there, poking him in the chest, "What the hell are you doing here in a tux? Where's Lizette?"

Before LaStanza can answer, Lizette called out. She was standing a few feet away, naked and wet from the hot tub as she wrung out her long hair.

"Did you know he was here?" Jodie asked Lizette.

"No. He escaped. Again!"

"Wait," LaStanza told them. "This is my dream."

"So," Jodie and Lizette answered in unison. "Does that make you think you're in charge?"

"Yeah," called out Shelton Turner, III, with his Danny Glover smile, ogling Lizette as he approached wiping his hands on a rag.

"Nice outfit," Fel told Lizette, checking out her ass.

"Gol-damn!" Snowood choked on the wad of tobacco as he pointed at Lizette's boobs. Snowood's face turned red and LaStanza eyes snapped open as he realized he was dreaming. He looked down at Lizette and laughed to himself and closed his eyes again.

Easter Sunday, March 30, 1986

8:40 a.m. – Milan Street

"Second District's calling for Homicide."

When the phone rang, Cody jumped off the bed and ran out of the bedroom.

"Candy-Ass," Jodie said as she walked around the bed to catch the phone before the third ring.

"Detective Kintyre?" A hollow female voice with radio chatter in the background. *Headquarters.*

"Yes." Jodie's heart sank as she sat on the bed.

"We have a Signal 30 at 439 Walnut Street. Second District's calling for Homicide."

Jodie picked up the note pad next to the phone and wrote down the address, then asked the operator for the item number, time of the call, who called and the name of the first responding officer. Then she called her mother next door and told her she wouldn't be going with them to Easter Sunday mass.

"Oh, dear," her mother said. "We can go to afternoon services."

"This could take all day," Jodie said as Shane jumped up on the bed and looked around for what had caused his brother to run off. Jodie hung up and kicked off her white heels, pulled off of her peach colored skirt and climbed into a shorter gray skirt, which was not as snug as her black one.

She pulled her off-duty 9mm Smith and Wesson Model 669 out of her purse and slipped it under her pillow. Reaching into her closet she grabbed a light-weight black jacket and her shoulder rig with her Beretta already in the holster. A pair of low rise black shoes later, she tucked her handcuffs into the back of her skirt and the notepad into her briefcase, turned on her LFR and notified Headquarter she was in route to Walnut Street.

8:57 a.m. – Walnut Street

"Ferocious cats. Predators!"

It took Jodie sixteen minutes to get to Walnut, turning off Magazine Street. She found the line of squad cars along the Audubon Park side of the one-way street, half a block from Garfield. Jodie climbed out of the unmarked Ford she shared with her partner and looked between the houses at the oaks of Audubon Park. LaStanza lived in a direct line across the wide urban park.

She found the first officer who'd arrived at the scene standing at the bottom of the six brick steps that led to the open door of 439 Walnut Street. John Raven Beau nodded to Jodie, his normally dark complexion almost pale.

"Thought you were on the evening watch," she said, taking out her note pad to jot a quick description of the house. A freshening breeze from the river fluttered her note pad and rustled the tree leaves overhead. She smelled freshly cut grass.

"Shift change this morning," Beau said as he leaned against the black wrought iron rail next to the steps.

Jodie remembered she'd be back on the day watch Monday morning.

The house had two stories, gray stone walls, red-brown shingle roof and a covered front porch. There was a garage on the river side of the house and a driveway beyond that could almost be an extension of Garfield Street. A low stone wall ran in front of the house and around it to the back yard facing the park.

Jodie looked up from her notes and said to Beau, "OK, tell me."

He nodded to his police car with a woman in the back seat, doors open. "Daughter came by to take her mother to nine o'clock mass. Found the front door unlocked and followed the blood from the foyer through the living room to the kitchen in back. Looks like the mother was bludgeoned to death. I tried my best to not step in the blood. The daughter did and so did the killer. He was wearing sneakers. We secured the daughter and searched inside carefully. No one else inside."

"How old was the victim?"

"Daughter says fifty-five. A widow. While we were searching, her boyfriend came by to go to mass with them." Beau pointed up the street. "He's in the back of Left Sider's unit."

Jodie's eyes squinted. "Sider's first name is 'Left'?"

"What? No, Jimmy. LaStanza calls him 'Left'. Long story."

"*Lord.* That moniker will stick. LaStanza's always nailing people with aliases. Snowood's Country-Ass – forever. Even his wife calls him that now."

Jodie saw another patrol officer standing next to a marked car parked in front of Beau's with a man sitting inside.

Beau pulled out a set of keys. "The daughter's." He held up a brass one. "The kitchen door in back. It's still locked but you'll avoid the blood that way." He pointed to a blood mark on the porch next to the front door. "Killer came out this way, left bloody footprints outside the door, then cut across the grass." He pointed to the street. "No blood on the sidewalk or street."

"I need the usual out here," she told Beau. "License numbers of all cars in the area, four block radius. IDs of all passersby, including anyone in the park. Any neighbors stick their heads out, get their info. I'll get help to canvass the neighborhood."

Crime Lab Technician Val Avery stepped up with his camera case and black evidence case. Avery: forty-two, six feet tall and paunchy, with short cropped sandy hair and bifocals. Jodie led him to the front door and had him start with his pictures of the bloody footprints outside the door, footprints made by sneakers, leading away and into the grass as Beau had said.

"We'll need close-ups too."

"Of course," Avery put his cases down then pointed to the half open door. "I see blood inside."

Beau told him the blood started just inside the front door and went all the way back, splattered on the walls and streaked on the tile floor.

Jodie walked around the house to the kitchen door in back. It was a glass double French door. She peeked in and saw the body lying in a heap next to the kitchen table. She was about to open the door, then decided to follow Avery in through the front and went back around. A blue jay followed her, barking at her as it bounced from tree branch to branch. Probably a nest nearby.

Jodie Kintyre followed the crime lab tech through the front door. There was no damage to the door or dead-bolt lock which could only be opened by key. A set of keys were in the lock on the inside and Jodie could see a peep-hole in the door where the victim could see anyone ringing her doorbell.

While Avery took photos, she noted the blood splatter on the walls of the narrow foyer and the blobs on the floor and the smears where something had fallen, probably the victim, and the footprints. In the stuffy house, the thick smell of blood was sickening. Jodie only had coffee that morning and felt it churning in her stomach.

From the blood-splattered hall into the living room, the blood trail smearing the tan carpet and a green love-seat, the blood streaking the tile floor of the dining room, more blood splatter on the dining room table and an overturned chair, the blood leading into the kitchen. A woman's left high heel shoe lay in the archway between the dining room and kitchen. There were more bloody footprints of the same sneakers. Avery and Jodie stopped beneath the archway before the kitchen and the large pool of blood around the victim's body.

She lay flat on her back, arms and legs spread open. Her light green pants-suit soaked in blood, her right high heel standing between her feet. The stocking on her right foot was ripped.

Jodie eased around the body, stopping when she could get a good look at the woman's battered face and head, smashed beyond recognition. From the blood splatter on the room and walls, Jodie could see she was beaten as she lay. The woman's hands were severely battered, right wrist broken in a compound fracture, bone protruding through ripped flesh.

As Avery continued photographing, Jodie checked out the kitchen door. Nothing amiss. She spotted Beau approaching through the backyard. He stepped up to the back door and spoke through the door, "We checked all the windows. Locked."

She nodded and turned to Avery. "I want blood samples from every room, every surface." Jodie unlocked the back door. "I'll be back in a minute."

Avery pulled out his LFR. "I'm getting another tech over here."

"Good." Jodie walked past Beau and headed next door to use the phone. She needed help. Now. The blue jay followed her, chattering angrily.

"Shut the fuck up," she told the bird, "I have cats!" She lowered her voice, "Ferocious cats. Predators!" She stepped over the low wall for the neighbor's front door. "Just don't ring a phone around them."

9:35 a.m. – Exposition Boulevard

"It's bad or I wouldn't call."

Lizette was awake when the phone rang. Lying in bed, she was staring at the ceiling, wondering if her headache was a lack-of-sleep headache or a hangover headache.

"Let the machine get it," her husband said. A moment ago Dino was asleep, on his side facing her. His right eye was open now, brows furrowed.

"Headache?" she asked.

He closed his eye.

After the fourth ring the answering machine answered and she heard a sigh and Jodie's voice. "I'm sorry, Liz but I can't find anyone else." A sigh again. "It's bad or I wouldn't call."

Lizette picked up the receiver and told her friend, "You know you don't have to apologize. He's right here." She extended the phone. Her husband ignored her. She placed the receiver gently against his forehead.

"It's for you, Inspector Clouseau."

LaStanza snatched the receiver and growled, "The fuck is this?" She saw him swallow, then say, "OK. No problem. Really." His eyes were still closed. "What? It's in walking distance?"

A quick shower later, LaStanza stepped out of his front door, running a hand over the stubble on his chin. He'd wanted to wear the tux again, just to see Jodie's reaction, but Lizette hid the tux pants when he was in the shower. So he put on a pair of tan pants, Dockers, white dress shirt, gold tie and a blue blazer. Lizette had bought his entire outfit, even the shiny brown loafers with the rubber soles.

In his left hand he carried the tan leather case Lizette had given him for Christmas. First time he'd used it. Inside was a thick note pad with lined gray paper and a Mount Blanc ball point pen with baby blue ink inside. There was also a slot for business cards. LaStanza's magnum lay in a leather holster clipped to the waistband of his pants, handcuffs tucked in the rear of the pants, LFR in his left rear pocket.

His gangster glasses blotted out most of the sun's strong rays as he crossed Exposition Boulevard and walked across the grass of Audubon Park. Bright sunlight streamed through the oaks, like beams in a dusty cathedral, there was so much pollen in the air. LaStanza had no allergies so the pollen never affected him, ever.

Stepping across the blacktop road that circled inside the park, he slowed to let a couple on racing bikes speed past. Heads down and wearing dark goggles, they probably didn't even see him. The blacktop was neatly divided by a thick white line. Joggers to the right, bicyclers to the left. No cars, except police cars, allowed. It had been two weeks since LaStanza had run along the blacktop and that frustrated him, reminding him he had to find time to exercise.

A miler at Archbishop Rummel, LaStanza had lettered all four years in high school and still loved the solitude of long distance running, the steady plop-plop of feet, the rising heartbeat, air rushing through his lungs.

He walked over the stone bridge just beyond the blacktop, crossing the man-made lagoon that separated the golf course from the rest of the park, and started across the course, watching out for golfers. Easter Sunday and the sun was shining and he was heading to a scene Jodie described as gruesome. Someone of her experience calling a scene gruesome was chilling, at the least.

He looked up at the pale blue sky and smiled, remembering the time he'd started the narrative on a police report, back when was a rookie patrol officer, "On a balmy spring day in the City That Care Forgot, a rat-bastard stole two children's bikes from the front yard of –" The report was rejected by his sergeant, of course, and he had to rewrite the narrative.

He'd caught the bastard the next day. Jackass took the bikes to Finkle's Bicycle shop on Magazine and tried and pawn bikes to a bicycle retailer. LaStanza had already alerted old man Finkle, who jotted down the rat-bastard information from his driver's license and held the stolen bikes "on consignment" for the thief, called the Sixth District station for LaStanza and the case was as simple as that.

A warm breeze rustled the trees as he moved off the golf green. Audubon Park was about a half mile across at this point. Keeping a wary eye for anyone, he saw no golfers but spotted a elderly man sitting in one of the green gazebos next to a smaller lagoon.

The man looked up from the paperback he'd been reading. LaStanza opened his coat to show his badge. "Police," he said. "Have you seen anyone else around here this morning?"

The man took of his thick glasses and pulled a different pair of glasses from his shirt pocket and blinked at LaStanza who pulled out his ID folder and showed the man his credentials. Of course the old man had to put on his reading glasses again.

He turned out to be a World War II vet who lived on Garfield, near Broadway and had seen no one, except LaStanza, and nothing out of the ordinary all morning. LaStanza wrote down the man's info from his driver's license before leaving the man to his book.

10:09 a.m. – Walnut Street

"She knows LaStanza. They almost kissed."

Crossing the blacktop again, LaStanza approached the house Jodie had described, gray stone walls, red-brown shingle roof. He spotted Jodie standing just inside the back door. Unlike LaStanza's mansion, which faced the park, the houses along Walnut had the park as an extension of their backyards.

Jodie turned as he stepped in and let out a long sigh. She moved aside and nodded to the body. LaStanza took a long look and said, "OK, tell me."

She laid it out as he stared at the victim's pulped face, twisted arms and bloody pants-suit. Jodie asked him to go around and interview the daughter, then the boyfriend. "Beau's out front," she said as they stepped out and almost bumped into Fel Jones.

"Just finished my autopsy." Fel held up his LFR. "Heard all the chatter."

Fel wore an outfit that almost matched LaStanza's, a blue blazer, tan pants, loafers, only with a blue tie.

"Thanks," Jodie said, tapping LaStanza on the arm. "You better canvass. Fel can take the family."

It went without saying and all three knew. Better to send LaStanza around to the rich, white, uptown neighbors. In Homicide – you took the easy road, although LaStanza would prefer to send Fel around and fuck the lily whites.

They'd done that often enough when they were partners as patrolmen. Whenever a white face tried to pretend Fel wasn't there and only talked to LaStanza, he'd tell them Fel was the senior partner and step back. It was worse in the black areas. The women talked to Fel with no problem, but the brothers often ignored him worse than the uptight whites. Fel got used to it and eventually calmed down his hot-headed Sicilian partner, who wanted to tell them to get fucked. But it wasn't easy.

An angry blue jay followed LaStanza around the house, bouncing from limbs and chattering loudly and for a moment he was eight years old again, with his big brother Joe in City Park where a host of blue jays ran them out of the neatest hiding place, tall bush-trees surrounding the huge defunct Pop's fountain. The jays swooped at them like dive bombers.

Joe got so mad he threw his baseball cap at a jay on a branch and to the their surprise, the cap fell on the jay and brought the jay to the ground. Joe pounced on the hat before the jay could get out, carefully reaching in and wrapping his thirteen-year-old hand around the jay.

The jay tried to peck him and squawked for a while before Joe gently rubbed its belly. The jay finally calmed down, but kept glaring at Joe who started petting its head.

"Hope I didn't hurt the little fella," Joe said, sitting down with the bird who became even calmer. It was such a pretty bird with so many different shades of blue feathers and some black and some white. When Joe let the bird go, it bounced twice on the ground, looked around and flew off. Both boys were glad they hadn't hurt the bird and found a different hiding place, at least until spring ended and the jay's left their nests.

Stan Smith was out front of the victim's house now, standing with fists on hips, posing actually, as he called Beau over from across the street. He handed Beau's notes to Left Sider and told him to get the license plate numbers.

"You're the rookie," he reminded Sider. He sent another rookie into the park to stop joggers or anyone else he spotted.

"No need to talk to the old man in the gazebo," LaStanza said, turning them all around. "I already talked to him."

Stan folded his arms, flexing his muscles and said, "Another bad one, huh?"

LaStanza nodded and told him he was taking Beau along and crossed the yard, over the small brick wall to the next door neighbor's house.

"Forgot to get the victim's name from Jodie," LaStanza thought aloud.

"Helen Collingwood," Beau said. "Fifty-five. A widow."

Without looking back, LaStanza said, "Yep, you'll make a good homicide man one day. You poor bastard."

The door opened before LaStanza could ring the bell.

"Police," he said, showing his badge. "I'm Detective LaStanza, Homicide Division. This is Officer Beau."

"What's going on?" The neighbor was about sixty, a tall woman with dyed red hair, on the orange side.

"Did you see anyone around your neighbor's house this morning?"

"Just y'all. What happened?"

"This is important, ma'am. Did you see anyone around the house before the police?"

"No. Please tell me what's happened?"

"I'm from the Homicide Division ma'am. Something happened to Mrs. Collingwood. Did you know her well?"

Tears welled in the woman's eyes and she choked back a sob, holding on the door frame.

"Is there anyone else in the house?"

She nodded and stepped back.

"May we come in?"

She led them into a formal living room with matching sofas and love-seat, all three covered in white brocade. The woman plopped in the nearest sofa. The carpet was off-white and the room smelled of furniture polish. No one with bloody shoes came in here.

A young man in his mid-twenties, eating a Hubig's fried pie, stepped in and stopped immediately.

"Mom?"

For the next fifteen minutes, LaStanza interviewed the pair, securing info from their driver's license. The son was a junior at the University of New Orleans, majoring in police science. Wanted to be a cop when he grew up. He kept eye-balling Beau's uniform. Beau pretended not to notice.

Neither had seen anything or knew anyone who would hurt Helen Collingwood. Neither remembered seeing any suspicious persons in the neighborhood recently. Neither knew of any visitors to the house next door except for the daughter and Helen's boyfriend.

LaStanza asked to see their back door and was led to another kitchen with a rear-facing French doors and a wooden deck outside. No blood on the deck and it was dry. Hadn't been washed recently.

On their way out, LaStanza asked, "Who cuts Helen's grass?"

"Wilson's Lawn Service. They cut ours too." The woman's eyes widened. "You don't think they had anything to do with this."

LaStanza did not respond but secured the address and phone number of Wilson's as the son asked, "What happened to her?"

"She was killed," LaStanza said.

"In her home?"

"Yes." He left it like that.

Stepping out on the sidewalk, LaStanza turned right and led Beau back past the victim's house. They moved up two blocks to Benjamin Street where the houses on the victim's side of Walnut ended at an extension of the park. He pointed across the street and told Beau, "Go up to St. Charles and take that side of the street, working back this way. I'll go back down this side to Prytania, cross over and meet you on the way back up."

"Sure."

LaStanza didn't have to say it. Homicide rarely relied on patrol officers to conduct interviews, but Beau was an exception. As the tall patrolman crossed the street, LaStanza called out, "Keep an eye out for blood."

Beau backed away with a, "Naturally."

LaStanza came upon a shirtless man standing next to a lawn mower on a freshly cut lawn three doors up from the victim's house. He'd smelled freshly cut grass earlier. The man was in his late sixties, still in pretty good shape, stomach flat and arms toned. He had greenish-black tattoos on both arms, good ones, an anchor and a sailing ship, both somewhat faded.

Another WWII veteran, a navy man who'd served on the *Yorktown* at Midway and later on the *Enterprise*. Friendly, in an authoritarian way. With a snap, he presented his driver's license and retired military I.D.

"So what happened?" he asked.

"Your neighbor was killed this morning."

The man shook his head and dug the toe of his tennis shoe into the grass and told LaStanza he barely knew the victim and had seen nothing. He'd cut his backyard first that morning. While he was cutting his front grass, he'd seen the daughter arrive, then the police. He'd seen plenty of suspicious people in the neighborhood all the time, but not that morning.

LaStanza pressed him for descriptions of the suspicious persons and found most were young, most were male and most probably students from Tulane or Loyola just across St. Charles. They carried books as they lounged around the park and walked up and down Walnut Street, very suspiciously.

"It that pretty blonde policewoman in charge or something?"

"Yes, she is."

The old man nodded approval. "She's a looker all right."

"I'll tell her."

LaStanza moved to the next house.

Fel Jones watched him pass as he sat in the car with the victim's daughter. Both passenger doors were open, Fel in front, arm up on the back of the seat, the daughter in the back seat. A light breeze came through and Fel caught a whiff of the daughter's perfume. Belinda Collingwood was an elegant woman, thirty-five, a teacher at Delgado Junior College, married, no children, husband a chief pilot for Delta Airlines. She always used her maiden name. Saturday night her husband flew off to Jamaica on his normal Caribbean round trip.

A petite woman, couldn't be taller than five-two. Her long, light brown hair was pinned back with gold barrettes. She wore a light green dress. A pair of green high heels lay on the grass next to her open door. They were covered with blood.

"My mother called at seven and woke me. I oversleep a lot. I grunted and she said I'd better get up for mass. Then she said she thought there was someone at her front door." Tears rolled down Belinda's narrow cheeks. "That was –" She sobbed, covering her face with her hands. "– the last time – I'll ever hear her voice again."

Fel looked at her driver's license again and made sure he'd copied her address correctly in his notes. She lived on Oak Street, just off Carrollton, a good mile and a half away.

Belinda dug another Kleenex from her purse, wiped her face and focused her red-rimmed, brown eyes at Fel.

"Who has keys to your mother's house?"

"Me. My mother and Frank." The boyfriend, still waiting in the other police car. "That tall officer has my keys now." *That would be the Cajun-looking cop, Beau.*

Fel could see the strain in Belinda's face as she struggled to control her emotions and he found himself hurrying, but didn't want to miss anything. Not surprisingly, Helen Collingwood had no known enemies, no problems with any neighbors, not even a jilted ex-boyfriend.

"What I can't fathom," Belinda concluded, "is who she would have opened the door for. It had to be someone she knew."

"Or felt no threat from," Fel added, digging out a business card and jotting Jodie's name on the back. "She's the case officer, but you can also call me if you think of anything else, or just want to talk. We're at the same phone number."

The boyfriend, Frank McWilliams: sixty-six, five-nine, two hundred pounds and completely bald, was an attorney with the law firm of Segundaga, Scootaput and McWilliams.

Is he fuckin' with me? Fel thought as he asked for the spelling.

McWilliams passed him a business card that looked genuine. Law firm on Poydras Street, just down from the Superdome.

"Not surprised you've never heard of our firm," McWilliams said. "We specialize in maritime law."

"How long have you known Helen Collingwood?"

He'd met her two years ago at a Knights of Columbus dance. Helen loved big band music. "We'd trip the light fantastic all night long," Frank said.

"The what?"

Frank raised his left hand and formed his right arm as if he was holding a woman. He rolled his shoulders slightly, mimicking dancing. "We'd dance the night away."

Ten fruitless minutes later, Fel climbed out of the second police car as Frank went over to the first to talk with Belinda. Fel stretched, turning his face to the strong sun, eyes clamped shut. He felt the heaviness return to his heart, remembering the faces of the parents of Monique Williams, his uptown square victim. The police chaplain had come along to tell the parents they'd never see their daughter again. Monique's father stood rock still, while his wife clung to his arm. The excruciating pain in their eyes as their life collapsed around them was pitiful. No matter how many times Fel saw this collapse, he never got used to it. Couldn't ever.

Looking to his left, he spotted LaStanza crossing the street and heading back this way, so he went to help with the canvass.

LaStanza saw Fel crossing the street as he noticed Beau moving up to another house. He waited for his old partner and Fel arrived with an, "A.F.D.!"

LaStanza, "Another fuckin' disaster."

Fel, "Close enough."

They took the next house in line together. By the time they linked up with Beau, LaStanza had two note pages full of names, addresses and driver's license numbers but no useful information. Beau handed him two pages of the same as patrol officer Sider hurried up with his list of automobile license numbers.

LaStanza turned to Beau and pointed to Sider. "Left Sider, right?"

"Right."

Sider went, "Huh?"

LaStanza took his sheets and thanked him and asked them to come back to the murder scene.

The daughter stood in front of the house in her stocking feet, arms folded in front, legs slightly parted as if she had to steady herself. She turned to the approaching men and wiped her eyes with a Kleenex. She blinked and took a hesitant step toward LaStanza.

As he passed, she stuck a hand out and said, "I know you."

Fel moved past LaStanza, shaking his head.

"It's Dino, isn't it?" Belinda said, a sad smile crossing her lips.

"Yes, ma'am."

"Don't 'ma'am' me. We're the same age. We went to Holy Rosary together."

"We did?"

Fel moved behind the daughter, still shaking his head at LaStanza. Beau joined him, but didn't shake his head. Left Sider stopped behind Beau and looked around, as if he didn't want to hear this.

"We square-danced together at the school. You tried to kiss me once at recess."

Jesus. LaStanza kept his face stiff as Fel rolled his eyes at him.

"I ran across the playground to get away from you."

Fel covered his mouth to stifle a laugh.

Jesus H. Christ.

"I'm sorry," LaStanza.

"Don't be. I wanted you to kiss me. Just not in front of my friends. I wanted you to follow me, but you didn't."

Fel laughed then coughed to try to cover it and moved away quickly. Sider followed but Beau stayed. Thankfully he kept a serious look on his face.

A cloudy memory blinked in LaStanza's mind and he smiled. "You wore pig-tails."

"Until I went to high school. Cabrini. Where'd you go?"

"Rummel."

So this lady and LaStanza were separated into an all-girls and all-boys high schools. Never to see each other again, until this sunny Easter, drawn together by death. LaStanza looked down at his shoes.

"This is nothing but a big small town," Belinda said.

LaStanza had said that enough times. They both turned to the sound of brakes squealing. The coroner's office white van stopped in the street just in front of the house, two large black men exited, went around back and pulled out a gurney with a black plastic body bag atop.

The daughter seemed to tilt, so LaStanza grabbed her elbow.

"You all right?"

She nodded as her mother's boyfriend hustled over to help her to the back seat of Beau's unit. LaStanza and Beau led the coroner's men around the house to the back door where Jodie stood.

A thin man in a shirt and tie, dress black pants, approached from the park. He had a reporter's skinny note pad in hand as he approached Jodie. He opened his mouth, but she cut him off.

"Don't come in the yard. This is still a crime scene."

The man stopped just outside the low wall.

"I just need the basics."

Jodie waved him away. "Talk to the Public Information Officer, whenever the fuck she gets here."

"But –"

"Can't talk to you." Jodie turned her back to the reporter who looked at LaStanza.

"She isn't the P.I.O. officer?" the reporter asked.

"Nope," LaStanza snapped. "She's a real cop." He grinned coldly. "Don't cross that fence."

Jodie watched Avery finish bagging the victim's hands, putting rubber bands around her wrists to keep the paper bags in place. Standing he nodded to the coroner's men, who stepped in with the body bag.

"Why bag the hands?" Beau whispered to Jodie.

"At the autopsy, we'll scrape beneath the fingernails and swab the hands carefully. She might have scratched her assailant. Might have gotten some of his blood, hair."

A movement behind Beau caught Jodie's attention as the daughter came around the house. LaStanza moved to cut her off and Jodie stepped past Beau toward them.

LaStanza stood in the daughter's way so she couldn't see the coroner's men stuffing her mother into the body bag. He passed her a card as Jodie stepped up and introduced herself as the case officer, giving the daughter her card.

The victim's boyfriend came hurrying around the corner and moved up behind the daughter.

"You need to get some rest," Jodie told her. "We'll lock up when we leave, but we can't let anyone inside for a day or so. OK? I'm also going to need your shoes for a while."

"I don't want them back."

The daughter nodded as the coroner's men came out carrying the body bag, putting it on the gurney and strapping it down before taking it away. A bald man rushed around the side of the house with a clipboard in hand. Jodie recognized him as a coroner's investigator and told the daughter she would have to speak with him.

As Jodie stepped away, the daughter asked, "What are the chances you'll catch who did this?"

Jodie glanced wearily at LaStanza, who said, "Want me to answer that?"

She shook her head. She didn't have LaStanza's perfect record. "We'll work our asses off," Jodie said. "You can count on it."

The boyfriend guided the daughter to a concrete bench away from the back door while the coroner's investigator got his initial information from Jodie.

As the investigator moved to the bench to talk with the daughter, Fel pointed to LaStanza and said, "S.K.L.T.A.K."

Jodie sighed, her shoulders slumping.

LaStanza shrugged at Beau.

Fel nodded to the daughter, "She knows LaStanza. They almost kissed."

"Just now?" Jodie stammered.

"Back in fourth grade," explained LaStanza. "At least I think it was fourth grade." He pointed over his shoulder. "Man cutting his grass says you're a *looker.*"

"Jesus."

"Daughter's a very pretty woman," Fel said. "She has a husband, however. Pilot. Delta Airlines. Although he does seem to be gone a lot."

"She's not LaStanza's type," Jodie said. "Her dress is a foot too long."

She saw a confused look on Beau's face.

Left Sider looked even more confused. Jodie was too tired to explain.

"You should see LaStanza's wife," Fel told Beau. "Princess of the mini-skirt. Wears dresses up to her butt."

LaStanza, "Sometimes higher."

A tiny smile came to Jodie. "When we play tennis, she wears skimpy panties under the shortest tennis skirts she can find. Distracts the hell out of all the men."

Stan Smith, who had eased up behind Jodie cut in, "Jesus. Tell me next time y'all play. I love tennis!" He jabbed his right index finger into Left Sider's chest. "And I love Lizette's ass. You ever see it?"

Left Sider rubbed his chest. "Why is everybody joking?"

Stan's eyes bulged but it was Beau who said, "Rookie. The worse it gets, the more we joke or we go nuts. You'll learn."

4:45 p.m. – Exposition Boulevard

"Who the hell would she open the door for?"

LaStanza punched in the alarm code and the kitchen door popped open. He let Fel in but didn't go in as he saw Stan park his personal car along Garfield. Stan led Beau over. Both were off-duty now, but still in their uniforms.

"Did you say something about beer and pizza?"

"That's the idea." LaStanza had invited everyone over, even Left Sider, who was in a hurry to get home to his wife and kid. Jodie thought she'd salvage what was left of Easter with her parents.

As LaStanza was about to step into the kitchen behind Stan and Beau, he spotted Lizette's sea-foam green Maserati turn the corner. He waited as the garage door raised and she turned into the garage.

She called out, "Can you give me a hand?"

He went around and found his wife leaning in the trunk. She wore a fitted black minidress which rode high up her ass as she bent over, the tops of her thigh-high stockings and bottom of sheer white panties exposed. He smiled.

"I brought food," she said, backing out with two large tupperware containers. He gently patted her ass before reaching in for an aluminum foil covered tray.

"Get the trunk, OK?"

He closed the trunk and followed her around to the kitchen door, still open. Whatever he was carrying smelled wonderful.

"Where'd they go?" he said when he didn't spot anyone.

"Who?" Lizette put her containers on the counter.

"Fel, Stan and Beau. I was gonna call out for pizza."

They put the food on the kitchen counter. She pulled the foil from the tray in his hands. "Brulie's jambalaya." She pointed to the two tupperwares. "Bisque and etouffee. More than enough for four."

When she turned back to him, he moved close and could smell her perfume. He put his hands on her hips and gave her a feathery kiss on those full lips. She raised her hands to his shoulders.

"Hey! Hey! The livin' doll's here!" Stan came out of the dining room with Fel and Beau trailing behind. "I was just showing Beau the place."

Lizette smiled at them, her arms wrapping around her husband's neck for a moment.

"I brought food," she said.

"Got a kiss for me?" Stan stepped up and pursed his lips, like a constipated goldfish.

Lizette laughed and moved around her husband to sit on one of the bar stools. "Y'all dig in," she said. "I'm not serving you."

Fel moved around and kissed Lizette on her bare shoulder.

"Hey!" Stan snapped. "He gets to kiss you?"

"He gets to do more than that." Lizette shot Stan a smug look.

Fel chuckled and Stan looked confused as hell.

LaStanza pulled plates from the cupboard and big spoons and pointed to the microwave.

"Hi, I'm Lizette," she told Beau and LaStanza apologized for not introducing her. Lizette crossed her legs and twisted away from the counter, facing Beau as he waited with his empty plate. Stan was the first to dig in, Fel pressed right behind him. LaStanza went to the fridge for beer, St. Pauli Girls, Abita and Amstel Lights.

Lizette saw Beau glance at her legs and decided to give him a little show. Looking down, she uncrossed her legs and pulled up her thigh-highs, one at a time, all the way up, giving him a nice view of her panties. She felt her heartbeat shoot up immediately.

When she looked up Beau looked up too and smiled shyly. She winked and climbed off the stool.

"I'll be right back," she said. "Have to take the LeGris's from Loyola to Professor Jefferson's house. Won't be a minute." She stepped back to her husband and brushed his lips.

"I miss anything?" he asked, factiously. An Easter egg hunt at Loyola, of all fuckin' things.

"You would have been bored. Except at the egg hunt. I bent over a lot."

He laughed and kissed her back and watched her breeze out.

Stan elbowed Beau as he went around the kitchen counter with his over-flowing plate. "Told you she was hot."

Beau looked at LaStanza and didn't react.

LaStanza shrugged and, "She's a handful, all right."

The food was delicious and the four men gobbled it down without conversation. Everyone went for seconds, LaStanza less than the big guys. He stopped at one beer, switching to Barq's, as did Beau.

Finishing first, LaStanza opened the French doors to the rear deck and fired up the Jacuzzi, putting it on lukewarm. "It's relaxing," he told Beau. "Believe me."

Stan needed no coaxing, undressing down to his boxers.

"Don't worry, son," Stan told Beau. "It's big enough where we won't touch each other."

Fel thanked LaStanza for the food and said he was going to salvage what was left of Easter with his Wanda. LaStanza had his shirt off when Fel came back inside fuming.

"Goddamn piece a' shit unit! Fucker won't start."

"Need a jump?"

"It's the starter. Just replaced it Thursday!"

Fel snatched up the phone and called headquarters for a wrecker.

LaStanza put his shirt back on and told Fel to leave the keys in the car. "I'll drive you to Wanda's."

"You sure?"

"I gotta put miles on the new car. You wanna just take the Maserati?"

"No," Fel said, heading back for the door. "I don't wanna drive that."

"Hey!" LaStanza called to the two in the Jacuzzi. "I'll be right back."

The engine of LaStanza's Maserati was so quiet it was hard to tell it was running until he touched the gas pedal, lightly, and it sprung to life.

Fel sat back with his eyes closed and said, "W.A.F.W."

LaStanza tried but only came up with, "The second to last word is fuckin'. Right?"

"What A Fuckin' Weekend!"

"You tellin' me?"

LaStanza felt that old closed-in feeling. The Senoré Case was his and he'd done little or nothing and the first twenty-four hours of the case was long gone.

"Walnut," Fel said. "Who the hell would she open the door for?"

Jodie's case now had its moniker. Walnut. LaStanza's was Senoré and Fel's would be The Square. LaStanza nodded as they passed St. Vincent DePaul's Sanitarium on Garfield, on the way to Magazine Street.

"The boyfriend didn't do it," Fel said, eyes still closed. "He was having breakfast with two judges, Edkins and DeSoto, at Ye Olde College Inn before going to meet the victim and daughter for mass. Sure they'll confirm it."

LaStanza tried to keep his mind from making a mental list of the things he had to do – running the license plates, checking on the names of everyone stopped, checking on anyone arrested in the vicinity of Claiborne and Carrollton for the last several years. Canvass again and again.

LaStanza took a left on narrow two-way Magazine and gunned it for a few seconds, slowing nicely behind a bus and followed the bus from the Second District into the familiar territory of the Bloody Sixth District.

Fel still had his eyes closed so LaStanza shut up until he pulled up in front of Wanda's small apartment house just off Magazine on Josephine Street. Wanda was sitting on the porch swing, staring at them. She wore a dark green dress, a matching ribbon in her long hair. She took a long drag on a cigarette and folded her arms across her chest.

"Jesus," Fel said as he opened the door. "She's smoking. I'm in the shithouse."

LaStanza waved at Wanda. She ignored him, turning her dark brown eyes on Fel as he approached. LaStanza got the hell out of there.

5:55 p.m. – Josephine Street

"You know she sweats you man, big time!"

"Should've known you'd be with that bastard." Wanda had her legs crossed, leaning forward now, all bunched up. Wanda Summers: twenty-eight, five-six, one-twenty pounds, with tawny brown hair straightened long and a reddish-brown complexion, full, sensuous lips and wide eyes.

They'd been dating for two years, talking about marriage the last six months but stopped when Fel was sent back to Homicide after he and LaStanza got in another damn shootout. Wanda was an assistant manager of D. H. Holmes Department store on Canal Street, the highest African-American in management in one of the city's oldest stores. She made twice Fel's salary.

They'd met on I-10, when Fel stopped at two a.m. to help her with a flat tire. She wouldn't get out of her black Saab, even when Fel showed her his police ID through the window. She yelled at Fel to call AAA if he was really a cop. He did. It took them forty-five minutes. Same time a marked police car pulled up and the patrolman convinced Wanda that Fel was indeed a cop.

She apologized three times as the AAA man changed her tire and insisted on taking Fel to lunch and that's how it started. Eye-flirting over butterfly shrimp, holding hands crossing the street back to Holmes.

Fel had played it smart, not moving in quickly, letting Wanda set the pace until she attacked him in her living room and they'd been making love three times a week, most weeks, until he went back to Homicide.

Fel stepped through the gate and up the five wooden steps to the gallery.

Wanda stuck out her chin. "Didn't you say, 'I'll be here right after the autopsy?' And don't tell me an autopsy takes all damn day!"

How many times have we been over this – Fel thought wearily as he said, "I went to help my buddies."

"Anything for LaStanza!"

Fel sat next to her on the swing, planting his feet to keep it still. "Jodie caught a bad one. Uptown woman butchered in her home."

"Jodie?" Wanda stood up and flipped her cigarette all the way to the street. Fists on her hips now. "Miss blonde perfect?"

Jesus, why did I mention Jodie?

"You know how I feel about *her?* You just trying to hurt me or something, leaving me alone on Easter to be with *her?*"

Fel kept his voice low. "I wasn't with her. I barely saw her."

"You know she sweats you man, big time!"

Fel stepped around Wanda to the edge of the porch and looked up at the bright sky, wishing a fuckin' airliner would just come down right on them, wipe him out right now. Only planes rarely flew over the city, skirting it to the airport out in Kenner.

"You and your friends!" Wanda stormed into her house and slammed the screen door. "Go back to them!" she called out from her living room. "Go shoot someone else with that Wop so you'll end up a school guard, or go bang Miss blonde perfect. Just go!"

He was too tired to argue, too tired of everything, so Fel went down the steps, taking out his LFR as he moved though the gate.

He called LaStanza, "3128 – 3124."

"Go ahead."

"Can you 10-19?"

"10-4."

"At the corner?"

LaStanza clicked twice as a response. The Maserati was back in two minutes, LaStanza not looking at him.

"You were waiting around the corner?"

LaStanza nodded. "Didn't like the look in her eyes."

"Me either." Fel climbed in and said, "Can you take me home?"

"No problem."

Fel could see LaStanza knew, but wasn't talking. Three silent blocks later, Fel said, "A.F.D."

"Another fuckin' disaster," LaStanza said without looking at his old partner.

"Fuckin A."

6:10 p.m. – Exposition Boulevard

"I think I'm evolving."

Lizette walked out on the deck with three chilled St. Pauli Girls. She kicked off her heels, bent over and handed a beer to Stan, then Beau. Stan eased around in the hot tub to look up her dress.

"Join us," Stan said, grinning.

Lizette gave Beau a long look, the tall cop's light brown eyes staring at her. He had the look of the hawk about him, even taller than Stan, his muscular arms up on the side of the tub now, beer in his left hand.

"You gotta be naked," Stan said.

"In your dreams." She laughed and reached around to unzip her dress. The two men seemed to hold their breath. She loved to do that to men. How many times had her husband told her? She had the body – she had the power. Just a hint of a flash and she had the undivided attention of most men. She'd known that since she was fourteen, when she and her twin developed earlier than most girls.

At twenty-five, Lizette knew exactly what effect she had on men as she climbed out of her dress, sat on the bench next to the Jacuzzi and pulled off her stockings, draping them over the back of the wooden bench. She went back inside to the closet, just within the kitchen door, for three towels and barrettes for her hair. Standing over the men in her lacy, low cut bra and thin white panties, she pinned her long hair up.

"You're not getting naked?" Stan squawked.

"These get wet and you'll see enough," Lizette said as she slipped into the hot tub across from the men. She sank to her neck then sat up higher and looked at her chest. The tiny nipples of her oversized breasts were already pointy and clearly visible through her bra, so was her light pink aureoles.

She took a sip of beer as both men stared at her chest.

"I've seen your luscious babies before," Stan told her breasts. He glanced up at Beau. "Last Mardi Gras. Caught her and a blonde girlfriend flashing two motorcycle cops."

Lizette rolled her eyes.

Stan lifted his legs to show off his boxers, as if Lizette wanted to see.

"They wore masks so the people taking their pictures couldn't positively ID them," Stan said. "Lizzie wore a white jacket with nothing under it and a black miniskirt. She sat on one of the bikes and opened her jacket, then leaned back and let everyone see the front of her panties, with her legs wrapped around the motorcycle's gas tank."

"It was Mardi Gras," Lizette said, then stretched her legs out and let them rise, drawing her hips to the top of the gurgling water. It was as if she wore no panties, plastered as they were against her dark bush.

Both men let out a long breath. She sank back down and took another sip of beer, her heart pumping now. She wasn't teasing, exactly. She was getting as turned on as they were. Nice, casual flashing of friends who appreciated it.

"So what's your wife doing at the moment?" Lizette asked Stan.

"Easter with her parents. She's more than fully clothed right now."

"What about you?" she asked Beau.

"Not married."

Then she remembered about his dead girlfriend and felt bad.

"Where do you live?" she asked and Beau told her on an old houseboat in Bucktown.

"You serious?"

He took a hit of beer.

"Where are you from?" she asked, knowing full well his accent was from the bayous.

"Little village called Cannes Bruleé near Vermilion Bay."

"Burnt cane," she told Stan who was still leering at her breasts. "That's what the village name means in French."

Stan pointed his beer at Beau but didn't stop looking at Lizette's chest as he said, "You part Mexican, ain't ya?"

Beau looked surprised and smiled, "Everyone else at the district knows. Surprised you don't. My mother is Lakota. Sioux to the white man and my father was Cajun."

"I'm in love with her." Stan pointed his beer at Lizette and finally looked into her eyes. "Almost like a brother only I'd do her if she'd let me."

"She won't," LaStanza said from the open kitchen door. Lizette turned and saw that familiar deadly-serious Sicilian look on his face before he winked at her and went back inside.

Lizette climbed out and ran a towel over herself before going into the kitchen. She dried herself as best she could, leaving her wet bra and panties on as she draped the towel over a stool.

"Nice outfit," LaStanza said, looking her up and down.

She glanced over her shoulder as Beau came in, towel wrapped around his waist.

"Gotta go," he said. "Thanks again for the chow." He smiled at Lizette. "Best Easter present I've had in a while."

She faced him and let him have a good look as she removed the barrettes, shaking out her hair.

Stan came in saying, "Better get home before the old ball-and-chain calls missing persons."

They left quickly.

As Lizette started to remove her bra, LaStanza told her, "What do you have in mind, little girl?"

She dropped her bra and climbed out of her panties. "You can't do me with them on." She took his hand and led him up the back stairs to their bedroom where she lay on the bed, spread eagle and watched him take his clothes off.

"You've been naughty?"

"I've been very naughty, letting men see my panties, letting your friends gawk at me. You see Beau with the towel around his waist. Hiding a hard-on, or what?"

Lizette raised her knees and reached down to finger her clit. "What's taking you so long?"

He moved even slower as she started without him, watching his wife finger herself, getting herself nice and wet by the time he moved his lips to her thighs. He licked the soft skin of her thighs, licked his way up to her bush and kissed her silky pubic hair. He kissed around her pussy as she withdrew her hand. He breathed on it, but didn't touch it. When he moved his kisses around for the third time, she yanked his head, shoving her pussy against his mouth and his tongue began to work her clit. He slipped his right middle finger into her pussy as he continued licking her.

Lizette's hips rose as she gyrated against his tongue. Waves of passion seared through her as he reached up and grabbed her boobs, kneading them as he licked. *Who said a man can't do two things at once?*

When she got close, she gasped, "OK. OK." Meaning now, but he wouldn't stop. She pulled his hair but he wouldn't pull his tongue away and she got closer. She grabbed his ears and yanked but he wouldn't stop and suddenly it hit her like a wave, running through her thighs and she quivered and bucked to the climax.

Still he wouldn't stop and she could only collapse until he was good and ready, climbing on her and pressing his dick against the hot folds of her pussy. She cried as he worked it in and said, "Yes. Yes. Come on. Fuck me!"

He tried to hold back, stopping in mid-stroke several times, but she wanted none of that, bucking with him, fuckin' him back until he gushed in long, hot spurts in her, his balls slapping her ass. When he finished, she kept bucking, wanting more but settling for a nice inside climax.

As they lay next to one another, catching their breath, she told him, "I think I'm evolving."

"Evolving?"

"Into a nymphomaniac."

He took in another deep breath and said, "That's a load off my mind."

Lizette snuggled against him and they both fell asleep with the late-afternoon orange sunlight streaming in through the French doors of their bedroom balcony.

Monday, March 31, 1986

9:50 a.m. – Detective Bureau

"He used a piece of wood."

As Jodie stepped into the Homicide squad room, she noticed three things out of place: a black woman with a shoulder rig standing next to her desk; Snowood and his partner actually working, or appearing to be working; and Kelly smiling at her from the coffee desk.

Edward Kelly: twenty-four years old, six feet tall with a weightlifter's build and dark blond hair cut short, looking like a young Robert Redford. It was the first time she'd seen him out of uniform, standing there in a dark blue suit and a deep red tie.

Jodie dropped her briefcase on her desk and noticed LaStanza's open briefcase on his desk, his navy blue suit coat draped over the back of his chair. She turned to the black woman and extended her hand.

"Jodie Kintyre."

"Sheila Glapier." Glapier seemed to notice Snowood for the first time as she shook Jodie's hand, her jaw dropping. She leaned closer to Jodie and whispered, "What's he wearing?"

Jodie took a closer look at Snowood who wore another of his U.S. Cavalry outfits, blue shirt with two rows of gold buttons down the front, a yellow neckerchief, white cowboy hat on his desk as he slowly typed a report. Sucker had his gold detective's badge pinned to his chest, like a goddamn Tombstone sheriff.

"He thinks he's in the cavalry."

Glaiper's brow furrowed above her deep set brown eyes. Sheila Glapier: thirty, stood five-three, a full-figured gal with dark brown skin that reminded Jodie of brown velvet, her hair done up in long corn-rows. She wore dark green pants and a white blouse, a dark green jacket resting on the chair next to Jodie's desk.

"Sergeant Land told us to wait out here." Glapier nodded toward Kelly as he approached with two mugs of coffee. Kelly's eyes continued staring into Jodie's as he approached.

Jodie asked Snowood, "Where's LaStanza?"

"Computer," Snowood said, not looking up from the report he was slowly typing. Snowood's partner, Steve Stevens, yanked the sheet of paper from his typewriter, balled it up and threw it at his trash can and missed. Stevens: thirty-five, five-eleven, a pudgy two-forty with light brown hair chopped short, a cleft chin and mismatched light blue eyes. His left eye was crooked, usually pointing at his nose until he flipped out, which happened often, then his eyes would straighten, freaking everyone, even LaStanza, who'd pointed out Stevens' left eye was actually larger than his right eye.

Stevens smiled at Jodie and said, "Hey there, Baby Cakes."

Jodie turned back to Glapier and waved at Snowood and Stevens, "If you stand close enough to them, you can hear the ocean."

Kelly passed the extra mug to Glapier and smiled again at Jodie.

"Nice seeing you," he said in that deep voice.

"You too." And then it hit her. "You must be our back-up."

"That seems to be the plan." Kelly raised his mug. "Coffee?"

"Let me check on my partner."

Jodie found LaStanza in the computer alcove, typing in another name on the police computer, the dot matrix printer spitting out another page. He was in a pale blue dress shirt, short sleeved, and a silver tie with navy blue specks to go with his navy blue suit pants. Jodie smiled, remembering Lizette showing her the suit, along with three others she'd bought for him. Liz sure got a charge out of dressing up her man.

LaStanza admitted to Jodie the only clothes he'd bought for himself since the wedding were Levi's and Wrangler jeans, and his running shoes, of course. Couldn't even buy his own underwear because he'd find new packages on the bed before he wore out his old drawers. Lizette liked him in colored jockeys. But, with a sly smile, he said he didn't complain. She let him help her pick out her lingerie.

LaStanza looked up and said, "So you saw Kelly out there."

"Yeah, why?"

"Your face is flushed."

"No, it isn't." She felt her face flushing *now*. Son-of-a-bitch could always read her with those cardsharp eyes. He missed nothing.

He went back to typing.

"How's it going?"

"I'm on page three of fifteen." LaStanza jutted his chin at the lists of names and license plates from Claiborne and Carrollton. He looked back and asked how her autopsy went.

"Took three hours." She told him about both broken arms, one broken in three places, and the seven broken ribs, sternum fractured as were both clavicles. "Most of the bones in her face were broken. We've accounted for all of her teeth, including the seven we found in the living room and hall.

"Jesus." LaStanza typed in another name.

"He used a piece of wood."

"Baseball bat?"

"No. There was bark and wood splinters. A tree branch."

"Or a whole fuckin' tree."

Kelly stepped in and said Mason was waiting for them. LaStanza scooped up his notes while Jodie tore off his print-outs. They passed Fel Jones, standing by the coffee desk. He also wore a navy blue suit.

Lt. Rob Mason stood leaning his butt against LaStanza's desk, a mug of coffee in his right hand, his left fingers drumming the desk in another nicotine fit. Mason: five-nine, weighed one-fifty, with a lean, triangular face and Marine Corp flat top, dark brown hair graying now. He'd been trying to expand his wardrobe mixing sport coats and dress slacks, today in tan coat and navy pants and matching tie. Always the white dress shirt and penny loafers.

Mark Land came out of his tiny office as Jodie and LaStanza arrived at their desks. Mark also in navy blue slacks, doing his impersonation of an over-sized LaStanza with a silver tie. Bad enough they looked like brothers, but Lizette's touch was here too, taking Mark's wife shopping to spruce up *her* man's looks.

"The two new faces," Mason began, "are follow-up officers. Sheila Glapier from the Sixth and Edward Kelly from the Fourth District. They're on loan to us while we wade through this fuckin' Easter carnage."

Mason nodded to Jodie. "Tell us about your post."

She told them the results of her autopsy. Glaiper's eyes widened but Kelly kept his from reacting.

"Motha fuck," was the only reaction, this from Steve Stevens, until Snowood decided to add, "Hey, last night I saw an episode of *Hee Haw* I ain't never seen 'afore. Thank God for cable TV."

Mason shot a needle-glare at Country-Ass. Mark's eyes doubled in size. Jodie said, "Hard to believe he beat a hundred-thousand other sperm."

Mason's voice rose, "I'll handle the computer work. All of you give me your canvass names and license plate numbers." Looking at LaStanza now. "I'll compile photo lines-ups for your witnesses. I'll go to Robbery and get photos of all recent 64-men. And I'll get the same from J.P." Jefferson Parish wasn't far from Claiborne and Carrollton.

Looking at Kelly and Glapier now. "You two will assist LaStanza, Kintyre and Jones on these Easter Killings." Turning to Snowood now. "You and Stevens are up for everything and I mean fuckin' everything. You don't like it, I'll pack you off to the fuckin' Sniper Task Force." He paused a moment to let that sink in. "Mark and I will back you. If it gets worse, we'll call in burglary detectives."

"Fuck," Stevens said because they all knew most burglary dicks were pretty worthless. Fat fucks who would have been in Vice if they had more of their teeth.

"Actually," Fel said. "N.G.Gs over there."

LaStanza, "Not – um?"

"New Good Guys," Fel said. "They have some new guys over in Burglary. Used to be district follow-up and are pretty damn sharp."

"The fuck," Stevens again.

"Look who's talking," LaStanza again. "You don't even know how to spell burglary much less anything else."

"I fuckin' do."

LaStanza yanked the daily from Stevens' typewriter and pointed to a word. "It's height. Not *heigth*," spelling it out. "That's not even a fuckin' word."

Stevens looked at his partner and said, "This is gonna be hard work, man."

"Hard? Hell, this ain't hard work. I used to dress monkeys in a travelin' circus. That was hard work."

LaStanza turned to his partner, with his mouth open.

"The fuck you talkin' about monkeys?" Mark said.

"Seriously. Hardest work I ever did. Right outta high school. Joined the Ringling Brothers when they came to town. Got a job dressin' monkeys. Little bastards would bite, spit, scratch, kick, anything so's you had to hold them down and force the clothes on 'em."

LaStanza to Jodie, "I don't fuckin' believe this."

Jodie had her hands over her mouth to keep from laughing and encouraging Country-Ass.

"Didn't matter if it were nice clothes, either. Keen little suits with ties. Didn't matter to those little bastards. Oh no! I could understood if we dressed 'em up like Stevens here, like a clown with all the mis-matched colors.

Tears were in Jodie's eyes now.

LaStanza had to cut in, "I can see it – big galoot holding down a little monkey – shoving on a shirt – little hands and feet scratching and kicking."

"And screeching!" Snowood again. "Bastards sound like a kid getting skinned alive."

"All right," Mark boomed. "Enough. I'm going with Jodie back to Walnut. Newbies go with Fel back to the Square. LaStanza's got a funeral this morning."

Mark caught Jodie's eye, "I assume you're going through the house, room by room. I'll re-canvass."

Snowood had an announcement as the meeting broke up. "Hey, I got a new license plate slogan for Mississippi – "Litracy ain't ereting." He spelled out the mis-spellings, cornering Kelly to explain he and Stevens were coming up with new license slogans for every state.

"You have Louisiana?"

Snowood grinned, showing off his tobacco-teeth. "Louisiana – the banana republic."

LaStanza tried his best not to enter into it, but couldn't help himself. "It should be "Louisiana – where the weak are killed and eaten."

"No," Jodie disagreed. "That's the slogan for New Orleans. Louisiana is 'a state of confusion'."

11:30 a.m. – St. Vincent's Cemetery

"This looks like an assignment for a man named Beau."

It was a small cemetery by New Orleans standards, two narrow blocks in an uptown neighborhood with shotgun houses and duplexes on three sides and a private high school along the backside. LaStanza parked the unmarked Ford on Soniat Street, next to the four-foot brick wall surrounded St. Vincent de Paul's Cemetery. Slipping on his suit coat, he stepped through the wrought iron gate, LFR in his left hand.

The brilliant sunlight, reflecting off the concrete, had him squinting even behind his dark gangster-glasses. The typical above-ground cemetery, known in New Orleans as a "little city of the dead," with its whitewashed sepulchres and cement tombs, had no grass. It was wall-to-wall cement.

Moving through the crypts, LaStanza stopped next to a raised plot of forty-seven headstones marking the burial site of forty-seven Sisters of Charity of St. Vincent de Paul. They'd tried to grow grass on top of the raised plot. It looked more like moss. He sat on the low wall surrounding the plot and looked up at a large walled-tomb along the back of the cemetery. Atop the wall stood a life-sized stone crucifix, Jesus on the cross. At His feet were three bronze statues of women praying for him.

Just to the left was the Louvier family crypt, an immaculate mausoleum where Lizette's twin sister was buried five years ago on an overcast afternoon. Lynette Anne Louvier was twenty when the Slasher caught her between a stand of dwarf magnolia trees along Exposition Boulevard.

Closing his eyes, LaStanza remembered the first time he saw Lizette. It was the night after her sister's murder. She was standing in her father's darkened library, now *their* library in *their* mansion, standing beneath a painting of Lynette.

LaStanza had been resting his tired eyes, sitting in her father's easy chair in the library when he woke to find Lizette, thinking she was an hallucination. He didn't know Lynette had a twin. He'll always remember Lizette's face that first moment he saw her, a sliver of light falling on her, those large, topaz eyes staring at him, those full lips, the line of her cheek.

"Who are you?" she'd asked.

He told her he was a detective.

The wide eyes hardened when she said she'd heard The Slasher had killed three previous women. "Why haven't you stopped him?" she cried, tears streaming down her face.

"You're useless," she said. "*Useless.*"

And she was right.

Even when he and Mark caught The Slasher, it didn't help the Louviers. It couldn't. Lynette was gone.

LaStanza opened his eyes when he heard a car door slam, but it wasn't the Senoré's funeral procession yet. He'd purposefully avoided the wake, arriving here before the funeral to have a quiet moment with Lynette.

The memory still hurt, Lizette's anger, the feeling of inferiority he had around the Louviers. Hell, he always felt out of place, even now in his own house, like a little boy with his face pressed against the glass, looking in at the rich.

But slowly, ever so slowly, Lizette warmed to him. Hell, he'd warmed to her immediately, falling for her but it took her a while until she took his hand one day, then kissed him later, softly on the lips.

LaStanza had stumbled in and out of love before but nothing like his feelings for Lizette. Emotionally and physically, he loved her completely. He'd love her forever. If she ever stopped loving him, just seal him away in one of these walled tombs. What would be the point of love if he couldn't love her?

Mr. Tough Guy. Mafia Killer. Man with the perfect solution record. Always gets his man. The fuck! Seal him away. Without Lizette, what would be the point of it all?

He spotted Beau coming through the gate. In a black suit and wrap-around Ray Ban sunglasses, Beau walked straight to LaStanza and said, "The procession's right behind me."

LaStanza stood. "You went to the wake?"

"Couldn't get in. The place was packed."

Beau looked at the tomb LaStanza had been staring and asked, "Somebody you know?" He didn't miss much.

"My wife's twin sister."

"Oh."

"My first case in homicide."

"Damn." It took a good half hour for the entourage to park and the mourners to stream through the gate and collect around a small sepulchre near the center of St. Vincent's. The place suddenly reeked with the sickly-sweet smell of roses. LaStanza hated that smell. Too many funerals.

Standing in the background, LaStanza checked the periphery.

"What are we looking for?" Beau whispered.

"Anyone looks out of place. Mason solved two murders over the years when killers visited the funeral. See their handiwork."

"Jesus."

"We also want the family to see we're still on the case."

A whiff of incense came their way as the priest swung the silver incense burner over the polished wooden casket. LaStanza spotted Pauli and his wife up front, dressed in all black, their heads bent.

The service was short and quiet.

He waited as the people streamed away, watching Pauli lift his mother from a folding chair and guide her slowly away from her husband's sepulchre. Lori Venetta stepped from behind her father and came toward LaStanza and Beau. Her hair in long, wet ringlets, her lips glistening with deep red lipstick, almost maroon, she wore a black knit dress, cut at mid-thigh, showing off her slim figure.

Beau let out a long breath.

Lori stepped up to LaStanza. In her heels she was a good two inches taller than him. LaStanza noticed tiny freckles on the bridge of her small nose and along her delicate cheek bones when she took off her sunglasses and stared into his eyes.

She pulled a note pad from her purse and a small silver pen and jotted on the pad, showing it to LaStanza.

"Any progress?"

"No, but we'll find them."

She shifted her weight from one leg to the other and finally looked away from LaStanza's eyes to jot another note, which read,

"Can you come by my office sometime?" She handed him a business card made of parchment with her name embossed: Lori Venetta, Executive Director of the Chickima Foundation with a St. Charles Avenue address.

"Sure," LaStanza said as she handed a card to Beau and pointed to his chest, him too, obviously. LaStanza waited until she looked back at him before telling her he needed to speak with her and her father as soon as it was convenient.

She wrote, "Tonight. At my mother's. Eight o'clock? The visitors should be gone." Then she added, "You both look tired."

LaStanza read the note and showed it to Beau. Looking back at Lori, her eyes held his again for long seconds. Then she reached over to brush an unruly strand of hair from his eyes. He needed a haircut, no doubt, but it was the intimacy of her brushing that told LaStanza more than he wanted to hear.

She touched Beau's arm, giving him another long stare before following her parents through the cemetery.

Beau let out another long breath.

"I must be getting old," LaStanza said. "I don't remember her being so – beautiful."

Beau whispered, "That's a fuckin' understatement."

The detectives moved through the crypts, both watching the gentle sway of Lori Venetta's slim hips as she moved, with almost feline elegance.

"This looks like an assignment for a man named Beau," LaStanza said.

Beau shook his head. "She's outta my league."

"The fuck."

"Too sophisticated for my Cajun side and too white for my Sioux nature."

"Yeah? Then you tell me how in hell the richest heiress in Louisiana, ten generations of wealth, sophistication and beauty marries a little greaseball like me? My grandfather *fell* off the fuckin' banana boat from Sicily."

Stepping through the gate, LaStanza added, "You wanna come to the Venetta's tonight. I'm just gonna talk to them about the autopsy."

"Got plans," Beau said. "Dinner with an ex-girlfriend."

"From the funeral right into the pyre."

"You've had experience."

"Fuckin'A."

1:22 p.m. – Claiborne Avenue

"We don't talk to Wops!"

LaStanza parked in the same cab stand, leaving his coat behind, his gold badge clipped to his belt and LFR in his back pocket, revolver exposed in its canvas holster on his right hip, note book and Colibri in hand. He crossed Carrollton and stopped momentarily at the spot of the murder. A homeless black man in his sixties, sitting against the back wall of K&B, watched LaStanza approach. His right hand gripped the paper bag with his bottle inside as he struggled to get up.

LaStanza took his elbow and help him up, then gave the man a ten and asked if he'd heard about the murder. The man shook his head as he stared at the ten dollar bill as if was some alien object.

"Ask around," LaStanza told him. "I'll be back. Come up with something useful and there's money in it."

The man blinked his bleary eyes.

"Tell your pandas. We're looking for two black guys in their twenties." LaStanza ran off the descriptions, which didn't seem to register. The old man hurried away with his newfound wealth.

LaStanza returned to the murder spot. Someone had cleaned up the blood. He stood where the walker had lain and looked at the uneven cement, the oil stains where cars had parked, two crumpled candy wrappers. A gust of wind sent the wrapper spiraling and LaStanza looked up at dark rain clouds moving in from the west, angry clouds moving quickly.

An empty Sprite can rolled past him and he felt something in his chest as he watched it re-trace the steps the killers had taken as they fled Shoe Town, stopping momentarily to murder a ninety-one year old man with a walker. What he felt inside grew and he recognized it and wanted it. The leopard again, pacing now, in anticipation of the hunt.

As he looked around, LaStanza felt his killer instinct rising, like bile from his liver. He felt his eyes narrowing as he moved to the corner of the K&B, pressing his back against the corner to watch the flow of traffic along Claiborne, to watch the occasional pedestrian across the street, to watch the people waiting for the bus.

He crossed to the neutral ground and questioned the people at the bus stop, then went up to Carrollton to question the people at the streetcar stop before moving into Palmer Park. A leopard was patient and this was just the beginning of the hunt.

After canvassing the park, speaking to nine people, LaStanza took the houses surrounding the park before returning to the drug store, Skate Town, Shoe Town but first, the fire station. Three firemen sat on folding chairs outside the fire house with their legs spread and arm folded. As LaStanza stepped up a voice boomed from inside the fire house, "We don't talk to Wops!"

The three firemen didn't react. LaStanza waited as a shadow came out of the fire house and with it, a face from the past. Eddie Landis, who'd gone through the police academy with LaStanza, grinned broadly and said, "I was a better cop than you, a better shot than you, better lookin' too." This brought chuckles to the firemen.

Landis: six feet, two-seventy, balding with a pasty complexion and horn-rimmed glasses. He stopped in front of LaStanza with his hands on his hips. "I was a much better shot."

"On the pistol range," LaStanza said. "It's different when they shoot back."

Landis laughed. "How many you killed?"

"I lost count."

Landis laughed even louder and slapped LaStanza's shoulder, sending him sideways a step.

"When did you get back in town?" LaStanza asked.

"Three years ago. Nobody leaves New Orleans, permanently. You know that." Landis had quit the department and the city for Wisconsin some years back. He and his wife had lost a baby. S.I.D.S.

"Come inside and eat," Landis said. "Just finished a pot of gumbo."

"No thanks. I'm here about the murder around the corner."

"Murder?"

LaStanza looked at the other three firemen and each shrugged.

"We sent someone around and spoke to y'all."

"We just came back on duty today from four days off," Landis said. "The other crew was here."

LaStanza dug out business cards and passed them around, explaining to them how the murder went down. He finished with the usual. If any of you hear anything, let him know.

"Ask around," he said and that brought more chuckles. One of the sitting fireman said nobody talked to them around here, 'cept the bums mooching.

"Those are the ones I mean," LaStanza. "They're always around. The might have seen something."

He told them he was serious and thanked them and they all nodded in that bored fireman-with-nothing-to-fuckin-do-look. Then again, these were the same guys who saved the Cabildo when a roofer accidentally set it ablaze. The image was indelible, fires hoses raining down on the old seat-of-government building from every angle, additional hoses wetting down St. Louis Cathedral next door too keep the flames from spreading, firemen running in and out of the Cabildo, now a museum, carrying out paintings, priceless historical documents, including one of the copies of the Louisiana Purchase and the death mask of Napoleon. LaStanza had watched from atop the sea-wall along Decatur Street, certain they'd only manage to save the slab and was amazed when they saved the entire structure, except the roof, which was under repair to begin with. A-fuckin-mazing, when you put a spark to their asses, those guys could deliver.

The manager of Skate Town, above the Shoe Town, could have been Landis's younger brother. His named was Sanders.

"I wasn't around. Most of the crew were part-timers for the Skate-a-thon. Usually work weekends, Friday and Saturday nights and Sundays."

LaStanza spoke to everyone in the place, passing out cards, feeling the leopard pacing as he moved from one group of skaters to another. No one saw or knew anything but all would check around. Some sounded sincere.

Evangelista Luz greeted LaStanza with a blink of her eyes and a wide smile. She was in all white, dress a little too tight, white heels a little too high. She looked nice. Behind the counter sat a short man with an olive complexion and a harsh look on his face.

Evangelista introduced her husband who folded his arms as he stared at LaStanza.

"The security guard quit. So did Andy Pitney. They too shook to work here." She nodded toward her husband, who was listening. "Luis wants me to quit too, but I'm *no* quitter."

A tall man came out of the back room, with a clipboard in hand.

"That's our regional manager. He's working with me while he interviews replacements."

She introduced LaStanza to a Mr. Wesley, six-two, two-hundred, sandy hair and a weak chin. He had an even weaker handshake.

"You're not from here are you?"

Wesley's smile was hesitant and he answered, "No. Cleveland. How'd you know I wasn't from –"

"Where's your security guard?" LaStanza asked.

"We're still setting up another company –"

"Get one right away. And not some old guy. Get off duty cops, or ex-policemen."

"Huh?" Obviously the regional manager didn't like taking instructions, so LaStanza put it plainly. "Anyone from here knows you don't open your doors around here without a security guard."

"Well that's a corporate decision."

LaStanza leaned closer, making the big man inch backward.

"Yeah? And when one of your employees gets hurt, I'll be the first on the witness stand on the lawsuit against your corporation and you personally, telling a New Orleans jury how I warned you and you didn't listen." LaStanza smiled. "I'm good in front of juries. Get a guard in here. Anything happens to Mrs. Luz, I'll be very angry, then I'll kick your ass in court. Capiche?"

Wesley went back into the back room.

Evangelista hid her giggle behind her hand. Her husband wasn't placated but that was fine with LaStanza, who heard his call sign on his LFR and pulled his radio from his back pocket.

"3124 – go ahead."

"Got some line-ups for you. 10-20?" It was Mason.

"Shoe Town."

"In route."

Evangelista moved behind the counter and leaned her elbows on it. "Did you see them in the video tape?" she asked.

"Saw the tops of everyone's heads. Unless they look up at the camera like Chevy Chase did in that movie, we'll never see their faces."

"What movie?"

LaStanza couldn't remember but the scene was memorable, Chevy forced to rob a bank and looking up directly into the security camera for a long look.

LaStanza moved to the door to the back room and peeked inside. Wesley was taking some kind of inventory. LaStanza tried a different tack, apologizing for his earlier anger and bringing Wesley back out into the main room where he pointed to the video camera.

"It needs to be lower, right behind the cash register area so we can see the *faces* of the robbers. Just a suggestion. But you might make some points with your corporate people. Tell them it was your idea."

Wesley didn't seem mollified, but LaStanza saw him making note as he went back into the store room.

When Mason came in, he held the door open for a pretty blonde and a muscular black guy with short cropped hair, a small gold earring in his left ear. Mason followed them in and both moved up to LaStanza.

The blonde spoke first, "I'm Emily Reese, here for my interview." She smiled and stuck her hand out to LaStanza, who shook it and smiled back. In her late twenties, Emily was five-one, ninety pounds, slim and perky.

"I'm Jim Saxon," the big man said, extending his hand.

LaStanza shook it. "Where'd you play ball?"

Saxon grinned. "St. Aug."

"I'm Detective LaStanza, Homicide Division. Y'all want to step toward that back room for Mr. Wesley."

Saxon seemed amused, Emily confused for a moment before they went to the back. LaStanza introduced Mason to Mr. and Mrs.

Luz.

They used the counter to lay out the line-ups, one at a time, seven photos in each. Mason had come up with twenty sets. Evangelista studied each photo carefully and shook her head. Nothing. Zero. Zip. LaStanza thanked her.

Stepping outside, LaStanza stretched and Mason said, "How about supper?"

"Sounds good to me. Where'd you park?"

"Next to yours."

They headed around the corner. LaStanza gave the leopard another long look around.

"Where you wanna go?" Mason.

"Lizette's taking the entourage to Galatoire's."

"Don't let me hold you up."

"Too late. Anyway, I've never been and don't wanna go."

"Why not? It's one of the best. If not *the* best."

LaStanza looked at his lieutenant closely, noticing his shirt under his coat for the first time.

"Is that a pink shirt?"

"It's light red. Your wife picked it out for my wife."

"Didn't you have a white shirt on earlier?"

"Spilled coffee on it."

"Come on. Follow Me," LaStanza.

On the way Mason called Jodie and Fel and told them to bring the newbies.

6:40 p.m. – Oak Street

"Beside, I don't like eating with those people."

The Veranda Restaurant occupied the bottom portion of a narrow two-story townhouse at the corner of Monroe and Oak Streets, just across from a run-down mechanic shop, once a filing station, its old Esso sign leaning against the side fence.

LaStanza led the way through the front dining area, through the kitchen where four women worked over a grill and two black ovens, to a long table on the covered back porch. He sat facing the restaurant, letting Mason face the back yard, lit by two yellow lights. There were more tables in the back yard.

"Smells great," Mason nodded back to the kitchen.

"It's real Mexican food only they're all from Honduras."

A girl with chocolate skin brought out two large glasses of ice water, slice of lemon in each and a menu for Mason. She smiled shy.

"Ciao, Consuela. Comé sta?"

She laughed and said, "I'm not Consuela. I'm Lucy," and left them alone on the porch.

LaStanza called out behind her, "We've got others coming."

"Since when do you speak Spanish?" Mason opened the simple paper menu.

"That was Italian. I keep trying it on them but it doesn't work."

Mason crinkled his brow. "You not eatin'?"

"I know what I want. Try the burros, burritos actually, and the soft tacos. The chimis too. Everything's big here."

He turned to look at the back yard at the banana trees and camellia bushes just as a wave of cool air breezed over them, the air smelling of rain. The rest came in together, Jodie leading the way, towing Fel and Glapier, Kelly bringing up the rear. Jodie and Fel came around to sit on LaStanza's side.

LaStanza leaned back, watched and listened to his friends talk over each other, telling Mason about their canvasses, discussing the menu, Jodie giving hints since she'd eaten there with her partner before. He watched Kelly, sitting across from Jodie, looking at her, smiling when she looked at him. Glapier frowned at everything on the menu. Jodie guided her to the soft tacos.

The rain started slowly, then built up, peppering the tin roof over the porch, stifling the conversation, sending a fine mist over the overworked detectives. LaStanza closed his eyes and let it flow.

His usual chicken burro, Spanish rice and refried beans were especially good that evening. The owner came out to check on them, a tiny woman with gray hair, dark face wrinkled and bright brown eyes.

"This is Mama," LaStanza told the group. "This is her place."

"Is everything OK?" Mama's voice was deep and velvety, with only a hint of an accent?

"Perfetto," LaStanza in Italian.

"Perfecto," Mama corrected him before signaling to Lucy for drink refills as Mason explained to Fel how LaStanza was trying to teach them Italian.

"Man," Kelly finally spoke. "This place is great."

"Yep," Mason agreed, "but I'd still be at Galatoire's with my wife."

Jodie put a hand on LaStanza's shoulder. "Lizette was expecting you at Galatoire's?"

"As if."

She let out a long sigh, looked up at Kelly and explained. "For some goofy reason, he dislikes fancy restaurants."

LaStanza picked up his water glass. "It's not goofy. It's called usury. They charge a hundred bucks for a dish should cost fifteen at the fuckin' most. And don't give me all that ambiance shit." He waved at the dripping back yard. "This is beautiful and peaceful and the food and service are fantastic. Besides, I don't like eating with those people."

Fel suddenly laughed. "You're fuckin' incredible."

"Rich people give me a royal pain."

"You're rich," Jodie said.

"I'm just a gigolo. Ask my wife's family."

Glapier had a puzzled look on her face, hard to tell apart from her usual scowl, so Jodie explained, "He married the richest woman in Louisiana. They're loaded only he hasn't faced up to being rich."

"The fuck. I just paid for this meal."

Jodie slapped his shoulder and Fel complained but Mason knew better. He stuffed two pieces of Juicy Fruit into his mouth. Poor bastard wanted a cigarette so fuckin' bad.

Jodie tried to get a check but Mama explained, "Señor LaStanza has an account here. Direct deposit from his bank. It works rather nicely."

He slipped Lucy two twenties on the way out.

"One is for Consuela."

"I'm Consuela."

"Then one's for Lucy." Consuela and Lucy weren't twins, but they looked so much alike.

It was Lizette's money and she kept stuffing his wallet, so –

8:01 p.m. – Dublin Street

"Only, there are a lot of robbers in this city."

Lori Venetta unlatched the screen door to let LaStanza in. When she looked behind him, he told her, "Beau can't make it."

She nodded and closed the wooden door, setting the dead bolt. She'd changed into a dark gray skirt with a charcoal gray top, her hair pinned up on the sides with barrettes. She looked – delicate – elegant again.

Pauli was still in his black suit and shook LaStanza's hand. Voices echoed from the rear and Pauli said his mother was with older relatives in the kitchen.

"Have you made any progress?" Pauli asked.

"Nothing yet. We're working hard. We *will* find them."

Gail came in carrying a tray with a coffee carafe, cups and saucers. She put them on the coffee table in the living room and filled four cups. LaStanza sat in one of the easy chairs while the Venettas sat on the sofa facing him, Pauli in the middle.

When Lori crossed her legs, LaStanza saw her dress was a wraparound and her entire right leg was exposed before she closed it. LaStanza couldn't help notice her long slim leg, but that's what she wanted. He knew that and kept his face blank. But he couldn't stop his heartbeat from rising a little.

Looking at Pauli, he told them he needed their help.

"Anything," Pauli said.

"Your father wasn't shot." LaStanza let that sink in.

Gail said, "But the paper –"

"Was wrong," – LaStanza. "And right now only the killers, the pathologist, a few cops and y'all know this. We want to keep it that way because sometimes a secret like this will bring the killers and us together."

Lori was jotting furiously and uncrossed her leg to pass the pad to LaStanza, her skirt opening to show both thighs. She written: *They might tell people and you can pick up their story?*

"Exactly." Then he told them how killers always talk and often correct newspaper stories. He could see in their eyes they understood.

Pauli, – "So if we hear of anyone around here's saying he wasn't shot, we'll get a hold of you immediately."

LaStanza nodded and took a sip of coffee. For the next ten minutes he told them what he'd been doing, putting in long hours canvassing, running line-ups, researching through files for crimes of similar M.O.

"Only there are a lot of robbers in this city."

Lori passed him another note: *We're not to correct anyone about how he died, right?*

She was a sharp as she looked. LaStanza passed the note to her father and said yes, don't correct anyone. Let everyone think it was a shooting.

Through the entire meeting Lori stared into LaStanza eyes, reaching into them, almost intrusively. He kept his eyes from reacting, knowing exactly what was happening. She was nice to look at and his heartbeat and stirring dick had minds of their own, but he knew this could be trouble.

He thanked them for their time and told them he'd keep them in the loop. Lori had another note and she went to the door behind him to hand it to him: *Thanks for staying in touch.* And she took his hand and squeezed it. He felt his heartbeat again, nodded and left, confident he could handle the situation as he handled everything.

Yeah, a little voice in his inside said. *Right.*

Tuesday, April 1, 1986

11:00 a.m. – Exposition Boulevard

"Where are we doing this?"

"Coffee?" Lizette asked Sam Edkins as his stepped into the kitchen. Fel's Uncle Sam was six-two, two-fifty, with the same blue-black skin as his nephew, brown eyes and close-cropped salt-and-pepper hair. He also had the same wide grin as Fel. He'd told her he was sixty, but looked younger.

Sam put the box he was carrying on the counter and sat up on one of the bar stools as Lizette poured them each a mug of coffee-and-chicory. Sam took cream and sugar. Lizette took hers black. "How'd they come out?" She pulled the box closer. She was dressed casually in red jogging shorts and a white tee-shirt and white running shoes. Sam wore a black shirt and black jeans.

She opened the box and slowly leafed through the proof sheets of eleven different poses she'd taken for the pin-up calendar she was putting together for her husband. It started out to be a boudoir calendar, but Lizette had some ideas for outdoor shots, so after taking six bedroom scenes of Lizette in various nightgowns and negligees, Sam took his camera gear outdoors.

Lizette stopped at the two sheets of bra and panty pictures taken at Pop's Fountain. It was a bright, beautiful day with a freshening breeze from the lake that lifted Lizette's dark hair.

"I like that shot the most." Sam came around and pointed to a pose of Lizette with her hands behind her head. In a diaphanous lacy French bra and matching white panties, she looked almost nude. With her hair flowing and the pouty look on her face, it was a very provocative picture.

"The kids on the bikes liked that outfit too," Lizette joked, remembering the three boys stopping to watch. They even tried to peek at her when she'd gone into Sam's van to change into a different bra-and-panty set.

In the next series she wore a white tennis outfit as she sat provocatively on a bench. Instead of bloomers, she'd worn sheer pink panties. The last set was quite sexy, Lizette in a tight red mini-dress sitting up on a shoe shiner's platform in an old shoe shine parlor, her left leg extended straight down while right foot was lifted high on the shoe pedestal while a very old shoe shine man pretended to buff her red high heel. Sam had moved around to get different views, some with the other customers, all men, staring at her open legs, some shots showing the tops of her thigh-high stockings and the see-through white panties, her bush clearly visible.

"This one." Lizette pointed to one of the shots which showed her panties and a haughty, uncaring look on her face, a nonchalant look as if she sat like that all the time. You could see the shoe shiner's arms in the picture and part of the back of his head. He wasn't looking at the shoe.

Lizette looked through the sheets again as they finished their coffee. When she looked at Sam, who'd gone back to his stool, she said, "You ready?"

"Always." The big grin.

Lizette took the proofs into the dining room and slipped them into the bottom drawer of one of the four china hutches. As far as she knew, Dino had never noticed any of the hutches.

"I'll get dressed," she told Sam on her way back through the kitchen and up the back stairs. When she came down twenty minutes later, Sam's eyes lit up. The black mini-skirt was so short it barely covered her ass. The tops of the black thigh-hi stockings were visible. The white jacket had one button in front which managed to cover her breasts, a hint of her pink areoles peeking out.

Sam carried her bag out to his van, parked just outside the kitchen. Climbing in, Lizette's skirt rose, exposing the entire front of her sheer white panties. Even tugging the skirt down didn't cover the panties.

"You look hot, Lady."

She had her hair fluffed in long curls and wore light make-up with dark brown lipstick. Sam grinned at her before going around to he driver's side. He glanced at his watch. "Good. Our motorcycle cop will meet us in a half hour."

"Where are we doing this?"

"Behind the fire station just down from my studio. The firemen won't mind."

Lizette laughed. She'd met Fel's uncle by accident two month's earlier. They'd bumped into each other in Marquette Hall at Loyola, Lizette hurrying to one of her classes, him looking for the photo lab. Lizette's class was cancelled and she found the big man still looking for the lab ten minutes later.

She took him to the administration, then led him to the Dana Center and along the way discovering his nephew was Felicity Jones. They had coffee first, in the student union, where Lizette broached the idea for the calendar. She'd been looking for a professional photographer she could trust. Sam promised he would never let his nephew know anything about their arrangement, which was strictly business and highly confidential. It didn't take more than one session for Lizette to realize she'd made the right choice. Sam was a true gentleman, although there was always an appreciative gleam in his eyes when she posed with very little on.

"This motorcycle cop doesn't know my husband or your nephew."

"He's a rookie. Doesn't know much."

12:12 p.m. – Claiborne Avenue

"That was steamin'."

Lizette laughed again as Sam pulled the van behind the firehouse on Claiborne, just down from his studio at the corner of Claiborne and Orleans Avenues. Sam went into the firehouse and a couple minutes later a motorcycle cop pulled off Claiborne and parked. He took off his helmet and was young and black and built like a linebacker. Sam came out of the firehouse with three firemen. He waved to Lizette who climbed out and all the men became statues, all staring, grins on their faces, eyes wide open.

Sam referred to her as Liz and the cop was Larry. It took a minute for Larry to position his bike to face the firehouse with the van blocking its view from the street. Sam brought out his Hasselblad camera, the same model Lizette had bought Dino last Christmas. One of the firemen had a video camera, another a 35mm.

"Mind if we take some pictures too," asked the man with the 35mm. He was in his fifties and looked a little like Dino's father, except heavier.

She shrugged, her heart stammering now as Sam waved her to the bike. She climbed on and with her legs open, sat up, hands on the handlebars. She could see the men positioning themselves to get a good shot of her panties.

Sam set up and focused and said, "OK. Open it."

She unbuttoned the jacket and it opened automatically, freeing her breasts, just as she had last Mardi Gras when Stan spotted her. Sam began snapping pictures, his strobe flashing. He had her lean back, lift one leg, then the other.

"Pull up a stocking," he told her and she lifted her leg and toyed with the top of a thigh-hi, then the other. She took off the jacket. Eventually, he had her lay back on the bike with her knees up and open, her head back, face pointing to the sky. The men moved around to get every body part on film and she felt her heart thundering in her ears, knew her nipples hard a hint of dampness between her legs when a breeze came.

She climbed off the bike and Larry asked for a picture with her. They stood together, arms around each other's waist, and smiled at the camera. Then Larry looked down at her breasts and Sam took another shot. She felt Larry's fingers rising slowly from her waist to touch the bottom of her left breast.

"Wow," Larry said as they disengaged and he brought his hands around to softly brush against her nipples, sending a shudder through her.

"Hold on," Sam said. "You gonna touch 'em, lets get those dark hands against that white skin." He stepped in for a close up and asked Lizette to put her hands behind her head again.

Larry stared at her breasts as if he'd never seen a pair and slowly, softly drew his fingers around them, cupping them, caressing them as Sam took pictures. Larry began kneading her breasts and Lizette's breathing rose for several delicious moments until Larry pulled away and wiped his brow.

"Whew. Hope I can climb on my bike now."

Larry thanked her and left. There were six firemen now and the one with the 35mm asked if she'd pose on their fire engine. Sam quickly reloaded his camera and film packs.

"I'm Jim," said the 35mm man as he guided her to the side of the shiny engine. "Since we've seen your panties, would you mind climbing out of that skirt?" His face was redder now and beamed at Lizette who shrugged and unzipped the skirt, ooching it down. She tossed it to Sam and climbed up on the side of the engine.

And for the next scintillating fifteen minutes, Lizette posed for the firemen and Sam, standing, sitting, bending over. Sitting in the passenger seat of the cab, toyed with her panties, pulling them aside to show more of pubic hair, pulling them up again, silky strands of hair sticking out the sides now.

The panties didn't hide much and she felt so hot, so naughty. The men were so attentive, so appreciative, so captivated, she thought. Moving to the rear tailgate, Jim asked if she'd remove her panties. She was so excited, riding such a high, she almost did.

"You can see plenty already," she gasped and watched them focus on her, feeling their leers as if they were touching her.

Before leaving, each fireman asked to pose with her, arms around waists, each leering at body parts from up close. Jim was the last and the only one brazen enough to ask to touch her and she let him. This was one man who'd had plenty of experience feeling up a woman's boobs.

By the time she climbed, almost naked, back into Sam's van, she was nearly panting.

"That was steamin'," Sam said.

"You telling me?" Lizette worked the miniskirt back on and the jacket and tried to catch her breath.

Jesus, where's Dino right now? She was so hot, so wet, she needed him – *now.*

Lizette closed her eyes and tried to think of something else, anything else but she could see still feel the hands on her breasts, could see Larry's dark fingers brushing her nipples, Jim's strong hands squeezing her boobs, sending shocks of passion through her.

She's posed nude before, back at Brown, and her classmates had lust in their eyes, but not like these men. Back in college she was in control of them and herself, she was the southern-belle-vamp that made most of the milquetoast Yankee girls look like skinny, underfed boys. She felt herself shivering inside and knew she wasn't in control of herself as before.

She's come out of her shell in college, graduating from being a little neighborhood tramp on Exposition Boulevard, to a real whore, loving every moment of it. She'd explained it all to Dino. Her promiscuity. She liked calling herself a selective whore, when she felt the calling. It gave her a thrill, always did. She was a rich, uptown, classy little slut and right now, she needed her husband.

She needed a good fuckin'.

She looked at Sam's hands on the wheel and bit her lip. No. She couldn't do it. She could tell herself sex was sex and love was love. But no. She would have to get out the vibrator. Maybe she could call Dino, get him home for a quickie. Maybe she could go meet him, pull him into the backseat of her Maserati. To hell with the vibrator. She wanted Dino.

What she didn't figure was for him to be pulling up in his unmarked unit just as Sam parked next to their mansion.

2:08 p.m. – Exposition Boulevard

"A school boy's fantasy."

Sam climbed out while Lizette tried to close the jacket even more. She watched her husband look at Sam, then at her, then back at Sam again. Then he smiled slightly.

"Fel's uncle, right? Sam, isn't it?" LaStanza shook Sam's hand and looked back at Lizette. "What are y'all up to?" There was a wily look in her husband's eyes and Lizette let out a long breath.

"I'm taking some portraits of her for you," Sam said as Lizette climbed out and LaStanza blinked and started laughing, laughing so hard he had to hold on to the porch railing. Thank God he was in a good mood.

"What the hell kinda outfit is that?"

Lizette put her hands on her hips, which caused the button on the jacket to almost pop.

LaStanza finally stopped laughing. "It's an April Fool Day outfit?"

"The men who were watching didn't think it was I was a fool."

"I guess not."

She reached in for her bag and LaStanza said, "Jesus, you musta put on some show."

Lizette moved up to her husband and brushed her lips across his, then nibbled his lower lip. Then she took off the jacket and handed it to him before turning back to Sam and pecking him on the cheek.

"Thanks, Sam."

"Thank you."

Lizette went into the kitchen. Sam drove off and LaStanza followed his wife into the house.

"Hey, why don't you ask Sam to find a black guy to screw

Mrs. LeGris?"

"It's set up at his studio. This Thursday. Wanna come watch?"

LaStanza moved up behind her and cupped her breasts and began to rub them gently. She leaned back against him.

"This what you came home for?" Her voice sounded like a purr.

"I need one of those Colibri pen refills. Are they in your desk?"

She started grinding her hips against him and he felt the dick already hard and throbbing. He was about to pull away when she turned and started yanking at his tie.

"Slow down," he said, trying to help. "You're choking me."

So she grabbed his belt and let him take care of the tie and shirt.

"Don't drop the gun," he was panting now.

Her mouth moved up to his and her hot tongue pressed against his and he grabbed her ass and guided her to the floor and did her with his pants around his ankles, shoes and socks still on. She guided his dick to the folds of her pussy and he sank in and she started rocking immediately, gasping and crying and even when he tried to slow down, she wanted no part of it. She was so hot, she damn near broke his back, her arms and legs wrapped around him.

She came quickly bucking and crying out and then slowed down as he got his second wind and began some long, grinding strokes.

"Oh, Babe," she moaned. "Yes. Yes. Yes!"

He looked at her lovely face and her eyes were closed, her mouth open in pleasure and he gushed in her in long spurts. She continued bucking, her pussy muscles sucking every drop from him. Finally, he sank on her and tried to catch his breath.

"That hit the spot," she said.

"All I wanted was a ball point refill."

"Well you hit the jackpot, Slick."

"Speaking of slick." LaStanza knelt up and then sat back and pulled off his pants and shoes and socks.

"I'll turn the Jacuzzi on," she said, getting up.

"Won't have time."

"A quick soak." He watched her fine ass move to the French

doors and out on the patio.

What the hell? He was tired of canvassing so he went out. Lizette was already in the tub. He went to check the temperature and she told him it was already on lukewarm. He climbed in and let the churning bubbles do their work.

"We should do this more often in the afternoon," she said, her face glowing in that post-intercourse look she got when she'd been good and screwed. He liked that look.

They both closed their eyes.

Two quiet minutes later, Lizette said, "Is that your radio?"

"It's in the back pocket of my pants. They aren't calling me." He realized he'd been listening.

"I heard the word 'homicide'."

"Yeah, but unless you hear 3124, it ain't me."

They remained silent for the next ten minutes before Lizette got up. "I'll get the towels."

He watched her climb out and wring out her hair just as Professor LeGris stepped through the open French doors with three young men, who all stopped in their tracks and stared at the naked lady. Of course LeGris would have the alarm code. He was their guest.

Lizette let out a little gasp, then put her hands on her hips and said, "Well, I'm not diving back in."

The first young man, tall and blond pretended he wasn't looking at her, the second, smaller and skinnier with café-au-lait skin looked Lizette up and down, then looked away, then looked again. The third, a thick Hispanic-looking guy stared unashamedly at her body parts.

"Gee, Miss Louvier," the third one said, "nice outfit."

She laughed and introduced her husband to Billy, the blond, Freddie and Jose, the big Hispanic guy.

"Why are they here?" LaStanza asked and LeGris answered. They came to get the notes for tomorrow's symposium. Jesus, the three boys gaping at naked Lizette were students in the class she was teaching on her fellowship.

Lizette went in for a towel and dried herself in front of her new audience, then brought a towel out for LaStanza, winking at him and he knew by that look on her face she wasn't about to wrap a towel around herself.

"They've seen it all already," she said softly, reading his mind.

She tossed her towel on the kitchen counter on her way back through, leading the four into the dining room on the way to the library.

Getting out and toweling off, LaStanza noticed he had a blue-veiner, on the way to another diamond-cutter erection. He wrapped the towel around his waist and went through the kitchen, dining room, foyer and into the library where Lizette was bending over pulling something out of her desk drawer. LeGris stood next to her, the boys behind leering at her ass.

Lizette stood and turned and passed sheets of paper to the three boys, then stood there, relaxed and natural, naked, and talked to the boys about the symposium. She spotted LaStanza moving into the library and winked at him.

That was when LaStanza remembered his camera case in the corner and went over to dig out his Hasselblad. It was already loaded with only two shots taken of God knew what. He slipped on the strobe unit, focused and took a picture of his naked wife talking to three students and a French professor.

The boys finally noticed him.

"You don't mind if I take a picture of my nude wife with y'all, do you?"

"No," Jose said, smiling as he moved closer to Lizette and put his arm around her waist. Freddie moved to the other side, while Billy and LeGris went to either side. They faced LaStanza and smiled. He took three pictures and quickly took a fourth when Jose turned to Lizette's breasts and Freddie leaned over to get a closer look at her bush.

"OK," Lizette said, "you've seen enough. Y'all can leave." She shooed them out. LeGris asked if he should turn on the alarm when they left. Lizette reminded him it reset itself automatically as the boys each turned for one more look.

Lizette went back to the desk as LaStanza readjusted the towel. She brought his Colibri refill, handed it to him and yanked off the towel, pushing him back into the easy chair.

"I need a refill too."

She climbed on him, guiding his stiff dick to her pussy and

sank slowly on him, taking in a deep breath then started moving up and down on his dick. Cupping those heavy breasts in his hands, he nibbled each nipple and sucked and she started bucking on him.

"That was quite a show you put on, little miss teacher." he said.

She gasped, gnawing her bottom lip.

"A school boy's fantasy," he said in a voice husky with pleasure.

"Fireman's fantasy too," she said, bouncing now. "Except I wore panties."

"That's – a – relief."

"They got – to cop – a feel – too."

"You let some horny-toad firemen feel you up?"

"Just – my tits." She kissed him, tongue hot and hard pressing against his. The second time around always took longer and Lizette road the pleasure coming twice before her husband came again.

3:16 p.m. – Claiborne and Carrollton Avenues

"I shot the cowboy outside the Second District Station."

"3126 – 3124." Jodie calling LaStanza just as he was pulling away from the mansion.

"Go ahead 3126."

"Can you 10-19?"

"10-4. Be right there."

He was there in six minutes. She was waiting at the curb outside her victim's house on Webster, notepad under her arm, hand on her waist. Jodie wore pale green today, another skirt-suit with a white blouse, her .9mm in her right hip for a change. Nobody wore a shoulder rig *every day.*

"Claiborne and Carrollton," she said climbing in.

"My case?"

"No. Mark's got a police shooting. He's been you calling on the radio."

"Jesus." LaStanza hit the accelerator and slapped the blue light on the dash.

"Thought you were going home to get a pen refill." He saw her lean forward to get a better look at him. "What happened to you?"

"Whaddya mean?"

"You're all messed up. Tie crooked. Hair's a mess."

LaStanza tapped the siren as he zipped across the neutral ground on St. Charles and took a hard left, punching it.

"Is that lipstick on your neck?"

"Probably." He tapped the siren again to warn a car about to ease through a stop sign in front of him. "My wife attacked me when I went to get the refill."

"Attacked? Oh!" Jodie let out a long sigh. "You guy are like rabbits sometimes."

"Hey, she attacked *me*."

Carrollton was surprisingly traffic-less and LaStanza made good time. He spotted flashing blue and red lights from four blocks away and had to park two blocks away, across from Palmer Park. As they approached on foot, he took in the scene.

Police cars blocked off the wide intersection, turning traffic around a block away, uniformed officers blowing whistles and waving arms. An ambulance sat parked beyond the end of the streetcar line with two EMTees standing with their arms folded. Mark Land stood in the center of the intersection in a tan suit. At his feet lay a man in tee-shirt and jeans and tennis shoes.

Several other police cars stood haphazardly in the wide intersection. LaStanza spotted Stan Smith barking orders to several cops. John Raven Beau leaned against the door of one unit and watched them with those steely eyes of his.

"So what do we have?" Jodie asked as Mark looked up from the body.

The man had three holes in him, one in his left shoulder, one in his belly and one in the right side of his face, exit wound just below the left temple.

"64 ass-hole stuck up the K&B. Three units responded. Five cops fired God know how many fuckin' rounds. I think Officer Beau over there was the only one who hit him."

LaStanza looked back at Beau and recognized that expressionless look on the tall cop's face. Beau was keeping his eyes from focusing on anything specific. LaStanza had been there, more than once.

"Did he have a weapon?"

Land pointed with the toe of his right shoe at the butt of a handgun sticking out from beneath the dead guy's torso.

"He fired several shots. Took out one of Beau's windows."

LaStanza could see it now, a window was missing from Beau's car.

Mark waved his hand around. "We got witnesses galore. Cops shot up two passing cars, a van and the streetcar sitting at the end of the line."

"Jesus, anyone hit?" Jodie.

"No, thank God." Mark. "Fel's dropping off both newbies but he's gotta go back to the Square. S and S have a dumped body in Algiers." He tapped LaStanza's shoulder. "Take Beau to the office for his statement soon as the lab gets here."

"Let me stay," LaStanza said. "This is *my* intersection."

"Yeah, you're right." Mark turned to Jodie who was already nodding and starting toward Beau. Looking back at LaStanza, Mark said, "What happened to you?"

"Huh? Oh. Fuckathon."

"Jesus. I hope you're talking about your wife."

"Of course."

LaStanza took out the Colibri and the refill and refilled the pen as a voice called out. He looked over at fireman Landis strolling their way, tugging up his uniform pants with both hands.

"Guess what? We seen the entire fuckin' thing this time!" He pointed toward Beau. "That guy's a dead shot. Three shots. All hits. First time I ever saw bullets hit someone. Fuckin' cool!"

Jesus H. Christ. I sure hope these weren't the firemen Lizette posed with.

Jodie watched Beau's face as she walked up. She'd seen that look before on her partner's face after he'd shot Casey Aloysius under the St. Claude Avenue Bridge and again after he and Fel gunned down Kaiser Billyday. It was an insulated look, as if he was in there all right, but wearing his face as a mask now, showing no expression, keeping it all inside.

He nodded as she stepped up and said, "You know the routine. Only speak to me."

Stan Smith took that moment to pass by and wave. He knew better than ask Beau anything.

"I'm taking you to the Bureau soon as the crime lab gets here."

"I know."

"This isn't your first time is it?"

"No. I shot the cowboy outside the Second District Station."

Jodie pulled out her note pad and remembered. The other platoon handled it but the story got around fast. Man in a cowboy outfit, ten-gallon hat, double six gun rig, boots, even spurs, approached several cops outside the Second District Station at shift change. He challenged them to draw. One of the cops drew a stick figure on a piece of paper. Beau heard the laughter as he started across the street and watched the cowboy pull out both six guns and open up. Fortunately he only killed two police cars and the front window of the stationhouse. Beau dropped him with two shots. The story got around fast – injun kills cowboy.

Man had been just released from a mental hospital. Called himself the Waco Kid because he had a passing resemblance to Gene Wilder of *Blazing Saddles* fame. Only he couldn't shoot. Thank God.

"You want to tell me how it went down?" Jodie asked.

"Briefly."

"64 in-progress at the K&B. I was the third unit to arrive. Man was running across the intersection, shooting at Sgt. Douglas and Left Sider, then he shot at me as I climbed out and I fired three rounds and he went down. Checked him for vitals. Came back to my car to wait for y'all."

Two crime lab technicians arrived, one started taking pictures, the second came over to Beau and secured his weapon and swabbed his hands for a neutron activation test to see if he fired a weapon. Jodie moved Beau away, just as vans from Channel 4 and Channel 6 squealed up.

"Yoo Hoo! Yoo Hoo!" A tall blonde in a tight red dress and spiked heels, silver star-and-crescent badge clipped to her waist, came bouncing up to Jodie and Beau. "I need to talk to the officer who shot the guy."

"No you don't." Jodie stepped between the woman and Beau.

"I'm *not* a reporter. I'm the –"

"I know who you are," Jodie said in an even voice. "Officers in police-involved shooting talk to Homicide only."

The blonde looked as if she'd been pinched. "I just want background –"

"Sergeant Mark Land's in charge. He's over there." Jodie pointed to Mark as she moved away with Beau.

"Next to the dead man?" The blonde's nose crinkled.

"How long you been a cop?"

Public Information Officer Alice Walker, no relation to the writer, didn't answer.

As LaStanza went down on his haunches next to the body, Mark said, "Think he's one of yours?"

"Don't know. Criminals are stupid enough." To return to the scene of the crime.

Only this man had a cross on his right cheek. Evangelista wouldn't have missed a six inch tattoo. And he looked short, shorter than LaStanza who knew he had to wait for the coroner's investigator before searching the body. Hopefully the fool had some ID on him. Standing, he looked around and headed for the biggest crowd of spectators with his pad and Colibri with its new refill. He'd need it.

Fel Jones wasn't content to park three blocks away and just let the newbies into the scene. He walked in with them, past the growing crowd to find Mark Land standing with the crime lab tech as close-up pictures were taken of the body.

Mark ran down the incident to them before sending Glapier and Kelly in opposite directions to interview witnesses. Glapier, in her lime-green pants-suit, headed straight for a group of firemen standing just inside the cordoned off area. Fel wondered as he watched her move away, if the girl had a full-length mirror at home. He wasn't sure, but red shoes didn't seem to go with lime green.

Kelly, on the other hand, wore a navy blue blazer over light gray pants and looked as if he'd stepped out of the pages of *GQ*. Not that Fel have never seen an issue of *GQ*, but he was sure that's what a *Gentleman's Quarterly* man looked like as Kelly walked to the K&B Drug Store, scene of the armed robbery that sparked the present shenanigans.

"Where's Jodie?" Fel asked Mark.

"Just took the shooter to the Bureau."

"Kelly'll be disappointed?"

"What?" Mark gave him a sharp look.

"He sweats her, big time."

"Sweat? The fuck you talking about?" Mark was transforming into his grizzly persona.

"He likes her."

Mark looked around, his eyes bulging now. "I got a police shootin' and you wanna talk about detectives liking each other."

"Secretly, I thought you'd wanna know."

Mark moved his face right in front of Fel's. "Aren't you supposed to be back at the Square? Or you want me to give you something to do here?"

Fel backed away, hands up in surrender. He spotted LaStanza and walked toward him as his old partner moved away from the crowd at the end of the streetcar line.

When he got close enough he said, "A.B.D.A.T.O."

"Another bad day at the office?"

"You getting' good. Who's the shooter?"

"Beau."

"Jesus, didn't he shoot someone already?"

"I don't know." LaStanza moved toward the group standing at the bus stop next to the bank, catty-corner from the K&B.

"When you and Liz were in Paris. Right after we killed Kaiser Billyday."

"I killed Billyday. You wounded him."

Fel laughed as he backed away, calling out, "N.W.T.A.S."

LaStanza tried ignoring him, but Fel explained anyway, "Not What the Autopsy Said. I inflicted a fatal wound too."

LaStanza rubbed his eyes.

"You look strange, man. You all right?"

"What?" LaStanza suddenly looked like a mini-grizzly.

"You look messed up, like you been takin' a nap."

LaStanza was about to give Fel a good ole *fuck you* sendoff when he spotted Lori Venetta in the crowd and froze, which also stopped Fel in his tracks.

4:02 p.m. – Detective Bureau

"You're getting a reputation."

They didn't use a video camera to tape an officer's statement in a police shooting, nor a tape recorder. Jodie sat at her desk behind her typewriter and typed Beau's statement. If the cop was nervous or stumbled it didn't show up on paper. Beau, however, wasn't nervous and didn't stumble one bit, giving her the facts in that slight Cajun accent of his.

"You know, I've never been able to fire *expert* on the range," he told her as she slipped a new sheet of paper into the typewriter carriage.

"I have," she said. "My partner tells me it's different when the target moves."

"And when they shoot at you." He blew out a long breath.

Several detectives came into the rear of the Bureau, robbery and burglary detectives, all looking at Beau as they passed.

"You might wanna talk to my partner when this is done."

"Yeah?"

"He's shot four."

Jodie guided him back to the statement and it ended at three pages. Short and sweet with no problems. She told him so. Then she warned him that a witness or two may pop up to dispute the facts.

"Witness?"

"Sometimes a shithead'll come forward and say the guy had his hands up or you stood over him and executed him. Especially an interracial shooting. That's why we gotta dot every *i*, cross every *t*. Actually, it's the same when a black cop shoots a white boy."

Another group of detectives filtered through the Bureau, stealing glances in their direction.

"You're getting a reputation."

Beau looked at the bay of windows at the far end of the wide squad room, the sunlight streaming through the peeled-away green tint, causing his eyes to squint.

"When I was little, living back on Vermilion Bay. I used to

dream of being someone when I grew up." He turned back to Jodie. "I shoulda been more specific."

She had to smile and for a second he smiled back and Beau had one of those smiles that lit up his face, one of those dreamy smiles. If he wasn't so damn young. He was good looking all right and had that quiet, dark, dangerous side that made her want to reach over and – if she weren't old enough to be his big sister.

"It started out to be a good shift," he said, leaning back now, maybe relaxing a little. "I arrested the plant fiend."

"The what?" Jodie leaned back in her chair and put her hands behind the back of her head. She crossed her legs and Beau automatically glanced at her legs. She like that predictability about men.

"Been having calls about someone stealing potted plants from porches along Fern Street, between Spruce and Hickory –"

"Wait. Stealing plants? Fern, Spruce, Hickory Streets?"

"Yep. Stolen ferns too. Go figure. I never thought potted plants were that expensive, but the victims were all ladies and they had receipts."

Jodie's phone rang and she answered before the second ring, "Homicide, Det. Kintyre."

"Jodie? Jim Morris here from the superintendent's office."

"Yes, captain."

"You have the officer who shot the robber down there?"

"Yes, sir."

"Good. Keep him there. The Chief wants to do the superintendent's hearing this evening, no matter how long it takes for y'all to get finished. He's leaving on vacation tomorrow morning. Six a.m. flight."

Jodie explained that Mark was still processing the scene and witnesses were still being interviewed.

"No problem," Morris said, his voice surprisingly friendly. "Just have Sergeant Land give us a call when he's ready. I spoke with him a few minutes ago. Says it looks like a good shooting. No sense making a big deal over it." Morris hung up.

Jodie explained what just happened to Beau.

"You don't mind hanging around do you?"

"Nope."

Jodie reached for her mug. "Want some more coffee?"

"Sure."

"So what happened with your plant fiend?" She led the way to the coffee pot and had to start a fresh pot of coffee-and-chicory. "Lady this morning showed me where her ficas disappeared to. My plant fiend had her two ficas on his front porch on Hickory Street. Still had the Walmart tags attached. Typical low-life criminal came to the door stoned outta his mind. He was still wearing the same tee-shirt and shorts my victim had described.

"So I put the cuffs on him and he insisted he had to have his wallet with him to go to Central Lockup. He forgot he'd given me a phony name but his ID was in his wallet."

"Don't tell me," Jodie said, arms folded now as she leaned against the table, waiting for the coffee to drip, "outstanding warrants?"

"Four. Two from Plaquemines and two from Jefferson for aggravated burglary. But the topper. He had fifteen rocks of crack in his wallet and three tabs of PCP."

"In jail for a long time."

"Hopefully."

Jodie put two Equals in her coffee. Beau took his black. She warned him it was strong. He nodded, took a sip and smiled.

"I wonder if the guy you shot's connected to LaStanza's case," Jodie said.

Beau shrugged. "He didn't fit the script, but you never know."

"What about your plant fiend?" Jodie sat and crossed her legs again, resisting the urge to push down her skirt.

"He's white," Beau said. "Douche-bag named Dudley. Dudley Rich. Only known criminal associates are other white boys. All in jail. Just like Dudley now."

"Good."

"Stupid bastard insisted on bringing his wallet, as if we wouldn't find the dope."

4:40 p.m. – Claiborne and Carrollton Avenues

"She thinks I'm her personal detective."

Lori Venetta stood above the crowd on one of the concrete benches at the bus stop. Her large brown eyes were wide and staring at LaStanza for a long moment before she looked down at a kid, about eleven with skin as dark as the black Saints tee-shirt he wore. She took his hand and he helped her down, the crowd backing away as her dress rose up her thigh, mostly men hawking out Lori's legs. In a short beige skirt-suit, Lori's legs looked even longer than usual in tall, brown high-heels. She eased through the crowd, her strawberry-blonde hair hanging in long wet-curls and her face made up like a cover-girl model. The eleven-year-old tailed behind her.

She moved up to LaStanza, eyes locked on his and handed him a note that read: *Are you all right?*

"Sure." LaStanza said, stepping a little closer. "You shouldn't be here."

"What's in the note?" Fel said, tapping LaStanza's shoulder.

Lori looked at Fel, then back at LaStanza, who glared at his friend then introduced them, explaining Lori was mute before Fel said something stupid.

"So what's in the note?" Fel.

LaStanza showed him the piece of paper.

Fel nodded to Lori. "Yeah. He looks bad, don't he? Kinda worn out."

LaStanza caught a movement in the corner of his eye and saw Mark stomping up. The big sergeant pointed an angry finger at Fel and Fel took off, waving a quick good-bye to Lori and calling out, "S.F.B."

Lori shrugged to LaStanza and he told her, "He puts things in initials. Probably meant 'She's freakin' beautiful'."

Mark's grizzly persona faded quickly as LaStanza introduced his sergeant to Lori. Mark apologized and pulled LaStanza aside to tell him the superintendent's hearing was going to be this evening, so if there were any good witnesses, snap to it and don't drag it out.

"Sure." LaStanza eased back to Lori, Mark still with him.

"What's in the note she gave you? She didn't see something, did she?" Mark smiled at Lori who shook her head.

LaStanza's shoulders sank as he showed the note to Mark who

coughed immediately. Lori passed LaStanza another note: *You look different.*

"Huh? Oh. A hard day."

Mark said, "Why don't you tell her the truth? Why you look so beat."

LaStanza turned his back to Lori and glared at Mark who backed away and ran into the coroner's investigator with the dead guy's wallet in hand.

LaStanza wheeled to face Lori who had yet another note: *You look nice. Hair messed up.* She reached up and brushed strands of hair from his forehead, then straightened his tie.

"You don't really want to see all this. Your car around here?"

She pointed down Claiborne where two bored patrolmen were standing next to their police car in the middle of the street. He took her elbow and led her back through the crowd to her car, a light blue Saab.

She passed him another note before climbing in: *Does this have anything to do with my grandfather's death?*

"I don't think so. But I'll find out if it does."

"LaStanza!" It was Mark with hands cupped around his mouth.

"Gotta go. I'll come by your office tomorrow."

He watched her climb in as he backed away, her skirt rising high as she got in. He felt a throbbing in his loins and shook his head. *First Lizette now this. Jesus.*

Mark was waiting with his own note, Sheila Glapier standing behind him in Christmas colors.

"We got an ID on the dead guy." Mark handed him the note. "I want you to go talk with the family."

Looking at the note, LaStanza realized he could walk there. Dumb ass robber lived two blocks from the K&B, right up Dublin Street from the Senoré's house.

"All right." LaStanza.

Glapier leaned in and said, "You O.K.?"

LaStanza nodded, gritting his teeth as Mark instructed Glapier to pick up the canvass where LaStanza had left off. Mark followed LaStanza.

"What's with the redhead brushing your hair?"

"She's a little proprietary about her grandfather's case at the

135

moment."

"Pro what?"

"She thinks I'm her personal detective."

Mark stopped next to the coroner's white van, which had just pulled up. LaStanza kept moving, but Mark called out, "Hey."

He turned, still backing away. He saw the look on Mark's face and said, "I can handle it."

"All right. Just don't do anything dumb."

LaStanza had to smile at the concern on Mark's face and remembered Mark as his partner when he met Lizette and knowing he was falling for her and wondering if she would ever even like him. Mark was there for that anguish, pulling for him but warning him not to do anything dumb. LaStanza felt a momentary shiver.

He stopped and called back to Mark who was watching two coroner's assistants roll the dead guy into a black plastic body bag.

"Hey!"

Mark looked up.

"I can handle it!"

"Good. Why you still here?"

6:03 p.m. – Dublin Street

"Was his first name Andrew?"

The man shot by Officer John Raven Beau grew up in a wooden shotgun house on Dublin Street two houses up from Apple Street, little over two blocks form the Senoré's. Andy Portier, alias Andy Peters, alias Andy Jones, alias Andy Gonzales was twenty-one, stood five-five, weighed all of one-forty pounds. He had fourteen arrests for burglary, theft, armed robbery and various drug offenses, been in and out of jail since he was twelve.

"He's been in parish prison the last three months," said a surprised brother-in-law, the only occupant of the house on Dublin Street when LaStanza knocked on the door. Andy Portier's mother died two years ago, father long gone, only sister was at work.

"She's gonna take this bad," said the brother-in-law who didn't invite LaStanza inside.

"Do you know who Andy hung around with?"

"Nope. He and I didn't get along. He's a criminal." The brother-in-law was a former longshoreman at home on a permanent disability. "Cargo container hit me on the head."

"When's the last time you saw Andy?"

"Two. Three years ago. My wife told me he was in jail. He don't come around here much.

"Where does he stay when he's not in jail?"

"Beats me."

"Was his first name Andrew?"

"No, Andy. Like Andy Jackson."

Whose name was Andrew you head-butted numbskull.

LaStanza left his card and asked for Andy's sister to call him. Then he canvassed his way back to the crime scene. People were friendly, even talkative, but no one knew anything about Andy Portier or anyone who could have pulled the robbery at Shoe Town.

6:20 p.m. – Detective Bureau

" – and have a plan to kill everyone you meet."

Jodie watched Snowood lead his partner into the squad room and unconsciously pushed her skirt down before Country-Ass stepped up. In a brown shirt with gold buttons, gold denim pants and tan cowboy boots, Snowood wore a white Stetson and a wide tan leather belt with a huge brass buffalo head buckle.

He gave Jodie a "Heidi" as he dropped his briefcase on his desk and headed straight for the coffee pot. Steve Stevens, in a bright red shirt, blue tie, brown pants and black shoes, followed his partner to the coffee table. Stevens looked tired as hell, but it was hard to tell with his normal hangdog expression.

Beau shot Jodie a look and she said Stevens was color blind.

"No fuckin' kiddin'."

Jodie started laughing and couldn't stop, which got Beau chuckling and drew an angry look from Stevens, who figured he was the butt of the joke. Snowood seemed oblivious as he mixed his coffee and seemed to notice Beau only when he returned to his desk. He blinked twice at the tall patrolman.

"You the one part Sioux, ain't ya'?"

"Lakota," Beau corrected him.

Snowood raised his hand as if in third grade, then looked at Jodie as he said. "Righty-o. Sioux is what their enemies called them, meanin' 'snake in the grass' 'cause the Lakota were so formidable an enemy." He looked back at Beau for approval, raising his coffee cup. "I been rentin' documentaries from the video store. Did y'all know polar bears are left handed?"

Beau took a hit of coffee and said, "I'm only half Sioux. I like the name Sioux better actually. Sounds fiercer."

Snowood extended his hand to shake. "You can call me Doc, as in Holliday."

Beau shook his hand and turned a wary eye to Jodie who just grinned and took a sip of her coffee.

"You see, Crazy Horse. My old partner LaStanza is the re-incarnation of Wyatt Earp. He's a gunslinger and I'm his life-long buddy, even though he's got a filly to ride the range with now."

Jodie watched the expression leave Beau's eyes as he stared at Snowood for several seconds before saying, "His name was Curly before the vision, before he attacked the Arapaho as Crazy Horse."

Snowood nodded slowly, staring back at Beau's deadpan face.

Beau turned to Jodie. "My great-grandfather claims we're direct descendants of Little Hawk, brother of Crazy Horse." He lifted his mug to Snowood. "They both fought at the Little Big Horn."

Snowood whispered, "Jesus Hillybilly Christ! A direct descendant?"

Jodie felt goose bumps. The book she was reading, *Red Hawk,* was about an Oglala Sioux warrior and a blonde settler woman. This was what LaStanza called a "Twilight Zone Moment."

Stevens, who had moved up behind Beau, said, "Didn't you kill a cowboy not long ago?"

Mark Land and the others decided to enter at that moment, banging open the squad door. Mark, in full grizzly mode, stomped ahead of a grinning Kelly, a confused-looking Glapier and LaStanza, who still looked like he'd just got out of bed. Mark waved Jodie into his tiny office.

LaStanza nodded to his partner and picked up the phone on his desk to call Lizette. "I'm gonna be late," he told her. She said O.K., no problem. He looked at the receiver before asking if she was all right.

"Sure, big guy. You did me right." She hung up.

Jesus.

When Jodie stepped back into the squad room, someone had made a fresh pot of coffee and everyone was sitting around LaStanza's desk, even Fel Jones, each with coffee, each listening to Beau and LaStanza talking about shooting people. She and Mark freshened their coffees and slipped up to listen.

" – only thing worse than a miss is a slow miss," Beau said. "You gotta be quick and accurate."

LaStanza came right back with, "Only hits count." He raised his cup to Snowood who'd never hit anyone he'd shot at in his life. Fel grinned widely.

"Anything worth shooting," Beau said, "is worth shooting twice. Ammo's cheap."

"And it doesn't matter what ammo you use, departmental regulations or not." LaStanza again. "Ten years from now nobody'll remember the details. Just who lived."

"Don't worry about their eyes," Beau told Snowood. "Watch their hands. Hands kill."

"The faster you finish a gunfight, the less shot up you'll get." LaStanza.

Jodie thought they were joshing, a light-hearted discussion but she could see in both faces, they were dead serious.

Beau said, "Never drop you guard. Ever."

LaStanza stood and stretched. "Be polite and professional and have a plan to kill everyone you meet."

That seemed to suck the air out of the room until Snowood said, "Did y'all know an ostrich's eye is bigger than its brain?"

"I know people like that," LaStanza raised his mug to Country Ass.

"I got the license plate slogan for Alabama," Stevens announced. "Hell yeah, we got 'lectricity!"

"Got Utah," Snowood said, "Our Jesus is better'n your Jesus."

"All right," Mark's voice boomed. "Let's coordinate this shit and get Beau in and outta the superintendent's hearing before

Memorial Day."

Jodie watched LaStanza and Beau as Mark went through the checklist of what still had to be done. She saw both as hunters, that peculiar male pathology, planning a hunt, stalking their prey, lashing out with sudden violence. Then again, she was also a hunter, encircling her prey, tracking them down.

She noticed Kelly staring at her and gave him a sad smile. His smile was bright and quick. He was so full of energy, he seemed to bounce in his seat.

" – one more thing," Mark said. "The goddamn FBI-led task force for The South Louisiana Sniper Case will be moving some people over here to the Bureau, so cut 'em some slack and don't get in their way or they'll draft more of us for that circle jerk."

Snowood stood up and announced, "Speakin' a circle-jerks. Did y'all know humans and dolphins are the only species who have sex for fun?"

"You think sex with a porpoise is fun?" Sheila Glapier snapped, which caused Stevens to spit up the coffee in his mouth all over his desk.

Wednesday, April 2, 1986

10:00 a.m. – Uptown Square

"You're getting everyone pretty shook up around here."

Fel Jones climbed out of his unmarked car, parked in the same spot he'd parked on the evening of the murder. He stood looking at the buildings of Uptown Square and his shoulders sank. He gazed around at the neighborhood he'd been canvassing since the killing. Two kids in the playground waved at him, the now-familiar detective.

"Useless," he muttered on his way to the square. As he ascended to the second level of the square, he hoped Mason would come up with something in his computer checks of robbers, thieves, carjackers, someone fitting the brief description of his killer.

He was met at the top of the stairs by a tall man with silver hair. The man wore a pristine navy blue suit. Fel had left his blue blazer in the car. His .357 magnum rested in its black canvass holder attached to the black belt holding up his gray pants, badge clipped to the front of the belt.

The man excused himself and introduced himself as the general manager of Uptown Square.

"Nice to meet you," Fel extended his hand and the man reluctantly shook it.

"I have a request," the man said.

Fel waited as the man let go of his hand.

"You're getting everyone pretty shook up around here," the man said.

"Good."

The general manager sighed. "How long is thing going to go on? Asking people if they saw anything when they weren't around."

Fel wanted to get up in the man's face, but decided LaStanza's normal reaction wouldn't be appropriate, so he tried to Jodie the man. "Not much longer. I'm not just asking if they saw anything, I'm asking if they know anyone who fit the description of the killer and the car he left in." An idea came to Fel and he was suddenly glad he took the Jodie way. "You can actually shorten this for me."

"Yes?" A doubtful look on the man's face.

"If you could send a memo to every store manager and have them put my questions to their employees, I won't have to go from store to store."

The man nodded slightly and Fel was sure he seemed to shrink an inch or two.

"Please," the man said, stepping aside and opening his arm. "Come to my office for some coffee and we'll put together a memo with my secretary."

Awfully white of the man. Fel smiled and agreed.

The man's secretary was a sister, older than Fel, but with reddish hair remarkably like Wanda and for a moment Wanda came to mind, that pretty face smiling at him, the smile transforming into a frown and then a grimace as she'd dismissed him, like he was a houseboy. Go away and don't come back until you've changed.

Quit being a cop and maybe I'll love you.

It didn't work that way. And both knew it. Suddenly there was a period at the end of their relationship that made Fel feel sick.

He settled in the padded chair across from the general manager's desk and thought, *back to work, homeboy.*

10:15 a.m. – St. Peter Street

"O.K., what'd I miss?"

Evangelista Luz's husband insisted on coming along. He sat up front with LaStanza, Evangelista in the back seat of the unmarked Ford. Freddie Luz was actually smaller than LaStanza but much broader with slightly darker skin and black hair. He wore faded jeans and a Gold's Gym sleeveless tee-shirt so show off his shoulders and biceps. Evangelista, also in jeans, wore a frilly pink blouse.

"This is the Quarter," Freddie said, looking around Chartres Street as LaStanza had to slow down behind a horse-and-buggy full of wide-eyed tourists. "What kinda artist is this?" He shot LaStanza another angry look.

"Police artist," LaStanza explained patiently. "He has a photo studio, sells still-life pictures but he's also an artist."

He wanted to bring the newbies so they could watch the police artist at work, but Jodie needed Kelly and Glapier at Helen Collingwood's funeral, to help her build her background on her victim, locate all associates, anyone Helen may have opened the door for, including all relatives, casual associates, anyone who worked at any place she frequented from grocery stores to restaurants. She'd been focusing on neighbors, so far.

LaStanza parked in the "Police Only" zone next to St. Louis Cathedral on St. Peter Street. He slipped the blue light up on the dash and the laminated "Officer on Duty" card next to the light. He climbed out and stretched. In a light gray suit, white shirt, black tie and black loafers, LaStanza thought of the days back when he wore sports clothes, blazers and casual pants, Dockers. That was before Lizette started buying all his clothes. Now he wore suits most of the time, suits that cost more than a month's salary.

"We're up the street," he told the Luzes and led them up St. Peter toward Royal Street. The Starving Artist's Gallery was sandwiched between a touristy seafood restaurant and an antique shop. The narrow doorway led to a narrow hall and three small rooms of black walls adorned with black and white prints in plain wooden frames, pictures of the French Quarter, St. Louis Cemetery and the riverfront. They were very nice prints. Lizette had two of the starving artist's prints hanging in one of their upstairs spare bedrooms. The place smelled a little musty, usual for the old Quarter.

The starving artist himself, Johnny Dee came down the back stairs to greet them, pointing to the video cameras in the corners, "Saw you come in." He shook hands with LaStanza. "Nice to see you again, detective."

LaStanza introduced Evangelista and Freddie.

At six-two, weighing one-seventy, Dee was a stork of a man with curly brown hair. LaStanza figured him to be in his mid-forties.

"You take all these pictures?" Freddie said. Evangelista poked him in the kidneys.

"Just the black and white ones." They were all black and white. Dee, in faded khakis, shirt and shorts, led the way up the back stairs to his apartment above. He even moved like a stork, head bobbing, long neck.

"You own this place?" Freddie asked as they stepped into a foyer area with a sofa and bookcase crammed with record albums and paperback books.

"I rent. Nobody sells places in the quarter anymore," Dee explained, showing them into an office area that opened into a large studio. "Property's too expensive to sell." The place was well-lit by rows of windows facing Royal and St. Peter Streets. One of the windows was open and two pigeons were perched there watching them.

Dee sat behind an artist's table, tilted at thirty degrees. There was a white drawing pad with drawing pencils in a case next to it.

"So who's the witness?"

Evangelista stepped forward and Dee patted the stool next to where he sat. One of the pigeons few off with a flurry.

"Detective LaStanza mentioned on the phone we're doing two sketches," Dee told Evangelista who nodded. Freddie went to the window, scaring away the last pigeon, leaned his elbows on the sill and watched the man talk to his wife, making sure that was all he was up to.

LaStanza found another stool and sat behind Dee and watched as Evangelista closed her eyes and envisioned the first robber, describing his face to Dee's prompts. Slowly the face took shape, first in pencil, then in charcoal, then in ink until a human face emerged.

"That really looks like the big one. One who put his gun to my head," Evangelista declared, waving Freddie over just as the door opened and a willowy blonde woman came in.

Dee turned and smiled, "You're an hour early." The woman was about five-three, thin, wore a loose-fitting white cotton dress and sandals and carried two Styrofoam cups. "I brought coffee. Sorry I didn't know you had company."

"We're not company." LaStanza stood as she stepped closer, giving her the stool. "Y'all want some coffee?" he asked the Luzes. Evangelista said yes and he went down the stairs and back out to the street. He was heading for Café du Monde when he spotted the French café at the corner of Chartres and St. Ann. The scent of freshly-baked bread drew him in. le Madelaine turned out to be an old fashioned French bakery. He bought five warm croissants and three tall coffees.

Passing in front of the cathedral, he had to dodge a mime who was being chased by an invisible creature. He edged closer to the artists whose works were hung from the tall, wrought iron fence surrounding Jackson Square. Most were New Orleans scenes, some of them with eye-catching Van Gogh color schemes. He remembered walking around with Lizette and commenting on the paintings. She thought it was nice the way he liked almost everything, but he wasn't discriminating enough to purchase art. She had the eye and from the stuff decorating their mansion, she was right, including the urns in the foyer and statues of Napoleon, Murat and General Bernadotte. LaStanza grew up on South Bernadotte Street.

When he stepped back into the studio, Dee was nearly finished the second drawing and the blonde was naked. He stopped as she looked at him and smiled.

"OK, what'd I miss?"

Dee answered without looking up. "Mindy is a professional nude model. She's just getting comfortable for our shoot."

Freddie Luz pretended he wasn't staring at Mindy as she stood in front of him, pulling her long hair back and munching on a croissant. Evangelista winked at LaStanza, "Freddie ain't seen a naked blonde girl before."

"What makes you think I don' see a naked blonde before?" Freddie was up on his toes now.

Evangelista laughed. "Go ahead and look. It's a free country."

Freddie folded his arms and looked Mindy up and down. She did a slow turn for him, giggling and for a moment LaStanza thought of Lizette, naked in front of her students. He was getting excited. Naked Lizette always turned him on, no getting around it.

He tried not to stare at Mindy but she kept moving in front of him and Freddie, who kept checking out that patch of blonde pubic hair between her slim legs.

10:45 a.m. – Metairie Cemetery

"Why is that woman laughing?"

It was once a race track, but as the story went, some rich guy was kicked off the grounds of the Metairie Race Course one day and vowed he'd buy the track and turn it into a cemetery. Shortly after the Civil War, he did, turning the race course into Metairie Cemetery. It lay at the western edge of the city, up against Jefferson Parish. It was the biggest little city of the dead in New Orleans with rows of concrete sepulchres and crypts and a huge mausoleum overlooking I-10.

Jodie and Kelly walked into the large funeral parlor, easing around the rock pool in the center filled with goldfish and aquatic plants under a skylight. They eased toward the left rear parlor where Helen Collingwood lay in a closed casket. There were twenty-two people in the parlor, mostly women, mostly middle-aged or older. Jodie spotted Helen's boyfriend, attorney-at-law Frank McWilliams of Segundaga, Scootaput and McWilliams. He sat in a group of middle-aged women.

Kelly nodded toward him, "Did we check his alibi?"

"Yep. At breakfast with two judges."

Belinda Collingwood, looking even more petite in a black dress, hair pinned up in gold barrettes, stood at the foot of the coffin. Jodie was in one of her slimming outfits, a charcoal gray pants-suit. Kelly was in a funeral black suit. An eight-by-ten picture of Helen Collingwood stood in a wooden frame atop the coffin. She looked forty in the picture.

Kelly whispered to Jodie, "Which one is the victim's ex-husband?"

"You didn't read the daughter's statement Fel took, did you?"

"Yes, I did." Kelly shrugged.

"Mr. Collingwood died ten years ago."

Belinda stepped up and tried to smile as she thanked them for coming. Jodie pulled her aside.

"We need some help."

"Anything."

"We'd like a copy of the sign-in book and everyone's address you can get."

Belinda's brow furrowed. "You think someone here –"

"No. But they might know someone who your mother would open the door for."

"Oh." Belinda didn't look convinced. She glanced at Kelly then asked Jodie, "Isn't Dino LaStanza working on the case?"

"We're all working on it. He's on another case right now."

Jodie didn't peg Belinda as a woman who thought a man should be in charge and when Belinda reached over and squeezed Jodie's arm and smiled sadly, she knew she'd figured right.

"Thank you Detective Kintyre. I know how hard you're working on this."

Jodie and Kelly eased away from the coffin and family and remained out in the foyer in case anyone wanted to tell them anything.

Kelly – "Does she know LaStanza?"

"He tried to kiss her."

"What?"

"Back in fifth grade."

"Oh."

Kelly returned a smile to a middle-aged woman in a mini-dress and black stockings. Jodie shook her head and reminded him to keep an eye out for anyone suspicious looking.

Kelly nodded, still glancing around. "Including flirty older women?"

She poked him in the ribs.

"How about dinner tonight?" Kelly asked, still looking around. Jodie looked at his face in profile, the square jaw and Bob Hope nose, only not as severe a ski-jump to it.

"That would be nice."

"No sex, though," Kelly said in a lower voice. "I'm saving myself."

"For what?"

"That's the part I can't figure out." He turned his blue eyes to her. "My mother keeps telling me I should save myself."

She had to move away to keep from laughing out loud.

They stepped outside when the priest arrived. Jodie didn't want to hear all that holy stuff. They waited by their car and followed the procession through the big cemetery to the sepulchre, remaining in the background, checking around to see if any suspicious-looking bastard was lurking nearby, maybe checking out his handiwork.

On their way out of the cemetery, Jodie spotted a billboard across I-10. The huge billboard featured a laughing middle-aged blonde lady with hands raised, fingers open in glee. The caption below read, "We Celebrate Life at Metairie Cemetery!"

Kelly asked about the billboard just as Jodie thought it had to be some ad executive's idiotic idea on how to market a cemetery.

"Why is that woman laughing?" Kelly said.

"Because she just buried her husband and gets to spend all his money. She'll outlive him twenty, thirty years."

"Oh."

As they accessed I-10, Kelly asked, "What's next?"

"We spread out in the neighborhood. Glapier should be out of court by now."

Nodding, Kelly said, "Who the hell would she open the door for?"

"Question of the year." Jodie paused a beat. "Where are we going to dinner?"

"I'm a man. You can't expect to have it all figured out yet."

That brought another smile to her face. Maybe that's what she liked best about him.

11:40 p.m. – St. Peter Street

"They want to turn the Quarter into a theme park for tourists."

LaStanza figured it was another parade as a street-full of people turned up St. Peter from Chartres Street. There was a parade in the city just about every fuckin' day. Only the signs were a dead giveaway. It was a demonstration. About a hundred people, mostly in well-worn clothes, carried placards reading: Give Us Our Back Our Benches; Jacks Is A Jerk; Recall Jacks; We Can't Even Play Jacks at Jackson Square.

"What's this about?" Evangelista asked LaStanza as they waited by his car for the demonstration to pass.

"Councilman Sidney Jacks. The 'unofficial mayor' of the French Quarter." LaStanza pointed toward the front of the cathedral. "He had all the benches removed so street people can't sleep on them."

"Why?"

LaStanza had seen it on TV the night before, the evening news featuring silver-haired Jacks explaining the midnight removal of the benches.

"He's on a crusade to clean up the Quarter. Make it like it was in the forties."

"What was it like in the forties?"

"A slum. Ever see *A Streetcar Named Desire?* Rundown apartments. People yelling all the time."

A woman with burgundy hair and breasts the size of footballs and carrying a sign that read *Jacks is a Douche-Bag*, gave LaStanza a saucy look as she passed. "How ya' doin' Baby?"

"All right," he answered. "Are there many behind ya'?"

"Shit yeah."

He turned to the Luzes. "Y'all want some lunch?"

Evangelista looked at Freddie who said, "You buyin'?"

"Yep."

"Is that a ticket on your car?" Evangelista pointed to the orange parking ticket under the windshield wiper.

"Yep."

"You gotta pay?"

"Nope. Meter maids love ticketing police cars. We just throw them away."

"They won't boot your car?"

"After five tickets we switch the license plates." LaStanza pointed to the plate on back of his car. "That's a stolen plate anyway. Took it out of the motor pool a month ago."

Freddie stepped between LaStanza and Evangelista as he led them around the Cathedral. Freddie tapped LaStanza's shoulder. "You wanna run that by me again. The demonstration shit."

Passing Pirate Alley, LaStanza caught a whiff of something pungent and thankfully, unidentifiable. "It's part of the Disneyfication of the Quarter."

"De what?"

"They want to turn the Quarter into a theme park for tourists."

That only seemed to confuse Freddie more. "What about Bourbon Street? That's why some people come here."

"Exactly." And LaStanza remembered the sticker Lizette had on one of her book bags. It was quote from Ernie Pyle, who lived in the city a while. It went something like: *When you get within a hundred miles, you begin to feel a little drunk just on the idea of New Orleans.*

"I still don't get it."

"Jacks wants to get rid of the street people, vagrants, shoe-shiners. " LaStanza waved at the art along the Jackson Square fence. "Street musicians and artists will be next. Nobody slept on benches in the forties."

"They didn't?" Evangelista. "Where's the bums sleep then?"

"Under the wharves." LaStanza's father told him all about the hobos who lived under the Toulouse Street Wharf, Tchoupitoulas

Street Wharf, hell every wharf. The good ole days.

Turning down Madison Street, LaStanza led them toward the river, a steamboat's calliope echoing over the tile rooftops. It took a moment to recognize the tune, "Marian The Librarian" from *The Music Man*, the only musical LaStanza could sit through, except maybe *Camelot*.

Evangelista said, "I love Greek food," as she followed LaStanza into Mr. Gryo's Cafe, Madison corner Decatur Street. Freddie hesitated at the door. LaStanza looked back. "You eat meat?"

"Sure."

"You'll love the gyros. Come on."

Freddie came in reluctantly, but only after his wife stood too close to LaStanza who was already ordered three gyros with fries.

2:10 p.m. – St. Charles Avenue

"I'll wait until you're ready."

It was once a single family dwelling, a two story Italianate with four ionic columns in front supporting a second-floor gallery with an overhang above, lots of gingerbread trim and a double wooden front door. A small brass plaque next to the doorbell read: Chickima Foundation.

He rang the bell and a woman's voice asked who it was. He spotted a video camera above the bell. Straitening his tie he said, "Detective LaStanza to see Lori Venetta."

The door buzzed and he pushed it open, stepping into a pristine foyer, hardwood floor covered in a Persian rug, two huge vases on either side of a staircase with an elaborate brass banister. Footsteps turned him to the left as a tall woman with short gray hair came though an open doorway. She wore a long brown dress and practical tan shoes.

"This way please," without an introduction. She led him through a wide office with several desks occupied by women, mostly middle-aged, all busy typing, not even bothering to look up. Some at computers.

"Please wait here a moment," the woman said, pointing to

several easy chairs assembled in a waiting area before she went through a door with a brass plaque marked: Director. The place smelled of furniture polish and he noticed the door and walls, all hardwood, were gleaming with wax. He was tempted to push aside a rug, kick off his loafers and go sliding.

The door opened and the woman with gray hair came out and said, "You may go in," without looking at him.

Lori Venetta sat behind a desk the size of Delaware, a large brass lamp at either end, a personal computer at the far end of the desk, a telephone on the near end where a teen-aged girl with blonde hair sat. Lori smiled and made hand signals, the girl interpreting, "Thanks for coming."

LaStanza looked around. "Nice office. It's bigger than my first apartment. What do y'all do here?"

A long, leather sofa rested against one wall, a kitchen ran along the other wall. Behind Lori was a picture window opening overlooking a colorful rock garden full of flowers.

Lori signaled again and the girl explained. "Chickima is a foundation that supports the handicapped. We're over a hundred years old."

"Oh."

"What are you carrying?" The blonde girl said to Lori's prompts.

LaStanza opened the folder, showed her the two sketches. "These are the men who robbed Shoe Town and killed your grandfather." He had to reach across the huge desk to place them in front of Lori who examined them carefully.

"What's your name?"

The blonde girl, sitting stiffly in a green sundress told him she was Sally. She couldn't be twenty.

Lori signaled again and Sally interpreted immediately. "These sketches are very detailed."

"We have a good witness. Someone from Shoe Town."

Lori via Sally – "Please sit." Lori waved to the two thick chairs in front of her desk. LaStanza sank into one, placing his LFR up on the desk.

Lori via Sally, "How's Officer Beau?"

"He'll be OK."

Lori's eyes narrowed and her fingers worked again. Sally, "It must have been traumatic for him."

LaStanza nodded. "I'll tell him you asked about him." He didn't feel like going into it, that sickening feeling the next morning when you wake up with it, killing a man, even one who deserved punishment. Different being the actual executioner. Everybody, even your partners, look at you differently. You're a killer. Then again, he and Beau have gone through it before.

LaStanza could never forget his mother's sad eyes the morning after he'd shot his first man. That look, that empathy, that hurt in her eyes pleading with him, asking if this was still her little boy.

Lori via Sally – "How is the investigation going?"

LaStanza nodded to the sketches. "That's the latest since I saw you yesterday. Still haven't found anyone in the area who saw anything, but I'm optimistic."

Lori via Sally, "Optimistic locating a witness or catching the criminals?"

"Both."

Lori made more signs and Sally stood and nodded to LaStanza on her way out. He heard the door close behind him. Lori came around the desk slowly, moving like a cat again, not purposefully but casually, as if she always walked like a predator. In a long, double-breasted red coat-dress that hugged her slim figure, she looked elegant again as she stopped and pressed her rear against the desk. He noticed her stocking feet. She'd kicked off her heels.

She gave him another long stare and he asked, "How's your family holding up?"

Lori reached for her note pad and flipped it to a new page and wrote: *We didn't expect him to live forever, but it was so sudden, so brutal.*

"And deliberate," LaStanza. "They didn't have to hurt him. He was just in their way."

She wrote: *You're still angry.*

"That's the way I work."

She flipped the pages back and tore off a sheet she'd already written on and handed it to him. It read: *I want to kiss you.*

152

He tried his best to keep from reacting as he stared at the note, thinking, *I don't believe I'm this fuckin stupid! Walked right into this one.*

When he looked back into those velvety brown eyes, her long stare was enough to tell him his eyes weren't hiding much. He brushed down his moustache with his thumb and index finger, climbed out of the chair and picked up the *I want to kiss you* note.

"I'll make sure Beau gets this."

She shook her head and pointed to his lips, then took a step closer. Without heels, she was only about an inch taller now. He leaned back against the chair and said, "This is a bad idea." He said it but was sure his eyes weren't following suit because the way she stared at him caused his chest to constrict.

Finding himself folding his arms in a defensive position, he said, "Lori, you're vulnerable right now."

Wrong! Never start a sentence with her name, you dummy. Shows intimacy. She was seeing right through him and that was disconcerting.

"When I say I'm a happily married man, I mean I'm a *very* happily married man." He took in a breath. "You're my victim's granddaughter. There's no way you and I can become involved."

Her stare continued and his heart kept stammering.

"Lori, you are a beautiful woman, but I'm going to keep this on the professional level."

Lori jotted another note, showing it to him now: *Do you think I want this? I can't stop myself.*

He shook his head. *Great. Just fuckin' great.*

And he remembered the vulture mobile above his bed when he was a baby. He struggled to find the right words, suddenly wishing Lizette was there. She was the brains of the operation. He may be street-smart but Liz was the one with the words.

Lori surprised him again, her eyes changing, suddenly revealing absolutely nothing. She was good at hiding her emotions too. Her Sicilian nature, he was sure. She jotted another note and handed it to him before walking back around her desk. He read it: *I'll wait until you're ready.*

There was only one thing to do. He picked up the sketches and got the hell out. Climbing into his car, he realized he was still holding the notes. He shoved them into his coat pocket to lose them later.

3:30 p.m. – Detective Bureau

"Did you just sneeze on me or is that your name?"

Lizette leaned over to plug the computer into the floor socket next to her husband's desk and was glad she'd worn jeans to the Bureau the way Steve Stevens was hawking out her butt. The fool had actually argued with her when she introduced herself at the front desk, computers on a dolly behind her.

"You LaStanza's *wife*?"

"Want to see my driver's license?"

"No," he stammered, ogling her with his misaligned eyes. "I thought you were a high school kid."

Lizette almost smiled. In a pink polo shirt and faded jeans, white tennis shoes, with her long hair in a pony tail, she did look young, but not a high-schooler.

As she stood up, Snowood, resplendent in a rawhide vest over a denim shirt, string tie, black denim pants, black boots and a black Stetson tilted back on his head, handed her a mug of coffee.

"So these are those new fangled personal computers?"

"Macintosh SEs." One piece models, the computers looked like portable TVs.

"What's in the other boxes?" Snowood asked as she put her mug on her husband's desk and picked up the box cutter.

"Printers."

Stevens kept staring at her with that lecherous gleam and she remembered a similar look in the eyes of the firemen she'd posed with, but they were strangers. Stevens was just strange.

She'd just connected the second printer to Jodie's computer when she spotted her husband crossing the squad room carrying his briefcase with a folder under his arm. Behind him tagged a heavy-set man in a gray jumpsuit. She put her hands on her hips, waiting for Dino's reaction only he kept that damn expressionless look on his face.

He moved up and said, "Don't I sleep with you?"

She rolled her eyes as he leaned over and kissed the side of her neck before telling Stevens, "This man's looking for you."

Stevens pointed to the folding chair next to his desk, picked up his coffee mug and headed for the coffee pot. The man in the gray jumpsuit sat hesitantly.

Lizette lowered her voice, "Does he always dress like that?"

"Color blind," LaStanza explained, "or just retarded."

She slapped his shoulder. Putting down his briefcase, LaStanza seemed to finally notice the computer and printer on his desk. He gave Lizette a hooded-brow look.

"You and Jodie now have computers," she said. "Word processors. Better than any typewriter." She pointed to the printer. "Print out your dailies. The computer will check your spelling and you can back-space to edit as you type. No more liquid paper."

"Gol' darn," Snowood said.

"Where am I gonna find time to learn how to use it?"

"There's one at home." Lizette pulled out the instruction manual. "And you can read. I've seen you."

"Excuse me, sir," the man in the jumpsuit said in a heavy accent, raising a finger to LaStanza.

"Yeah?"

The man stood and leaned forward, "I Vada Ganoush."

"What?"

The man patted his chest. "I Vada *Ganoush!*"

"Did you just sneeze on me or is that your name?"

"I come from Algiers for de police to see me. But I speak de bad English."

"Hey, Greek man!" Steven called out from the coffee area. "Just sit down!"

Vada nodded and sat again.

Snowood leaned in with, "He's the one found our dumped body in Algiers. Don't speak too good. 'Jew hear the way he talks?"

"Jew?" Lizette said.

"Western gibberish for 'Did you'," LaStanza explained.

Stevens came back, angry now. "You better learn English quick," he told Vada, who looked at Lizette and LaStanza for help.

Lizette opened her mouth to respond but her husband put a

finger over her lips.

"If English was good enough for Jesus, it's good enough for everyone," Stevens said.

Lizette's jaw dropped and she turned to her husband as he pulled out a pile of flyers from the folder.

"My killers from the Senoré case. They robbed Shoe Town."

"Got 'em copied fast, didn't ya?" Snowood.

"Fresh from the crime lab." LaStanza passed one to Snowood, "They're still warm."

The *Wanted for Armed Robbery* flyers had the two drawings, descriptions and LaStanza's name to contact at the Detective Bureau.

"Why aren't they wanted for murder?" she asked.

"My eye-witness is from the robbery. First things first." He had two smaller stacks of black and white photos of the drawings, picked up several with a stack of flyers and headed for his lieutenant's office. Turning around he explained to Lizette, "Mason has to write a press release and pass them out to the TV stations and papers."

Lizette sat at his desk and tried to ignore Stevens trying to communicate with Vada Ganoush. Neither seemed to be speaking English.

When LaStanza came back, she showed him how to turn on the computer. She was showing him how to access the word processing program when Jodie entered the squad room, followed by a tall blond man and a short, scowling-faced black woman in a purple pants-suit two sized too small for her.

Snowood's phone rang and he picked it up, "Heidi. Dis here's Homicide." The smile left his face immediately and his shoulder's sank.

"Bad news?" LaStanza.

Country-Ass pulled the receiver from his ear so they could hear the shrill voice on the other end. "The old lady," he said.

Lizette thought Jodie's eyes were lit up from getting the computer and printer, but quickly discovered it was the tall blond detective. It was subtle, but she knew immediately. This must be Kelly.

She waited until they all put their briefcases down to ask Jodie for an introduction. It was Kelly from the Batture Murders. Lizette remembered the talk about him. The black woman gave her a disapproving look as she was introduced, staring at Lizette's chest as men usually do before moving off to the coffee pot.

Lizette realized her nipples were erect and protruding. She turned around and Snowood covered the mouthpiece and said to her breasts, "Hey, looky. High beams."

Jesus.

Jodie had the computer manual in hand and was already reading. "You didn't have to do this," she said.

"Yes, I did." She listed her reasons raising a finger with each. "This will make your paperwork faster. I'll get my husband home sometimes. And I figure you'll learn it quickly and can teach him."

Snowood put the receiver on his desk and took his mug to the coffee pot. "Any y'all want a refill?"

His wife's voice echoed from the phone, still shrill and ranting. Snowood pointed to it. "Makes ya' wish the goddamn phone would just automatically cut off after thirty seconds, don't it?"

"What she mad about?" Stevens asked.

"Who the hell knows? I think I woke her up by mistake this mornin'."

Jodie, Kelly and LaStanza huddled around his desk as Lizette showed them the word processing program. Her husband seemed in a good mood and picked up on the computer quickly and Lizette was glad she'd pulled off this surprise.

She leaned close to LaStanza's ear and said, "Baba Ganoush is a dip."

"Looks like a dip-shit."

"No. Baba Ganoush is an appetizer. Eggplant, lemon juice, minced garlic, sour cream, pine nuts and olive oil. Get it at any good Mediterranean restaurant."

LaStanza just laughed, looking over at Stevens and Ganoush.

Snowood finally hung up the phone, took off his hat and wiped his brow. "And to think I woke up in such a good mood this mornin'."

"I woke up with a creek in my neck," Stevens looked at LaStanza as if he wanted to know how he woke up, as if LaStanza would answer.

Kelly said, "I woke up feeling pretty good." Lizette caught the slight smile he gave Jodie.

"Sometimes I wake up grumpy," Snowood said. "Other times I just let her sleep."

Thursday, April 3, 1986

8:30 a.m. – Uptown Square

"Where the fuck is big brother when you need him?"

"We can't call LaStanza," Mark said. "He's passing out flyers and Jodie's got a some leads on neighbors on her case. But you got me and Kelly, soon as he gets here."

Of course, Fel thought. LaStanza would be at his scene already with his flyers.

"Jodie got anything promising?"

"Who the fuck knows?"

Felicity Jones took off his suit coat and tossed it into his car. The day he decided to wear his new tan suit, it was already approaching ninety before nine a.m. What ever happened to spring? Typical New Orleans. He remembered it was cool on St. Patrick's Day in March and then two days later, it was as if God opened an oven and the heat and humidity belched out like a breath from hell. His white dress shirt was damp with perspiration.

"So what are these hot tips?" Mark asked.

Fel showed him his notes. "Apparently, there's a hard-assed habitual robber lives a block from here."

"Big surprise there."

"Fuckin' A. The ever *inefficient* criminal justice system kept more robbers on the street than in parish prison."

"I been meaning to check with the parole office on your case and LaStanza's." Mark said.

Fel shook his head. "Dino and I went there Tuesday morning. Met a typical G.A.L.B. who had no fuckin' idea how to look up the information. There's no central list. Neither does the parole board in Baton Rouge."

"G.A.L.B.?"

"Goofy Ass Looking Bastard."

Mark almost smiled. "What about the other tips you got?"

"Two GM model cars used in previous robberies in the area, a purse-snatching and a hit and run. Leads came from the guys working the South Louisiana Sniper Case. Apparently, they've been inundated with anonymous calls."

"At least Jodie's leads didn't come from the task force." Mark took off his blue blazer and put it inside his car, parked in front of Fel's. He also wore a white shirt, blue tie loosened, tan slacks and brown penny loafers, but still looked like a bear inside tan Dockers and loafers.

"OK, where to first?" Mark asked impatiently.

Fel pointed away from the parking lot, up Broadway. "We can walk."

So they did, LFRs in their left hands, coats locked in their cars, .357 magnums on their hips.

"They got any video cameras at the Square?" Mark asked.

"In some of the stores but not the exteriors."

"Where the fuck is big brother when you need him?"

Kelly called on the radio just as they arrived in front of a two story house on Broadway that had long ago been divided into apartments.

Mark told him to stand by the Square.

Their hard-assed habitual robber named Murphy lived in a rear apartment with 4C written in pencil on the door. Standing on either side of the door, the detectives tapped on it with their LFRs.

An elderly woman peeked out a window behind Mark and said, "He ain't there." She turned out to be the landlady, Gertrude Lavoisier, seventy-one, a very white woman who wouldn't even look at Felicity Jones, talking to Mark instead.

"He's dead," she said.

Mark began rubbing his eyes as Fel took notes.

"Got his ass hit by a police car in Jefferson Parish. Don't y'all cops talk to each other? They came by here yesterday. Lef' me a card." She showed Mark a business card from the Jefferson Parish Sheriff's Office Traffic Division. Fel leaned over and copied down the deputy's name on the card.

"He was drunk and walked in front of a police car, the dumb shithead." Gertrude finally looked at Fel and said, "Excuse my language."

"No problem, ma'am." Fel said, stepping back and poking Mark in the back.

Mark picked up the hint. "Did the J.P.'s go inside his place to search?"

"Nope. I gave them his mama's name and address in Georgia. Y'all wanna go in?"

"Yes ma'am."

"Y'all New Orleans police, right?"

Mark pointed to his badge clipped on his belt. So did Fel, who also took out his I.D. folder and showed her his credentials. She took a long look at it before passing them the key to the apartment.

The place smelled like a locker room that had been locked up for a month with no ventilation. Mark stepped outside right away and told Fel he'd go get Kelly and they'd look for those two GM cars.

"Gimme the notes," Mark said, remaining outside the door.

"Y.A.N.G.!" Fel handed him the sheet.

Backing away, Mark snarled, "What's that mean?"

"You Ain't No Good." Fel snarled back, then stepped into Murphy's stink. Surprisingly there weren't many roaches even with the empty Chinese food cartons and leaning tower of pizza boxes stacked in the corner of the bedroom, next to an expensive looking stereo system atop a beat-up bookcase filled with videotapes and audio cassettes.

It took him a half hour to find the first gun.

9: 20 a.m. – Walnut Street

"Don't know hardly anyone still alive."

Jodie Kintyre sat in her unmarked Ford with Sheila Glapier and studied the house at the corner of Walnut and Prytania, two blocks down from the Collingwood house. She shook thoughts of last night and Kelly's blue eyes staring at her from the across the table at Ralph & Kakoos Seafood Emporium. Delicious food followed by delicious kissing that almost went the distance.

"So what's the lead here?" Glapier asked.

"LaStanza interviewed the man who lives here on our initial canvass." Jodie nodded to the two-story chalet-style house with the green shingled roof. "Alfred Mueller, white male, sixty. Claimed he saw nothing but failed to mention to LaStanza he knew Mrs. Collingwood quite well, danced with her often at big band mixers."

"Mixers?"

"Where older singles get together to dance. V.F.W. Halls mostly. They have a regular dance at the auditorium at Loyola's School of Music."

Jodie climbed out and slipped on her light-weight beige jacket. She was in another skirt-suit while Glapier wore an orange pantsuit that looked a lot like the jumpsuits worn by prisoners at parish prison.

"What's V.F.W. mean?" Glapier asked.

"Veterans of Foreign Wars." Jodie took a close look at her. "You didn't know that?" Immediately she wished she hadn't asked that as Glapier became immediately defensive.

"No!"

Jodie let it drop as she led the way up the brick walk and rang the doorbell. Alfred Mueller, in a dark green tee-shirt, tan Dockers and sandals, opened the door and smiled immediately. About six feet, rail thin, with short hair, black as the darkest hair dye could make it, Mueller had blue eyes and a wide smile.

Jodie showed her badge and introduced herself and Glapier and asked if they could come in.

"I never refuse a pretty face," he said, opening the door wide.

An hour and two cups of coffee later, Jodie led an even angrier Glapier back to their car. Jodie tried to ignore Glapier's fuming until they'd pulled away.

"He didn't mean any harm," Jodie said, which again was the wrong thing to say.

"Don't give me that shit!"

"He was flirting with me too."

"Yeah. Well he didn't look at you like you were one of his house wenches, a slave girl called up from the field for plowing."

Jesus, where'd that come from?

"Men like him raped my ancestors like clockwork back when we slaved for them."

Jodie was going to let it drop but something made her remind Glapier. "Mueller's family emigrated to America after World War I, a good fifty years after slavery ended."

"You might be a hot shot detective, but don't tell me about slavery."

Now Jodie was hot but clenched her jaw and dropped it for now.

"He doesn't have an alibi," Glapier said.

Jodie was going to put it to her, ask if she was paying attention but instead of grilling Glapier, she just said it. "His hands and arms. No injury. We found two different blood types at the scene. The killer cut himself or gouged himself. And Mueller feet are too big."

Glapier stared at her, paying attention at least.

"Our killer wore a size eight shoe. Mueller wears a ten or an eleven."

"Oh," Glapier, barely audible.

Their next lead took them over to Hurst and Pine Streets, three blocks from Mrs. Collingwood's, to a run down two-story house with peeling green paint. Jodie rang the doorbell. No answer. The blinds were drawn.

Stepping off the front porch, Jodie looked around.

"An elderly recluse lives here," she told her partner. "Walks around the neighborhood every day, carrying a big stick and mumbling to himself."

"He crazy?"

Jodie shrugged. "Might be sad enough looking for Helen Collingwood to open her door for."

Glapier nodded.

"Let's look around for him."

It took them fifteen minutes before Glapier spotted the man hustling up Lowerline Street. As they followed the man moving along the sidewalk, Jodie studied his purposefully but hesitant gait.

The man was old and slightly stooped with a mass of unruly white hair piled atop his head and a grayish white unkempt beard. His black tennis shoes had holes in them, his red jogging shorts were faded into pink and his tee-shirt was baggy, collar almost falling off his skinny shoulders. In his right hand he swung a sawed off broom handle. He seemed to be mumbling as he walked.

Jodie trailed him as he turned down Dominican Street.

"He's awfully bony," said Glapier.

"Looks like a wild man."

"We gonna stop him?"

Jodie shook her head. "I'd rather see the inside of his place. We'll wait 'til he gets back home."

"Good idea." Glapier sounded calmer now.

Suddenly the man fussed at a passing dog who didn't seem to notice the man until he swung his stick toward the mutt, which scampered across the street. They trailed him until he turned down Pine, then moved ahead and parked in front of his house, watching him turn the corner, then went up to wait for him on his porch.

He didn't notice them until he reached the porch, stopped and blinked up at Jodie as she presented her I.D.

"Police," she said. "We'd like to talk with you, Mr. Smithers."

"Damn," he replied. "Why the hell not?"

The house was even more run down inside, the living room looked like the inside of an antique store with too many old fashioned lamps, bookshelves lining every wall. There were some books on the shelves, but most of the shelves were piled with magazines, empty Avon cologne bottles, old black telephones, clocks that weren't running and dozens of statues of Napoleon.

Smithers plopped down in one of the six sofas in the living room, none matching, all looking like leftovers from the 1920s. At least they looked clean. Jodie sat across from Smithers and looked at the man's wild eyes and wondered if anyone would open their door for him?

"Do you know a woman named Helen Collingwood?"

"Don't know hardly anyone still alive," he said. Looking at Glapier, he said, "Have a seat ma'am. Y'all want something to drink?"

Jodie took a look at the man's feet. Big. Very big, maybe a size twelve shoe and his arms and hands showed no wounds. She took her time anyway, establishing his usual routine, waking early and reading the newspaper, the entire paper. His morning walk started at eight o'clock sharp and usually took and hour and a half. He made three circuits, walking right past the Collingwood house on Walnut Street.

"Easter Sunday morning. Did you walk up Walnut?"

"Yeah – no. Not Easter Sunday. I went down to the Y on Lee Circle for the Easter breakfast. Took the streetcar. Stayed for lunch. Read my paper at the Circle."

A few more questions determined he'd caught the streetcar at seven a.m., down St. Charles straight to Lee Circle. For proof, he dug out Monday's newspaper and there he was, in a clear black and white photo, standing in line inside the Y.M.C.A. getting ham and eggs.

Jodie pointed to the front page of the paper to the photo of Helen Collingwood beneath the captain, "Murder on Walnut Street."

"Yeah." Smithers sat back on his sofa with the paper. "A policeman in a uniform stopped me the other day. Monday or Tuesday. Took down my name and address. Is that why y'all are here?"

Jodie nodded. She's found Smithers name in Left Sider's notes after the tip came in from suspicious neighbors about the old man walking around with a stick.

Glapier cleared her throat before asking, "Why do you carry a stick when you walk?"

"Dogs." He leaned toward Glapier. "Don't mean to sound abrupt ma'am. You ever been bit by a dog? A big dog?"

"Actually yes."

"Hurts like hell, don't it?"

Glapier almost smiled.

9:40 a.m. – Carrollton Avenue

"I thought I was your star witness."

LaStanza took the British racing green Maserati, parking it in the parking lot behind the Carrollton fire station where the firemen could keep an eye on it, remembering how his midnight blue Maserati had been stolen from Jackson Avenue a couple years back. He'd never forget rounding the corner and seeing an empty space where he'd parked the sports car not a half hour earlier. Never found a trace of it. According to the Maserati dealer, this *new* Maserati 450I was virtually theft proof, unless towed away, something about the drive shaft disconnected from the engine unless the super-secret coded key was in the ignition.

Theft proof? Nothing was theft proof in New Orleans. He made sure the firemen locked the parking lot gate before stepping into the station with his flyers and two dozen warm Krispy Kreme glazed doughnuts.

As the firemen attacked the doughnuts like ravenous wolves, he showed them the flyers.

With half-a-glazed doughnut protruding from his mouth, Landis mumbled, "Don't look familiar to me." But he was good enough to tack a couple copies in the stationhouse. LaStanza walked to the bus stops at each corner of Carrollton and Claiborne, using a staple gun to tack flyers to the telephone poles along the way and to the wooden supports of the tiny bus shelters. Twelve people were waiting for the buses but none recognized the faces in the flyer. Neither did any of the seven people waiting for the streetcar.

He tacked flyers to every telephone pole surrounding Palmer Park and spoke with six people there with the same result. By the time he returned from circling the park, the bank across Claiborne was open so he went there, then back across to K&B. Results negative. It was as if he was showing portraits of Martians. No one knew anyone who even looked like these guys.

At Shoe Town, Evangelista was so proud of her work she took extra flyers to take home.

"How's Freddie?" LaStanza asked.

Evangelista grinned. "All he's talked about was you and the artist and the blonde woman. He likes you a lot."

"He does?"

"Once he realize a man's not gonna put a move on me, he trust him."

"That's a load off my mind."

Evangelista taped two flyers inside the glass display case by the case register, then turned to LaStanza with a pout on her face.

"My name's not on this." She pointed to the part which said call NOPD with any information, listing LaStanza's name and the police department phone number. He thought she was joking and laughed only she wasn't.

"I thought I was your star witness."

"You are." And then he realized. "You haven't been telling people you're a star witness? You haven't been telling people you went to the police artist, have you?"

He could see the answer on her face.

"You can't do that. For you own safety."

Jesus. Another example where a cop had to think of everything. Didn't she read the newspaper, watch the news on TV? Eye-witnesses got whacked in New Orleans almost as often as there were parades and there were parades every fuckin' day.

He felt the anger rising in his chest. Anger at himself. He hated to make mistakes. *Dammit to hell.* He should have warned her from the start.

"Where's your security guard?"

"Who knows?" Evangelista let out a long breath. "I might be leavin' here."

"What?"

"I takin' a job on Magazine Street. Closer to my house."

It was his turn to let out a long breath, glad she hadn't meant leaving town.

"Hispanic record store," she said.

"Down the block from the Second District Station?"

"Yeah." She seemed surprised he knew the place. "I'll be day manager. The owner is Freddie's cousin, wants to stay open late and work the night shift."

LaStanza pulled out a new series of photo line ups with a photo of Andy Porter, alias Andy Peters, alias Andy Jones, alias Andy Gonzales, the robber from K&B that Beau shot, along with every known criminal associate of Porter.

"No. It isn't any of these guys."

LaStanza still simmered at his mistake. He told Evangelista he'd be around the area for a couple more hours and asked her to call her district manager and get a security guard over there. Before going upstairs to Skate Town, he reiterated she needed to quit bragging about what she'd seen.

As he stepped outside, he made a mental note to tell her to keep especially quiet once he nabbed the fuckin' killers. The system worked in their favor too many times in this goddamn city. Defense lawyers got the names of the witnesses and suddenly their stories changed or worse, they end up dumped along Airline Highway.

Lori Venetta's face suddenly came to mind as he ascended the stairs to Skate Town. He was going to mention it to Lizette, casually, so it wouldn't come as a surprise if it ever came up again. Lori putting the move on him. He had nothing to hide.

But why do I feel guilty? Because I want to kiss those lips, run my hands along that slim body, run my fingers through her long red hair? Damn. LaStanza shook his head and returned from fantasy land as he stepped into Skate Town. He found Sanders the manager flirting with two juvenile girls, both wearing cut off jeans and mid-drift tops, looking punkish with dyed orange and red hair respectively.

Sipping Cokes through straws they became very excited about the flyers, although Sanders was annoyed at being interrupted by the detective. The girls didn't know anyone who looked like the faces in the flyer.

"They really bad?" the taller of the two girls asked.

Jesus. "They're no good, rotten cowards. They murdered a ninety-one year old man, smaller than you." He pointed at the nose of the smaller girl.

LaStanza remained patient as Sanders barely looked at the flyer.

"Mind tacking a couple up?" LaStanza asked.

Sanders shrugged. "Most of my crew are part-timers for the Skate-a-thon. Usually work weekends, Friday and Saturday nights and Sundays."

LaStanza loved feeding them the Terminator line, "I'll be

back."

Sanders gave him a hang-dog look. He brightened immediately when LaStanza told the girls as he walked away, "He's a helluva guy."

"Tomorrow's our big night," Sanders called out.

Tomorrow would be Friday. Same night as the murder. Hopefully, some of the same people would be there. Hopefully.

10:22 a.m. – Claiborne and Orleans Avenues

"Can you keep an eye on my book?"

Lizette led the way up the narrow stairs to Uncle Sam Edkin's photo studio, Valerie LeGris right behind with the professor trailing, carrying the video camera case and tripod. Valerie wore a red Japanese kimono and red spiked high-heels. Beneath the kimono, she wore a white lacy French bra, matching panties and white thigh-high stockings. She'd made her face up, crimson lipstick on her lips, eyes highlighted with blue eye-shadow.

Lizette wore a snug denim dress with zippers in front and white sandals, her hair in a pony tail. Her dress nearly reached her knees but could be un-zipped upward to show her legs and down to show cleavage, only she wasn't showing much. She wasn't competing with Valerie and planned to leave before the action started. Lizette's heartbeat rose, surprising her.

Valerie looked back at Lizette and winked, a smile on her lips, like they were conspirators up to something mischievous.

"Here they are," Sam Edkins announced from the top of the stairs. He stood waiting with a wide grin on his face. He was in a green tee-shirt and jeans, his salt-and-pepper hair freshly cut. He stepped back into the studio.

"You parked in back?" He asked Lizette.

"Yes. Next to your van." Hard to steal a car you couldn't see. Lizette had squeezed her sea-foam green Maserati between the buildings and parked it in the back yard on the other side of Sam's van.

As Valerie stepped in, Sam's eyes lit up.

Sam's studio occupied a large, sun-filled room with a skylight above and a row of windows overlooking Claiborne Avenue. The elevated interstate ran along the neutral ground, about fifty yards beyond the windows.

Lizette introduced, "Valerie LeGris, meet Sam Edkins." They shook hands as Professor LeGris stepped in. Lizette introduced him and Sam stepped back to wave over three other men in the studio. All were in their early twenties, all dark skinned, two with their shirts off to show their finely-sculptured chests and arms. The one with his shirt still on was Rod, Sam's assistant photographer, the other two were models, Mike and Eddie.

Lizette could feel the electricity between Valerie and the models who checked her out carefully as she stepped forward to shake their hands. Sam set up his lights, and the models led Valerie to a plush, blue love-seat near the center of the room, just beneath the skylight.

Professor LeGris looked nervous and excited as he set up the tripod and attached the video camera atop. Lizette stepped over and made sure he'd turned the camera on correctly.

"How long does ze battery last?" LeGris asked.

"Each one lasts two hours and you have three."

He also had a spare tape and the electric cord to plug the camera into a wall socket if this went on and on. As soon as everyone was ready, Sam asked his models to stand aside and took several full length photos of Valerie before bringing the models back to pose standing with her.

Lizette checked the viewfinder of the video camera and made sure the tape was recording for LeGris before stepping away. The models removed Valerie's kimono and stared at her body parts as she did a slow turn for them.

The models kneeled next to Valerie and ran their hands up her legs to her panties as Sam snapped away and LeGris recorded his wife getting felt up. Mike and Eddie slowly pulled Valerie's panties down, faces only inches from her bush.

As soon as Sam stopped to change film, Lizette tapped Sam on the shoulder and said she'd be back. He looked disappointed that she wouldn't hang around, but she didn't want to be anywhere near what was about to happen.

Breathing a little heavy as she climbed into the Maserati, Lizette pulled out on Claiborne and hooked a u-turn to head back uptown. She stopped at a light, threw back her head and laughed. There was always a first time for everything. She'd just brought a woman to a gangbang.

It took a half block for her to realize the truck next to her was struggled to keep up, gears straining. Looking down, she saw the bottom zipper had opened, almost up to her panties. She shook her head, hit the gas and left the truck and its driver in her wake.

An hour later, sitting in C.C.'s Coffee Shop at the corner of Jefferson and Magazine Street, Lizette caught a man trying to peek up her dress. She was reading an advanced French language galley of Professor Albert Soboul's new discourse on Louis Antoine Saint-Just, the infant terrible of the French Revolution, reading how the twenty-two year old revolutionary helped write the Declaration of the Rights of Man and the Citizen with his friend, Robespierre.

The peeker was in his sixties, heavy-set with pallid skin. He wore a denim work shirt and faded jeans. She had just uncrossed her legs when she spotted the man's head lean away from his newspaper. He was reading the sports section.

She smiled to herself. With the zipper down, he wasn't getting much of a view. Then she remembered the stunt she'd pulled with Beau in her own kitchen and felt her pulse rising. Today she wore thin pink panties. If she went for it, he would get quite a view. She sat still for a solid minute before getting up with her empty coffee cup.

She looked at the peeker and said, "Can you keep an eye on my book?"

"Sure."

She went for a refill, came back and put her coffee next to her book and went to the ladies room. There wasn't a full length mirror so she couldn't see how high she needed to unzip the bottom zipper, so she brought it up to about an inch below her crotch.

She thanked the peeker with a smile and sat down, inching her chair to the right to give him a better view. She crossed her legs to make sure the dress rose. There was a wall behind the peeker so only he would get a look.

After a heart thumping minute, she uncrossed her legs. Glancing down she saw her dress was open enough for her to see a hint of her panties. From his position, he had to see all of it. She felt her pulse rise even higher as she pretended she hadn't noticed. Slowly she moved her knees apart.

Over the top of her book she saw his head tilt and then watched him shift his chair to get an even better view. After another hot minute, she put her right hand on her thigh and scratched it momentarily before bringing her hand up, pulling her dress even more open to scratch an imaginary itch higher up.

She left her dress higher. Peeking down she could see her panties. Yawning, she looked around and no one else was near, so she twisted her chair and brought her right foot up on her left knee, sitting cross-legged like a man as she unconsciously toyed with the instep of her sandal but only for a moment.

10:30 p.m. – Broadway

"Murders? Thought y'all were robbery dicks."

By the time Mark Land and Edward Kelly returned to the apartment of the now dead hard-assed habitual robber named Murphy, a Jefferson Parish Sheriff's sergeant was just pulling up in a marked police card with "traffic unit" emblazoned inside a lightning bolt on the side.

Mark introduced himself to the uniformed sergeant. J.P. deputies wore navy blue uniforms much like L.A.P.D. with a large silver shield and a baby blue patch on each shoulder. Sergeant Newit was about six feet tall with a quick smile and friendly handshake.

"Landlady called and said y'all were here. Thought I'd drop by, see if y'all needed any info on the dead guy."

Mark was glad to have Murphy's death confirmed, since they were searching the place. While he was checking out the other leads with Kelly, he had a flash of worry that Murphy wasn't dead and Fel would find his murder weapon and everything would get thrown out of court. All on the word of an old landlady.

Mark asked Newit how it happened.

"The fool was stone drunk, stepped right in front of one of our beat units on Airline Highway, middle of the afternoon. We have nine eye-witnesses."

Newit gave Mark their report item number and said he'd forward a copy.

"No need, unless we can link him to the murders we're working on."

"Murders? Thought y'all were robbery dicks."

"Nope," Mark said, "Homicide."

He led the three to the door of the apartment as Fel stepped out with a prosthetic leg.

"Oh yeah," Newit said. "He had one of those. That must be a spare."

Mark shook his head.

Fel announced he'd found nine guns in the apartment.

"Any .38 calibers?" Mark asked.

Fel led them to the sofa where he'd lined up the hand guns and pointed to a Taurus .38 and a snub-nosed Charter Arms .38 Off-Duty model. The rest were .22s and .25s.

Mark told Kelly. "Victim at the square was shot with a .38 Smith and Wesson. Security guard from LaStanza's case had a .38 Smith, Combat Masterpiece stolen."

Kelly, "What about the guy Beau shot?"

"He had a .25 caliber. P.O.S."

Wasn't one of Fel's initials. Everyone used P.O.S. – piece of shit.

Kelly was writing furious notes and asked, "Broadway. Is it an avenue or a street?"

"It's just Broadway." Mark said.

Fel asked about the two GM cars. Mark explained the Pontiac was sold two years ago to a woman in Shreveport and the Buick was up on cinderblocks, been up for a while. So much for tips.

"Shit," Fel said as he stepped to a narrow door behind the couch. "Didn't see this door." He opened the door and fell back grabbing for his weapon, but not pulling it out.

"Jesus."

Mark and Kelly moved over as Fel leaned aside to let them see into the narrow closet where three large heads hung, each mounted on boards, one tacked to either side of the tiny closet, one hanging from a clothes pole.

Fel said the obvious. "Why the fuck would a city boy have three stuffed razorback heads in his closet?"

The heads were hideous, mouths open, baring razor-sharp tusks, squinty eyes, dark gray bristly hair with a band of white hair surrounding their necks.

"They aren't razorbacks," Kelly said. "They're javelinas."

"The fuck you know that?"

Kelly pointed to a brass plaque on the mounting board of the head in the center. The plaque read: Javelina or Collared Peccary of North America. In smaller letters: Property of Tucson Native Mammal Museum.

Mark had to laugh, which brought a laugh from Newit. "The crap you see in police work."

Then Mark asked Newit, "Did the douche-bag have anything on his body we need to know? Besides a prosthetic leg?"

Newit chuckled. "All he had was a wallet with a driver's license, couple business cards, twenty bucks."

Fel went down on his haunches and pointed to a stack of wallets and four purses at the bottom of the closet.

Mark tapped Kelly's shoulder. "Call Robbery and get someone over here." He turned to Newit. "I'm sure they'll get with your Robbery Division. Probably clear up a shitload of 64s – armed robberies."

It was Newit's turn to state the obvious. "This place stinks."

"T.T.B., buddy. T.T.B." Fel said as he stood and led everyone outside to wait for the Robbery dicks.

Newit asked Mark, "What's T.T.B.?"

"You got me."

Fel supplied, "You think it stinks? Then T.T.B.– Try the bathroom."

3:30 p.m. – Jefferson Avenue

"And this is how you eliminate suspects."

Jodie and Glapier waited out front for their last appointment of the day to walk up from the school. Jodie spotted him a block away, another six footer, this man was portly and balding and was already winded from walking half a block from the school where he taught math and algebra.

"Think that's our man," Jodie told Glapier and read off the information she had on him. "Alfred Cromarty, IV. Teaches math and algebra at Newman High School right down Jefferson. He was 'let go' from an all-girls catholic high school for 'undefined reasons'."

"That don't sound good." Glapier said.

"According to Belinda Collingwood, he went out with Helen Collingwood a couple times last year. Nothing serious, according to the daughter."

Jodie closed her notes. "This is what comes of building a biography of your victim." The man reached the gate to his house, looked around and hurried inside.

"Why didn't we just drop by the school?" – Glapier.

"If he's innocent, no sense in getting the school all riled up."

Jodie climbed out of the car. Glapier climbed out and said, "That's one thing I'm gonna have to learn as a detective. When to push and when to be subtle."

Jodie smiled at her. She was thinking all right. She led the way up and rang the doorbell. Cromarty answered, a hesitant smile on his face. He had a weak chin. Jodie produced her credentials and introduced herself and Glapier.

"Come in," Cromarty said, as he brought them in to his living room, Jodie observed no visible injuries on his hands and he wore a size ten or eleven shoe.

"Thanks for seeing us right away," Jodie said as they sat in matching blue sofas facing Cromarty across a chrome coffee table. The living room was immaculate and smelled of pine cleaner.

He offered coffee.

"We've been on it all day," Jodie said.

She went through some background information. Cromarty was a native, was raised uptown, went to Newman, then Tulane, then Vanderbilt for his graduate degree.

Jodie watched his eyes when she asked about Helen Collingwood. Cromarty leaned forward, elbows on his knees and stared Jodie in the eye. He'd met Helen at a fund raiser dance for the museum. They both had gone alone to the dance. He asked her out and they went out twice, dinner and a movie. They kissed goodnight once. He could tell she wasn't interested and didn't call her again.

"She is – I mean *was* – a strong willed woman. Confident. I liked her but I could tell I lit no spark in her."

"Which museum."

"N.O.M.A."

The New Orleans Museum of Art in City Park. Jodie asked if he knew the date of the fund raiser. Her shoulders slumped. Following up on that would be a headache. Hundreds of people could have gone.

"It was the annual Christmas fund raiser. Just before Christmas."

"Why were you dismissed from St. Agnes?"

He leaned back, still looking at her eyes. "You already know the answer to that." He took in a breath, smiling weakly and said, "I had an affair with a former student."

"How former?"

"She was at Tulane. A sophomore. Her father howled to the nuns at St. Agnes and once they found out, well, it was better I leave. I resigned."

Alibi for Collingwood 30? None. He was home alone all Easter Sunday.

"You ever been inside Helen Collingwood's home?"

"Inside? No." His eyes narrowed momentarily before he said, "If you want my fingerprints, hair, fibers, anything. I'm willing. I had nothing to do with this."

"No need for your prints. I saw your honorable discharge on the wall in the foyer."

She'd put his name on the list for FBI lab to compare his prints to the latents taken at the scene.

"What's your blood type?"

"O positive."

"Have an insurance card or anything to substantiate that?"

He dug in his wallet and produced a Blue Cross Health card and sure enough, he had type O Positive blood.

"What size shoe do you wear?"

"Ten and a half."

Jodie closed her notes and took out a business card.

"Do you of anyone who would have hurt Helen?"

He shook his head.

"Anyone suspicious at that dance?"

He kept shaking his head.

"Any waiter or movie ticket taker that paid inordinate attention to Helen?"

"You are fishing for anything, aren't you?"

Jodie stood and passed him her business card.

"We just being thorough." She nodded to the card. "If you think of anything else, give me a call."

She thanked him on their way out.

Getting back in their car, Jodie asked Glapier if she had any questions.

"What was that about fingerprints?"

"All military personnel are fingerprinted. FBI's got his prints."

"Didn't know that."

"And the blood type?"

Helen had AB positive blood, her killer O negative, remember?

Glapier seemed a little embarrassed.

Jodie cranked up the engine and said, "And this is how you eliminate suspects."

4:00 p.m. – Magazine Street

"Very nice meeting you."

Lizette called Uncle Sam's studio from a pay phone on Magazine, just down from Hergert's Used Bookstore she'd just visited. It took Sam nine rings before he answered in a breathless voice.

"It's Lizette," she said. "All finished?"

"No. She – won't stop. I had to call in reinforcements."

"Jesus." She hoped LeGris brought enough condoms. Lizette could hear a high-pitched squeal in the background on the phone.

"Gotta go," Sam said. "I'll bring them home after, OK?"

"Sure."

He hung up and she could just imagine. She took in a deep breath, switched the bag she was carrying to her right had and started back for the Maserati parked at a meter a block away. Passing a tiny ladies shoe store, she spotted a heavy-set bald man sitting behind the small counter. He looked bored, but seem to notice her as she passed. She stopped a few steps later, took in another deep breath and thought she'd give him a thrill. Her one as well. She pulled the zipper down in front to show more cleavage and up from the bottom of the dress again, almost to her crotch.

She turned and almost bumped into a man who smiled and said, "Well, hello there."

Dino's father stood grinning at her and right behind him stood her peeker from the coffee shop. Captain LaStanza glanced down at her chest and said, "You're about to pop outta there, young lady." He stepped back and looked down Magazine Street. She yanked up her zipper while the other man winked at her.

"Supposed to be a bookstore 'round here," the captain said.

"I'm Jersey," the peeker said, extending his hand. "Fred Jersey."

"This is Lizette, my daughter-in-law," the captain said. "I think that's the bookstore." He pointed at the green Hergert sign outside the old bookstore.

"You're the one married Dino?" Jersey said as they shook hands. Dino's father's thick moustache looked like it needed trimming, so did his mop of wavy gray hair. Captain Anthony LaStanza was olive skinned with a solid, thick body.

"I was just in there," Lizette said.

"Good, then you can help me find a book." Captain LaStanza stepped over and opened the door for her and Jersey.

"It's called *A Terrible Thunder*. About the New Orleans sniper back in '72. Howard Johnson's."

"Red cover," Lizette said as she stepped in and turned right for the local interest section of the bookstore. She'd just seen the book. She went right for it and pulled it out for the captain.

"Yep. That's it." He took it and opened it to the pictures in the middle. "Been out of print for years." He showed her a picture of several cops hiding behind a police car, each cop wearing a helmet. "That one's me," the captain said. He pointed to the next cop. "That's him."

He flipped to the index in back and showed her the name LaStanza. "I'm mentioned a couple times."

Lizette remembered the day. She was in grammar school, Holy Name of Jesus, sixth grade. Sent home early, she watched it on TV. A sniper shooting cops and civilians from the roof of the downtown Howard Johnson's on Loyola Avenue. It was racial. Angry black man killing whites. Same guy had set fire to the Rault Center a few days earlier, sending a bunch of women from a high rise beauty parlor plunging to their deaths to escape the inferno.

Sitting at home as a child and watching the TV, she'd imagined a race war with all the reporters talking doom and gloom. Only the killer wasn't from New Orleans. He was from Kansas. Even the most militant Afro-Americans of the city denounced the lunatic.

"Joe was up on the interstate, diverting traffic, thankfully." The captain rarely mentioned Dino's big brother. No one in Dino's family talked much about Joe, except Dino and only late at night.

"Where was Dino?" she asked.

"In the army." The captain closed the book. "Imagine he was dodging bullets 'bout that same time. Freakin' Viet Cong." He looked at her and his voice deepened. "He talk much to you about Vietnam?"

She shook her head.

The captain took the book up to the counter and was startled to discover the book cost thirty bucks.

"Damn."

"It's rare," the bookseller said.

Dino's father explained he'd paid retail for it back in '72, maybe nine bucks, but he'd loaned the book to another cop who loaned it to another cop and it disappeared.

"You have another one for my friend?"

The bookseller didn't.

"That's OK," Jersey said. "I'll just read yours."

"The hell you will."

As they left the store, the captain pointed up Magazine and asked Lizette, "Wanna join us for a beer?" He laughed before she could say no and led Jersey away.

The captain turned and said, "Saw your husband a little while ago. Over on Claiborne. Flagged him down. He's canvassing that old man murder case."

Lizette nodded.

"Take care," said Captain LaStanza.

"*Very* nice meeting you," said Jersey with a smirk.

Of all the people I could flash, I picked this guy. Lizette laughed at herself as she unlocked her Maserati.

5:50 p.m. – Exposition Boulevard

"They lick your shoes?"

Aunt Brulie amazed Lizette again. How she knew LaStanza would call asking if he could bring some of the guys home for supper was beyond Lizette's comprehension. Obviously, the professor and wife were expected, but not the entire Homicide entourage. Yet Brulie had prepared a feast – a huge pot of chicken gumbo, a pork roast simmering in its juices in the oven, a tuna casserole, candied yams, and Dino's favorite home-made blackberry pie. All Lizette had to do was turn on the electric rice cooker and slip the garlic bread into the oven and warm up the rest.

At six o'clock, the kitchen door opened and Professor LeGris came in with Uncle Sam. Both men carried camera gear. Pulling up the rear was a thoroughly worn-looking Valerie LeGris, no lipstick, no makeup, a distant look in her eyes. She gave Lizette a weak yet evil-looking smirk and started up the back stairs.

"She gonna make it all right?" Lizette said as LeGris hurried after his wife. "Oh, yes. She's just – as we say – exhausted."

Uncle Sam was grinning, arms across his chest.

"You missed quite a show."

Lizette raised her hand. "No details, please."

Uncle Sam moved back to the kitchen door. "I'll have your latest proofs ready tomorrow."

"Don't rush," Lizette said as he left.

Ten minutes later, as Lizette had everything heating nicely, her husband came in the kitchen door with Mark Land. She hadn't seen Mark in a while and missed his big-bear hug. Mark was Dino's partner when they'd met and was the first to see their mutual attraction, prodding Dino to pursue her, even if he thought she was beyond reach.

She gave her husband a warm kiss and he hugged her tightly for a long moment.

"Boy, does this smell great. Use your phone?" Mark pointed to the phone.

"Sure."

He called his wife, telling her he'd be late. "Naw, everything's OK. I'm at the LaStanzas." He stayed on the line talking to the kids a few minutes.

Lizette moved to the rice cooker and checked it as LaStanza climbed up on a kitchen stool and leaned back. He looked beat.

"Rough day?"

He nodded. "Legs are shot."

"The hot tub'll help."

He yawned and asked how her day went. She had the small of her back against the center counter, hands up on it behind her and looked very nice to LaStanza, with those zippers tantalizing down up top and up from the bottom of the nicely fitted denim dress.

She kept her voice low. "Valerie LeGris had her session with Uncle Sam."

LaStanza shrugged.

"Remember how I said she wanted to get tapped by a black man?"

He laughed.

"Well Uncle Sam had a couple hunks waiting in his studio and the professor videotaped the action."

"You watched?"

"No way. I got out of there." She didn't say she was sure the action would have turned her on and she didn't need that, with all those naked bodies around her.

"Ran into your father."

"Me too. Where's you see him?"

"Old bookstore on Magazine Street. I found that Elmore Leonard book for you."

"All right."

"He hadn't been drinking, at least didn't seem that way." She told him how the old man asked if she wanted to go to a barroom with her.

LaStanza laughed again. Since retiring, Captain Anthony LaStanza had focused most of his attention on the pursuit of liquor. Being interested in a book might be a good sign.

"What book was he looking for?"

She told him and he nodded.

A knock at the kitchen door brought LaStanza off the stool. It was Fel and Kelly, followed almost immediately by Jodie and Glapier, her face not as scowling as she looked around the kitchen.

"I'll give 'em the tour," LaStanza said, leading Kelly and Glapier away as Fel moved up and pecked Lizette on the cheek. Mark hung up and asked Jodie for an update. As Lizette checked the food, she told her sergeant about her day.

"So how was your day?" Lizette asked Fel, looking him in the eye, wondering if his uncle had broken his promise and let Fel in on her posing. But Fel gave no indication of that.

"We chased bogus leads all day. Do I smell funny?"

Lizette shook her head.

"Spent most of the day in a stink house."

"Your Uptown Square Case?"

"Hard-assed habitual robber. Only he wasn't my killer. He's dead, but that ain't why. He had an artificial leg and my guy ran off after shooting my victim. He also collected razorback heads."

"What?"

"Javelinas," Kelly said as he came back in and Lizette caught the knowing smile on Jodie's lips. "They were javelinas. Collared peccaries. They look smaller than razorbacks."

"He collected –" Lizette's sentence was cut off by Fel who explained about the Tucson Native Mammal Museum plaques. It was then she noticed the eye exchanges between Kelly and Jodie.

"So when do we eat?" LaStanza.

"Set the table," Lizette told him and he immediately went back out into the formal dining room with Fel, Kelly and Mark while Jodie stepped over to help Lizette.

"What can I do?" asked Glapier.

Lizette pointed to a cabinet. "Glasses in there. Ice in the refrigerator door. You can ask what everyone wants to drink. We have beer, soft drinks, iced tea, bottled water in the fridge."

Glapier smiled, seeming glad to be included.

The chatter died away as everyone dug in. Sitting at the long, rectangular cherry wood table, beneath a huge crystal chandelier, and eating off fine earthenware, the group seemed muted. Lizette noticed that these normally loud cops seemed to quiet down while at her table. She took that as a compliment, having dined with them in cafés and smaller restaurants where they were loud enough to irritate most of the other diners.

LaStanza told her it was because no one wanted to accidentally break anything. She scoffed but the more they came by, and they came by often enough, the more she noticed they were different here in the mansion.

"So," Mark said, coming up from breath. "No shop talk, OK?"

Nobody was talking anyway.

He looked at Lizette and said, "Read any good books lately?"

Lizette cupped her chin in her hand, elbow up on the table and said, "I'm reading Soboul's new discourse on Saint-Just, Infant Terrible of the French Revolution."

Mark smiled and turned to LaStanza. "You read any good books lately?"

LaStanza finished chewing his mouthful of chicken gumbo and leaned back. "Funny you asked. The very day before we caught all these fuckin' murders, the wife and I went to three bookstores looking for a good Joe Wambaugh, Ed McBain, or Elmore Leonard I hadn't read and all we found in the mystery section were a buncha little-old-lady-solving-murder-mysteries. Fuckin' librarians , chefs and maids solving murders."

Fel snorted. "T.B.T.F.D."

Glapier's brow furrowed.

Fel leaned over his plate of roast pork. "T.B.T.F.D."

"Why you addressin' me?"

LaStanza took a bite of garlic bread. Lizette sipped some gumbo. Jodie and Kelly continued their eye talk.

Mark snarled. "All right. Decipher!"

"That'll Be The Fuckin' Day," Fel.

"What?"

"T.B.T.F.D." Fel spoke as if talking to a child. "That'll Be The Fuckin' Day."

"You are so bizarre," Mark growled, then turned to Jodie and asked if she'd read anything lately. She hesitated. "OK, just no one tell Country-Ass."

She made sure everyone nodded before she told them about Red Hawk of the Oglala Sioux. "It's quite good. Historical."

Mark nodded to Kelly. "Read any good books lately?"

"*Nicholas Nickleby.*" He was serious, staring at Jodie again.

"What about you?" Mark asked Glapier.

She said, "*Nicholas Nickleby.*" She pointed her fork at Kelly. "We read it together."

Kelly looked puzzled.

It took LaStanza a full second to realize. "Hey, y'all. Sheila Glapier made a joke!"

Everyone applauded and Glapier's face became even darker for a moment before she smiled.

"So," Lizette leaned toward Mark when the laughter died down. "What have you read lately?"

He waved an index finger in the air. "Which is the point of this questioning. My wife is driving me stone-fuckin-nuts reading mysteries *solved by cats*! He stood, almost knocking his chair over. *The Cat That Solved The Strangler Murders. The Cat That Caught The Serial Killer.* She can't stop reading them and can't stop telling me about them!"

Fel coughed up some water.

Lizette, "Are they comedies?"

"No. Serious. Cats solving mysteries!"

"My two cats can't solve the mystery of where's the water dish." Jodie smiled at Kelly. "They can find the toilet bowl, can find my shoes to lick but let the phone ring or my beeper go off or anyone knock on the door and they run under the sofa." She turned to Mark. "Shane got lost the other day in the corner of the living room. Sat there crying like a kitten until I turned him around and showed him the rest of the house was still there."

"They lick your shoes?" LaStanza asked his partner.

"Just the insoles. Disgusting. Lick them until they pull the insoles out. Have to keep my closet closed."

LaStanza went into the kitchen and brought out the candid yams and blackberry pie.

Jodie was still going on about her cats. "I bought one of those coffee grinders. Got some fresh beans. Both cats up on the counter, having to check out anything new in the house. I hit the grinder and they dove. Cody knocked over a chair. Shane ran into the wall." She took in another breath. "Cats solvin' murders. Next they'll have dogs solving murders."

Mark looked up from his roast. "They have them too!"

When the roaring abated, Fel asked Mark, "Say, why didn't you ask me if I read any good books lately?"

Mark leaned toward Fel. "What's the title of the last book you read." He put up a hand. "A book you finished."

Fel grimaced, looked around and said, "*The Great Gatsby.* Back in high school. Still don't know why he thought that ditzy Daisy was so fuckin' hot."

Lizette tapped her husband's hand as he cut the blackberry pie. "Before I forget," she said in a lower voice. "I want to remind you about tomorrow night."

"What about tomorrow night?"

Lizette's eyes bulged. "Antoine's. The LeGris's last night in town."

"I can't go."

She pulled her hand away.

"It's Friday," he said. "One week since the Senoré was killed. I have to be there for the skate-a-thon. Most of those people go there only on Friday nights."

Lizette looked at him incredulously. She grabbed his hand and dug her fingernails into it. "Could you please come into the kitchen."

"Sure." He followed her, looking at the red marks on the top of his hand.

She wheeled and poked him in the chest with her finger. "This is the *one* event you promised not to miss."

He gave her that inexpressive poker-face.

Her fists went to her hips. "You're not going to answer me?"

He closed and rubbed his eyes. "I have to canvass tomorrow night."

"You *promised* me, mister." She slapped his shoulder, hard, as she went back into the dining room.

I did promise. He remembered her excitement about Professor LeGris coming and all the events, especially that last supper with just the professor, his wife, Lizette and LaStanza.

He looked back into the dining room.

I did promise.

But that was before the Senoré found himself in someone's way and got his face crushed. That was before.

Friday, April 4, 1986

10:05 a.m. – Detective Bureau

"And Baba Ganoush is an appetizer!"

LaStanza called Lizette after he finished his first look through the huge stack of paperwork Lieutenant Mason had compiled from the list of names and license plate numbers from the Senoré crime scene, which included forty-two men with criminal records. Mason had tried to locate a match with the names and numbers from the Square and Jodie's Walnut Street scene because you never know until you check. There was no match.

When Lizette answered, he asked, "Why don't we have a fancy lunch with the LeGris's? I can get away for a long lunch."

185

She let out a sigh. "I just cancelled the reservation at Antoine's. I suppose I could call back and see if we can do lunch there." She sighed again. "They're pretty well packed up."

"I don't have to be at Skate Town until around four."

"I'll call you back." She hung up without a good-bye or an I love you. She was still simmering.

LaStanza slipped the notes into the bottom drawer of his desk and began packing his briefcase.

Jodie looked over from her computer screen and said, "This is great. I get my dailies done in no time."

He nodded. He'd turned his computer on, started up the word processing program and had Jodie help him set up a template for his daily reports, but that's as far as he'd gotten.

His phone rang and he snatched it up before it rang again. It was Lizette. They were on for noon.

"I'll be right there," he said. Hanging up he told Jodie what he was up to, since Mark wasn't around as he turned off his computer.

"Good," she said and didn't mention it was her idea for him to do lunch with the professor and wife.

"Only I have to go to another goddamn fancy restaurant."

"Don't start that. It's worth the price."

"No it isn't. No meal for two people should more than a minimum wage worker earns in a week. Since we'll be four that's double."

Jodie shook her head and told him he was sounding more like a liberal Democrat every day. "Maybe even a socialist."

"Yeah. Yeah."

"Face it. You're stinking rich."

The squad room door banged open and two men came stumbling in, both handcuffed behind their backs. One was huge, had to be six-six and weighed a good three-hundred. The second as skinny and short. Both had straight black hair, olive skin and wore dirty gray tee-shirts and rough-material black denim pants.

"Ya' fuckin' morons!" Steve Stevens bellowed as he herded them toward his desk. "Can't even fuckin' walk."

Paul Snowood, resplendent in a blue cowboy shirt, two rows of brass buttons and white fringe, tight-fitting black denim pants, silver snake-skin cowboy boots, a white ten-gallon Stetson perched on his head. Snowood carried his briefcase in one hand, a white Styrofoam cup in the other. His NOPD badge was clipped to his shirt again.

"Ole Vada Ganoush!" Snowood announced as he arrived and Steven shoved the two men into gray folding chairs between his desk and Snowood's. "Ole Vada Ganoush," Snowood repeated, "done solved this one for us. These are our Algiers killers. Desperados from south of the border. Way south. *'Farners.'*"

It took LaStanza a moment as hurriedly closed his briefcase. *Farners?* Foreigners.

"Fuckers have no ID" Stevens called out, "Hey big guy, what's your name?"

The big guy didn't even look at him.

Stevens kicked the chair. "Hey. What your *nomay? Nomay?*"

LaStanza shook his head. The big guy, looking around, met his eyes and LaStanza asked, "Cómo se llama?"

The big man raised his chin. It was then LaStanza caught a whiff of the men, sweat and the musty smell of mud.

"Cómo se llama?"

The big man snarled, "Se llama, Piso Mojado."

LaStanza turned to the smaller man and asked his name.

"Prohibito Fumar."

LaStanza blinked and turned to Stevens. "Don't write that down."

Steven looked up from his notes. "I can't even spell it."

"Call Immigration." LaStanza picked up his briefcase. "They have ways to identify people. These guys could be from anywhere, Central America, South America, the Antilles."

He could see it wasn't registering with Stevens so he glanced at Snowood who was spitting in his cup. "Call Immigration." LaStanza waved good-bye to Jodie and stepped away.

"What? That ain't their names?" Snowood.

LaStanza wheeled, still backing away and told him. "Unless the big one's name is 'Wet Floor' and the little one's 'No Smoking'."

Snowood coughed up brown spit, which almost fell on his nice shirt. He wiped his chin immediately and roared at his prisoners, "You fuckin' wit' the wrong cowpoke!"

LaStanza opened the squad room door, called back over his shoulder. "And Baba Ganoush is an appetizer!"

"What?" Snowood and Steven together.

Jodie had her hand over her mouth as S and S looked at one another, head bobbing like those plastic dogs glued to dashboards of beat-up Chevys in the Magnolia Housing Project.

Jodie turned off her computer and hurried out as S and S searched for a telephone book in order to call Immigration. Their two prisoners checked her out as she moved away from her desk. She ignored them, resisting the urge to push down her snug skirt.

She wore a navy blue skirt-suit, skirt a little too short, another outfit she was urged on by Lizette to purchase. Her hair turned out nicer than normal, fluffed with the blow dryer. She felt good today, looking good, knowing how she must look to those men.

As she moved out of the squad room, she was flagged down by the desk sergeant who pointed to a thin, balding man sitting against the wall.

"Detective Kintyre," desk sergeant Braun called out. "This man's here to talk to you about your case. Walnut Street."

Jodie stopped and looked at the man, who adjusted his horn-rimmed glasses. She noticed two band-aids on his right arm.

"He's here to confess," Braun said. "Says he did it."

Jodie stared into the man's dark eyes and he swallowed and started to stand up.

"I already searched him," Braun said from behind the desk.

The man stood and smiled weakly. He was about LaStanza's height, five-six but weighed even less, maybe one-twenty. He wore a tan Izod polo shirt and brown slacks and brown penny loafers.

"I seen you searching around," he said. "Knew you'd find me sooner or later." He bounced on his toes. His feet looked small.

"I'm Detective Kintyre."

"I'm Wilhelm von Knyphausen." He shrugged his small shoulders. "It's an old Hessian name."

Jodie hoped that last name didn't mean smoke or floor or something.

She took a step closer. "You have any I.D.?"

"Got it over here," Braun called out, holding up a black wallet. "Ran him already. No record."

She took the wallet as Braun winked at her, then showed Wilhelm von Knyphausen back through the Detective Bureau and into one of the tiny interview rooms, seating him behind the small table on the uncomfortable wooden folding chair whose front legs had been shaved down a half inch, so he would have to lean back to sit straight up, keeping him on edge, uncomfortable. There were no windows. The only other objects in the room, besides the light switch and harsh fluorescents, was a large tripod with a video camera atop, an electric clock behind von Knyphausen's head, which would be seen in the video, and a black telephone on the edge of the table, also seen on the videotape in case an interviewee claimed he was held incommunicado. Hell, there was a phone right in front of him. The phone had to go through the desk sergeant's switchboard, but few, if any interviewees picked up the receiver.

Jodie left him there to simmer a while. She went back to her desk for a blank videotape, a waiver of rights form, notepad and pen. She watched S and S take their suspects into two other interview rooms and leave them inside. They were still cuffed.

A movement caught her attention and she spotted Fel Jones leading two men into the Bureau, one Chinese, the other a big man with light brown hair, in his twenties, about five-ten. Kelly and Glapier pulled up the rear. Glapier in another tight-fitting pants-suit, this one electric blue, and it occurred to Jodie she must have bought most of her clothes when she weighed less. Kelly looked sharp as usual in navy blazer and off-white pants.

"Put them in the interview rooms," Fel told Kelly.

"Only one left," Jodie told them, pointing to the last door on the end. "What you got?"

Fel looked tired. "Task Force found these two for me. Both want to confess to my murder."

Jodie looked at the Chinese man, who stood about six feet tall, was thin and had graying hair. The man wouldn't meet her gaze. She turned back to Fel who instructed Kelly to put the other man in the last interview room and then pointed to the chair next to his desk for the Chinese man to sit.

"Hey," Snowood called out as he and Stevens were about to go into their interview rooms. "Watch out for their names. They might be appetizers!"

Jodie explained to Fel.

It took six minutes to eliminate Sammy Foochow as a suspect. Obviously, he'd read about the case in the newspaper but got all the details wrong. The woman he killed was white. He shot her on the wrong side of Uptown Square. She was wearing blue jeans. He escaped on foot and didn't get into a car.

Fel sent him on his way with a stern warning.

Glapier asked, "I thought the shooter was white and the driver black."

"Me too." Fel headed for the coffee pot with Jodie and Kelly. They decided to send Kelly in with Jodie for her interview and Fel would take Glapier in with him. Each took fresh coffee in with them, an extra cup for their interviewee.

Wilhelm von Knyphausen sat behind the table with his arms folded. Jodie slipped the videotape into the recorder but didn't turn it on. Instead she put her portable tape recorder on the table, turning it on, took out the waiver of rights form and read the man his Miranda rights, having him put his initials next to each right and signing the bottom of the form.

Kelly had to stand as there was only room for two chairs in the tiny room. He stood leaning against the door. His mission was to watch and learn and say nothing. After introducing herself on the tape as well as Wilhelm von Knyphausen and Kelly, she gave the date, time and location before asking Wilhelm some background questions.

She got to the point as quickly as she could.

"Are you here to confess to a crime?"

"Yes, ma'am."

"You'll have to speak up." Jodie pointed to the tape.

He repeated his yes ma'am louder.

"What crime would that be?"

"The murder of Helen Collingwood at 439 Walnut Street."

He got the name and address correct. Jodie watched his eyes as he stared straight into hers, unblinking most of the time behind those horn-rims.

"How did it happen?"

He started breathing heavily, his eyes filling with tears. "I – there was a – rage – inside me. I was jogging and it just hit me, brought me to her door. I rang the bell and she answered and I asked for a drink of water. When she opened the door a little wider I hit her in the face and hit her again and again. She stumbled back and I kept hitting her until we got to the living room and I found a poker, like from a fireplace and kept hitting her."

He sobbed and buried his head in his arms atop the table.

Jodie looked at Kelly who just shrugged.

When Wilhelm recovered, somewhat, he sat up and said, "Then I raped her." He went into a detailed, sickening account of the ways he stuck his dick into her, fuckin' her after she was dead. Heis eyes were steely now as he looked for a reaction in Jodie, but received none.

When he paused to take in a breath, Jodie asked him to describe the layout of the house. He started shaking again and became confused.

She pointed to the band-aids. "How'd you get them?"

"Huh?"

"How'd you cut yourself?"

"Thorn bushes outside my house."

"What's your shoe size?"

"Huh?"

"Come on, I'm speaking English."

"Uh, eight."

"OK. What room did you leave the body in?"

He looked at Kelly and chuckled. "You ever fuck a dead woman?"

Jodie turned off the recorder, left Wilhelm in the room and went out to her desk to fill out an arrest form to book the stupid fuck with falsifying a police report.

"Will the D.A. prosecute him?" Kelly asked.

"I doubt it, but I want his prints on file."

"Jesus, what a sick bastard."

"He's playing out a fantasy." She looked up into Kelly's blue eyes and he gave her that warm smile. She winked and felt the rising anger Wilhelm had stirred begin to slip away. She snatched up her phone and called the Sex Crimes Unit.

"You need to send someone over here. Got a live one for you."

She went on to explain Wilhelm's rape fantasy.

"We'll be right there."

Kelly sat in the chair next to Jodie's desk. "Tomorrow's Saturday isn't it?" His eyes twinkled at her.

"Yes."

"How does dinner sound?"

She leaned back in her chair and said, "Actually, I was going to roast a juicy capon. Make wild rice, get some fresh sourdough bread, add a little cranberry sauce and peach cobbler for desert. You interested?"

"Absolutely." He leaned back and put his hands behind his head. "What's a capon?"

"Castrated rooster."

His Adam's apple moved up and down with his audible gulp.

"Makes the chicken very juicy."

He snickered.

"What's so funny?"

"How do you castrate a rooster? They have balls?"

She'd never thought of that before and said, "You got me."

Fel Jones also used a tape recorder and a waiver of rights form. He went carefully. This man fit the script of his killer. Theodore Sience was twenty-seven, born and raised in the city, no criminal record. He was a jewelry salesman.

First thing out of his mouth was to make sure Fel spelled his name correctly. "It's not *science*, it's Sience."

Most products of the Orleans Parish Public School system could barely spell, much less understand the larger words on the waiver of rights form without a cop going over them three times, however, Theodore Sience had gone to a magnet school, one of the academically high-standard schools, which meant he was only a couple notches below Catholic School standards.

Fel, who had played football while receiving a good education at St. Augustine, let Sience brag about his football days at Ben Franklin High, before cutting him short to get the rest of Sience's background information.

He let Sience tell his story of the murder at Uptown Square, while Glapier stood against the wall, arms crossed, a determined look on her face. Sience had some of the facts right, how he'd approached the victim who refused to give him her purse, how he'd shot her, then panicked and ran for his getaway car, which he drove off.

"Did you take anything?"

"No."

"Where did you shoot her?"

"Behind the Square."

"Where on her body did you shoot her?" Fel.

"In the back. Three times."

"Why do they confess?" Glapier asked as she and Fel left a handcuffed Sience in the interview room.

"Some want their names in the paper, some are bored with life and this is exciting."

"But they could wind up in jail, at least for a while."

"I think most know we'll trip them up. Some just want to go though the shit they see on T.V. Get into a shouting interrogation with the cops."

"But we don't interrogate," Glapier said, almost smiling again. "We interview."

She was learning quickly.

"They watch cops slap around suspects on TV and think it's real."

"Yeah." Glapier scooped up the coffee pot and re-filled both their cups. "We beat people around like that we be in front of the Grand Jury every week."

"Exactly. Now we book the lovely Mr. Sience with filing a false police report so he gets to go to jail for a while. Wouldn't want to disappoint him, the fuckin S.A.B."

"The what?"

"Stupid ass bastard."

Fel started back for the interview room, turned and added, "I knew he was a lying bastard the minute he started talking."

"You that good?"

"Ben Franklin doesn't have a football team."

3:30 p.m. – Claiborne Avenue

"She's starving to death, you morons!"

193

LaStanza was just parking his unmarked car in the cab zone next to Palmer Park when Mason called him on the radio.

"10-20?" Mason asked his location.

"Palmer Park."

"Need you to go around the corner. Sycamore and Dublin. Got a bad one and 3122's in court. He'll be there ASAP."

"10-4." LaStanza cranked up the Ford and zipped around Palmer Park. He spotted two marked units in front of a two-story brick double at the corner of Sycamore and Dublin Streets. The front of the house faced Palmer Park. An ambulance pulled up behind him.

A young-looking patrolman came out of the right side door and leaned to the side and retched. LaStanza moved past him and stepped into a dark house the reeked of mildew. Too much furniture crowded the living room, four sofas, two shelf units with two TVs, a stereo and several large speakers. He followed the voices around two recliners in the center of the room to a narrow hall and a bedroom where a woman with grayish skin and frizzy graying hair sat on the edge of a bed. Another young-looking patrolman stood next to her.

LaStanza opened his suit coat to show his badge and the cop pointed down the hall. "They're in the kitchen."

He passed an unoccupied bedroom, a filthy bathroom, and stepped through a dining room with two tables and barely enough room to pass the chairs and went into a kitchen where a young-looking black officer knelt next to little girl sitting on the floor.

The girl stared straight ahead as if blind, her stringy black hair hung limp around a sunken face. She wore a ratty gray dress, her legs extended straight out. She was barefoot and her legs and arms were rail-thin. LaStanza felt the acid in the stomach bubbling.

A tall EMTee stepped behind LaStanza and the cop moved to let him at the girl who appeared to be about ten. The cop, whose name tag read Adams, told LaStanza, "She's this way." He led LaStanza out the back door.

"I think the little girl in the kitchen punched 911 on the phone. We got no answer and the front door was open. We found the old woman sleeping in the bedroom. Little girl in the kitchen just pointed out the back door."

In the tree-filled backyard, overgrown with brush, there was a shed of sorts, a tin thing with a sunken roof. Inside, amongst rusted lawn mowers, broken rakes, shovels and two old washers, lay another little girl in another ratty dress. This one was younger. Six, maybe seven years old.

"I checked for vitals," Adams said. "She's dead."

LaStanza went down on his haunches and pressed his fingers against her throat, then tried to find a pulse on her wrist, but she was cold and stiff and there was no pulse. He studied the child for a minute, the gray skin tight around her bones, as if it had been painted on. LaStanza felt the skin on his arms tingle and his heart stammering in his chest.

"Can't figure if these people are black or white." Adams said.

LaStanza stood and brushed his pants leg, acid rising in his esophagus.

"Don't see any trauma," Adams told LaStanza.

"She starved to death," snarled LaStanza as he hurried back to the kitchen. He found both EMTees hovering over the little girl, trying to get her to talk.

"What the hell are you doing?" LaStanza glared at the EMTees. "Get this child to the hospital! Now!"

The taller EMTee stood up to LaStanza who shoved his face in the EMTee's face.

"Are you insane? Get this child outta here! She's starving to death you morons!"

The smaller EMTee stood up. "I'll get the stretcher."

"To hell with the stretcher!" LaStanza scooped the girl up and rushed through the house. She didn't weigh fifty pounds. He held her tightly, intending to put her in his unit and drive her himself to Charity, only the big EMTee was right on his heels calling out, "We'll take her."

LaStanza stopped by his car and the big EMTee put out his arms. "Give her to us. We'll take her. We'll get a line started in her arm."

"Go open the fuckin' ambulance!"

The EMTee did, his partner hurrying to the driver's door. LaStanza wouldn't give up the child until he climbed in and put her on the stretcher inside the ambulance. Climbing out he shouted, "Get her there! Now!"

The red lights flashed and the siren wailed and the ambulance pulled away as the big EMTee was yanking the back door closed.

LaStanza went back into the house. The cop from the bedroom, whose name tag read Hill, met him in the overstuffed living room. He nodded in the direction of the ambulance. "They were asking her how she felt and how many fingers they were holding up."

Jesus. LaStanza shut his eyes and fought to control his rage. His stomach was gurgling now.

"3122 – 3124" Mark calling on the radio. LaStanza pulled is LFR from his back pocket and responded.

"I'm in route," Mark said.

"10-4."

A loud bang turned LaStanza and Hill around as a large man stomped into the living room. About six-three, a solid two-fifty, the man wore a muscle shirt and dirty jeans, tattoos on both arms.

"What the hell's goin' on?" the man's voice boomed. LaStanza felt his breath slip away as he realized he recognized him.

"What are y'all doin' in my house?"

Hill stepped forward, right hand raised, palm out. LaStanza leaned forward, slipped his handcuffs from his belt and rushed past Hill, slammed his shoulder into the big man's belly, sending them both to the floor. LaStanza had the man's right hand cuffed and was twisting it behind the man's back before the big man could react.

"What! What!" the big man shouted, trying to roll LaStanza off. He only succeeded in freeing his left hand for LaStanza to cuff behind the man's back. Climbing off, LaStanza avoided the man's kicking feet.

"What's goin' on?" The man bellowed.

"You're under arrest," LaStanza gasped, feeling a belch of acid in his mouth. He couldn't catch his breath. The thought *panic attack* flashed into his mind. He pointed to the man and managed to get Hill to understand to search him as LaStanza hurried back through the house to the bathroom where he vomited his portion of the three hundred dollar lunch they'd had at Antoine's – French onion soup, chateaubriand, French bread, bananas foster and fine burgundy wine – down the toilet.

Flushing the "exquisite" lunch, he leaned over the sink and splashed water on his face and slowly his gasping subsided and his heart quit slamming in his chest. His eyes shut tight, letting nothing in except the vision of the little girl's skinny arms. While he'd stuffed himself, she'd starved. While he lived in luxury in a fine mansion, she lived here.

How long does it take to starve to death?
How much pain did she endure?

He splashed more water on his face. He couldn't control his heartbeat but could control his breath. He held on to the sink, tilted his head forward and breathed in short bursts and slowly breathed deeper until he felt his breathing returning to normal. God, he hated losing control. But he knew it wasn't a panic attack. It was anger. It was the leopard. He stood and held his hand against his chest and his heart rate seemed to have decreased.

By the time he returned to the living room, Mark was standing there. The big man was on one of the sofas, leaning forward as he sat next to the old woman, who was also handcuffed behind her back.

"He attacked me!" the big man bellowed at LaStanza.

"Shut the fuck up!" Mark bellowed back.

LaStanza went straight up to the big man and spoke, his voice scratchy from stomach acid. "I canvassed this house twice in the last week. Talked to this fat bastard and those little girls were inside, starving to death."

He felt another surge of acid moving up his throat, coughed it up and spit it in the man's face. Mark stepped over and guided him back toward the bedrooms where LaStanza told him what had transpired since arriving.

"Come on." He took Mark to the body.

On their way back into the house, LaStanza said, "I'll talk with the neighbors. See how many of them knew the girls were here."

"No. Go get a soft drink. Relax. Go to Skate Town. S and S are coming." Mark pulled out his LFR and called for the crime lab before LaStanza could protest.

On his way through the living room, the big man screeched at him. "Wipe off my face!"

"Fuck you, ass-hole!"

Sitting in the Ford, hands on the steering wheel, LaStanza squeezed so hard, his hands turned white and then numbed. He sat there until he saw Snowood's unmarked car pull up and pulled out of there before he had to talk to S or S.

A chilly Coca-Cola later, from K&B, LaStanza belched several times as his stomach settled, somewhat. He watched the rear parking lot behind K&B fill and followed the people up to Skate Town for the Friday night skate-a-thon. He peeked into Shoe Town to check on Evangelista and found an unhappy looking regional manager Wesley behind the counter. He told LaStanza Evangelista Luz had quit.

"Where's your security guard?"

"We're still working on that."

"Hope your home office has the phone number of your next of kin so we can notify them to come pick up the body."

Wesley blanched and LaStanza stepped out.

Manager Sanders of Skate Town gave him a weary look as soon as he entered. The two juvenile girls were there with their dyed orange hair and dyed red hair and exposed mid-drifts. Sucking Coke through green straws, they hurried to LaStanza and introduced him to their boyfriends, skinny boys with spiked hair and vapid stares.

Two grueling, unproductive hours later, LaStanza stood next to the shoe counter as Sanders passed out yet another pair of hideous-looking shoes with white skates.

"You look beat man."

LaStanza's stomach still churned but surprisingly, he felt hungry.

"Want a Coke? It's on the house?"

LaStanza thanked him but declined. "I'm sorry if I disrupted your business," LaStanza apologized, which felt funny coming out of his mouth. He rarely apologized for anything.

"No problem," Sanders said. "Actually you've been a draw." He waved his arm in the air. "They been talkin' about the murder and some came just to meet you."

At least they were talking about the murder. Too bad no one had seen anything a week ago. LaStanza had passed out enough flyers and business cards. "Any regulars missing tonight?" he asked.

"Funny you should ask. Couple regulars aren't here tonight."

"You know their names?"

Sanders nodded and reached down for a card file, flipped through the index cards and passed LaStanza two cards. He could barely read them, but was able to glean two names with their addresses and phone numbers. One was Lenny Evans who lived on General Ogden Street, the other, Dana Barret of Monticello Street in Jefferson Parish. General Ogden he knew. Bad area. Monticello ran along the levee dividing Orleans from Jefferson.

Dana Barret. Why did that name sound familiar? He made a note to run both names through the computer as he descended the stairs to the street where he jumped when a loud noise shook the building. Lightning flashed outside and another thunderclap shook the building.

He peeked out the glass door and it was dry outside. He sniffed the damp air and felt the sudden coolness of nearby rain. Stepping out he looked around and saw it. Torrential rain falling in Palmer Park.

Dammit to hell.

He ran for his car, trying to beat the rain there. As he crossed Carrollton, fat rain bounced off the roof of the Ford. He managed to get inside just as a wave of torrential rain peppered the car. He sat and watched as for a minute before closing his eyes to listen to the strike of the heavy rain drops.

It took a few seconds to realize Jodie was calling him on his LFR.

"3126 – 3124."

"Go ahead."

"10-20?"

"Palmer Park."

"Need any help?"

"Negative."

"We're in route to the Camellia for 10-40. Wanna join us?"

"Let me see if 3122 needs any help."

Before he could call his sergeant, Mark called, "3122 – 3124. That's negative. I'm taking the 10-15s to the Bureau." Mark was heading to the Bureau with his two prisoners.

A few seconds later Jodie came back on. "3126 – 3124. You comin'?"

His rubbed his belly and felt pain in his stomach. Maybe he should try some toast or something, so he told them he was coming. It took longer than usual with traffic piled up. New Orleanians needed driver's re-training as soon as it started raining, as if they were suddenly on another planet and everything was too fuckin' wet to do anything but stay home.

6:20 p.m. – Carrollton Avenue

"Hell, that's the perfect woman!"

LaStanza found an open meter a half-block up from the Camellia Grill, dug the umbrella out of the backseat and got out. The wind-whipped rain drenched him before he reached the white columns in front of the old building that once was a fine antebellum home and now housed the finest grill in town. Jodie, Kelly and Glapier were already seated at the far left side of the long "W" shaped counter. Only Kelly looked wet and it didn't take a rocket scientist to figure he'd dropped them off in front and then parked the car.

The place smelled wonderful, meat sizzling on the grill. His appetite must be returning. As LaStanza wiped his face with a towel provided by a waiter, someone bumped into his back. Snowood and Steven stood grinning and dripping behind him.

Who invited them?

"Why aren't you helping Mark?"

"He run us off," Stevens said defensively. "Felicity is still at the Bureau to help him." He stepped aside as a couple moved from the right side of the counter to let them pass.

"Detective LaStanza," a deep voice called out and LaStanza leaned around Snowood, who was wiping off his Stetson, and spotted Pauli Venetta and Lori standing there. She wore a snug pale yellow minidress a light-weight white sweater over her shoulders. Pauli was in a pullover and jeans and for the thousandth time LaStanza was reminded New Orleans was just a big small town.

Pauli extended his hand and they shook, LaStanza staring into Lori's dark brown eyes that looked nearly black. "My daughter forced me out of the house," Pauli was saying. "Lori loves this place." He went on to say something about his wife staying with his mother so he could get out, but LaStanza felt Lori's eyes holding his, pulling at him and he swallowed hard and forced himself to look at Pauli.

He explained about the canvass of Skate Town and Pauli thanked him again and said they should be going, not wanting to be away from his mother took long. He reached around to the cash register to pay for their meal. Lori edged closer to LaStanza and he smelled her perfume. He expected her to give him a note, but her staring continued and he saw such emotion in her eyes, it made his breathing come shallow. Her face remained serious, eyes searching his even after Pauli stepped up with a large umbrella and said goodbye.

LaStanza watched her leave, watched the sway of her hips, watched as she turned back with that penetrating gaze before they stepped out into the rain. Turning to his partners, he saw everyone watching him. He went to take the end spot but Jodie shoed Glapier over and called him over next to her.

Before she could start on him, he looked at Glapier and said, "Just saw a dog and two cats bounce off the roof of a car out there."

"Cats? Where?" She looked toward the windows.

A weary smile crept across Jodie's concerned face. She knew what he was doing.

"What ya' mean she can't talk?" Snowood asked Kelly who leaned back from whispering the information to Country-Ass.

Jodie looked over. "She's mute."

Snowood craned his neck in case Lori was still in view and whistled loudly. "Mute? As in she really can't talk?"

"Exactly."

"Gol' damn! Hell, that's the perfect woman!"

"What?" Jodie snapped.

"Freakin' gorgeous and can't yap all the time!"

Jodie slapped his shoulder.

Snowood looked at LaStanza. "Come on. You tell me there ain't a man who hadn't pointed his TV remote control at his old lady and hit the mute button." He raised his right hand, left hand over his heart. "On the off chance God is watching and lets it work. Just once!"

Stevens laughed, which wasn't a pretty sight, bobbing on his stool.

"I'll bet you even done that with da' Princess," Snowood challenged LaStanza. "Lizette's close to perfect, but if she were mute! Gol' damn." Snowood looked back at the door again. "That was some luscious looking redhead."

Jodie stared at LaStanza until he looked back.

"Wish I could use a mute button on him." LaStanza nodded toward Country-Ass.

Jodie's stare continued until he shook his head.

"I saw all that eye contact," Jodie said. "What's going on, *partner?*" She dragged the last word derisively.

"Not a damn thing." He steeled his eyes. "I'm not stupid."

Thunder rolled outside, followed by a loud clap that rattled the glass on the front door. Thankfully the smiling waiter stepped up and everyone started ordering. LaStanza stuck to his toast idea and ordered another Coke.

"Then what was all that ogling about?" Jodie wouldn't let it rest. "*I'm* not stupid, either."

"Hey, Wyatt," Snowood called out. "You tappin' that or what?"

Jodie wheeled and Snowood put up his dukes in defense. "Don't mess wit' me lil' Filly. I ain't humpin' her."

LaStanza buried his face in his hands. "Everybody just calm down."

That seemed to work until everyone's food came and Snowood put it in a direct question. He asked Stevens first.

"Would you tap that?"

"In a freakin' heartbeat?"

Snowood said, "I would, fastern' a heartbeat. If she ever looked at me like she did ole Wyatt, I'd be dry humpin' her against the cash register."

LaStanza noticed Kelly was holding Jodie's hand now and trying to stay out of it.

Looking at Glapier, LaStanza said, "There goes another dog and another cat."

Glapier looked at the driving rain.

Jodie snapped, "Enough with the cats and dogs already."

"3122 – 3124." Mark calling LaStanza who answered immediately.

"White Street's flooded," Mark said, obviously warning any of them thinking about going to Headquarters. "How's the rain over there?"

LaStanza answered, "I just saw Superman walking on the sidewalk."

Kelly appreciated it, slapping the counter. Glapier was still looking outside until Stevens had to tell her.

"It's rainin' cats and dogs! Get it?"

Glapier turned and glared at LaStanza.

Snowood continued with, "OK, Wyatt. Serious now. You don't expect me to believe you wouldn't do her if she offered. Man-to-man. You not gonna pass that up."

LaStanza looked around and the only other customers were too far away to hear much, he hoped. The man behind the cash register was enjoying the jabbering, so were the waiters and at least one of the grill cooks.

"Come on," Snowood wouldn't give up. "I ain't askin' Kelly cause his Squeeze is right here." He ducked away from the spoon Jodie threw at him. "But Wyatt. You can't look me in the eye and tell me you won't tear off a piece 'a that pretty Filly. Come on. Man-to-man."

In the ensuing silence, LaStanza realized everyone was waiting for his reply. He washed down a bite of toast with his Coke, took in a deep breath and spoke to the counter.

"Sex is one thing. But that isn't what she wants and I'm not going there."

Jodie announced, "You're a man. Your brain doesn't work right all the time."

"Actually mine does." Even when he was falling apart in the house facing Palmer Park, it had worked. He didn't shoot the fat bastard. He lowered his voice. "My brain works all the time. Do you think I'd actually do that, take advantage of my victim's grand-daughter?"

He looked Jodie in the eye. "She's lookin' for a love affair and I'm not touching her. Period." He almost added, "OK, mother?" But figured he'd stop while he was ahead, stop while Jodie seemed to believe him. He hoped he did and went back to his toast, wishing his heart wouldn't ache when he looked at Lori.

At that point, Stevens gave his perspective. "A hard-on has no conscious."

"That's conscience," Jodie said through gritted teeth.

"First time you ever agreed with me," He opened his mouth to show Jodie the chewed-up omelet in his mouth.

"The perfect woman," Snowood said again. "You can sit on the sofa with her and watch a football game and she can't jabber at you through the good parts because she can't talk. At all."

LaStanza waited to catch his eye.

"Idiot. You won't be able to watch the TV at all."

"Why not?"

"You have to watch her sign language."

"Huh?"

And with that, LaStanza left, dropping a ten on the counter for the waiter and not waiting for his change from the cashier on his way out. Three steps into the deluge he realized he's left his umbrella but wasn't about to go back for it.

Jodie's shoulders slumped and Kelly squeezed her hand.

Stevens turned to Jodie, his bad eye straightening out, "See, you done drove him straight to the redhead. Bet that's where he's headin'."

Jodie scooped up her steak knife, but Kelly stopped her from plunging it into Stevens.

Saturday, April 5, 1986

9:15 a.m. – Exposition Boulevard

"Biggest circle jerk you'll ever see."

After starting a pot of coffee, LaStanza checked the morning paper, as he'd done every day since the Senoré's murder to make sure some enterprising journalist hadn't stumbled across Grosetto Venetta's autopsy results and told the world the old man wasn't shot.

There was nothing about his case, the headlines focusing on *Terrorist Bomb Berlin G.I. Hangout.* LaStanza read the lead article about the La Bella Club Disco where U.S. Army personnel congregated, two Americans killed and one hundred and fifty-five wounded. Libyans were suspected.

There was an article about Jodie's case, citing how detectives continue to saturate the Walnut Street area searching for clues and witnesses. He smiled at the word "saturate" figuring the reporter must have seen Jodie, Kelly and Glapier going around. There was some background information on Helen Collingwood, but nothing Jodie didn't already know. He tore out the article in case Jodie missed it. There wasn't a thing about Mark's case. Not yet, but LaStanza couldn't imagine the paper missing a story of a girl starved to death. He moved to the sports section as he drank a quick cup of coffee.

Ten minutes later he went out the front door. On their wide gallery, LaStanza stretched his legs and started his controlled breathing. In a Columbian blue Archbishop Rummel High tee shirt, John Churchill Chase's raider-on-a-horse emblazoned in white on his chest and a pair of crimson running shorts, white Nike running shoes, LaStanza loped across his yard. He jogged across the double-wide sidewalk of Exposition Boulevard, through the oaks, dodging puddles from last night's torrent, keeping to the right side of the concrete road that looped around the man-made lagoon and golf course occupying the center of Audubon Park.

He moved off the concrete to run alongside the road, keeping on the grass, to jog the one and three-quarter mile jaunt around the park. Grass was easier on the knees, but he had to run up on the concrete often with all the puddles next to the roadway.

The warm air was filled with the musty scents of the oaks and pecan trees and the fresh scents of the magnolias and sweetgums. Spanish moss, dripping from the oaks, waved in the spring breeze. Passing a long row of wild roses, he picked up their sweet scent as he turned to run parallel to St. Charles Avenue, a green-brown streetcar clanged along the neutral ground past the towering spires of Loyola University.

It took a while for his breathing to even out. A miler at Rummel, LaStanza loved to run, loved to feel the rush of air forced in and out of his lungs, the warm burning of his legs, the thumping of his heart. He took it easy however, since it had been a while since he'd run.

He wasn't alone on this pretty morning. Many joggers, mostly women, took to the track with a number of bicyclers zipping past along hugging the left side of the road. LaStanza eased around two women speed-walking with strollers and for a moment he was reminded of that painting Lizette had showed him at an art gallery in the Quarter. It was an Audubon Park scene from the 1890's with people picnicking next to the lagoon, men in heavy pants and striped shirts running and women with long dresses walking strollers.

Passing the rear of Helen Collingwood's home on Walnut Street, he looked over there, shaking his head as a flash of the sudden violence that had destroyed Helen and her daughter's life came to mind. That's when a snapshot of Lori's face came to him, those dark eyes, her long. lustrous red hair framing that lovely face, those lips.

He shook his head again and increased his pace, pushing himself to outrun the vision as his Nikes pounded the ground. The vision of those lips, those sleek legs followed him for several minutes, but he pressed it from his mind, thinking about last night, how he came home soaking wet, took a hot shower, went down to find Lizette and the LeGris's on the sofas downstairs watching TV.

He'd curled up with his wife on one sofa, while Valerie fell asleep with her husband on the other. Lizette found *Amadeus* on HBO. LaStanza didn't want to see it, with all that classical music and especially opera until the first chords stuck and he was hooked, like a freakin' trout. The movie was incredible, the music even better. F. Murray Abraham certainly deserved his Academy Award and Tom Hulce had grown up since his Pinto role in *Animal House*. It was nice evening, calming and warm with the rain outside.

By the time he jogged up to his gallery, LaStanza's heartbeat was stammering and it took a couple minutes to catch his breath. He turned and looked back at the park and felt as if maybe he'd left some of his problems back there along the run. Maybe.

Lizette sat at the kitchen counter, morning paper laid out in front of her, coffee cup in her right hand. She was in a white polo shirt, jeans, no shoes, hair wrapped up in a white towel atop her head. He kissed the back of her neck and she smelled shower-fresh.

She didn't react and he stiffened.

"What?"

"Mason called. He wants you to call him on the radio."

"Seriously?"

"I ever joke about that?"

He moved to the phone as Professor LeGris stepped in with two suitcases, smiled and left them at the back of the kitchen before going back up stairs.

"On the radio," Lizette repeated as she turned the paper without looking up. He went up the front stairs, with LeGris using the back stairs with his suitcases, and scooped his LFR from the nightstand.

"3124 – 3120."

Mason answered right away, asking LaStanza where he was.

"Home."

"I'll call you on a land line."

LaStanza sat on the edge of the bed. Less than a minute later the phone rang and he scooped it in the middle of the first ring.

"The sniper struck again," Mason said. "We need everyone out here at the Marina."

"The sniper?"

"The South Louisiana Sniper just shot Councilman Sidney Jacks."

"You serious?"

"As a fuckin' heart attack. Shot him in the head as he stood on his sailboat, yacht actually." There was a commotion behind Mason, voices rising. "It's a real circle jerk around here." Mason lowered his voice. "If you can't make it, just tell me only I can't find anyone except you and Fel. Mark's coming after his autopsies."

LaStanza told him he'd come and just before hanging up asked where at the marina.

Mason laughed. "Just follow the fuckin' crowd. You won't even be able to turn off West End Boulevard. Biggest circle jerk you'll ever see."

LaStanza had one more question. "How do we know it's the South Louisiana Sniper?"

"He called the Task Force just before he popped Jacks."

"Jesus."

"If I had him," Mason snarled, "I wouldn't need you."

LaStanza was in the shower when it hit him. Mason said Mark was at his autopsies. *Autopsies.* The little girl in the kitchen didn't make it. As the hot water beat down on him, LaStanza felt his heart sink and a hollow feeling in his belly. He could see the little girl's blank face, feel her as he carried her out of the death house. She was just hanging on to life, had been hanging on for all the time it took to starve her to death and LaStanza had knocked on that door twice.

He climbed into a silver blue suit, white dress shirt, navy blue tie with white designs, black loafers. As soon as Lizette saw him walk into the kitchen, briefcase in left hand, LFR in right, she covered her face with her hands.

"I'm sorry, Babe. I really am."

She didn't answer. He was supposed to help take the LeGris's to the airport.

"City Councilman Sidney Jacks was just assassinated," he said.

LeGris stepped in with another suitcase, nodded to LaStanza and went back up the rear stairs. LaStanza leaned over and kissed his wife's neck. As he pulled away, she reached back and squeezed his hand.

"I'll be back as soon as I can."

She nodded but didn't meet his eyes. He watched her shoulder sink as he opened the kitchen door and went around to the garage for his Maserati. As he turned on the engine, Fel called on the LFR and asked for a ride.

10:33 a.m. – New Orleans Marina

"You'll learn cops can make *good* money here."

Three marked police cars blocked off West End Boulevard just beyond Robert E. Lee Boulevard. An over-zealous patrolman waved LaStanza's Maserati away and became immediately furious when LaStanza inched his car closer.

"You stupid or something?" the cop growled. He was big and burly and young, red-headed and red-faced. "Now back up!" The cop slapped the hood of the Maserati. Before LaStanza could get his driver's side window down, a sergeant grabbed the big cop and pulled him back.

LaStanza held out his ID folder and recognized Sergeant Sam Buras, a real old timer, who waved him past. Turning to the right, LaStanza pulled the Maserati up on the levee and parked it. He and Fel climbed out, each pulling on their coats, each sliding their LFRs into back pockets, note pads in their left hands.

"Hey," LaStanza called out to Buras. "Tell the rookie to watch my car."

The red-headed rookie opened his arms and said, "How am I to know detectives drive sports cars?"

LaStanza stepped up to him and said, "Just watch my car, Rookie," followed by a cold smile.

"Nice suit," Fel said as they took the center of West End up toward the lake. Fel wore his new black suit. LaStanza made sure he'd worn his best, both looking sharp on purpose. They didn't get to play police with the FBI every day and LaStanza knew he would be wearing the most expensive suit out there. The fuck if he and Fel were going to do the dirty work for the feds, like climbing over boats or searching under buildings.

They each slipped on a pair of super-dark reflective gangster sunglasses as a warm breeze blew off Lake Pontchartrain with the scent of salt water. Gulls glided above the restaurants along West End, across from the levee. LaStanza and Fel passed seven more marked units and two dozen unmarked police cars parked in the street, some NOPD but mostly fed cars, which were easy to spot because they were newer and cleaner. Nice having federal prisoner trustees wash your car every day.

Lake Marina Drive looked like a parking lot, including a fire engine, three ambulances, an assortment of vans and marked police cars from NOPD, the Levee Board Police, Harbor Police, Orleans Parish Sheriff's Office and one Jefferson Parish Sheriff's car.

The two J.P.s were leaning against their car and watching the crowd outside the opening in the sea wall that protected the city from the lake water, the opening led to the Marina.

"Y'all lost?" Fel asked the J.P.s.

The older of the two said they couldn't get out. The younger one said they would probably get suspended. Not only out of their beat they were out of their freakin' parish and caught at it. Curiosity killed the cat and suspended enough cops.

They passed the S.W.A.T. van, exchanging bored looks with nine men in all black, including Kevlar helmets and bulky bullet proof vests.

"Hot enough for ya'?" Fel again.

"Go to hell," one of the S.W.A.T. men grumbled.

There was even a hot dog vendor across Lake Marina Drive from the Marina. A semi-crowd surrounded the vendor, including three cops. They found Mason just outside the opening in the sea wall. His tired look turned into a smirk when he saw them. He was in khaki pants and a white shirt and brown tie. No coat. A tall FBI man, in black suit pants, neat tie with his white shirt, wearing a blue windbreaker with FBI emblazoned in bold yellow letters on it stood next to Mason.

"These your men?"

Mason introduced them to Special Agent Dicks who flipped through sheets on a clipboard and told Mason, "I'll need them to go through the sheds, inside, outside, on top and under the two on the far end."

"Hey," LaStanza said before Mason could answer. "See this suit. I'm not climbing on or under anything." He nodded over this shoulder. "You got anyone going through that high-rise?"

Behind them stood a new condo high-rise of fifteen stories, balconies facing the lake and the marina.

Agent Dicks blinked at LaStanza and turned to Mason. "Your men don't follow orders?"

The smirk was on Mason's face again. "We're here to assist you. Not do your dirty work. Who you got assigned to the high rise?"

Dicks let out an exasperated breath and flipped through his sheets. He shook his head.

"OK, pencil in Detectives LaStanza and Jones. They'll canvass the high rise."

Dicks nodded and moved away. A yellow dog raced up and barked at him, causing him to hop skip away, waving his clipboard at the dog.

"Dog!" Fel called out, going down on his haunches. "Get over here."

The dog turned, bent its head low and barked twice before wagging its tail and creeping over to Fel for a good petting.

"How'd you know its name was Dog?" LaStanza asked.

"He looks like a dog."

"Enough," Mason said and gave them the run down. Just before seven a.m., a man called the Task Force from the pay phone outside Aaron's Seafood, corner West End and Lake Marina, gave the code word that identified him as the South Louisiana Sniper and said he was going to shoot another politician this morning. He left the receiver off the hook so they could trace the call. Five minutes after seven three people at the marina heard a gunshot and found Councilman Jacks dead on his yacht. Head shot, took off the top of his skull.

Mason pointed over his shoulder at the marina. "Yacht's near this side of the marina and can be seen by anyone on that side of the seawall and over here from the levees and high-rises, any place over two stories."

"Anyone see anything or hear where the shot came from?" Fel.

"Nope," Mason.

"Code word?" LaStanza asked.

The smirk was back on Mason's face. "This is top secret but the sniper's been calling the Task Force and they set up a code word for him to give so they know it's him every time he calls and no one puts him on hold."

As they were about to leave, Glapier called Mason on the radio. He asked if she could join the show and she said yes. LaStanza took out his radio and told her to wear a dress and high heels.

"10-9," she asked him to repeat it and Mason took over.

LaStanza and Fel crossed the street for the high rise and spotted four FBI men heading for the crowd atop the levee running along West End Boulevard.

Sheila Glapier joined them by the time they reached the third floor of the high-rise. She wore a black dress and high heels, her hair back in a bun. LaStanza immediately apologized for the cats and dogs thing.

She seemed surprised at the apology.

"I was just fooling around," he said.

She almost smiled and said it was pretty funny actually. "Can't believe I'm that dumb sometimes." A moment later, she asked, "Why'd you want me in a dress?"

"You wanna climb under wharves? Get all muddy?"

"Nope."

"That's why you're in the high rise and not down at the Marina."

They took one floor at a time, knocking on doors, getting names of occupants, asking if they heard or saw anything or saw anyone who didn't belong around the building that morning.

Out on the balcony of a fifteenth floor condo, LaStanza looked down on the Marina. A sniper had a clear shot from there. The marina was so crowded he could barely make out Jacks's yacht. Even with his sunglasses, he had to shield his eyes with his hand to look out at the lake's gray-brown water and bright blue, cloudless sky. Dozens of sails dotted the lake. People were fishing from the steps along Lakeshore Drive, others picnicking along the levee while FBI men kept up their canvass. It was a beautiful day. Except for the 'unofficial mayor' of the French Quarter and for a moment LaStanza remembered the protest parade along Chartres Street and the sign: *Jacks is a Douche-Bag.*

"Maybe the homeless will get their benches back now," LaStanza told Fel and Glapier in the elevator on the way down to the first floor. He had to explain about Jacks's campaign to clean up the French Quarter.

"Don't y'all watch the news on TV?"

"Sometimes."

They called Mason on the LFR and rendezvoused by the hot dog vendor where Fel and Glapier and Mason ordered dogs. LaStanza was hungry but not that hungry.

More cops were arriving. A line of robbery detectives in polo shirts and jeans, badges and guns on their belts and a line of burglary detectives, also in casual clothes, baggy enough to hide their oversized bellies, headed for Special Agent Dicks and his clipboard.

LaStanza was about to mention how those boys were about to get dirty when he spotted Snowood and Stevens, in polo shirts, jeans, casual shoes came out of the marina. Both were filthy and heading their way.

Snowood stopped at the curb to wipe mud from his shoes.

"Glad I didn't wear ma' boots."

"Where y'all been?" LaStanza asked innocently as Mason and Fel tried not to choke on their hog dogs.

Stevens answered, "Under a buncha fuckin' sheds. Wit' spiders and shit!"

Snowood added, "Mighta' found somethin' worsen' dressin' monkeys in a Traveling Circus."

S and S ordered two dogs each from the vendor as LaStanza chuckled.

"You find Kelly and the Filly, yet?" Snowood asked Mason.

Apparently he was unable to locate Jodie and Kelly. Then again, it was their day off, and it appeared they were smart enough to know how to disappear.

"Good for them," LaStanza said. "Someone oughta miss this fuckin' circus."

Mark Land materialized next to LaStanza as if he'd popped in from one of those Star Trek transporters. He was dressed casually and looked miserable. He shared his misery, telling them about the Koch family who lived at the corner of Sycamore and Dublin Streets.

The old woman was the aunt of the girls, their mother serving time in Parish Prison on a crack cocaine charge, second offense. The fat guy was the aunt's son.

"Fuckin' evil," Mark said. "Whole fuckin' Koch family. I'm not talking scumbags or even ass-holes. I'm talkin' evil. They had those little girls chained in the kitchen. I found leather straps they used around the girls' wrists and ankles with blood and dried skin on them. They had enough room to get to the sink and slurp water."

Mark began rubbing his weary eyes.

"Fat fuck said the girls were bad, wouldn't listen, had to be tied down or they ran amok. Those little innocent girls." He took in a deep breath. "You shoulda seen their little bodies covered with sores."

Mark wheeled, took two steps over to a concrete and wooden bench next to a bus top and kicked the back of the bench, splitting the top two-by-four, then split the second two-by-four, before turning around and sitting on the bench, taking in deep breaths.

Mason sent LaStanza, Fel and Glapier to the restaurants along West End, where LaStanza bought a club sandwich to go as they continued their canvass. Mason sent S and S back into the marina pit and sent Mark home.

At four p.m., LaStanza and Fel were released, passing their notes to Mason before leaving. They found an FBI agent next to the Maserati. He was talking on his own LFR. Buras called them over and said the FBI's running LaStanza's license plate. "I tried telling him who it belonged to but The FBI knows it all."

LaStanza moved to his car and opened the back door, turning around the FBI man, who was leaning against the front fender.

"Mind getting off my car." LaStanza took off his coat and laid it on the back seat.

The FBI man glanced at LaStanza's badge clipped to his belt.

"This is *your* car?"

"Didn't the sergeant tell you that?"

"I thought he was joking." The FBI man took a step away from the Maserati.

LaStanza opened the driver's door as Fel climbed in. "How long you been assigned to New Orleans?"

"Three months," the agent answered.

LaStanza shot him a devilish look. "You'll learn cops can make *good* money here."

He and Fel climbed into the Maserati and pulled away.

"Stupid fuck's already on his radio," Fel said.

4:40 p.m. – Exposition Boulevard

"We have greyhounds in the kitchen."

LaStanza stepped into his kitchen and found two greyhounds staring at him. For a second he thought they were statues, one tan, one spotted gray and white sitting perfectly still until the spotted one tilted its head to the side and gave a light, "Woof."

He found Lizette in the library at her Macintosh computer. She was still in the polo shirt and jeans, hair in a pony tail now as she typed.

"Hey, Babe," she said in a voice that didn't sound as upset as he'd thought she'd be, him talking all day at the marina.

He waited for her to look at him before saying, "We have greyhounds in the kitchen."

Her eyes lit up. "Aren't they beautiful?"

He waited for more, but she wasn't volunteering, so he said, "*You* must have let them in."

She turned in the desk chair and folded her arms across her breasts.

"I didn't see any keys in their paws and I don't think they know how to punch in the alarm code."

He got nothing from Lizette.

"They spending the night, or what?"

She sighed, her shoulders sinking again. "I told you about the adopt-a-greyhound program. Remember?"

He tried but he couldn't and she could see it in his eyes.

"From the Mobile Greyhound Race Track. Dogs still young but not fast enough anymore. Put out to pasture. They are so gentle. All the wildness has been run out of them."

"The spotted one 'Woofed' me."

"You never listen to me. I told you at least three times about the adoption program."

"I listen to you. Only my brain can handle just so much information."

She went back to her typing.

The worrisome part of all this was LaStanza didn't remember anything about greyhounds. *What else have I missed? Jesus.*

The greyhounds were waiting for him in the foyer, like statues again, just sitting there staring at him. He tilted his head to the side, furrowed his brows and said, "Woof."

"Woof," the spotted one responded, then stood up and wagged its tail wildly.

"I don't know what I just said to them," he called out to Lizette.

"What?"

"They're out here in the foyer now and I went 'Woof' and the spotted one answered and now he's rubbing his snout against my leg."

She came in.

"They're awfully tall," he said as the spotted one stood up, its head almost reaching LaStanza's face. Lizette petted the dog's head and the other one came over quickly to get his pets.

"They're both males but have been neutered. We don't want them peeing around the house, marking territory." She showed him the collar on the tan one. "They both have collars and these tags have LaStanza and our address on them and the red tags show they've had all their shots."

Both dogs nuzzled her as she pet them and she had to balance herself.

"They're quite affectionate," she said. "Let them run in the front yard, but make sure the gate's closed while I get ready."

"For what?"

"We're going to the pet store. We're going to need food and water dishes, muzzles so you can take them jogging with you." She beamed at LaStanza. "They're inside dogs but need a lot of exercise."

LaStanza took them out front, checking the gate before going back to the gallery to lean against the rail and watch the dogs run back and forth, sniff at everything then pee on everything they sniffed.

Lizette came out with tennis shoes on now, her hair combed out.

"Get outta that suit, mister."

She and the dogs were waiting for him in the kitchen when he came down in jeans, a black tee-shirt and black tennis shoes. He pulled on a short-sleeved blue shirt to cover his off duty weapon, shoved into the back of his jeans at the small of his back.

"They're not coming are they?"

"No." She gave him a look as if he was retarded. "They wouldn't fit."

"How'd they get here?"

"They were dropped off. Come on." She handed him a note pad and pen, scooped up purse and headed for the kitchen door.

On his way out, LaStanza looked back at the spotted one and said, "Hey, don't burn the place down."

The dog went, "Woof."

On their way to a pet store on Magazine, Lizette told him he'd have to name them.

"Why?"

"You like naming things, giving nicknames."

She was getting him involved and they both knew it. But he felt good about it. She nodded to the pad and pen and had him make a list: food, dog treats, dog bones, chew things, muzzles, leashes, canine shampoo, canine vitamins, dog toys.

"We already have flea drops." She went on the explain how you drip the drops on the back of the dog's neck and it kills fleas, flea eggs, even ticks.

"What about blow up dolls? You know, like poodles they can hump."

"What do you think neuter means?"

"Oh, yeah. I forgot. Poor guys." LaStanza reached over and rubbed his wife's shoulder. "How about we pick up some grub for us on the way home?"

"Let's call out for pizza after we get all this dog stuff settled."

"All right."

"Oh, one more thing." She hit her horn to warn a dummy backing out of a driveway. "I'm trading in this car for a Land Rover on Monday. We only have a two-car garage and I'm not parking a car on the street."

"Land Rover? Yeah, they're kinda cool-looking." He'd seen one in a movie.

"An off-road vehicle, but fancy. British. If it can navigate the jungles of Africa and the Australian outback, it can negotiate the pot holes of New Orleans."

"Don't be so sure."

5:10 p.m. – Henderson Point

"I don't believe we're here."

Bobbie's Restaurant sat on a shell road, half a block from a shrimp dock across the bay from the small town of Bay St. Louis, Mississippi. The décor was straight out of the 1940s with a kidney-shaped bar along one side of the single story restaurant, a low ceiling and tables lining the windows that faced the brown water bay.

Jodie Kintyre and Edward Kelly were the first customers, early for the dinner trade, even on a Saturday night in semi-rural Mississippi. Jodie, in a yellow skirt suit with a diaphanous white blouse covered by the suit jacket, had her blonde hair fluffed and face looking radiant in the diminished light. Kelly, in an off-white linen shirt and navy blue pants, looked especially sharp with a slight touch of mousse in his hair, pushing it back from his chiseled, handsome face.

"I don't believe we're here," Jodie said as Kelly dipped a chilled shrimp into his cocktail sauce.

"I always wanted to eat here when I was little."

Kelly, who'd lived three years on Henderson Point, had fished in these waters, had swam in the nearby Gulf of Mexico, had walked past Bobbie's everyday on his way to catch the school bus. She picked at her salad, not wanting to spoil her appetite for baked redfish, as Kelly told her the story everyone around there told, the night of Hurricane Camille. His family had evacuated to Pass Christian High School on higher ground away from the gulf. The Category Five hurricane hit them directly. Incredibly the huge tornadoes that had bounced in off the gulf had missed the high school. Instead of the couple hundred dead, there would have been nearly a thousand.

Henderson Point, that peninsula separating the bay from the gulf, was devastated. Only a handful of buildings, all gutted, remained. Kelly's house wasn't one. Bobbie's was. Kelly was seven when his family moved to New Orleans.

Jodie's redfish arrived with Kelly's trout almandine and they ate quietly, their eyes doing most of the communicating as the golden sun sank in the western sky, shimming on the bay's dark water.

A photographer came around with a large, speed-graphic camera and asked if they'd like a photo and for a moment Jodie remembered that scene from *The Best Years of Our Lives,* Dana Andrews sitting with his blonde wife and the woman he was really in love with. Jodie became a Dana Andrews fan, watching black and white movies on TV with her parents, *Laura, The Purple Heart, The Ox-Bow Incident.* Kelly ordered two prints and they posed, his arm around her, both smiling at the camera.

After the tasty meal, washed down with a bottle of Liebfraumilch, Jodie and Kelly walked back to their bed-and-breakfast. It was three blocks away and they walked hand in hand, sometimes looking at the shells on the road, sometimes looking out at the glimmering bay, sometimes glancing at each other.

Aunt Marian's Bed-and-Breakfast was a three-story ante-bellum style house with a long staircase in front, leading up from a wide front yard dominated by two huge oaks and several smaller magnolia trees. Jodie caught a whiff of magnolia as they went through the gate of the white picket fence.

Their room was downstairs to the left of the staircase. Kelly unlocked the door and held it open for her. They'd checked in earlier, had changed into their outfits, one at a time in the bathroom, but now as Jodie stepped in, her eyes looked to the queen-sized bed immediately.

Kelly flipped on a lamp atop the end table next to the bed and turned off the overhead light. He locked the door and they faced one another for a long moment before Jodie stepped up and brushed his lips with hers. He kissed her back and the kiss intensified into a French kiss, their bodies pressed against one another as they stood.

The kiss continued, arms around backs, pulling each other closer, hearts stammering. Slowly, the kiss became less intense, followed by pecks on lips. Jodie reached up and began to unbutton his shirt, then pulled it out of his pants to run her hands across his hairless chest.

He removed her jacket and smiled at the vision of her lacy bra through her diaphanous blouse, then slowly unbuttoned the blouse, dropping it on the chair next to the door. Jodie tossed his shirt atop it.

Kelly ran his fingers over her bra, then around back to unfasten it. He tossed it over his shoulder and stared at her breasts. Jodie closed her eyes as his fingers found her nipples, rolled over them. He cupped her breasts and rubbed them, tweaking her nipples. Her breath came out shallow now as she reached for his belt buckle.

He wore blue jockeys. She wore no panties beneath her pantyhose.

The slow choreography of stripping one another ended and they stood face to face again for another long kiss. She took his hand and pulled him to the bed, kicking off the covers, shoving down the sheets.

She lay back and let him make love to her, kissing his way down from her lips to her breasts. He ran his tongue around her pink aureoles and sucked each nipple before kissing his way down to her belly button, his hands moving to her breasts to gently knead them.

He kissed her bush, tongue flicking her clit and she opened her legs. He moved between them, still reaching up to feel-up her breasts as he tongued her clit. Her hips gyrated against him. He pulled a hand away from her breasts and slipped a finger through her pussy lips, tongue still working her clit and she gasped, her hips moving quicker now.

Kelly wouldn't stop, even after she came, hips rising off the bed, passion shuddering through her. She tried to pull his head up.

"I want you in me!"

He got the hint and moved his face to hers. She reached down, took his swollen dick in hand, pressing it against her wet pussy lips. He worked it in and she cried again with the deep penetration. They stopped for a moment when he was completely inside, Jodie looking up into his blue eyes. He smiled and began working his dick in her, pulling it half-way out, plunging it back in, then worming it inside her, sending her though another climax.

He certainly had stamina, pausing to keep from coming several times, French kissing her until they had to come up for breath, but eventually he couldn't stop and came in hot gushes in her.

They lay for a long while, next to one another, body machinery returning to normal before she grabbed his dick and he started in on her again. The second time took even longer, less frenzied, more loving and she came again just as he did.

Later, as he slept wrapped in her arms, the silent air conditioning cooling her body, Jodie closed her eyes and smiled to herself. Only later, in the dead of night just before dawn did she wake and felt such a heaviness in her chest.

In her heart she felt this wasn't permanent, this wouldn't last. They would not be like this when she was an old woman. In her heart she knew she would be alone then. She just knew it. She gently brushed Kelly hair from his face, brushed her lips across his cheek and snuggled closer and felt him pulling her close in his sleep.

Sunday, April 6, 1986

10:10 a.m. – Exposition Boulevard

"They'd – chew – you – to pieces."

The greyhounds didn't seem to mind LaStanza putting muzzles on them, then he realized they wore muzzles when they raced. They bounced in place, knowing what was coming, he guessed.

"How long will you be gone?" Lizette asked, standing in the foyer in the long tee-shirt she'd slept in, her arms folded, smiling as her boys were going for their first jaunt through Audubon Park.

"Huh?"

"How long will you be gone?"

"We'll be gone the whole time."

She blinked, then smiled. About time he got her with one.

The spotted one went, "Woof." And the tan one gave LaStanza two impatient woofs.

He opened the door and the dogs raced out into the fenced yard. As they sniffed around, depositing pee, defecating at different corners of the yard, LaStanza went through his stretching routine, today wearing a black tee-shirt with POLICE in white in front, gray jogging shorts and black Nikes.

Soon as he opened the gate the greyhounds bounded through it and raced for the lagoon and he wondered if they'd ever stop. They turned in either direction, the tan one running toward St. Charles Avenue, the spotted one racing toward Magazine Street and for a sickening minute he thought he'd never see them again.

Looking back and forth at each of the dogs as he jogged to the road next to the lagoon, he lost site of the tan one, but watched the spotted one do a long loop and come running back toward him at breakneck speed, passing two bicyclers who accelerated to keep up. The greyhound ran past LaStanza flat out.

"Hey," he called out and the dog turned on a dime and came running back up to him.

"He's fast," said the male cyclist as he slowed down.

"What's his name?" the woman cyclist asked with a smile as she went by.

"Flash," LaStanza said, patting the greyhound on the head. The dog was barely panting. They both loped up toward St. Charles and found the tan one waiting for them. LaStanza watched the dogs play tag along the front of the park and race up to every jogger to sniff.

When they reached a baby carriage, this one with a toddler sitting up in it, Flash ran up and LaStanza heard a squeal of delight from the baby. Its mother wasn't so amused and LaStanza had to run harder to get there to mollify her.

"He's just sniffing."

"He's too big to be off a leash." She was a thin woman with a shrill voice.

"He's muzzled, lady."

She noticed the emblem on his shirt and pulled her baby away.

"Come on, Flash." LaStanza continued his running, struggling when they turned parallel to Magazine. He slowed. No way he could keep up with greyhounds.

Several black boys tried to keep up with the dogs who bobbed and weaved through them, then turned back when the boys fell behind. As LaStanza passed the boys who were trying to catch their breath, one called out, "Those your dogs, mister?"

"Yep."

"They sure are cool."

"They greyhounds, right?" Another asked.

LaStanza nodded.

"Why they got muzzles?"

Gasping, LaStanza managed to say, "They'd – chew – you – to pieces."

The boys liked that and tried to catch up, but in their bulky jeans and sandals, they couldn't keep up with LaStanza, much less the greyhounds.

As soon as LaStanza turned away from the lagoon for his gate, the dogs turned and went straight into the yard to pee some more and wait for him. Pretty intelligent, he had to admit. He made sure to lock the gate when he went in.

Lizette came out with two cups of coffee. She was in another white polo shirt, red miniskirt and red sandals. He had to beg off the coffee for a minute to catch his breath.

"You name them yet?"

He nodded.

"Don't name them something stupid or gross."

"Gross?"

"Like your friend Stan Smith who named his son Shank, because he has one."

LaStanza pointed to the spotted one and said, "He's Flash." He pointed to the tan one. "And he's Thompson."

"Flash and Thompson?"

"I think Flash is faster and the other one looks like a Thompson."

Lizette gave him a knowing smile. "Flash Thompson was the bully who picked on Peter Parker in high school. I read some of your Spider-Man comics."

LaStanza didn't know why he was surprised. She had a mind like a steel trap that snared more information than any computer. And she had no trouble accessing the information. He sat on the top step and she sat next to him and they sipped coffee while Flash and Thompson continued to investigate their front yard.

"I unplugged the phones, hid your beeper," she said, "and took the battery off your police radio."

"Excellent."

"Just you and me and Flash and Thompson on a Sunday." She ran her fingers across the small scar on his neck but pulled it away immediately, dripping with his perspiration.

She stood. "You need a shower and I need a towel."

Flash and Thompson followed them in and LaStanza took off the muzzles and the boys headed for the water dishes and food bowls in the kitchen.

1:20 p.m. – Bay St. Louis

"– if we can go sit by the water."

The main street of the little harbor town was lined with seafood restaurants along the bay side of the street and antiques stores, hand-made jewelry shops, clothing shops and used bookstores on the other side.

Kelly, in a light blue pull over, faded jeans and brown sandals, picked up a three-foot model of a sailboat, shrugged and rolled his eyes at Jodie, who wore a short beige sundress and white sandals. She shook her head.

They weren't looking for anything in particular, had already been through a dozen shops. Moving together, Kelly took her hand and opened the door. The warm bay breeze flowed over them.

"Let's go over there." Jodie pointed to a sandy beach between two of the restaurants where she could see wooden benches overlooking the bay.

"In here first." Kelly pulled her to a small wooden building with Aleta's Jewelry in a white sign outside. She shrugged and went along but wasn't interested in much inside, until Kelly picked up a silver pin and said he wanted to get it for her.

He leaned over and whispered in her ear. "To remember this trip." It was a silver seagull with white semi-precious stones as wings. It was small, at least and Jodie checked the price tag, glad it wasn't too expensive.

"OK," she said, "if we can go sit by the water."

They crossed the narrow main street and found a bench without bird droppings on it and sat. They held hands and watched sailboats glide by on the dark water.

"Where's Bobbie's?" Jodie shielded her eyes from the sun.

He pointed across the bay. "Can't see it beyond the dock, but it's there. Can't see Aunt Marian's either surrounded by all those trees."

She put her head on his shoulder and he put his arm around her and they sat there for an hour at least, just sat there. Later, they took off their shoes and walked along the sandy beach. The breeze picked up, lifting Jodie's dress. She didn't bother with it until it blew up over her waist. She brushed it down and looked around but no one was watching.

They found a patch of grass and sat facing the bay. Leaning back on their hands, feet extended, they remained there. When Jodie looked at Kelly, his eyes were closed, his breathing even. She studied his face in profile, wind lifting his hair in gusts. He was a very handsome man, even more handsome when he opened those eyes, always filled with kindness, or when he gave her one of those mischievous pirate smiles. Finally, they stood and moved back to Kelly's Jeep, re-crossed the bay for Aunt Marian's. They had to turn in the key but only after another tryst in their room.

Supper at Bobbie's would be followed by the two hour return trip to the land of constant murder – New Orleans.

5:15 p.m. – Josephine Street

"I don't see us going much further with this."

Wanda Summers sat up in her bed, brushed her tawny hair from her face and lit a cigarette. Fel Jones, catching his breath as he lay next to her, waved his hand to shove away the smoke, got up and went to the bathroom. When he returned he sat at the foot of the bed and watched Wanda who wouldn't look back.

He watched her full, sensual lips wrap around the cigarette as she inhaled. They'd kicked the sheets off the bed, so she sat there nude, full breasts with her nipples still pointy, pubic mound still damp from their lovemaking.

She blew out another cloud of smoke and announced, "I don't see us going much further with this."

He'd been expecting it, but not right after making love, not right after her calling him God, or whatever. He'd been expecting it, but it still felt like a stab in his heart. He looked down at his pants on the floor and reached for his black jockeys.

"It was nice while it lasted," Wanda said.

He didn't want to hear any more, standing as he pulled up his jockeys.

"We're not incompatible. Our lives are, however." She looked at him and he blinked back at her eyes and shook his head.

She took another deep drag on her cigarette. "Don't blame me." Her voice deeper now, harsher. "And I don't blame you. I blame your job."

He pulled up his pants, zipped and snapped them, fastened the belt. He stuffed his socks in his pockets and slid his feet into his penny loafers, then reached for his shirt and gun.

"I don't see why you couldn't leave that in the car." She pointed her chin at the gun.

"You won't have to worry about it anymore." He pulled on his shirt and quickly buttoned it.

"That all you got to say?"

226

He finished buttoning the shirt and sat back down on the edge of the bed. "You really want to talk about it? I don't see that doin' much good. I'm a detective. That's *all* I am."

"And *that's* your problem!" She stabbed at him with the cigarette. "You're a man first and a cop second."

His head sank until his chin touched his chest. Of course he was a man first, of course he lived a fucked-up existence. He and LaStanza had talked about it so many times, even when they were partners as patrolmen.

Then one day, LaStanza said, "I may live in a fucked up world. Then again, there's Lizette."

Fel thought he'd found something like that with Wanda. It wasn't the first time he'd been wrong. He stood up and shoved his gun into his belt behind his back.

"I really don't want you to call me anymore." She sounded sad now.

"I won't," he answered softly.

"I mean it."

"Me too." And he left.

5:25 p.m. – Milan Street

"– ya' missed a good time at the old marina yesterday."

Jodie found three messages on her answering machine.

Saturday, 9:21 a.m. "It's Mason. Get me on the radio when you get home."

Saturday, 4:16 p.m. "It's Mason again. Disregard my last message. See ya' Monday."

Sunday, 10:09 a.m. "Doc here, Lil' Filly. Just wanted to tell ya' that ya' missed a good time at the old marina yesterday."

She scooped up her phone to call Mason, hesitated and called her partner instead. It rang but there was no answer and LaStanza's answering machine didn't click on. She'd try him later. The last thing she wanted to do was get on the LFR. An hour and nine unanswered phone calls later, Jodie put on jeans and a white-tee shirt and climbed into her Saturn and drove to LaStanza's.

"I'll get a sandwich for supper on my way home," she said aloud. Any excuse to tool around in her Saturn that still had that new car smell inside.

6:40 p.m. – Exposition Boulevard

"More than once, right?"

Lights were on in the mansion as Jodie parked the Saturn against the curb at the dead-end of Garfield Street. She went up the back steps to the kitchen door and through the window saw LaStanza by the sink. She tapped on the door and he opened it. He was in a tan tee-shirt and black shorts, no shoes.

"You just got back home?"

"No."

"What's wrong with your phone?"

He laughed as he realized, "We unplugged it this morning." He opened the door for her to come in. "Tired of getting called out." He was suddenly serious. "You're not here on business?" She wasn't dressed for work.

"No. I've got a couple cryptic messages on my answering machine from Mason and a retarded one from Country-Ass. I didn't abandoned y'all to something bad did I?"

"No. You took a day off on your day off. You're the only smart one." He told her about the shooting at the marina. "We had *too many* cops."

He leveled those light green eyes at her and said, "So you and Kelly had a good time?"

"What makes you think we were together?"

"My badge has the word 'detective' on it." He could see he was right by the look in those hazel, cat eyes. She looked away but too late.

"We went to Mississippi."

Both turned as Flash came in and sat and stared at Jodie who was amazed at seeing a big dog in the kitchen.

Flash went, "Woof."

"When did you get a greyhound?"

The padding of more feet turned Jodie as Thompson came in and sat next to Flash and stared at her.

"Tell me there aren't any more."

Lizette answered from the dining room doorway, "There aren't any more."

Jodie put her purse up on the counter, stepped over to the dogs and petted each on the head. They stood, tails wagging and nuzzled her.

"Did you call Fong's yet?" Lizette to LaStanza.

"Yep." He had just hung up the phone from ordering Chinese delivery when Jodie tapped on the door.

"Good. Want some Chinese?" Lizette asked Jodie. "We always order the dinner for four and microwave the leftovers for days."

"Sure."

LaStanza headed out of the kitchen, turned and said, "Jodie and Kelly did it in Mississippi." He pointed a finger at Jodie. "More than once, right?"

Jodie eyes bulged.

He moved the finger to Lizette and said, "More than once. Y'all talk until the Chinese arrives but I don't wanna hear about it over supper."

Lizette stuck her tongue at him.

Monday, April 7, 1986

9:15 a.m. – Detective Bureau

"Watch out for Peter Parker and Matt Murdock."

As soon as everyone was settled with their coffees, Mason leaned against LaStanza's desk and said, "The Task Force is running papers this morning in Gentilly. They got a lead on their goddamn sniper."

Mason was in his typical black slacks, white shirt, narrow black tie, black penny loafers. Standing next to him, Mark also wore black pants and a white shirt, only his wife must have bought his tie that looked a little like a black and white Dali painting. He looked tired.

229

"For those of us who haven't paid attention, that's the fourth politician the South Louisiana Sniper has popped. Two more and he wins a free trip to Disneyworld." Mason paused to take a sip from his mug.

LaStanza looked around and no one even smiled.

"Hey! Mason just tried to tell a joke. Come on, a little laughter here." He laughed. No one else did. LaStanza wore a black suit that morning with a gray shirt and a black tie with white and gray overlapping ovals and new extra-comfortable black shoes Lizette found for him, soft leather shoes with rubber soles for running. How she could buy shoes that fit him perfectly was beyond him.

Mason continued his debriefing on the shooting at the marina. The FBI lab found the bullet. It has gone through Jacks' skull and landed on the next yacht.

"They are good," Fel said. He looked even more tired than Mark. Black pants again, white shirt, dark gray tie, his dark face looked almost pale.

LaStanza watched Jodie and Kelly as Mason went on about the marina. Jodie looked almost calm and not as stiff as usual in a pale green skirt-suit and black high heels. Kelly, in a dark blue suit, white shirt and pale green tie that almost matched Jodie's outfit, exchanged looks with Jodie as he stood on the far side of the group.

Glapier was the only one taking notes. LaStanza studied her face for a moment and she was so focused on the briefing, she didn't notice. She was a serious one and the way she went through her interviews in the high-rise showed LaStanza she was a very sharp cop, asking direct, pertinent questions. She'd need that if she wanted to stay in Homicide.

She could be abrasive, a little loud, confrontational, opinionated – a lot like him. When she glanced his way he lifted his cup to her and she gave him a quizzical look. He pointed to her note pad and gave her a thumbs up and she shook her head, a smile playing at the corner of her mouth as she refocused on Mason. She also wore black today, a black pants suit.

Mason was saying, " – and he's using a Mauser Model 68, 30-06 caliber. A hunting rifle."

He looked up from his notes but no one had a smart-assed remark so he went on. "I know I don't have to say this, but I want y'all to avoid them like the fuckin' plague. The Task Force tried to take Jodie away this morning, but I told them to fuck off. So they tried to take Fel." He shook his head. "He ain't goin' nowhere, either."

"G.F.T.," Fel said and LaStanza interpreted right away, "Good Fuckin' Thing."

"Damn, they got half the bureau, already" Mark snarled.

Mason nodded. "I tried to give them Snowood but nobody wants a Country-Ass."

Paul Snowood opened his arms in protest, a squirrelly look on his face. His black Stetson tilted back on his head, he wore a silver cowboy shirt with fringe, a black rope tie with a silver longhorn clasp and black denims, black cowboy boots.

"What about me?" Stevens asked. He was typically multi-colored, brown pants, yellow shirt, red tie.

"Nobody knows you work here," Mason answered. "You wanna go over there?"

"Hell no!"

Stevens looked around, his crooked eye finding LaStanza, "What about LaStanza?"

"They wanted anyone except him. They don't know about Kelly and Glapier so nobody tell them."

LaStanza turned in his chair and raised his hand to Fel for a high five.

Mason spent the next twenty minutes going over information he'd gleaned from the police computers about the license plates numbers, driver's license numbers of all the people in the canvasses of their Easter weekend murders, the Senoré, the Square and Walnut Street.

"Not one match." So no one car or person was at any two of the scenes, which was something, LaStanza guessed. Mason had more line-ups for him and leads for Jodie and Fel.

As Mason broke up the meeting, Snowood stepped up with a hurt look. "You really tried to give me away."

"Get outta here."

LaStanza headed for the police computer to run the names of the two skaters who'd missed at Friday's skate-a-thon. Lenny Evans, black male, twenty-two, who lived on General Ogden Street, had no criminal record, not even a traffic ticket. Dana Barret, white female, twenty-one of Monticello Street in Jefferson Parish, also had no criminal record or traffic offense. He confirmed their addresses then went back to his desk.

Jodie was at her desk and typing furiously on her computer.

"What's the lead?" he asked.

"Another man who danced with Helen Collingwood at a mixer. Convicted felon."

"For what?"

"Criminal damage to property."

"A vandalism *felon*?"

"He broke forty-two car windshields in a parking lot Mardi Gras Day when he was seventeen. Amounted to thousands of dollars in damage. A real desperado."

"You never know," LaStanza. "He may have used a tree trunk to break all those windshields."

"Peachy keeno," Jodie. "Just peachy keeno."

Peachy keeno? Jesus.

Fel was huddled with Kelly by his desk. LaStanza called out, "What's your lead?"

"Douche-bag in parish prison says he knows who did it. Even gave Mason a name. Name's got no record, not even a D.L. I'm taking Kelly with me. Show him where the bad boys live."

Glapier stepped behind Jodie who nodded and said they'd be off in a minute. Looking up from her typing, she asked LaStanza, "What're you doin'?"

"Two people to run down from the skate-a-thon and line-ups for my 'star witness'."

"Star witness?"

LaStanza told her about Evangelista.

"Thank God she quit Shoe Town," Glapier said.

Snowood called out, as if anyone was interested, "I haveta' leave early. Gotta pick up my cougar."

"You bought a new car?" Glapier asked, causing Jodie to cringe.

"No. Mountain lion. It's arriving this afternoon."

"You bought a mountain lion? I thought it was illegal to own one."

"Oh, it is. I found a mountain man, regular Jeremiah Johnson, in Wyoming. He's driving it down in a minivan. It's only a juvenile."

"But it's illegal," said Glapier as LaStanza hurriedly packed his briefcase.

"You gonna turn me into the feds?"

Jodie cut in with, "Quit talking to him. He's so dense, light bends around him."

Which prodded Snowood into another fact he'd probably learned from the history channel, "Didja' know a flea can jump 350 times its body length? Be like a human jumpin' the length of a football field. And elephants are the only animals that *can't* jump."

LaStanza got up to leave, passing Fel and Kelly who held up the morning paper and showed him a headline – *Plane too close to ground.*

"Wouldn't that be true on any plane crash?" Kelly said, then pointed to the lead line of the article and read, "Something went wrong in jet crash, panel says."

"OK." LaStanza paused. "Here's a lesson for you. Those who can't write become editors. Those who can't edit become publishers. Those who can do none of those things, go into journalism."

Kelly showed him another article – *Italian prostitutes appeal to pope.*

"There's hope for the old man after all."

Fel held up the sheet of paper with the lead Mason had given him and asked, "Does this name sound familiar? Cranston Lamont?"

LaStanza shrugged and turned away. It hit him after three steps and he called over his shoulder, "The guy's fuckin' with you."

"What? Cranston Lamont's an appetizer or means *no smoking* in Scottish or Welch?"

"No. Lamont Cranston was *The Shadow.* As in the old radio show."

"Son-of-a-bitch!"

Before he reached the door, LaStanza called back, "Watch out for Peter Parker and Matt Murdock."

"Who?"

"Spider-Man and Daredevil."

"Real fuckin' funny!"

Waiting for the police elevator, LaStanza couldn't stop wondering what the hell was going on with the name games. Vada Ganoush, Piso Mojado, Prohibito Fumar, Lamont Cranston. He looked at his notes, at the name Dana Barret and had a funny feeling about the name again.

1:10 p.m. – Oak Street

"Damn, why you still workin'?"

LaStanza was already sitting at the long table on the covered back porch of the Veranda Restaurant, taking in the spicy scents from the kitchen as Jodie and Glapier came in to sit across from him. Consuela followed them with menus for the women.

"Ciao, Consuela."

"I'm Lucy."

"You ever get it right?" Jodie.

"Nope."

Fel and Kelly came in, Kelly sitting next to Jodie, Fel coming around to LaStanza's side of the table, their backs to the back yard. Lucy carried in a tray with five glasses of water, lemon wedges on the lips of the glasses. She slipped menus in front of Fel, then Kelly on her way back into the kitchen.

As soon as Lucy stepped back in with two large bowls of chips and several smaller bowls of salsa, everyone ordered right away and began dipping chips into the hot salsa.

"So how was Lamont Cranston?" LaStanza to Fel.

"Jerk at parish prison was Sammy Smith. A real G.A.L.B. He said Cranston Lamont was my killer. He wanted a deal for a reduced sentence."

"What's he in for?"

"Burglary. Twenty-one burglaries. Been in jail three months."

"Damn."

Kelly and Jodie were whispering back and forth, Glapier trying not to notice.

"The guy's full-a-shit?"

"Completely." Fel took a long drink of water. "Guy's a freakin' comedian. I ask him his date of birth and he says July first, so I ask what year and he says every year."

Glapier asked, "What's a G.A.L.B?"

Fel and LaStanza answered together, "Goofy Ass Looking Bastard."

LaStanza asked Glapier. "Your lead any good?"

"Nope. The guy's a bank Vice-President. No vandal anymore. He just got back from three weeks in Vail, Colorado."

"What bank?"

"Hibernia, why?"

"Lizette's father owns three banks. That ain't one."

"He's a bank president?"

"No, he owns them and so does Lizette, parts of them anyway. She also owns parts of banks in Switzerland and Luxembourg."

"Damn, why you still workin'?"

"Good fuckin' question."

Jodie waited for a pause in the conversation to ask her partner, "What about your missing people from the skate-a-thon?"

LaStanza finished chewing a chip before, "Guy named Lenny Evans is a basketball player at Xavier. Got a full scholarship and still works part time at Kinko's on Carrollton to help raises three sisters, all in grammar school. No mom. No dad. Guy's almost seven feet tall. He'll be entering the NBA draft as soon as the season ends." LaStanza dipped another chip. "Eager to help, but knew nothing."

He dipped another chip then said, "Woman named Dana Barret wasn't home. Does that name sound familiar to any of you?"

Jodie shrugged, so did Kelly. Glapier shook her head.

"Sounds familiar," Fel said, reaching for a chip as Lucy arrived with everyone's lunch. LaStanza had his usual chicken burro, Spanish rice and refried beans.

As everyone settled in, LaStanza said, "Lizette told me a joke last night."

"You kiddin'?" Fel.

"Not bad, you wanna hear it? Kelly probably needs to hear it."

Kelly smiled and Jodie glared at LaStanza who told Lizette's joke.

"A man walking on a beach in California finds a lamp half buried in the sand, digs it up and rubs it and a genie pops out. Only this one angry genie, tired of all the three wishes, says, 'You get one wish, buddy, so make it good.'

"The man looks at the ocean and says, 'I always wanted to go to Australia, only I'm too scared to fly and I get sea sick in boats. So I want you to build me a bridge to Australia so I can drive there. That's my wish.'

"The genie points to the Pacific and says it's impossible. The logistics. 'Do you know how far Australia is? How would the supports ever reach the bottom of the ocean? Look how much concrete we're talkin' about and the steel.' So he tells the man he'd better come up with a different wish.

"The man sits in the sand and say, 'OK. I've been married a couple times and divorced, had a lotta girlfriends over the years. All of them said I didn't understand them. So my wish is that I could understand women, how they feel inside, what they're thinking, why they cry sometimes. I want to *really* understand women and make at least one happy.'

"The genie replied, 'You want that bridge two lanes or four'?"

Glapier spit out the water she was swallowing. Kelly slapped the table. Fel even laughed. Jodie crinkled her nose at LaStanza who reminded her, it was his wife's joke.

Jodie raised her right eyebrow, which she did when she was about to say something clever. "Know why it's so hard for women to find men who are sensitive, caring and good-looking?"

LaStanza and Fel both shrugged.

"Because they already have boyfriends."

"Aha," from Fel.

"Why do men have a hole in their penis?" Glapier asked and got no response. "So oxygen can reach their brains."

Jodie laughed, Kelly too. Poor guy sitting next to his new girlfriend. He was having trouble eating.

Glapier raised a soft taco. "Know why food's better than men?"

No takers.

"Because you don't have to wait an hour for seconds."

"Depends on the man," Jodie said and Kelly actually blushed.

Fel pointed his fork at Kelly. "You dog."

"Do you know why men have bigger brains than dogs?" – Glapier again.

"We have bigger brains than dogs?" – Fel.

"So they won't hump women's legs at cocktail parties."

"I tried that," Fel said. "It works on the right woman."

"Me too," said LaStanza.

The restaurant's owner came out and checked on them. "How is it?"

"Wonderful, Mama," LaStanza answered.

"Bené," Mama said in Italian which lit up LaStanza's eyes as a loud voice with a country accent echoed from inside.

LaStanza cringed.

"Who invited him?" Jodie said. They all turned to the doorway as Mama went back in. A huge man in a white Stetson came out with a nasty-looking red-head in a turquoise miniskirt and a chest bigger than Dolly Parton's.

"Howdy," the cowboy said, leading his hussy to a table out among the trees in the back yard.

Glapier leaned toward Fel and whispered, "Wanna try humpin' her leg?"

"Can you believe Snowood with a mountain lion?" LaStanza said.

"How are your greyhounds?" Jodie asked so LaStanza had to explain about Flash and Thompson, keeping it brief.

"Kinda big ain't they? You ain't got a back yard," Fel said, "and not much of a front yard."

"Just Audubon Park."

"Good point."

"Where are S and S, anyway?" Fel asked.

"They're with Mark over on Dublin Street," Kelly said.

Starvation case.

LaStanza felt the acid in his stomach.

2:40 p.m. – Magazine Street

"So was Carmen Miranda."

Musica Botafuego occupied the first floor of a three story wooden building, sandwiched in a long line of store fronts along Magazine Street, just down from the Second District Police station by Napoleon Avenue. Painted a bright yellow, posters covered its picture windows. Loud latin music reverberated as LaStanza and Fel stepped in.

Evangelista Luz saw them immediately, reached over and turned the music down. She wore more make-up at her new job and was in a red minidress, stockings and red high heels. She looked very nice and smiled broadly at them. Two teen-aged boys, who were eyeing her from a rack of audio cassettes, tried to act casual as she bounded out to LaStanza and did a twirl, her dress rising high.

She lifted the front of the dress to show LaStanza.

"It's a white danskin," She said, showing the danskin covering her pantyhose. She nodded toward the boys and lowered her voice, "They think it's underwear." She leaned closer. "I been *seeing* a lotta records."

LaStanza introduced Fel and Evangelista asked about Beau.

"Told you, he doesn't work with us."

"I saw him yesterday." She smiled even wider. "He was comin' outta the district across the street." She patted Fel on the shoulder. "Beau's a dreamboat. Not that you guys are bad. He's just younger."

Christ. LaStanza dug the photo line-ups out of his jacket and laid them out, one at a time, seven pictures in each set. "Let me know if you recognize any anyone."

Evangelista examined the photos carefully, shaking her head and LaStanza could smell her perfume now, strong but not too strong. Four more teen-aged boys came in with two teen-aged girls.

"You have 'La Bamba'?" Fel asked.

"Huh?" Evangelista looked up.

"Ritchie Valens."

Evangelista gave him a strange look. Fel moved to a rack of tapes.

When Evangelista finished with the line-ups, LaStanza asked for the music store's phone number.

"You're still living at the same place?"

"Sure."

He gave her a serious look. "You stopped telling everyone you're a star witness, right?"

She stood up straight and saluted. "Si, señor."

"Good." LaStanza picked up the line-ups. "I'll be back."

"I know. We gonna catch 'em."

"What does Botafuego mean?" LaStanza.

"Hothead."

LaStanza smiled and told her to be careful. Fel followed him to the door, asking Evangelista if they had any Santana.

She shook her head. "Everything we got is in Spanish."

"He's Spanish."

"So was Carmen Miranda," LaStanza injected

"Who?" Evangelista.

God, LaStanza felt old.

3:40 p.m. – Exposition Boulevard

"We're holding your father ..."

LaStanza wedged a business card in Dana Barret's door, just above the dead bolt. He'd written on the back of the card for her to please call, then went home early.

Flash met him in the kitchen, followed quickly by Thompson and a pale Lizette who said, "Your mother just called. Your father's in jail."

The dogs nuzzled him for attention.

"In jail, where?" LaStanza plopped his briefcase atop the kitchen counter. Lizette said she wasn't sure.

Flash put his paws up on the counter and nuzzled the briefcase.

LaStanza scooped up the phone and punched in his mother's number. She answered immediately in that low, sad voice.

"He left a number," she said. It was a 455 exchange number. Metairie.

After he made sure his mom was all right, LaStanza called the number. It was the Jefferson Parish Sheriff's Office East Bank Lockup. The desk sergeant seemed to be expecting his call and put him through to a Deputy Foto.

"Is this Detective LaStanza?"

"Yes."

"We're holding your father ..." Foto's voice dropped away.

"Is he OK?"

"Yes. But he's been drinking and ran his Lincoln into a dumpster outside a barroom and insisted on driving it off, but it was too wrecked."

"What's he booked with?"

"I don't want to arrest a retired police captain, unless I have to. Can you come get him?"

"I'll be right here."

Foto gave him the address, "3300 Metairie Road but you can reach us off Airline Highway."

"I know. I'll be right there."

Lizette asked, "Is he OK?" She was bent over a rollicking Thompson rubbing his belly as he lay on the floor, paws flailing. In her minidress, the cheeks of her white panties were pointing at LaStanza. If that's what she wore to teach today, he wondered if any of the students were hanging around outside.

"Wait," Lizette said as he headed for he door with his LFR. "Don't you want to see the Land Rover?"

She hurried to the garage with him and he took a quick look at the British racing green Land Rover, which had tan trimming and a tan leather interior. He had to admit, it looked great and told Lizette.

Kissing her, he said, "I gotta go."

"OK."

He pulled out in his Maserati, leaving her behind the wheel of her Land Rover. She looked like a kid in her parents' car.

4.25 p.m. – Metairie Road

"Not drunk, huh?"

The traffic was heavy on Airline, but LaStanza zipped his way through it leaving the cars like they were parked. An Italian sports car had its advantages. Approaching the Causeway underpass, LaStanza gunned the Maserati past a state police car driven by a trooper who must have been catatonic or on his way to lunch because he didn't pursue. LaStanza had to brake hard to not miss the narrow turn in to the rear parking lot of the East Bank Lockup.

Deputy Foto was shorter than LaStanza, even shorter than Lizette who stood five-two and-a-half. She always claimed the and-a-half. Foto had thinning brown hair combed down in front and looked like a used chariot salesman, but was a rather serious cop.

"I have to write him a ticket, but I didn't run a breath-a-lizer test, so you can just take him with you."

Foto was cutting them so much slack, LaStanza thanked him more than once. When his father refused to sign the ticket, LaStanza had to ask Foto for another favor.

"Can you leave us alone a minute?"

Seated in an interview room even smaller than the ones in the Detective Bureau, Captain LaStanza didn't bother looking his son in the eye, sitting back with his arms folded. He wore a yellow polo shirt and black and brown plaid pants.

LaStanza asked him, "What's the matter with you?"

Captain LaStanza puffed out his chest, "What do you mean?"

"It's a traffic ticket. Sign it or they'll have to book you. You know that."

His father leaned both hands on the tiny table and looked into his son's eyes. "I'm not drunk." His breath could be lit by a match.

"It's a ticket for careless operation. They don't even take your license out here when you get a ticket."

"Oh." The captain stood up, a little wobbly and waved his hand. "In that case." He went around the table quickly, reached for the door, missed the handle and ran his face into the door frame.

"Not drunk, huh?" LaStanza opened the door and led his father to a desk next to Foto and watched him sign the ticket.

"We towed in the Lincoln," Foto said.

"We'll send for it." LaStanza thanked him again, gave him his business card and shook his hand. Captain LaStanza was at the Lock-up door trying to get it open. He hurried over.

"What the hell car is this?" his father said, standing next to the Maserati.

"Get in, Pop."

The old man's belly was so big the polo shirt barely covered it. He was probably still trying to wear a 'large'. He climbed in, which took some effort, until LaStanza reached in and moved the seat back.

"All right," the captain waved him back in. "Let's go."

The old man didn't say anything until they were on Bienville Street, heading for North Bernadotte.

"Where you takin' me?"

"Home."

The old man looked at his watch. "Drop me off at the watering hole. Gotta meet some people." He ran his fingers through his unruly mop of gray hair, as if that did any good.

When LaStanza turned on North Bernadotte, driving past his father's watering hole – Cella's Bar – the old man pointed at the bar and said, "You just missed it."

5:55 p.m. – North Bernadotte Street

"You're a lucky man, Dino."

LaStanza drove up to the house, parking in front of the two story, stucco where he was raised. He got out and glanced over at the dark oaks of City Park a block away, then went around to let his father out, who was having trouble locating the handle.

He helped his father up the steps where his mother waited in the open doorway. She took her husband inside and told him she'd just drawn a hot bath. His parents went into the back of the house and LaStanza closed the door and plopped down on the sofa. He closed his eyes and took in the familiar smells of home. Clean, it smelled clean. It always smelled clean even after his mother cooked. He could never figure how she did that.

Virginia LaStanza was a housewife, stayed home, took care of things, raised her sons, while Anthony LaStanza went out to play police. She was gray now, hair up in a bun, looking smaller each year, but her light green eyes were clear and bright. She was a lot smarter than his father gave her credit for, smart enough to catch LaStanza and his big brother Joe every time they pulled something and they pulled a lot of stunts.

For a moment, he felt that familiar heartache when he thought of Joe. Funny how most of the time he remembered Joe as a teenager, the mischievous boy with a devilish glint in his eyes. When Joe visited him in his dreams, he was always a teen, rarely the police sergeant who was gunned down in the line of duty.

LaStanza had said it so many times. He was happiest in his life during those long summers of his childhood when the world, City Park in particular, was a big playground for him and his big brother. Now, in his thirties he no longer felt that way because of Lizette.

The doorbell rang. It took him a second to recognize another retired cop, Fred Jersey in his own tight-fitting polo shirt and green plaid pants.

"Your father all right?"

LaStanza let him in, shaking his hand asking, "What's with the plaid pants?"

Jersey shrugged and said everyone at the watering hole was worried.

"He's OK. He's taking a bath."

"About time." Jersey seemed to lighten up, turning back to LaStanza with, "You're a lucky man, Dino."

"Because my father's an alcoholic?" He could smell beer on Jersey breath from twelve feet away.

"No, your wife."

"My wife?"

"I met her the other day outside a bookstore with your father."

LaStanza remembered Lizette told him. He still didn't remember any greyhound conversation, but he remembered the bookstore story.

"She's quite a gal," Jersey said with a smirk.

"I know."

"Tell her I said, 'Hello'."

His mother peeked in from the kitchen a few minutes later and said, "Coffee, son." She noticed Jersey and nodded to him.

They went in and joined his mother for coffee at the kitchen table. It was an antique, dark brown wood, shiny with furniture polish. His mother look worn out. LaStanza asked if she was OK. Sitting up straight, she looked him in the eye and said, "Of course. How bad is the car?"

"They had to tow it in."

"Give me the number and I'll have it towed to your Uncle Sammy's."

"I'll have it towed," he told her. Her brother Sammy had a garage, a converted filling station, where he worked on cars. Good body man with a car, good mechanic as well. Bad temper. Typical Sicilian.

She'd mixed his coffee perfectly and it was good. Jersey didn't touch his, probably longing for that next beer. He finally got up and said, "Well, I'm glad he's OK. I'll let myself out." And he did.

As soon as they heard the front door close, LaStanza's mother said, "Your father's not an alcoholic. He deserves to let loose after all the years he put in working." She was using that stern voice she'd used all of his life.

He shook his head.

"Thank you for going to get him. But I'll take it from here."

"Don't file an insurance claim on the car."

"Why not?"

"I'll pay for it."

"Why should you?"

LaStanza smiled, got up and went around and kissed her cheek. Then gave her a big hug, which made her shoo him away. He gave her his father's driver's license before leaving.

"You should hide it," he said.

"He'd just drive without it."

7:05 p.m. – Exposition Boulevard

"Don't start anything you're not gonna finish, mister."

Lizette sat on front porch swing while Flash and Thompson played tag in the front yard. In the setting sunlight, Audubon Park was golden as LaStanza sat next to his wife.

"Everything all right?" she asked.

"Just peachy keeno."

"What?"

"That's a Jodieism."

Lizette, now in a white tee-shirt and yellow shorts, no shoes, leaned her head against his shoulder. He put his arm around her. Flash noticed him and led the charge up the steps. Two cold noses pressed against LaStanza's arms, dog breath panting at him until he petted both.

Just was suddenly, the greyhounds raced off.

A siren echoed along St. Charles Avenue.

"Fred Jersey says, 'Hello'."

"Who?"

"He met you with my father at the bookstore."

"Oh." Lizette felt her heartbeat raising and felt silly. Her husband had seen her prance around naked in front of strangers. Only, this involved his father. She closed her eyes and blew it off. It was just her panties.

LaStanza's hand found her right breasts and he kneaded it.

"Don't start anything you're not gonna finish, mister."

He started unbuckling his belt and she laughed and led him back inside, having to call three times for the unruly youngsters. Flash and Thompson finally came bounding inside.

"Can we lock them out of the bedroom?" LaStanza asked.

"Why? We're doing it on top of the cherry wood table."

She wasn't kidding.

He managed to shut the dogs out, closing both doors and turning off the lights before Lizette stripped, standing naked next to the table, hand on her hips. He could barely see her in the darkness, but he found her.

7:10 p.m. – Milan Street

"I was just trying to make you feel better."

Jodie fought her nerves as she picked Kelly up to drive him back to her house for dinner with her parents. He was in a pale blue linen shirt and navy slacks. She was in a yellow sundress, longer than the one she wore in Mississippi.

As she tooled the Saturn down to Magazine Street, Kelly reached around to touch the back of her neck.

"You OK?" he asked.

She chuckled. "Twenty-seven, you'd think I wouldn't be nervous bringing you and my parents together."

He laughed.

She'd warned Kelly about her parents, them being prototypical protestants.

"I was raised Lutheran," Kelly said.

"You're Irish Catholic."

"I was just trying to make you feel better."

She slapped his leg. "My parent's view of Protestantism is derived from the haunting fear that someone, somewhere may be having a good time."

She turned up Milan Street and pulled into her driveway. Getting out, she took Kelly to her side of the double.

"I have to change shoes," she said. Darn new heels were already hurting her feet. Shane and Cody came running into the living room, skidded to a halt, jumped up and turned in mid-air and ran out as soon as they saw Kelly.

"What'd I do?"

"Nothing. They're retarded."

The cats peeked back in at Kelly when Jodie came back from her bedroom in a different pair of shoes.

Cody mewed, so she pet him twice. Shane cried so she gave him a pet too, before moving back to Kelly. As she locked her door, both cats stuck their heads through the Venetian blinds to blink out at them. Kelly waved.

She stepped over to the door of her parents' side of the double and reached for the handle.

"Your father doesn't look like Thor, does he? One of those big Viking-looking guys."

"We're Scottish, not Norwegian."

"That eases my mind. I know all about that wall the Romans built to keep the Scots out when their conquered England. Your ancestors were so fierce the Romans didn't want any part of them and the Romans conquered the world."

Jodie led the way inside where her parents stood at attention in the living room, both with stiff faces, stiff backs, piercing gazes and for a moment Jodie thought of the bed at Aunt Marian's and the noises she and Kelly made there.

She smiled and introduced her boyfriend.

7:40 p.m. – Philip Street

"Here's to you, Lady."

Fel Jones lived in one half of a shotgun house and like Jodie, his parents occupied the other half of the house at the corner of Philip and Baronne Streets. Painted pale green, the house was actually in the Garden District, although its small front yard was no garden, just grass.

Sitting at his kitchen table, a half-finished bottle of Budweiser next to the scattered notes from his Uptown Square case, he tried his best to quit thinking about Wanda. Maybe he should go out. Find a little action.

No, he thought. Then thought – *I must be getting old.*

He looked over at his address book. Plenty of phone numbers there. But the more he thought about it, the more he realized those were mostly rejects, rejected for a reason, or more than one reason. He took a hit of beer and picked up the recent picture of his victim that he parents were kind enough to loan him. He stared into the dark brown eyes of Monique Williams, skin as smooth as velvet, lovely face surrounded by reddish-brown hair. She had full lips, like Wanda, but her eyes were much kinder.

He felt that link again, that connection with his victim, that emotional bond between the detective and someone he never met until their death. Her parents loved her dearly and would miss her forever, friends mourn her, people were affected by her loss, but he was all she had left, all the vengeance that was left for her short life.

Monique Williams lived twenty-two years.

Felicity Jones would take as many years as needed to catch the bastard who killed her. He dreamed of shooting the bastard, putting two semi-jacketed hollow point rounds in the head. He raised his beer to her picture, wondering if she had been as sweet as her eyes, or bitchy like Wanda. He decided she was sweet.

"Here's to you, Lady." He drained his beer, put Monique's picture down and went to his refrigerator for a fresh beer.

Tuesday, April 8, 1986

6:22 a.m. – Monticello Street

"I think he was trying to break into a car. Praise Jesus."

Hoping to catch Dana Barret before she left home, LaStanza parked the Maserati just as a light came on in back of her apartment. He waited a few minutes, sipping coffee from a travel mug, before going up to the door and ringing the doorbell.

The curtain on the window next to the door moved and the head of a black cat looked out at him. It had yellow eyes, its nose pressed against the glass.

"Who is it?" a female voice beyond the door.

LaStanza held up his credential so she could see through the peep hole and identified himself. He took two steps back to not crowd her.

"What do you want?"

"I want to talk with you if you're Dana Barret."

The click of the dead-bolt was followed by the door opening slightly. A brown eye on a pale face peeked out at LaStanza from behind a chain lock. She was about Lizette's height.

"Sorry to drop by so early, but I left my business card on your door yesterday and I'd like to talk to you about something that happened near Skate Town over on Claiborne Avenue."

"Skate Town? Praise Jesus."

"Yes. There was a robbery at Shoe Town and a man was killed."

The brown blinked three times before she said, "I have an early class this morning. I attend U.N.O. Praise Jesus."

"This won't take long."

"I can't miss classes. I've two tests this morning. Praise Jesus."

"When will you be free?" He tried his best smile.

"Twelve-thirty. But I'll have to wait for my friend's classes to end. I ride with a friend. Praise Jesus." A phone rang behind her and she seemed to panic.

"Go answer it."

She nodded, closed the door. The dead-bolt clicked. LaStanza smiled. Nothing wrong with being careful.

The dead-bolt clicked two minutes later and the eye seemed troubled. "My ride's not coming so I have to hurry to catch the bus. Praise Jesus."

"I'll drive you U.N.O., Miss Barret. After your classes, I'll pick you up and drive you home."

He opened his light gray suits coat and showed her his badge and held up his credentials again for her to get a better look. When he withdrew them, she asked, "Is that your car?" She nodded toward the Maserati.

"Yes, ma'am."

She nodded slowly and closed the door, setting the dead-bolt again. LaStanza went back to the Maserati, sat behind the wheel with the driver's door open and drank his coffee.

He watched a few people leaving for work down the street. When a marked Jefferson Parish sheriff's car turned up Monticello from Jefferson Highway, he knew it was looking for him. He stepped out, went around to the front of the Maserati and leaned against it, his arms folded.

The Jefferson deputy looked young. He parked right in front of LaStanza and opened his door, stepped out, keeping the door between him and LaStanza and said, "You the man says he's a cop?"

LaStanza opened his coat to show his badge. "NOPD." He carefully pulled out his ID folder and showed the cop his credentials.

"That your car?"

"My wife's. She's rich."

The deputy's name tag read: Herion. He came over and took a closer look at the credentials, still seeming skeptical.

"Lady called. Said a man impersonating a cop was at her door."

"I'm going to get my radio." LaStanza went around to the opened door and reached in for his LFR sitting up on the dash.

"3124 – Headquarters."

"Go ahead 3124."

"Call J.P.S.O. headquarters. East Bank. And identity me to them. I'm on Monticello Street in Metairie with a Deputy Herion."

"10-4."

Less than a minute later Herion responded to his headquarters, "This is JP 108 – Go ahead."

"That's an NOPD Homicide Detective."

"10-4."

Herion apologized.

"Nothing to apologize for. Could you go tell her I'm a real cop?" LaStanza nodded to Barret's apartment. Herion went to the door. LaStanza stayed by his car, sipping more coffee. It took a couple minutes.

Herion came back shaking his head.

"I think she stores nuts for the winter."

"Squirrelly?"

"As a rodent." Herion stretched and yawned. "I'm tired of explaining my name isn't Heroin."

LaStanza thanked him as the deputy moved away. Herion called back, "Watch out for the 'Praise Jesuses'?"

"I know."

Dana Barret was a petite woman with ash blonde hair, pretty, and delicate looking. She wore a short-sleeved blue blouse and denim skirt, brown sandals and carried a green bag over her shoulder.

"Let me help you with that?"

She seemed reluctant to hand her bag over, but did. LaStanza put it on the back seat, went around to hold open the front passenger door for her. She climbed in, carefully pushing her skirt down when it rose above her knees.

"I'm sorry I called the sheriff's office on you. Praise Jesus," she said when he climbed in.

"No, problem. Nothing wrong with being careful."

She wore a light perfume and sat with her hands on her knees. As they pulled away she said, "Didn't know cops drove sports cars. Praise Jesus. And you don't look like a cop. Praise Jesus."

"What do I look like?"

"An Italian gangster. If you're Hispanic, I apologize. Praise Jesus."

No apology if he was Italian.

He went through the usual spiel about a rich wife and turned down Jefferson Highway which became Claiborne Avenue a few seconds later as they slipped into Orleans Parish.

"I saw that movie on TV about Ted Bundy. Praise Jesus. The one with Mark Harmon. He pretended to be a cop but didn't drive a police car. Praise Jesus."

"A Volkswagen. Did you hear about the robbery and murder I mentioned? It was Friday before last, around eight p.m."

She thought about it a moment and said, "I left early, around seven. Praise Jesus. I had to take the bus home. Praise Jesus."

That's why her name and Lenny Evans' name weren't on the list Left Sider had compiled the night of the Senoré's murder. Lenny had left early also.

Dana Barret saw nothing out of the ordinary around Skate Town that evening and didn't even know about the killing. LaStanza handed her a flyer. She took a long look at it, shaking her head, then handed it back.

"Keep it. Something may come to mind."

Something did, but not until LaStanza had turned up Elysian Fields. She had taken the flyer back six blocks earlier. She looked at it again.

"This one looks like a boy I went to school with. Praise Jesus. He was a few years ahead of me. Praise Jesus."

LaStanza waited but when she didn't volunteer the name, he asked.

"Jazz Boykin. I think his real name was Jasper. Praise Jesus."

"What does he look like?"

"Tall. Over six feet. And skinny. Praise Jesus."

"Dark complected?"

She nodded, running her finger over the flyer.

"What about the other face?"

"Jazz had a little brother. Praise Jesus."

"When was the last time you saw Jazz Boykin?"

"Praise Jesus. About a month ago. I think he was trying to break into a car. Praise Jesus."

LaStanza felt the hair standing on the back of his neck.

"Where?"

"Behind the K&B next to Skate Town. Praise Jesus. In the parking lot. He saw me and stopped and acted real friendly. Praise Jesus."

Fuckin 'A. Praise Jesus.

"What did he say?"

"He made a joke. Praise Jesus. Said he was looking for his keys. He looked all strung out. Praise Jesus."

"You sure it was Jasper Boykin?"

"Of course. Praise Jesus."

LaStanza turned off Elysian Fields into the university grounds, following Barret's directions to the Liberal Arts Building.

"Why kind of car was it? You remember the color?"

"It was dark, blue or green. Praise Jesus. Not a compact and not a new car. Praise Jesus." She pointed to a long brick building, telling him that's it.

"I'll pick you up here at twelve-thirty?"

She nodded as she climbed out, reaching into the back for her books.

"Thank you for the ride. Praise Jesus." And she walked off leaving LaStanza with goose bumps.

Just like a fuckin' criminal to try to steal a car, then come back later to stick up a store. He called ahead and found Glapier already at the Bureau. He asked her to check to see if any cars were stolen from the area of Claiborne and Carrollton over the last month.

8:15 p.m. – Detective Bureau

"Why is there a razorback head on Snowood's desk?"

There was the head of a razorback on Snowood's desk. Glapier was standing next to it, looking at the mounted head as if it had just beamed down from an alien world. She wore gray pants suit, the same color as LaStanza's suit.

She turned to LaStanza as he put his briefcase on his desk and laughed. "I thought I'd seen everything up here."

LaStanza couldn't think of a smart remark, so he turned on his Macintosh and asked Glapier if she'd come up with any stolen cars. She handed him a computer print out with three stolen vehicles: a 1982 red Toyota Carolla, a 1980 green Ford pickup truck and a 1977 Olds Cutlass – blue in color. The Olds was stolen on Friday, March 14, 1986, between nine and eleven p.m. from the parking lot behind the K&B drug store, corner of Claiborne and Carrollton and had never been recovered.

LaStanza went to the police computer and the goose bumps came back as the dot-matrix printer spitted out the arrest records of Jasper Boykin and his nineteen-year-old brother Telrey Boykin, both listing their residence as 2932 Hollygrove Street, right up against Jefferson Parish. No wonder the Boykins raided into J.P., like Vikings raiding the British Isles.

Glapier had come up behind him with her coffee mug. She peeked at the print out and said, "Bad guys."

"Stone fuckin' criminals."

In his twenty-five years of life, Jasper Boykin, Also-Known-As Jazz Boykin, AKA: J.B., AKA: June Bug, black male, twenty-five years old, was arrested seventeen times in all five parishes comprising greater New Orleans – Orleans, Jefferson, St. Bernard, St. Tammany and Plaquemines. His arrests included three simple battery charges, four theft arrests, two stolen car arrests, four simple robbery arrests, three armed robbery arrests and a peeping tom arrest. The armed robbery arrests were all in Plaquemines Parish.

He was convicted twice in Jefferson Parish, once for simple robbery, sentence suspended and once for armed robbery, which he was sentenced to ninety-nine years and served five.

Telrey Boykin, AKA: T.B., AKA: Tuber, black male, nineteen, was arrested twelve times in New Orleans and Jefferson Parish, eight simple battery arrests, one aggravated battery arrest, one theft rap and two armed robbery arrests. The armed robbery arrests were in Jefferson Parish. He was convicted of theft in New Orleans, sentence suspended and for simple robbery in J.P., reduced from an original armed robbery charge, sentenced to ten years, served two years.

The Boykin brothers had been released through the revolving-door at Angola State Penitentiary a month apart, January and February, 1986. Both were on probation, but neither had reported to their probation officer after their initial visit. Both were wanted men. Parole violators.

Asking Glapier to go to the record room for copies of their mug shots, LaStanza began the tedious work of getting printouts of every known criminal associate of the Boykin brothers, which numbered thirty-two. He'd needed to get their mugs too.

When Glapier returned with the mugs of the Boykins, the hair on the back of LaStanza's neck stood out, as well as the hair on his arms. The mugs were recent. The brother had been arrested together on March 5 for simple battery. They were in a bar fight.

"If they were probation violators, how'd they get out of jail March fifth?" Glapier asked.

"You got me." LaStanza picked up the phone and called parish prison, confirming the Boykins were not currently in custody, nor had been since March fifth.

He took the mugs back to his desk and laid them next to the original sketches of his killers.

"Looks like they posed for them," Glapier said.

"Exactly."

Mason came in and LaStanza waved him over.

"Jesus!" – Mason.

"Praise Jesus." – LaStanza.

"I've never seen a closer match," Mason admitted. "Like they posed for them."

Glapier grinned.

"Tell me how this came about," Mason said as Mark came in. LaStanza waved his sergeant over, waiting for his growl of approval after looking at the mugs, then told them about Dana Barret.

"I'm picking her back up at twelve-thirty. I'll get a statement. Then I'm going to see my 'star witness' with new line-ups."

"She still telling everyone she's your star witness?" – Mark.

"I hope fuckin' not."

"Why is there a razorback head on Snowood's desk?" – Mason snapped.

Mark shook his head. "He put in a bid for it from a dead guy's family. Apparently he got it."

LaStanza went back to his print outs, sending Glapier back to the record room for mugs of the thirty-two criminal associates of the wonderful Boykin brothers. Mason came in and said he'd checked with Jefferson, St. Bernard and Plaquemines to make sure the Boykins were not in jail nor had been on Good Friday. No need to explain the police computer wasn't always accurate.

Jodie, Kelly and Fel came in as Glapier was assembling the print outs and Mason was helping LaStanza put together line-ups of the Boykin brothers and associates. Thankfully, Glapier handled the inevitable questions as the detectives crowded around the mug shots and sketches as LaStanza typed his first memo on his Macintosh. He was finished so quickly, he figured he'd done something wrong until Jodie eased over and showed him how to print out the daily.

"It even corrected my typos." LaStanza nodded.

Jodie was in a black pants-suit. Kelly wore a black suit. Fel, at least wore gray like Glapier and LaStanza, who didn't know why he noticed such things, then remembered why. When he and Mark rode together, looking so much like brothers, he hated it when they wore the same color clothes, like their mother had dressed them.

When Snowood came in, Stevens trailing behind, Country-Ass boomed, "Yeah! I got it!" He jogged across the squad room, took off his gray Stetson with a flourish and kissed the mounted head on his desk.

"Well, hooka tooka ma' soda cracker!" Snowood beamed.

"The fuck kinda honky shit is that?" Fel said as he stepped up.

"Does your mama chaw tobbaca?"

"What!"

"Calm down," LaStanza told Fel. "It's from an old song."

Dammit. Now the song began to run through LaStanza's mind and he remembered how his brother, the first kid in the neighborhood to discover the Beatles, hated that damn song.

Snowood snatched up his coffee mug and headed for the pot.

Fel moved up to the desk and said, "I thought it belonged to a museum in Arizona."

Snowood called back, "The Tucson Native Mammal Museum went outta business six years ago."

Glapier asks LaStanza, "Why would he want a razorback head? It's hideous."

Fel said, "It's not a razorback. It's a javelin thing. It's on the plaque."

"A javelina," Kelly said.

Snowood returned. "It's a javelina or collared peccary, also known as a musk hog. It is the only wild, native, pig-like animal of the United States."

"What about 'dem pig-like things in the Calliope Projects?" Steven asked. LaStanza avoided looking at him in his yellow shirt, orange tie and green pants.

"You being racist, now." Glapier.

"No, the pigs are white. I'm serious. They gotta weigh three, four hundred pounds."

Snowood went on about javelinas being protected now, like buffaloes.

"If I had to eat things like this, I'd become a vegetarian." Glapier was needling him now.

Snowood took the bait. "Hell, I didn't fight my way up the food chain to eat celery. If we ain't supposed to eat animals, why are they made of meat?"

Completing his line-ups, LaStanza put the sketches away and cleared his desk. he asked Glapier if she'd come to U.N.O. with him.

"Sure."

Before they left for U.N.O., Fel Jones made the hair on LaStanza's arms stand out again when he said, "You know my killer was in a blue GM car, like and Olds."

"He was white, though."

"But the driver coulda been black. These Boykin ass-holes,

they got any white criminal associates?"

"They sure fuckin' do."

LaStanza sat back at his desk and went through his information with Fel.

Before leaving, he remembered to call a wrecker to pick up his father's Lincoln, then called the Jefferson Parish Courthouse, was forwarded to the First Parish Court and found out how much a ticket for careless operation cost and slipped a check into an envelope with his old man's ticket.

On their way to U.N.O., he dropped it at the post office.

12:25 p.m. – University of New Orleans

"We're the real police, mister."

As soon as LaStanza pulled up in the loading zone outside the Liberal Arts Building, a university police car pulled up behind the Maserati. LaStanza got out and stretched.

"You can't park here," the oversized university cop called out, head leaning out his car.

"We're not parked. We're waiting for someone." LaStanza turned so the fool could see his badge clipped to his belt and his revolver on his right hip. He'd left his coat hanging in the back seat.

The big cop got out and pulled up his uniform pants.

"You can't brings guns on campus."

"We're the real police, mister."

The cop gave him a mean stare, reach into his car and called someone on the radio. He seemed to get into an argument for a moment, climbed in and drove away.

A few minutes later another university police car drove up with a man wearing lieutenant bars on his uniform collar.

"Everything all right?"

LaStanza nodded, then recognized the lieutenant.

"Yep," said the lieutenant. "I retired four years ago. Sorry about that rookie bugging y'all."

"No big thing."

Dana Barret came out and went straight to the Maserati. Glapier climbed out and LaStanza introduced her and opened the back door for Barret.

On their way back to headquarters, LaStanza pulled into the parking lot of Jerry's Po-boys on Broad Avenue. "What kinda po-boys y'all want?"

Dana opened he purse.

"It's on me," LaStanza said. They both wanted shrimp po-boys. He went in and ordered a dozen shrimp po-boys, dressed, no pickles. He hated pickles and asked the preparer to go light with the mayonnaise. New Orleans restaurants were notorious for slapping on wide swatches of mayonnaise.

1:35 p.m. – Detective Bureau

"Why does your name sound so familiar to me?"

Glapier went for soft drinks while LaStanza stacked the po-boys on one of the empty desks and told everyone to grab one.

He motioned for Barret to sit in the chair next to his desk.

"We eat first, then we'll get down to business."

When Fel stepped up, Dana Barret smiled for the first time. She looked prettier when she smiled. Fel smiled back and introduced himself and started the charm, pulling up a chair to eat next to her. He had told LaStanza about Wanda and the man had keep in practice. When Fel told LaStanza about Wanda, he'd concluded with A.N.B.A.T.D. LaStanza still hadn't figure it out.

Kelly sat with Jodie. LaStanza made sure to face away from Stevens who ate the way LaStanza imagined a javelina ate. Lotsa noise. Snowood took his po-boy with him on his way to a preliminary hearing.

The first line-up of seven pictures included one of Telrey Boykin. Barret picked him out right away. "That's Telrey. Hadn't changed much."

She picked Jasper out of the second line-up. LaStanza had her initial the rear of each photo from the line-up and sign the back of each Boykin brother picture before putting in the date and time, then taking a statement from her, which he typed on the Macintosh, making sure to put in every "Praise Jesus."

Jasper Boykin was positively the suspicious person she'd seen behind K&B. She couldn't really say he was breaking into a car but that's what it looked like to her. He printed the statement and she signed it.

Mark came out of his office, went to Snowood's desk and snatched up the javelina head, taking it into one of the interview rooms before coming back, saying, "Damn thing gives me indigestion."

Fel asked to go along when it was time to take Barret home.

Glapier seemed relieved, leaning close to LaStanza to whisper, "Good. I'm tired of the praising Jesus."

Half-turned in the passenger seat, Fel talked with Barret all the way home. LaStanza counted fifty-five praises along the way. He wanted to just say it – Enough with the goddamn *Praise Jesus*. She was giving him a headache, but the way she and Fel were smiling at one another, he let it slide.

Then Fel said, "Enough with the 'Praise Jesus', Dana. I'm getting a headache."

LaStanza gave Fel a double take.

"OK," Barret said.

Before she climbed out, LaStanza thanked her again, then asked, "Why does your name sound so familiar to me?"

"*Ghostbusters*," she said. "The movie. The woman played by Sigourney Weaver. Only she spelled her name with one 'r' and two 't's."

So that was it.

As they pulled away, LaStanza asked, "All right, I give up. What's A.N.B.A.T.D.?"

"Ain't Nothin' But A Thing, Dude."

So much for Wanda. At least that's the front Fel was putting up.

3:35 p.m. – Magazine Street

" – and I'm gonna ruin his fuckin' life."

Evangelista, in a full denim mini-skirt, a white blouse and white sandals, smiled broadly when LaStanza and Fel stepped into Musica Botafuego and turned down the music right away. There were nine teen-aged boys in the place and one twenty-something year old woman in tight jeans, very tight jeans, who pretended to ignore the detectives.

"I have some more line-ups for you to look at," LaStanza said, pulling out the four-by-five inch envelopes with seven pictures in each. He handed the first to her, keeping his face emotionless as she started quickly to thumb through the pictures. He felt his heart rising, hoping she wasn't going too fast.

She let out a scream and dropped the pictures. "That's him!"

Jasper Boykin's was face up on the glass counter. Evangelista began shaking, hands on either side of her face. LaStanza moved around the counter and she buried her face against his shoulder, hands by her sides and wept.

Freddie Luz chose that moment to come in, saw his wife and LaStanza and hardened his eyes immediately.

LaStanza asked him, "Can you help your wife?"

"What's going on?"

"She just identified the man who robbed her." LaStanza pulled away and nodded to the pictures on the counter. He passed Evangelista to Freddie, patting the man on his shoulder. "She's a brave woman and we're gonna nail the bastards."

Freddie looked at Fel who said, "We got 'em now."

It took hot-headed Freddie a couple minutes to catch on, Evangelista longer before she could look at the second line up. This time, she just dropped the pictures and croaked, "That's the short one." Fuckin' Telrey.

LaStanza asked Freddie if he could get his cousin to come in, watch the store. He needed Evangelista and Freddie to come to the Detective Bureau right away. When Freddie balked, LaStanza held up Jasper's picture. "This man stuck a gun against your wife's head and I'm gonna ruin his fuckin' life. You with me, or what?"

It took the cousin a half hour to show up. He looked like an oversized version of Freddie only balding. He understood completely and said no problem.

Evangelista recovered somewhat on the way to the office, taking in a deep breath and declaring, "You sure found him didn't you?"

"*We* found him."

6:10 p.m. – Detective Bureau

"Hey, where's my javelina?"

LaStanza called Lizette as soon as he got a free minute and told her they'd identified the Senoré's killers.

"Oh," her voice caught.

Sitting at his desk, new coffee mug in front of him, he told her the whole story, how Dana Barret led them to the Boykins brother and Evangelista's identification and how he and Fel then went to the house of former Shoe Town clerk, fuzzy-headed Andy Pitney, who wasn't keen on cooperating until LaStanza took his elbow and started to lead him out to the car.

Pitney positively identified Jasper and Telrey. So did the sixty-six year old security guard, Thomas Eustis, who pretended he didn't even remember the incident until his wife stepped into their living room and snatched his can of Miller Lite, telling him he'd better cooperate with the police.

"Can't have enough identifications," LaStanza told his wife.

"So what do you do now?"

"We're putting warrants together. Fel and Glapier are over on Hollygrove getting a script of the Boykin house and the three cars parked out front for warrants. We won't go until after dark." None of the cars was the stolen Old Cutlass. LaStanza could only be *so* lucky.

The dogs barked and she shushed them.

"Call me when it's over," she said, her voice husky with emotion.

"We can talk a while. The computer's making this so easy."

"Good." She grew quiet.

"So, what're wearing little girl?"

She sighed. "I'm not in the mood."

It took a while, dragging simple sentences from her about her day, about her classes. Before they got off, her voice finally became animated. "Call me. I'll be up working on my computer. I don't care how late it is."

"I know, Babe. I love you."

"I love you," she said faintly.

Kelly was grinning at him from the chair beside Jodie's desk. Jodie was over by the coffee pot, fixing another pot.

"Why don't we get warrants for murder?" Kelly asked.

"Because we have positive IDs for the armed robbery. First things first. They're already wanted parole violators, but this new charge will keep them in jail, hopefully." LaStanza explained that with the search warrants, they can gather as much evidence and by keeping all the warrants simple didn't give the pain-in-the-ass defense attorneys any room to wiggle. "Put everything on one warrant and you risk losing everything if it's thrown out."

LaStanza picked up his mug and headed for Jodie, Kelly following.

"Where'd you get the mug?" Kelly asked.

"My wife." LaStanza raised his newest coffee mug, blue enamel with white letters, – *Don't Piss Me Off! I'm Running Out Of Places To Hide The Bodies.*

After getting the warrants, LaStanza called home again.

"Change of plans. We're gonna get a late supper and take a rest before hitting them around three a.m. I'd rather do it at home with you, eat with you, get everyone to rest there, stage it all there, instead of going to a restaurant, then waiting around here."

"Yes. Come on," she sounded up about it. "I'll have pizzas delivered. We have enough drinks. How many are coming?"

LaStanza counted quickly and told her six, maybe seven.

As everyone packed up, LaStanza called the Second District and asked for John Raven Beau's home number. Beau answered after the second ring.

"Beau, it's LaStanza, have you had supper?"

Beau said he was just thinking about it, so LaStanza invited him over for pizza, mentioning they were running papers at three a.m. on the robbers from Shoe Town and if he wanted to come along.

"Absofuckinlutely!"

"You know where I live, right?"

"I'll be right there."

"Oh, can you bring your uniform. We'll need uniforms there."

"Sure."

LaStanza picked up an extra bullet proof vest for the tall patrolman and followed Mark, Jodie, Fel, Kelly and Glapier. Snowood came in as they filed out. A moment later, they heard him yell, "Hey, where's my javelina?"

9:20 p.m. –Exposition Boulevard.

"First time anyone mistook LaStanza for a priest!"

Beau arrived, in uniform, just as the pizzas arrived and helped lay them out on the cherry wood table in the dining room. For an instant LaStanza remembered him and his wife up on that table, her naked ass slapping it as they fucked. The table glistened with fresh furniture polish, thankfully.

Lizette wore one of LaStanza's dress shirts over a one-piece black bathing suit. She fired up the hot tub so they could relax after eating.

She ate one piece and noticed her husband and Beau had only one piece.

"Don't give any pizza to the dogs," she warned Fel who dangled a piece of pepperoni over his head, Thompson salivating ready to jump.

Surprisingly, Sheila Glapier was the most talkative, telling Lizette all about the "Praise Jesus" witness who broke the case. "Actually your husband broke the case. He kept at it until he found someone who knew something."

"He is persistent." Lizette gave her husband a weak smile as he sat down at the far end of the table next to Fel, both with bottles of Barq's root beer. He looked a little tired. Lizette sat at the opposite end of the long table from her husband.

"He's like a bulldog," Glapier said, taking a bite of meat-lovers pizza.

"A leopard actually."

Beau sat with them as Lizette told how Captain LaStanza nicknamed his youngest son after Dino gunned down the La Cosa Nostra hit-man known as the Twenty-two Killer. Going to the hospital where Dino lay with a gunshot wound, a graze to his the side of his neck, the captain patted his son's head and called him, "mio leopardo piccolo." My little leopard.

Lizette explained, "A leopard is nature's most efficient killing machine."

Beau broke the pause with, "The Lakota feel similarly about the eagle. Silent. Swift. A most efficient killer. That's why the Sioux wear white feathers, where the Cheyenne and Crow wear black feathers. The Cheyenne wear feathers from the golden eagle but the Crow wear feather from carrion eaters, ravens and crows.

Lizette gave him a long look. "Why isn't your middle name Eagle, instead of Raven?"

"The raven is a survivor, able to adapt to most conditions. He is a friend of the coyote and the Sioux believe that when the world ends only the coyote and his brother the raven will be left."

Jodie and Kelly had moved up, Jodie listening intently to Beau.

"My ancestors had some great names, Eagle Elk, Flying Hawk, Fears Nothing, Red Feather, Crazy Horse and his brother Little Hawk, whom my grand-father claims direct descent from."

Beau looked around, a pirate-smile on his face now. "My father's name was Calixte, Cajun French for chalice. I'm just glad my first name's John."

He looked at Glapier and said, "Names can be funny. Know what *Glapier* means in French?"

"No?"

"To yelp."

Sheila Glapier laughed loudly, saying it fit her mother even better than her.

Jodie mentioned a book she was reading about a Sioux warrior but Lizette focused on her husband as he prepared himself, as he brought out the leopard. She could see it in his eyes, the way he moved. Lizette noticed no one was talking around her a minute later and saw Jodie, Kelly, Glapier and even Beau looking at her.

She nodded toward Dino, her voice low. "He's getting into leopard mode right now. He'll get quiet and I swear his eyes will seem brighter and he even moves more easily, fluidly, on the balls of his feet. Anticipating the hunt, I imagine."

There was a look in Beau's eyes that he understood better than the others and Lizette was glad he was going along on this raid.

Mark was the only one who didn't get into the Jacuzzi, opting for a nap on the couch. Jodie had put on one of the bathing suits she kept at the mansion. Kelly and even Beau got in, wearing two of the spare suits. Glapier barely fit into the spare Lizette found for her.

Fel, with only his legs in the hot tub because everyone couldn't fit inside, started the joking. Sitting next to her husband, Lizette watched them try to release the tension through their humor. Cops reached for comedy, any relief, to break the stress actually, bad jokes, sarcasm and sometimes liquor or women.

She picked up Fel's story in mid-stream. " – and I'm taking a recorded statement from this G.A.L.B. and tell him his answers must be oral. I ask him his name and he says, 'Oral'."

Lizette leaned against her husband's ear and asked, "G.A.L.B.?"

"Goofy Ass Looking Bastard."

Jodie said, "I took a statement from a man who'd suffered brain damage in a crane accident, asked him what was his IQ, and he said, 'I can see pretty well'."

LaStanza smiled. "Remember the Alzheimer's guy?"

Jodie chuckled and snuggled a little closer to Kelly.

"Poor man was so messed up, I asked him if his memory was impaired. He said yes. I asked him if it was Alzheimer's and he said, 'I forget'."

Jodie pointed an accusing finger at LaStanza. "That's not the end of the story."

LaStanza grinned guiltily. "After he said he forgets things, I asked him to give me an example of something he'd forgotten."

Jodie roared, "The man sat there for a good five minutes trying the remember an example."

"He finally looked back at me," LaStanza went on, "and said, 'I forgot your question, father'."

Jodie almost came out of the tub. "He made the sign of the cross and started 'forgive me father for I have sinned.' First time anyone mistook LaStanza for a priest!"

Fel waited for the laughter to die down before, "Remember the blonde with the see-through blouse?"

LaStanza, "Like I could forget. Walked into court with those jugs bouncing."

"The D.A. asked her, 'Is your appearance here this morning in response to a subpoena' and she answers, 'No, this is how I dress most of the time'." Fuckin' judge almost choked."

Then the group started in on the motel slogans they'd made up for the sleazy motels along Tulane Avenue.

Fel, Jodie and LaStanza bounced the slogans back and forth, rapid shot and Lizette suspected they'd been working on this routine – "You could stay somewhere nicer, but you wouldn't have money left for the hooker, " from Fel.

"We don't make the adultery. We make the adultery *better!*" – LaStanza.

"Because you deserve better than the back of a Chevy." – Jodie.

"You rented the room, now buy the video." – LaStanza.

"Not just for nooners!" – Fel.

"We put the 'ho' in hotel." – Jodie.

After drying off and changing, Lizette climbing into a tee-shirt and jeans, LaStanza put on a pot of coffee-and-chicory. They went over their plan in the kitchen, Fel and Glapier explaining the layout of the house and neighborhood and LaStanza went back into leopard mode again.

He passed around the pictures of his suspects and Lizette looked closely at the harsh faces of the two men. One of them murdered that old man. It occurred to her one or both could kill her husband and she didn't know how much more of this she could take.

Before they left, they all climbed into large black bullet proof vests and LaStanza kissed his wife good-bye.

Wednesday, April 9, 1986

2:48 a.m. - General Ogden Street

"You ain't no future hall of fame criminal."

The good news was 2932 Hollygrove had abandoned houses on either side, so no pain-in-the-ass neighbors could see the police surrounding the house and call the Boykins on the phone. "Hey man, you got cops!"

The bad news was someone was watching TV in the front room of the house. Fel did a walk by and told LaStanza when he met the unmarked Ford at the corner of Fig Street.

"Watching TV at three in the morning?" Jodie shook her head. They were in all-black now, except Beau in his uniform. Jodie wore black slacks and running shoes. All were uncomfortable in their bulky bullet proof vests. Mark looking more like a grizzly than ever.

They'd arrived simultaneously, LaStanza's car pulling up at Fig Street with one of the marked units carrying two Second District patrolmen. From the back seat Mark told Fel, "You know the plan," sending Fel back to his car on the other side of the Boykins' house.

Fel gathered his crew, Glapier and Kelly, for their back yard assault. Mark would kick in the front door with LaStanza going in first, Jodie right behind, Beau remaining in the doorway to secure it. The other uniformed officers, including the unit down by Fel's car, would cover the sides of the house, in case someone climbed out a window of the rickety wooden house in dire need of new paint and a new roof.

Climbing out of the car, they moved quickly and silently across the small front yard and up the three steps to the concrete porch as Fel led his group around to the rear. Mark didn't stop, lifting his big right foot as he reached the door, crashing it into the wooden door just above the knob. The door crashed in, taking the frame with it.

LaStanza went in low, right over the fallen door, his .357 magnum cupped in both hands. He pointed it at the figure on the sofa and shouted, "Police! Freeze!"

The only light came from the TV but LaStanza could see it was an old man with no shirt, just a pair of shorts, a can of beer cradled in his right hand. The old man raised the beer and his left hand, blinked at LaStanza, then went back to watching the TV.

Jodie came in high, moving to the other side of the small living room, which smelled of stale beer and faintly of urine. She watched her partner cover the man on the couch until Mark could search him. Beau moved into the doorway to cover their backs.

Fel had to kick the back door twice before it slammed open, Kelly going in low, Glapier high, Fel following them into a kitchen. Kelly took the first room on the right, Fel moving to the doorway while Glapier moved to the hall.

LaStanza went into the hall just as a figure jumped out of a bedroom and ran away from him.

"Coming your way!" LaStanza yelled, drawing a bead on the retreating figure.

Fel saw a figure in front of Glapier, someone tall and screaming, "Fuckers!"

Glapier stepped aside as a thin man punched her shoulder. She ducked and came with an uppercut that caught the man in the jaw, crashing him to the wall. He bounced and she kicked him between the legs and he went straight down, screaming, "Aaaahhhh!"

Fel was on him just as LaStanza arrived. He was young, tall and thin wearing white jockeys. Fell cuffed him behind his back and stood with his foot on the man's chest.

"What's your name, ass-hole?"

"Fuck you!"

When Glapier looked at LaStanza, he said, "Way to go, Sheila."

There was no one else in the house.

The old man told LaStanza, "That's my youngest son Edwin. He seventeen."

"Where's Jasper and Telrey?"

"Haven't seen Jasper in two weeks." The old man finally looked away from the TV and said, "Y'all stupid? Y'all got Telrey in jail."

"What do you mean we got Telrey?"

"He in jail." He took a sip of beer and went back to watching TV.

LaStanza felt sick in his stomach. "When was he arrested?"

"He called from parish prison 'round midnight."

"You got a phone?"

"Kitchen."

LaStanza found a green phone mounted on a wall and called parish prison, taking notes, shaking his head. Hanging up, he told them, "Some enterprising Second District officer nabbed Telrey shortly after midnight. He was a 107 outside a convenience store. Cop ran him and since he's a parole violator, took him in."

Fel was telling Edwin, "You better learn a trade. You ain't no future hall of fame criminal. A girl beat you up, boy."

Kelly, being the rookie, was elected to help Edwin into a pair of pants.

"I'm taking him with me," LaStanza told Jodie. "Y'all know what to look for." Since her name was also on the warrants, he'd let her search the house and cars outside.

He asked Fel if he'd go around and talk to the neighbors. Glapier went with him because you never know until you asked. Someone had to know where Jasper was. Maybe, just maybe, they'd talk.

LaStanza led Edwin outside and asked Beau if wanted to come along. "You already know how to search a house."

"Sure. Where are we going?" Beau holstered his weapon.

"Parish Prison then the Bureau." As he led Edwin to his car, he told Beau about Telrey. "Got to talk with him before he lawyers up. He'll be arraigned in a few hours."

"Say blonde lady," old man Boykin called out to Jodie who stepped back into the living room.

"Yeah?"

"Y'all gonna pay for that door?"

"See the big guy." She pointed to Mark.

3:55 a.m. – Detective Bureau

"An innocent man would be sweating bricks."

LaStanza put a handcuffed Telrey in one interview room and Edwin in another.

"Let 'em simmer a while," he told Beau who was already starting up a pot of coffee-and-chicory. LaStanza went to his desk and called his wife. She answered after the first ring.

"It's over," he said. "I'm at the Bureau. We got one of the brothers but the other wasn't there."

"Anybody get hurt?"

He told her about Edwin getting decked by Glapier, then told her he'd call later. Moving to the police computer he found Edwin had seven juvenile arrests and three already as a seventeen-year-old adult, the most serious was a pending burglary charge.

"Gets in a lotta fights," he told Beau. "The way Glapier cold-cocked him, he must lose a lot." They each drank a mug of coffee, then took some into the first interview room with them.

Telrey Boykin, in an orange prison jumpsuit, wouldn't look LaStanza in the eye as he sat across from him. Telrey wore a well-practiced jail-hardened look on his face. Beau stood behind LaStanza next to the tripod with the video camera. LaStanza freed Telrey's right hand, cuffing the other to the table leg. He didn't start recording yet, sliding a mug of coffee over to Telrey.

"I got nothin' to say." Telrey ignored the coffee.

"I don't want you to talk," LaStanza lied. "I just wanna show you something." He pulled the newest version of his flyer, this one with the drawings next to mug shots of Telrey and Jasper.

Telrey didn't look at it for a full minute as LaStanza and Beau drank their coffee. When he did, he stared at it, trying his best to keep from revealing anything. LaStanza watched the micro expressions on the harsh face, the eyes narrowing with a hint of realization.

"Like you and your brother posed for it."

Telrey keep looking at the flyer, his face even harder now.

"I've got you, plain and simple. You wanna tell me your side, fine. You don't. I don't give a shit. I'm not in jail. You are."

LaStanza got up and left with Beau, leaving the flyer with Telrey.

They went into the interview room with Edwin. No coffee this time, leaving Edwin cuffed behind his back, having to lean forward.

"The cuffs hurt," Edwin complained.

"They're supposed to," LaStanza answered. He'd double locked the cuffs so they wouldn't get any tighter. "Quit twisting your arms around."

"Why am I in jail?"

"Simple Battery and Resisting Arrest." LaStanza read Edwin his rights between Edwin's constant interruptions. When Edwin stopped to suck in air, LaStanza asked, "Where's Jasper?"

"Fuck you!"

LaStanza turned the light off on his way out. Let him sit in the dark.

A half hour later, he went back into the room where Telrey was sleeping, head back, mouth open.

LaStanza told Beau. "An innocent man would be sweating bricks. 'No, I didn't do it. I didn't do it!'. This mother-fucker's sound asleep." LaStanza slapped the table, then had to shake Telrey to wake him up.

Beau turned on the video camera and LaStanza read Telrey his rights once again, finishing with, "You understand these rights?"

Telrey nodded.

"Where's Jasper?"

Telrey shrugged then said the magic words that had LaStanza turn off the camera. He said, "I wanna talk to my lawyer."

Anything they recorded after that would be inadmissible. LaStanza asked him what he did on Good Friday, March 28th. "That's Friday before last."

"I wanna talk to my lawyer first."

LaStanza and Beau went out to LaStanza's desk to he could fill out the arrest reports for Telrey and Edwin.

"He's been handled so many times, his lawyers have finally beaten it into his head. Don't say anything."

A false dawn gave the sky a charcoal gray hue as they walked Telrey and Edwin around to central lockup, where LaStanza booked Telrey with armed robbery and Edwin with simple battery on police and resisting arrest.

"Why don't you book him with the murder?" Beau asked on their way back around to police headquarters.

"I will. I just want them to bring it up first. Hopefully Jasper won't be as sharp as his brother about lawyers although they've been handled enough, he probably won't talk. Telrey's a parole violator, he ain't going anywhere, especially with a fresh armed robbery charge."

"We have a good murder case, don't we?"

"A very good circumstantial case, but you know the D.A. They only get off on direct evidence. Eye-witness see them kill the old man or a confession."

6:05 a.m. – Detective Bureau

"You are one fortunate man, you know that?"

Beau went home to get a couple hours rest before returning to work.

LaStanza puts in an APB for Jasper Boykin and the stolen '77 blue Olds, in case the douche-bag did steal it, then got on the police computer, checking to make sure Jasper was not in custody somewhere. Then he ran all known criminal associates of the brothers Boykin again, their home address and all addresses where they'd been arrested so the search could begin for Jasper.

He'd just tore off the last print out when Jodie, Mark and Kelly came in. They'd found no money, except the thirty-two dollars in old man Boykin's wallet. No guns. Nothing that appeared stolen. Even the TV was old.

"We took two blue tee-shirts from a bedroom dresser," Jodie said. Evangelista said Jasper wore a blue tee-shirt during the robbery. She'd described Telrey's shirt as "dark."

Jodie sat heavily in her chair.

"We also took four pairs of jeans and three pair of tennis shoes. They're at the lab." She yawned.

The crime lab would check the clothes and shoes for blood. When the Senoré's head caved in there was enough blood splattered in the air. LaStanza went through his notes, found the coroner's office preliminary report. Grosetto Venetta had type B blood, genotype BB, Rh negative.

He reached into this bottom desk drawer and pulled out his

notebook from homicide school and leafed through it to the blood type chart. He smiled, making note that only two percent of the American population had B negative blood and less than one percent had B negative with genotype BB.

Slipping the notebook back, he recalled the three months he'd spent at the Southern Police Institute at the University of Louisville, two summers ago. Intense class work, he'd learned a lot of forensic information, and even a little practical homicide investigative techniques. In his class of thirty-four homicide detectives, he was the most experienced. Even the cops from Chicago and L.A. hadn't handled as many murders as he. Then again, they didn't work in the murder capital of America.

Kelly left before Mark. LaStanza told Jodie to go home.

"I'm out of here in a few minutes. Good work coming up with the clothes and shoes."

"Wish we'd have found that guard's missing gun."

"If he was smart, Jasper got rid of it. Then again, he could have it on him."

Jodie yawned and left as Lt. Mason came in, followed by a hang-dog looking Steve Stevens who bowed to Jodie as she breezed past.

Mason came straight for LaStanza for an update.

"I'll get the daily in later, but here's what you need for the press release." LaStanza handed Mason a print out from his Macintosh on Telrey Boykin's arrest and the wanted information on Jasper. "I'm going home for a little rest then I'll get to the Senoré's family before the five o'clock news."

"Good." Mason went into his office as LaStanza packed up. He felt Stevens watching, but didn't turn that way.

"Jodie always smells so nice," Stevens said.

"That's what comes with bathing regularly."

"It's more than that." Steven came over and sat in Jodie's chair, facing LaStanza across the two desks.

"You are one fortunate man, you know that?"

"The fuck you talking about?" LaStanza was thinking he could have gotten away cleanly if he'd left with Jodie. "No one up here is fortunate, up to our asses in murders."

"Not the work. Your partner. You get to ride around with Jodie. She's so damn beautiful. Get to be around those legs with those stockings. Just to be around her, man."

Jesus H. Christ. Not often was LaStanza at a lost for words.

"And, no offense, but your wife. She's gorgeous, like a teen-angel. You always around gorgeous women, man."

LaStanza tried shrugging.

"I don't mean no offense. I know Jodie's all Kellied up now. I'd just like to ride around with her sometimes. I mean I know she won't look twice at me because I'm cross-eyed."

And you dress like a fuckin' clown.

"Don't get me wrong, I get my share of women. Skanks mostly."

LaStanza stiffened his jaw to keep from laughing.

"No offense again," Steven went on, "but don't you get hard-ons riding around with Jodie?"

LaStanza felt a headache coming on.

"Just watching her cross and un-cross those long legs." Stevens shivered, took in a deep breath and stood up. "Good talkin' with you." He headed for the coffee pot.

Before LaStanza could make a getaway, Stevens called out, "Hey, what about that redhead from the Camellia Grill?"

LaStanza turned and spread his arms.

"Naw," Stevens said. "Not skanky enough."

Snowood came in, stopping LaStanza. "I'm gonna end up in Internal Affairs again."

"Fine." LaStanza tried to get around him.

"Lady just came outta the court building and pointed to this here new suede coat." Country-Ass fanned his jacket so LaStanza would notice. "Told me a cow was murdered to make ma' coat. So I told her I didn't know there was any witnesses, so now I gotta kill you too. She almost passed out."

11:00 a.m. – Exposition Boulevard

"Let's take a nap."

LaStanza went around to the front of the mansion to let the dogs out in the front yard. Flash and Thompson were waiting in the foyer in statue mode. Each stretched and walked through the open door, Flash giving LaStanza a, "Woof."

Leaving his briefcase on the foyer table, he went out and sat on the top step while the dogs did their business then started playing tag again, snapping at each other's tail and running away.

He was thinking maybe a jog after a good sleep when he spotted Lizette waking down Exposition Boulevard with someone. She was in an aqua dress not as short as her usual mini, but still short and looked nice with her hair in long curls, her legs looking especially nice. She wore white high heels.

She notices him and smiled, stopping at the gate as Thompson ran over wagging his tail and Flash barked at the guy with her who LaStanza recognized as Jose, the big Hispanic guy who'd caught naked Lizette getting out of the Jacuzzi. He remembered he had to get those pictures developed.

"Hello," Jose called out, handing Lizette her briefcase. LaStanza stood. Lizette slipped into the gate and waved at Jose, thanking him.

Flash followed Jose along the fence as he walked away. Flash gave him a couple, "Woofs."

Lizette breezed up to her husband and pecked him on the lips.

"He always carry your books home?"

"They take turns."

He couldn't read her face, odd for him. Maybe he was too tired or maybe she was just getting better at hiding things. She went in, leaving behind a whiff of her light perfume.

She called back, "They like to make sure I'm OK. They try flirting, but it doesn't work."

He looked at her just as Flash chased Thompson up the steps. She reached a hand out and said, "Come on. Let's take a nap."

They climbed naked into their bed and lay there atop the cool sheets. Lizette nuzzled against his shoulder and with the AC on and the ceiling fan, he felt almost chilly. She pulled him close and then became still and they fell asleep.

4:30 p.m. – Dublin Street

"You're not bad luck to me, you know."

No one was home at the Senoré's house on Dublin Street. LaStanza walked over to K&B, pulling out one of the pale green business cards he'd kept from the Senoré's wallet and called Venetta's Men Store on Magazine Street, hoping Pauli was there. He got the answering machine and left a message.

Damn. He didn't want them to hear it on the news and had no choice so he dug out Lori's business card.

"I'm sorry, Miss Venetta has left for the day," Sally said.

"I'm trying to get a hold of her father or step-mother. Do you know where I can reach them?"

"I think they're out of town. Miss Venetta is heading to their house to feed their cats. I can call her there and leave a message for you."

"Sure." LaStanza gave Sally the number to the Detective Bureau.

He needn't have bothered. Walking back to his car, he spotted Lori going into her father's side of the double house. He rang the bell and she peeked out a side window before opening the door.

"Hi, I have some information for you and your father."

Lori waved him in and moved to an end table to scoop up a pad and pen. She was in another slimming dress, this one olive green with a high slit that revealed most of her right leg. She jotted a quick note and handed it to him, moving closer so he caught her perfume.

The note read: *They took my grandmother across the lake to relatives.*

"Do you have a phone number where I can call them?"

She nodded and led him to a phone, punched in the number and handed the receiver to LaStanza. An elderly woman answered and passed him to Pauli.

"We caught one of the men," LaStanza said, watching Lori's eyes widen. She sat on the sofa. LaStanza explained about Telrey and how they'd charged him with the armed robbery of Shoe Town but will charge him with the murder as soon as they find his brother. "The other killer is Jasper Boykin, Telrey's brother. We're looking hard for him. I didn't want y'all hearing about it on the news."

A huge black cat jumped up on the arm of the sofa next to Lori and watched LaStanza with huge green eyes. Lori started jotting a note as LaStanza listened to Pauli repeating his message to Gail. Then Pauli explained they'd brought his mother to her sister's house in Covington to rest.

"We're supposed to stay here a week maybe. Should I come home?"

"No need. I'll let you know when we catch Jasper."

"Good luck, Detective LaStanza." Then he thanked LaStanza again, then asked, "How'd you find us so quickly?"

"I'm a detective," LaStanza joked, then admitted, "Your daughter dialed your number for me. I came to your house to notify you and she was here to feed the cats. Want me to tell her anything?"

"Have her get on the line."

LaStanza held the receiver out to Lori. "He wants you to get on the line."

She smiled and put the receiver in the end table and led him through the dining room into an office with a phone next to a small computer-like machine. She lifted the receiver off the phone slid it into a slot in the computer and started typing.

LaStanza read: Hi, Daddy. He said he'd get them and he did.

She paused a second and a printed message appeared on the screen: We'll be home tonight. Leaving your grandmother here –

LaStanza left them to talk and went back into the living room with the black cat following his every move. He tried to pet the cat but it moved away, remained out of reach.

"You're not bad luck to me, you know." Then he told the cat about the vulture mobile above his crib when he was a baby. The cat just stared back.

Lori came out and hung up the living room phone before passing LaStanza a note: *When my father gets back into town, we'd like you to come over and tell us how you found them. Nothing that would jeopardize the case, OK?*

"Sure."

She handed him another note: *When you said you always get them, I felt chills down my back. I feel them again.*

"We still have to catch the second one."

She jotted quickly: *Will he be hard to find?*

"He'll hide, maybe run, but criminals like him don't disappear. There are a lotta cops out there. I didn't solve this case by myself."

She gave him a long look, the eyes pulling at his again, but she kept her distance. He brushed his moustache with his fingers and knew he was nervous.

"I'll let you know when we catch the second one."

She nodded, her face suddenly sad and he thought she would cry but she took in a deep breath and smiled instead. He took a step back and she walked him to the door. Just as he was leaving, she passed him another note: *Please forgive me. I can't help the attraction. Maybe it's good you are strong.*

Yeah. Right. I'm a fuckin' oak.

He nodded, not looking back into those soft eyes and left. *That was a mistake,* he told himself. *I should have stared her down. I've stared down killers.*

Yeah. Right.

This was different. Very different

Thursday, April 10, 1986

11:55 a.m. – Magazine Street

"I don't want to die, but if I have to, I'm gonna die last."

Fel was the first to arrive at The Veranda and was led by Mama to a table in back. Jodie and Kelly came in as Fel started looking at the menu.

"I'm getting addicted to this food," Fel said but might as well be talking to himself with the way Jodie and Kelly were trying hard not to be cute together, her holding out the chair for him, he laying out her napkin for her.

Jodie finally looked at Fel and said, "No, luck?"

He shook his head.

LaStanza led Glapier in with one of the waitresses. LaStanza smiled at her. "Ciao, Lucy."

"I'm Consuela."

The rain, that had threatened all morning came with a vengeance, but there was no wind, so the rain fell straight down on the tin roof atop the porch where they sat. It was too loud to talk and everyone had to point to what they wanted for Lucy. A fine mist flowed over them from rain peppering the tables and trees behind the restaurant, typical semi-tropical New Orleans rain, fat rain, a hammering deluge. It felt good on Fel's face. He closed his eyes and waited for the food.

He smelled it as Lucy and Consuela brought it out to them, and finally opened his eyes. The rain let up enough for them to talk now and LaStanza learned from them that none had learned anything good about Jasper Boykin from the places they'd visited and people they'd spoken to.

Fel was tired of talking and sat there quietly. He was tired of talking shop all the time. Tired of worrying about his case. He had no lead, no idea, no clue. It was more than frustrating. Jodie, who had nothing going on her case, had Kelly at least, had something to distract her from her failing.

"I'm going back to re-canvass the Square," Fel said when there was a lull in conversation. "If super cop here can solve his case by persistent canvassing, then I'm gonna do the same thing."

"Super cop?" LaStanza's raised his eye-brows. "About time you acknowledged it."

Jodie threw a chip at him. "The chief doesn't think that."

"Why not?" Glapier said.

"LaStanza and Fel here are on the chopping block, especially our Sicilian sleuth," Jodie explained, then went on to share the warning LaStanza had received from the superintendent of police. Although all of his shootings were good shooting, justifiable homicides, the chief thought LaStanza's penchant for violence made him a marked man.

"And that was before he and Fel gunned down Kaiser Billyday not so long ago," Jodie went on. "So we're all waiting to see if the guillotine falls."

The rain blew up again and the noise on the roof was too loud for conversation. Fel dug into his tamales as Lucy and Consuela re-filled glasses with water or tea.

The rain suddenly stopped completely and not two seconds later the sun shined on the back yard.

Glapier said, "That's dangerous, hamstringing an officer like that. Don't dare shoot anyone."

"It hasn't slowed my partner down," Jodie said with a wily smile.

LaStanza repeated one of his favorite sayings, "Keep it professional, but have a plan to kill everyone you meet."

"Sounds like some kinda death wish." Glapier was truly concerned.

LaStanza chuckled. "I don't want to die, but if I have to, I'm gonna die last."

Jodie cut right in. "That's a quote from a movie, isn't it?"

"Robert Mitchum."

"Figured."

Everyone left a big tip for Lucy and Consuela because Mama still refused to bring a bill as LaStanza and his rich wife had an account at The Veranda. And, as usual, LaStanza had the last word, as they stepped outside to the wet sidewalk that steamed from quickly evaporating rain.

LaStanza touched Jodie's elbow. "If I get guillotined, Steve Stevens has dibs on getting you for his partner. You smell so nice and he likes the silky sound of your stockings when you cross those long legs.

Jodie shot her partner a look of incredulity and disgust.

LaStanza stepped away and turned. "So one of y'all better shoot Jasper before I do."

4:05 p.m. – Leake Avenue

"She has the jugs."

Retired Sixth District sergeant Louis Lewis was short and round and nicknamed "the Penguin" because he looked so much like Burgess Meredith who played the villain in the old Batman

TV series. After retiring, he'd bought a small warehouse across from the river levee on Leake Avenue, in a run-down area where the Mississippi made one of its turns around the city and turned it into an indoor firing range.

"You're losing it," Lewis told LaStanza as the target came back to them. "You got two outta the bull's eye."

Two of LaStanza's six rounds had only nipped the black bull's eye.

"I'm just getting warmed up." LaStanza replaced the ear muffs and reloaded his model 66, Smith & Wesson .357 magnum. Technically a snub-nose, with a two-and-a-half inch barrel, the stainless-steel revolver had been re-tooled by a S&W expert so the trigger had a silky smooth pull, allowing easy double-action firing.

Starting with low velocity wide cutter ammo, LaStanza reloaded with regular .38 ammo before moving up to .38 plus P ammo. Squeezing off each round, LaStanza slowly felt the leopard rising, brought out by the smell of gunpowder, the predator rising with the rush of adrenaline.

He'd reached that higher level of awareness where he felt he could see better, hear better, smell better, even taste the air. He slipped in .357 rounds and squeezed them off, the revolver recoiling much higher. The black rubber grip became damp with perspiration and tackier in his damp palm as LaStanza used the standard two-handed police stance.

He hit the bull's eye with all six rounds. After doing it a third time in a row, he let his weapon cool down before handing it over to Lewis for a good cleaning.

They sat on either side of the counter and sipped Cokes.

"These new algum sights are pretty nice, huh?" Lewis smirked. He'd recommended the new red front ramp sight, which was much easier to see, especially in the dark.

"When you gonna bring your pretty wife back here?" Lewis contorted his face in what he thought was a funny mug.

"Soon." LaStanza took a sip of Coke.

Lewis had gone a little wacko when LaStanza brought Lizette to the range for the first time. He'd bought her a S&W model 60, a five-shot revolver with a two inch barrel, stainless-steel which had also been re-tooled for a silky smooth trigger pull. He's added specially made rubber grips, thinner than usual for her small hands.

"She has the jugs," Lewis said.

Like Stan Smith, ignoring Lewis wasn't an option. He just kept rambling on.

"Tell ya' what. I'll let you see my wife's boobs if you let me see your wife's."

"They get a choice in the matter?" LaStanza.

"My wife would go for it. We went down to Bourbon Street last Mardi Gras and she started flashing her tits for beads. I took pictures. Wanna see 'em?"

"No." Before he could stop himself, LaStanza told him about Lizette climbing naked out of their hot tub just as three of her students came out of the kitchen.

"Completely naked?" Lewis almost fell off his stool.

I shoulda kept my goddamn mouth shut! LaStanza nodded.

"*Public* hair and all?"

Jesus.

"When you gonna invite me and wife into your hot tub?"

"Just clean my fuckin' gun, will ya'?"

4:15 p.m. – Exposition Boulevard

"How old are you?"

Lizette was in one of her husband's police gym tee-shirts and blue jogging shorts as she sat at her Macintosh putting the finishing touches on her latest paper about Saint-Just, the infant terrible of the French Revolution. The high-low ring of the kitchen doorbell, brought her back to the present.

She followed the dogs into the kitchen and saw Felicity's Uncle Sam through the panes of the glass top of the kitchen door. When she opened the door, Sam wasn't alone. There was a young teen boy with him. The boy with him was light skinned, Lizette's height and skinny. His name was Joe.

"I have the final proof for you," Sam said, handing her the pin-up calendar as they stepped in. Flash and Thompson sniffed each and Lizette had to tell Joe they weren't going to bite.

"Hope not," Joe said warily.

She put the calendar up on the kitchen counter and leafed through it slowly. Joe stepped closer to get a better look at the pictures. January and February had boudoir shots of Lizette in negligees.

"I have two proofs for March, the month of Mardi Gras next year."

Both pictures were of Lizette on the motorcycle. In the first one, sitting with her hands on the handle bars you could see her panties and most of her cleavage. In the second, she was leaning back, all of the front of her panties were visible as she sat with her legs around the gas tank of the hog and both breasts revealed as she'd opened her jacket.

Joe took in a deep breath.

"How old are you?" she asked.

Joe didn't look up. "Fifteen."

"I think the first one of these." Lizette flipped to April where she stood bent over picking up a tennis ball. Her butt looked very round in the sheer pink panties. In the May shot she was in the lacy French bra and panties by Pop's Fountain. June, July and August were more boudoir photos of Lizette in nightclothes, pretty provocative and very sexy looking with her face all made up.

September had a photo of her sitting up on the shoe shiner's platform in that tight red-mini dress, her left leg extended straight down while right foot was lifted high on the shoe pedestal while a very old shoe shine man pretended to buff her red high heel. The entire front of her panties visible and she had a nonchalant look on her face shown in profile.

October was yet another bedroom shot in a negligee. November she had stepped out of a shower with a towel barely covering her wet body, most of her breasts were seen, except for the nipples. December had her lying on her side in a very sheer red bra and panties.

"I have your check right here." She got up and went for her purse.

When she stepped back in Joe was looking at the boob shot again and Sam handed her a brown envelope with the outtakes from their motorcycle shoots.

"See you in two weeks," Sam said, picking up the calendar proof. "With the calendar."

She thanked him and Joe thanked her, very much, before they left.

Lizette took the envelope with the pictures into the library and sat at her desk, under the bright desk light and flipped through them. She felt her excitement grow as she relived the moments – the white jacket with one button in front, barely covering her breasts, hint of her pink aureole peeking out, hair fluffed in long curls. She especially liked the dark brown lipstick.

She slowly went through the shots of her sitting on the motorcycle with her jacket open and her breasts free. Then came the pictures of Larry the motorcycle cop standing next to her, then staring at her breasts, then his hand slowly rising as his fingers found her boobs and he cupped them, caresses them and began squeezing them. She had closed her eyes for most of those shots and now saw the pleasure on her face. His too, with those dark hands feeling her up.

Then came the photos posing for and with the firemen, her climbing out of her skirt, posing in her panties. Sam had stepped back and from a distance her panties hid very little, her thick bush clearly visible as well as the crack of her ass when she turned around and bent over. The pictures showed her posing for the firemen and it looked so damn sexy with her standing, sitting, bending over. Sitting in the passenger seat of the cab, she'd toyed with her panties, pulling the elastic aside to show more of pubic hair, pulling them up again, silky strands of hair sticking out the sides. She remembered how hot she felt, so naughty. The men were so attentive, so appreciative, so captivated. Finally came the pictures of her posing with the firemen, each smiling for Sam's camera, then looking down at her and Jim, their leader, taking his time giving her boobs a good kneading.

Breathing heavy now, Lizette slipped the pictures back into the envelope and went and put them with the others in the hutch in the dining room. She was just thinking how she'd move them tomorrow to one of her bank deposit boxes when she heard the front door open.

LaStanza came home to his wife, his dogs and the anticipation of a good, long run around Audubon Park in the warm sunlight. Flash was the first one to reach him in the foyer with Thompson sliding up to get his pets.

Lizette stepped in last with a familiar look in those topaz eyes and he knew he wouldn't be jogging anywhere. She had a better use for his energy.

Friday, April 11, 1986

7:40 a.m. – Tchoupitoulas Street

"You aware you have a 10-15 up here?"

Headquarters called LaStanza just as he was pulling the unmarked Ford into the police garage.

"620's calling for you, 3124. They just recovered that '77 Oldsmobile Cutlass you're looking for."

"10-4. 10-20?"

"Tchoupitoulas and St. James."

"10-4. I'm in route."

It took him twenty minutes. Sergeant Stan Smith stood leaning against the fender of his marked police car, just behind the Olds Cutlass, which was pulled up against the curb next to an abandoned warehouse. Arms folded across his chest, blond hair waving in the breeze from the river just across the levee. The wind smelled of bananas from a ship along the wharves. Stan grinned at his former junior partner and said, "I found it for you."

Stan-the-Man was sporting sixes on his collars again and 'splained to LaStanza that he was back in the Bloody Sixth just in time to locate the elusive '77 Olds Cutlass, blue in color. The license plate was missing, but the vehicle identification number checked out.

LaStanza didn't ask how Stan pulled this off, knowing the braggart would tell him in his own good time. They both turned to the sound of a vehicle pulling up. A crime lab van parked across narrow St. James Street, next to another abandoned warehouse.

"I took the liberty 'a summoning the lab, figurin' you'd want to process this here stolen vehicle," Stan explained as LaStanza recognized the crime lab technician whose mother thought it funny calling his brother Ira and him George.

"Gershwin," LaStanza called out. "I need the works on this one."

Gershwin nodded but LaStanza went over to make it clear. "I want you to swab the seats for blood residue, the carpet, truck too. Capiche?"

Blinking at an obviously excited LaStanza, Gershwin said, "Sure."

"And vacuum for fibers and hair, then dust the fuck out of it for prints. This is a murder vehicle, OK?"

"Yeah. I understand." The lab tech was mild-mannered enough not to seem to be annoyed by LaStanza's pushing, so he patted Gershwin on the back and thanked him.

"No problem," Gershwin said.

"3126 – 3124, what do you have?" Jodie calling.

"The '77 Olds."

"3128 – 3124, I'm right around the corner." Fel calling now.

"10-4."

Stan was still leaning against his fender and looking smug so LaStanza gave in. "OK, how'd you do it?

"By being good looking, intelligent and the best cop you've ever ridden with. And the fact the ass-hole pulled out right in front of me."

"Ass-hole? Someone was in the car?"

"3120 – 3124." Mason was calling now, so LaStanza held up a finger to Stan and answered his lieutenant.

"Go ahead 3120."

"You aware you have a 10-15 up here?"

Stan tapped LaStanza's shoulder. "I sent him to the Bureau."

"I do now," LaStanza told Mason. "I'll be right there."

"10-4. He ain't going anywhere."

LaStanza to Stan, "Who'd you catch?"

"Got his name in my clipboard." Stan pointed to his car.

"Jasper Boykin?"

"No." Stan started for his car just as Fel pulled up behind LaStanza's car.

"What'd he look like?" LaStanza asked.

"A fine citizen of Afro-American persuasion, fifty years old, five-nine, two hundred pounds." Stan reached into his car and pulled out his clipboard. "Name of Maurice Zedimore. Stays on LaSalle Street, right in the heart of the lovely Magnolia Housing Projects."

Fel made it for the end of Stan's remarks and said, "It wasn't Jasper?"

"Maurice Zedimore," Stan said

Fel looked at LaStanza, "That name ever come up?"

"Nope. Sounds familiar, though. But I'm going interview him. Can you stay and process this?"

Fel said sure.

As he backed away, LaStanza told Fel, "Talk to sergeant perfect here and see if he'd left out anything, like was there anyone else in the car and call me on the radio if you find the gun or a body in the trunk."

"Gotcha."

It took LaStanza seven minutes to make it back to police headquarters.

8:25 a.m. – Detective Bureau

"He bad. Real bad. I didn't know how bad."

Mason handed LaStanza a print out of his prisoner's arrest record. Maurice Zedimore, AKA: Mo, AKA: M.Z, AKA; Zed Man, was fifty-one actually, five-nine, two hundred pounds with black hair, brown eyes, dark complected, no scars, marks or tattoos. Last arrest was three weeks ago, drunk in public. Previous arrests were over twenty years ago, two simple battery charges and another drunk in public. This man was no hardened criminal of the Boykin sort.

"What the fuck was he doing with a stolen car?" LaStanza said aloud as he gathered his notes and a blank video tape before going into the interview where Zedimore waited.

He could see immediately this man was sick. Not drunk or strung out on drugs, but ill. LaStanza introduced himself, read

Zedimore his Miranda rights and asked the man if he wanted something to drink.

"Coke'd be nice."

LaStanza opened the door and asked Mason for two Cokes. Then he went around and uncuffed Zedimore, slipping the cuffs into his coat pocket, which he then draped behind his chair before sitting back down. Mason came right in with a Coke for Zedimore and a Diet Coke for LaStanza who gave him a strange look.

Mason said, "Lizette's orders."

Jesus. LaStanza was already losing the tiny love handles without her help.·

"Who's Lizette?" Zedimore asked.

"My wife. But that's not the question. The question is how'd you end up in a stolen car, Maurice?"

Zedimore took a long drink of Coke, wiped his mouth with the sleeve of his long sleeved shirt and said, "I want immunity. Complete immunity."

"For what?"

"For me to give you the killers, man."

"Killers?"

"Get your boss in here." It wasn't a command, more of a request, softly spoken and from the serious look in Zedimore's pained eyes, LaStanza knew it was no use being cute or arguing.

He opened the door again and called Mason back in.

"This is Lieutenant Rob Mason, commander of the Homicide Division."

Maurice took another sip of Coke, his hand shaking now. Putting it down he said, "I got a few months to live. Pancreatic cancer, spread to my stomach. Inoperable. Passed on the chemo 'cause I seen what it did to my friend." Zedimore looked from LaStanza to Mason, then back again. "I know I fucked up. Knew it would catch up to me. But I know who killed that old man behind K&B and I know who killed the lady by Uptown Square."

Zedimore leaned closer and said, "And I know who killed that lady by Audubon Park."

LaStanza felt his breath slip away as he stared back into Zedimore's deep-set eyes. Not only was the hair standing on the back of his neck, LaStanza felt goose-bumps the size of Mount Everest along his arms.

"Now," Zedimore said as he leaned back. "Go out and get my pain pills from that envelope you put it in." Nodding to Mason. "And get the D.A. over here and we'll sign the immunity form and I'll tell y'all everything I seen."

They brought Zedimore into Mason's office. It took forty minutes to get the Assistant D.A. in charge of major cases to come over, then another forty-five minutes for the D.A's staff to type up the formal immunity forms, and yet another thirty minutes to bring in a public defender and a court reporter.

Maurice "Mo" Zedimore, with only a few months to live, didn't want to spend one minute in jail, so he would give up the killers. Everyone was in agreement.

During the waiting, LaStanza called Jodie on the LFR and had her come in right away. He met her in the squad room, her in another yellow suit skirt, followed by Kelly in a Kelly green suit and Glapier in a tan skirt suit. LaStanza wore a navy blue suit today. He kept his face from revealing anything until Jodie stepped close.

"Stan Smith caught someone *driving* the '77 Olds. His name's Maurice Zedimore. We're waiting on the D.A. and public defender because we're going to grant him immunity. He knows who killed the Senoré and Fel's victim at Uptown Square and," LaStanza took in a breath and repeated what Zedimore had said, "and that lady by Audubon Park."

Jodie's eyes became cat eyes again, her hand slowly covering her mouth.

"If it's true," LaStanza shrugged.

Jodie just shook her head and moved slowly to her desk to sit down.

Fel came in ten minutes later to give LaStanza the breakdown on the Olds. Before he started, LaStanza told him. Fel's mouth dropped open. He looked at Jodie, who still looked a little shell shocked, then at Kelly and Glapier in case LaStanza was pulling his leg.

"Well. I.T.D.B.A.?"

LaStanza shook his head.

"Well. If That Don't Beat All," Fel explained, then gave LaStanza the breakdown on the Olds. Gershwin found blood residue on the front seat as well as on the carpet on the front passenger side of the car. He secured three canisters of vacuumed residue, one from the front seat area, one from the backseat area and one from the trunk, along with sixteen latent prints, most of them partials.

Before going into the big conference room, LaStanza asked Zedimore, "You know a Winston Zedimore?"

"Nope."

They brought the tripod and video camera into the conference room and Mason took charge of working the camera. Maurice Zedimore sat on one side of the long table next to his public defender, a frizzy haired man with pasty skin named Alfred Pankin. Across from them, with their backs to the camera were A.D.A. Donna Jamison, who's skin was only a shade lighter than Fel Jones, who sat next to her, then came LaStanza and Jodie. Fel and Jodie had note pads and pens, ready to pass notes to LaStanza, since he was handling the interview.

When Mason was ready, LaStanza began with "This statement was taken on Friday, April 11, 1986, at 11:02 a.m. in the New Orleans Police Detective Bureau. Interviewer is Detective Dino LaStanza, NOPD Homicide Division. I am the case officer in charge of the armed robbery of Shoe Town, a retail shoe store located at the corner of So. Claiborne and So. Carrollton Avenues and the associated murder of Grosetto Venetta, occurring at the same location around seven p.m., Friday, March 28, 1986. Interviewee is Maurice M. Zedimore, date of birth March 5, 1935, who resides at –" LaStanza gave Zedimore's LaSalle Street address, then read in Zedimore's social security number and Louisiana driver's license number before introducing the A.D.A., public defender and the court reporter who sat in the corner with her little typing machine.

"Also present in this room is Lieutenant Rob Mason, commander of the Homicide Division who is working the video camera. Also present is Detective Felicity Jones, NOPD Homicide, the case officer of the Monique Williams murder which occurred between five and five-thirty p.m. on Saturday, March 29, 1986, at

Uptown Square Shopping Center on Broadway, New Orleans, Louisiana.

"Also present is Detective Jodie Kintyre, NOPD Homicide, the case officer of the Helen Collingwood murder which occurred between seven and eight a.m. on Sunday, March 30, 1986, at 439 Walnut Street, New Orleans, Louisiana."

At that point A.D.A. Jamison explained about the immunity and public defender Pankin concurred.

LaStanza finally asked his first question, "How did you come to be here today, Mr. Zedimore?"

"Y'all arrested me for drivin' a stolen car."

"How did you come to possess this stolen car?"

"Jasper Boykin give it to me so's I can drive him and his bro around to rob people."

"When did he give you this car?"

"'Couple weeks ago."

"How many people have you robbed?"

Besides Shoe Town, the Boykins and Zedimore robbed three other people, people on foot, all in the uptown area. Zedimore gave the street names.

"How do you know Jasper Boykin?"

"I been knowin' him since he a kid. I know his daddy, but his daddy ain't no criminal. Jasper and Telrey, they stone criminals. And since I got sick and needed some spending money for my time left, I joined up with Jasper to get a little spending money."

"Are you ill?"

Zedimore explained about his cancer and said this was his dying declaration. LaStanza didn't rush the questions, watching Zedimore to make sure the man had the stamina.

Zedimore ran down the Shoe Town robbery in detail, how he'd parked the Olds on Carrollton behind the K&B while Jasper and Telrey went around to the Shoe Town. He couldn't describe what they were wearing but said Jasper had a silver colored revolver. He sat turned around in the driver's seat so he could see them come back around the corner. Telrey came first with the silver revolver in his hand, with Jasper right behind with a bigger revolver that was blue or black metal. Telrey had fallen down dodging an old man with a walker. Telry fell hard, yelled something. Jasper raised his gun and hit the old man hard on the head and the old man just crumbled.

"When they climbed in the car, Jasper had blood all over his hands."

"Did he sit in the front seat?"

"Yep. And I drove off for us to go and split the money. Only 'bout two hundred."

"Did they say anything about the robbery?"

Telrey was joking about an old man security guard and how they took his gun. Jasper was cussing the old man with the walker, calling him a stupid ass, too stupid to get outta the way.

Not wanted to exhaust the witness, LaStanza moved to the Uptown Square Case.

"That weren't Jasper or Telrey. It was another dude I know. Dudley Rich. He white. About twenty, twenty-two, my height but plenty muscles. He were raised in the Magnolia where I stays. He don't stay there now. Stays on Hickory Street. Has the word "tattoo" tattooed on his shoulder."

Jodie passed LaStanza a note: *That name's familiar.*

Maybe he was on one of the car registrations or was at one of the bus stops, LaStanza thought as Zedimore continued.

"He bad. Real bad. I didn't know how bad."

With Zedimore driving the '77 Olds, he and Dudley went looking for someone to stick up. It was Dudley who spotted the woman coming out of Uptown Square. Zedimore described Monique Williams perfectly and how Dudley ran up to her, how she pulled away and Dudley just shot her and took her purse.

"I was pretty upset about that. She was so young and pretty." Zedimore's hands shook but he sucked it in and continued with no prodding. "We got some crack with the money and I got all messed up. Slept by Dudley's and the next morning he woke me up early. I was in pain."

"What type of gun did Dudley have at Uptown Square?"

"He got two guns. A revolver and one of them semi-automatic that shoots a buncha bullets."

Zedimore drove again the next day, this time through residential streets. His head was aching he could barely drive, but Dudley had brought the gun and a big stick he kept playing with.

They almost jacked a couple pedestrians, but one was a jogger and joggers don't carry money.

"Then we passed this house by Audubon Park and this lady opened the door and looked out like she was looking for something. She was an older woman and left the door cracked a little. Dudley tole' me to stop and jumped out before I was stopped. He lef' the gun, but took the stick, using it like a cane, like he had a limp. The woman saw him when he was up her sidewalk and closed the door.

"He rang the bell and waited. He rang it again and started to limp back down the steps when the door cracked open and the woman peeked out. I rolled down the window and heard Dudley say something about bein' hurt and would she call for help. He limped closer and before the woman could close the door, he shove it in and go in.

"He in there a while and when he came out with the stick, he covered in blood. He wipe his shoes in the grass and run to the car and we left. Dudley had no money, nothin' from the house. He said to take him home to clean up and I can rest my head before we go out again. But when we get to his house and he get out with that stick, I drove off and ain't seen him since. He bad. He evil!"

"What kind of stick was it?" LaStanza asked.

"It was like a branch from a tree. Dudley likes plants and trees."

Jodie bolted upright in her chair and started writing another note, this one longer.

LaStanza asked his next question, "What did Dudley say happened in the house?"

"Nothin' and I ain't asked. But I saw the newspaper." Zedimore's face showed pain.

"What have you been doing since?"

"Laying low. I ain't even seen Jasper or Telrey. Hope I never see Dudley. I went to Jefferson looking for something to steal and went around town, but my disability check come in so I been livin' on that money."

Maurice Zedimore received a monthly disability check from an insurance company for a five-year old injury he sustained at Avondale Shipyards across the river. He fell from a scaffold.

"This Dudley, does he hang out with Jasper or Telrey."

"Far as I know, they don't know each other."

Jodie passed her note to LaStanza: I think Dudley Rich was arrested by Beau last week just before Beau shot that guy. Might still be in jail.

LaStanza felt his heart racing again as he jotted on the note: *Go check?*

Jodie went out quickly as LaStanza went back to asking for more details on the other people Jasper and Telrey and Zedimore had robbed. Then ran through the names of Jasper's and Telrey's criminal associates. Zedimore knew none of them.

LaStanza felt the leopard again, knowing the hunt was truly on now and fought to keep the heat building inside under control, so he asked a meaningless question, waiting for Jodie to return.

"Do you know a Winston Zedimore?"

"No."

"What about Ray Stantz?"

"No."

"Peter Venkman?"

"No.

"Egon Spengler?"

"Nope."

Glancing around, LaStanza could see none of them suspected and wondered if the juries would find his sick humor offensive or would laugh as he did inside, which seemed to calm the leopard down.

Jodie came back in with Dudley Rich's mug shot and another note: *Dudley Rich was released this morning. Ask him to describe the house on Walnut.*

Zedimore might have had a bad headache that bright Easter Sunday morning, but he knew the house was on Walnut Street, running next to the park, knew it was two stories with stone walls and a covered front porch and a low wall Dudley had to step over on his way back to the car.

LaStanza had Zedimore positively identify photos of Jasper and Telrey Boykin and Dudley Rich in front of the video camera, having him sign the backs of the mug shots.

After the statement's concluded, it was Fel who told LaStanza,

"Those last names. They sound familiar." Then he turned to A.D.A. Donna Jamison and said, "I've seen you around the courthouse but didn't have to courage to ask if you were involved with anyone because, frankly, you are so pretty you intimidate me."

Jamison smiled a knowing smile and shook her head. "That ever work with women?"

"No, but I keep trying."

She looked a Fel for a long moment, pulled out a business card and jotted a phone number on the back and handed it to him. "My home number. And if you'll get out of my way, I have to provide some witness protection for Mr. Zedimore here."

Fel smiled so wide, he looked silly and watched Jamison walk out of the room behind the public defender and court reporter.

Mason, who handed LaStanza the video tape to be entered into evidence, told Zedimore, "We'll bring you across the street to the D.A.'s Office."

"Anybody ever eat around here?"

LaStanza said he'd pay if they could talk one of the rookies to go get the food. As they moved back into the squad room, Fel and Jodie heading for their desks to fill out arrest warrants for Dudley Rich for each case, LaStanza heading for his phone to leave a message for Lizette, who would still be in class.

They sat Zedimore next to LaStanza desk.

"You sure you don't know Winston Zedimore?"

"How many time I gotta tell you? No."

"And you don't know Ray Stantz, Peter Venkman or Egon Spengler?"

"That's right."

Fel called out, "Who are those guys?"

"Ghostbusters. Figured there can't be that many Zedimores."

"Ghostbusters?" Fel was incredulous. "From the movie?"

Jodie's mouth fell open. "You put that on the tape?"

LaStanza nodded as he picked up his phone. "Winston Zedimore was the black guy, played by Ernie Hudson. He's from New Orleans, you know."

"Y.C.M" Fel said. "Y.C.M."

Lizette wasn't there, so LaStanza left a message that they'd broken Fel's and Jodie's cases. They knew the perpetrators of the entire the Easter weekend slaughter. He'd call later."

"OK, what's Y.C.M.?" he asked Fel as he handed Kelly two twenties for the food and Zedimore sipped another Coke.

"You Crazy, Man."

LaStanza felt the leopard still inside, sharpening its claws, but its fangs weren't bared anymore. That would come later. He started up his Macintosh, he needed arrest warrants for the wonderful Boykin brothers as well – first degree murder.

"Hey," he called Fel over. "The Praise Jesus girl. Dana Barret. *Ghostbusters*."

4:05 p.m. – Hickory Street

"Damn, this place stinks."

The plan was to kick in the front and back doors of Dudley Rich's last known address simultaneously. Only there was an elderly woman hosing the front yard. They sent a smiling Kelly to get her out of the way. She became immediately excited, saying she was the landlady and Dudley Rich wasn't home. She's seen him walk off about two hours earlier, heading up for the streetcar stop, Carrollton and Claiborne.

LaStanza and Glapier drove up there while the landlady let the rest in with a key to save the doors. Jodie and Fel each had a search warrant, for each case and with uniformed Second District officers guarding the doors, they methodically searched Dudley Rich's house, which stank of plant fodder.

John Raven Beau, who had arrested this man he'd described as the "Plant Fiend" received a invitation inside. He was on patrol that day and already in uniform and incredulous that he'd arrested a double killer for stealing ferns.

"You know he had a bandage on his hand," Beau told Jodie. "Hell, I thought he'd pricked it on a thorn."

"He cut it inside Helen Collingwood's house."

Beau looked sick, kept shaking his head. "Son-of-a-bitch had four outstanding warrants from two different parishes, fifteen rocks of crack cocaine and three tabs of PCP in his wallet and he's back on the street in little over a week."

Jodie showed Beau the mug shot of Dudley Rich. Once before the lab had screwed up mug shots, putting the wrong name to the wrong face.

"That's him, the ugly fuck."

Fel found the .38 under Dudley's pillow. It was Smith & Wesson Combat Masterpiece, same type of weapon taken off the security guard from Shoe Town. They didn't find the semi-automatic but found Monique Williams's purse, along with four other purses at the bottom of the bedroom closet. Monique's wallet with her driver's license was still inside, but the cash and credit cards were missing. The other wallets were the same, so Fel had more robbery victims to contact.

LaStanza and Glapier returned, peeling off their bullet proof vests before joining the search party.

"Damn, this place stinks," was Glapier's observation.

As soon as the crime lab arrived, they had the Combat Masterpiece dusted for prints. Two latents were lifted. They opened the cylinder and found six mis-matched bullets. LaStanza took the weapon straight to the crime lab to have it compared to the bullet from Monique Williams.

6:10 p.m. – Detective Bureau

"You sure he's the killer?"

The desk sergeant called Fel on the intercom. A man was waiting for him. Fel went out into the visitor's area and found Monique's father standing in a gray work uniform.

"I was heading to your house as soon as I finished here," Fel explained.

"I thought I'd save you the ride."

Fel led him into the squad room and then into Lt. Mason's office where they told him about Dudley Rich.

"Didn't want you to hear it on the news. That's why I left the message. We're releasing his picture to the media."

"You sure he's the killer?"

"We recovered the gun he used to kill your daughter from his house with his prints on it."

Fel went out to his desk and brought back Monique's purse.

"It's got fingerprint dust on it," Fel apologized. "And we can't release it to you until after the trial."

The big man leaned over his daughter's driver's license. His shoulders began to shake and a tear fell on the license, smearing the dust. Fel and Mason left him alone.

7:30 p.m. – Walnut Street

"I'm glad you two were on this case."

There was a For Sale sign just inside the low stone wall and a red Pontiac parked outside the garage. The front door of Helen Collingwood's house was new, a dark wood door now.

Jodie pushed the doorbell and stood back with LaStanza.

"Who is it?" a woman's voice on an intercom.

"Det. Kintyre."

The dead bolt snapped and Belinda Collingwood let them into the now pristine foyer and through a furniture-less living room. The acidic smell of new carpet made Jodie's eyes water slightly as Belinda led them through the empty kitchen. Belinda, in a black tee-shirt and designer jeans, led them out the French doors to the benches behind the house, illuminated by yellow lights.

"I'd offer you something to drink, but the refrigerator's empty," Belinda said, smiling sadly at LaStanza as she sat on one of the concrete benches, while he and Jodie sat on another.

Jodie began with, "We've identified the man who killed your mother."

Belinda took in a deep breath.

"As soon as we finish here, we're releasing his name and picture to the media."

"You haven't caught him yet?" Belinda looked more pale than usual. She looked back at the darkness of Audubon Park and sat up straighter.

"We'll get him," Jodie said. "It's only a matter of time."

Belinda began to breathe heavier. "Was it someone she

knew?"

"No. It was a random killing. He went up to her door faking a limp and she tried to keep him out but he shoved his way in."

The victim's daughter didn't seem to understand so Jodie explained how the killer was just driving around and how her mother had opened the door to look out, probably heard something or checking the weather and how the man had limped up and she'd tried to shut the door but he was too quick.

Belinda closed her eyes for half a minute and when she opened them, she asked, "Someone saw this?"

"Yes," said Jodie. "We have a witness."

She looked at LaStanza again and said, "I know y'all worked hard on this and I appreciate it."

Jodie added, "We'll notify you as soon as we catch him."

Belinda continued staring at LaStanza, but it was not intrusive like Lori Venetta's stare, not flirtatious, but friendly, warm coming from an acquaintance from long ago and LaStanza remembered her words, "We square-danced together. You tried to kiss me at recess."

They waited until she seemed calmer and helped her lock up the house she was selling, walked her to her Pontiac, waited for her to start the motor. She sat there a few moments, staring straight ahead and LaStanza was glad Jodie hadn't told her about the stick. She'd hear about it in court. They'd found the stick in Dudley's back yard, up against the back fence where he'd thrown it, blackened with dried blood and brain matter.

Belinda rolled down the window and said, "I'm glad you two were on this case."

Then she drove off.

Saturday, April 12, 1986

10:45 a.m. – Exposition Boulevard

"They act nice, but they're bad-asses."

They met at the mansion but Jodie made it clear LaStanza wasn't invited to come along.

"Stay home with your wife. We got it covered." Jodie snapped as they all sat around the cherry wood table in the dining room, all drinking coffee, Fel and Kelly nibbling Krispy Kreme doughnuts they'd picked up on the way. All were in jeans today, with tee-shirts and dress shirts worn unbuttoned to cover their badges and weapons attached to their belts, all wearing tennis shoes.

LaStanza, his coffee stopped mid-way to his mouth, gave his partner a long look. Technically he was the senior partner, but in actuality they were equal and Dudley Rich, who was a far greater threat than Jasper fuckin' Boykin, was her killer, hers and Fel's.

"We've got it covered." Jodie turned away from him and started divvying out assignments. They would be in two cars, Kelly with her, Glapier with Fel.

Yesterday, Jodie couldn't understand why Dudley didn't return home and had staked out the place with Kelly. Fel surmised he probably saw them hit the house, was probably in the area and knew the police were there. By Friday evening, after his picture was on all the TV stations, no way Dudley Rich would return home.

But the weekend plan was to make periodic checks and continue checking every address he'd been connected to, which were plenty, including every address of every known criminal associate.

They thanked LaStanza for the coffee and just left. He watched them leave and went into the library where Lizette was at her computer, Thompson sitting next to her, Flash sleeping next to the French doors that faced the park. He'd let them out earlier, now he was thinking about going for a long run.

"I'm staying home today," he told his wife, who was in a tee-shirt and shorts, hair in a pony tail.

"What?"

"They don't need me."

She looked at him for a second, then went back to her typing. He lifted her pony tail and kissed the back of her neck, then went upstairs to change into a Columbian blue Rummel tee-shirt and black jogging shorts, blue Nike running shoes. As soon as he pulled the muzzles out of the kitchen closet, the dogs raced in, tails wagging, toe-nails tapping on the hardwood floor of the dining room and the tile kitchen floor.

It was so bright outside, he went back in for the gangster glasses he'd started wearing while working the Twenty-Two Killer case, back when he tied up with the local La Cosa Nostra. He ran slow but picked up the pace as he turned to run parallel to St. Charles Avenue. Flash and Thompson ran off on their own, investigating smells, chasing squirrels up trees, then bounding back. Sometimes they'd let him get ahead, then race past him as if he were crawling.

Moving around slow runners, women with baby carriages and the walkers, LaStanza had to dodge two bicyclers going the wrong way. The dog chased them, barking loudly, but only for a while, returning to run with him.

Glancing at the Collingwood house, he saw the benches they'd sat on last night. The air smelled cleaner with a nice breeze coming off the river, shoving the hair from his face as he ran. When he turned to run parallel to Magazine Street, he ran flat out until the turn back toward his house. Slowing to a jog, he moved parallel to Exposition Boulevard.

It felt peaceful, tranquil and LaStanza knew this was the way it should be, this was the way most civilians saw the park. He saw it through dark lenses mostly. Lizette's twin sister Lynette was killed in this park. He'd gunned down the Twenty-two Killer in this park. Helen Collingwood had been a neighbor. But the sun shined today and people laughed, kids played together and his dogs chased squirrels that chattered back from the safety of the oaks. Blue jays swooped through the trees, a mockingbird going through a litany of songs because it knew all the songs, white egrets stood on their stilt legs at the edge of the lagoon.

Slowing once he'd finished a complete run around the park, LaStanza continued walking up to St. Charles to cool down. Coming back, he passed one of the wooden gazebos overlooking the lagoon. Thompson ran into the gazebo to a woman in a white dress who sat reading a book.

She seemed startled, then laughed and started petting Thompson. Flash ran to get his pets and LaStanza had to call them.

"It's OK," the woman said as he came closer. "They're beautiful. Why are they muzzled?" She was in her fifties, with silver in her reddish-brown hair, worn longer than middle-aged women usually wear it. Her dress was standard-issue uptown female long, almost to her ankles. She wore white sandals and was reading Elmore Leonard's *LaBrava.*

"Good book," LaStanza said. He wasn't panting any more, which meant he was getting his wind back. "If they aren't on a lease, they have to be muzzled. The law."

"But these guys wouldn't bite anyone." She managed to rub both greyhound heads, her book falling in her lap.

"Actually they would," LaStanza kept his face deadpan. "They act nice, but they're bad-asses. Bad to the bone. Aren't you Flash?"

That was a mistake. Hearing his name, Flash turned and jumped on LaStanza, whining like a puppy, wanting more pets. The woman laughed.

"It's so nice outside today," she said.

"The humidity'll be back with a vengeance."

She smiled as she picked up her book. Thompson bounded away, chasing another squirrel to an oak tree. LaStanza backed away and Flash joined Thompson for one more romp before they went back home and it occurred to LaStanza again, – this was the way the park was supposed to be.

Peaceful.

Without the blood.

Lizette was just coming out of the shower as he was getting in. She slapped his ass and reached for a towel. When he got out, she was in a bra and panties, putting on make-up while bright sunlight beamed through the French windows of their balcony overlooking Garfield Street. For a moment, he remember her standing nude out there one night, showing off as he left for his bungalow back when they were falling in love. She thought she was cute standing there naked and looked mighty sexy even after wearing him out in bed.

When she had stepped back inside, away from the moonlight, LaStanza spotted the eight-year old boy who lived across the street standing in his yard staring up at her balcony. The boy would be eleven now and had since moved away with his family but LaStanza was sure he would never forget Lizette's nude balcony scene. She would be that boy's sexual fantasy the rest of his life.

Just like her students, Billy, Freddie and Jose.

"Feel like going to the Quarter?" she asked as she applied eye-liner.

"Why not?"

"Good. It's such a beautiful day." No need to tell him how nice the French Quarter was during the day.

She pulled on a white polo shirt and put on a red mini-skirt, nice and short and full, not tight, put her hair back into a pony tail and climbed into a pair of white Nike jogging shoes. Planning to do a lot of walking.

LaStanza put on a black tee-shirt and jeans, pulling on a light blue short-sleeved dress shirt to hide his magnum in its canvas holster on his belt at the small of his back. He also wore white Nikes.

12:50 p.m. – French Quarter

"Or you can call me Piglet."

LaStanza parked the Maserati in a parking garage next to WWL-TV station on Rampart Street. When he carried his LFR around to the trunk, Lizette said, "I thought you were going to carry it."

"I have the beeper."

He made sure the radio was off and locked it in the truck, taking his wife's hand as they walked out of the garage. Soon as they turned down St. Philip Street, the breeze lifted Lizette's skirt and a passing man smiled.

They spent three hours in the French Quarter, moving along sidewalks locals called banquettes, because they became banks when the streets flooded, moving along buildings with front stoops and porches up against the banquette, wooden buildings, brick and stucco buildings painted in pastel colors. The Quarter smelled old, dusty, sometimes a little moldy. Lizette's light perfume made up for it in the river breeze.

Lizette led the way up Royal Street, to jewelry shops, antique shops, clothing stores, passing the tourist traps, the voodoo shops, tee-shirt shops, erotic clothing stores. Lizette was erotic enough.

He noticed she'd shove down her skirt when they were around women or kids, but left it fly around men and he wondered if she did it automatically, without conscious thought.

She'd showed him an article, back when they were first going out, a magazine article on how to make an impact on a man. If you have good legs, wear short skirts and high heels and don't be afraid to bend over; when you can, don't wear panties; always wear perfume; show cleavage; show your back and shoulders wearing backless dresses; accidentally flash your panties – Lizette had elevated that last point to an art.

They had lunch at a small Italian place and stopped in a vintage clothing store where Lizette tried on several dresses from the 1940, bought a dark red one that was nice and tight, along with a pair of high heels with straps that perfectly matched the dress color, then spent the rest of the time looking for a matching purse.

LaStanza was just thinking how peaceful the day was as they were stepping back into the garage when he spotted Fel and Glapier across Rampart Street. He stopped and watched them walk into a tattoo parlor.

"Wasn't that Fel?" Lizette said.

LaStanza nodded and continued into the garage where they'd parked the Maserati, taking his LFR out of the trunk and turning it on. He was about to call but Jodie would hear and he'd just get an ear full.

"Want to see what they're up to?" Lizette again.

LaStanza shrugged and looked back at Rampart. Glapier came out of the tattoo parlor. Jodie called Fel on the LFR.

"3126 – 3128."

"Go ahead."

"We're striking out over here."

"Same here."

"One more stop and we're heading back to Magazine."

Still holding her husband's hand, Lizette started toward the street. "You put up with all the shopping, I'll let you poke your nose in, but just for a minute. Capiche?"

"Capito."

Crossing to the neutral ground, LaStanza nodded to the tattoo parlor. "Dudley Rich has the tattoo of the word 'tattoo' on his arm."

She had to smile.

Fel spotted them crossing to their side of the street. A strong breeze lifted Lizette's skirt and he smiled broadly. Glapier did a double take.

"What the fuck are a couple dazzling urbanites like y'all doing in this funky neighborhood?" LaStanza said.

Fel pointed up Rampart. "That's Dudley's pool hall."

"Well, don't let us stop you."

"Nice skirt," Fel told Lizette and turned to walk two doors down to Sandor's Pool Hall with LaStanza.

Glapier followed with Lizette, leaning close and saying, "We can see all your panties with that wind."

"That's the point," Lizette said.

Glapier flinched.

"If your man spotted a woman's skirt fly up, he'd look. Human nature. My husband does the same thing. I'd rather be the focus of his attention." Lizette's skirt blew up again but not so high. "The point is to keep them attracted." She smiled at Glapier and added, "And off balance."

"You husband don't get jealous?"

"He's the only one gets to touch." *Which wasn't completely true*, Lizette thought.

Sandor's was a typical New Orleans pool hall, plenty of tables, a bar along one wall, benches along the other, smelling of cigarette smoke and beer. It was too early for the crowd, only a bartender and one man shooting pool at a table next to a steep staircase.

Lizette asked the bartender for the ladies room.

"Upstairs." The bartender was in his fifties, portly and bald.

Glapier went upstairs in front of Lizette, LaStanza watching his wife go up, seeing those lacy white panties as she ascended. The man at the table noticed too and stared.

Fel stepped over to him and opened his shirt to show his badge.

"Police."

The man batted his eyes and said with a sly smile, "I was – just looking."

Fel gave him a pained expression and took out Dudley Rich's

mug shot.

The man looked at it and said, "He's not – here today."

"He comes in here?"

"Yeah, and I usually leave – because he's a jerk." The pool shooter laughed and looked at LaStanza. "He's a – bully."

"When's the last time you saw him here?"

"Now that I think of it – it's been a while. A month. Maybe longer."

"You come in here often?"

"Every – day."

Fel moved to the bartender. The pool shooter nodded to LaStanza. "Want to shoot – a game?"

"No."

The man stuck out his hand, "I'm George – Effinger."

"The science-fiction writer?"

Effinger was surprised, smiling even wider. He was in his forties, long brown hair and a full beard and wore a well-worn gray tee-shirt and even older jeans.

"George Alec Effinger?"

"Yep."

"Read your book in Nam. *What Entropy Means To Me.* Made me laugh."

Effinger seemed delighted.

"Didn't know you lived here," LaStanza said.

"Came in '70 – for the Clarion workshop at Tulane – and haven't left." Effinger was a slow talker, carefully choosing his words. When he'd started talking, LaStanza checked out his eyes, thinking he might be on something, but Effinger's eyes were too sharp and lit up again when Lizette came back down the stairs, hand on the railing. Looking up, LaStanza saw the full rear of her panties as she descended. The science-fiction writer let out an audible sigh.

Glapier moved toward Fel. Lizette came over to her husband who introduced her to Effinger who went, "Whoa – Wow. Nice short skirt. Wanna shoot – a game?"

Lizette laughed, tucking her arm around LaStanza. Subtle sign it was time to leave.

"Nice meeting you," LaStanza said.

"Nice meeting – both of you," – Effinger to Lizette.

LaStanza called out to Fel, "This guy knows Dudley."

Effinger was still watching Lizette, smiled again, "Thanks for letting me gape at your legs."

Turning back, LaStanza said, "You still go under the byline *Geo* Alec Effinger?"

"I'm just plain George – now. Or you can – call me Piglet."

Lizette looked over her shoulder at the science fiction writer, flipped the back of her skirt up and laughed. So did Effinger.

Sunday, April 13, 1986

11:12 a.m. – Exposition Boulevard

"Anything to get out of lunch with my parents."

Just as Lizette and LaStanza were about to leave for lunch at her parent's Estate on St. Charles Avenue, the phone rang. He was going to ignore it, but Lizette scooped it up.

Her shoulders sank. "For you."

He rolled his eyes and took the receiver. It was Headquarters. The Orleans Parish Criminal Sheriff's Office just called. They were holding Jasper Boykin at Parish Prison. They had a number for him to call.

LaStanza reached for the note pad and pen they kept in the kitchen cabinet next to the phone and called Parish Prison for a Sergeant Courane who answered after three rings.

"Thought you might want to take him over to central lockup," Courane said.

"How'd y'all catch him?"

Courane sniggered. "He came in to visit a prisoner. We ran him on the computer."

"I'll be right there." LaStanza hung up. "I don't fuckin' believe this! Jasper went to Parish Prison to visit his brother. Had to identify himself. The guards snatched him."

"Anything to get out of lunch with my parents," Lizette tried to smile but her lips shook.

He took her in his arms. "Come on, Babe. I planned this?"

She let out a long breath and laid her head against his shoulder. He felt her shiver.

"What is it?"

"I don't know. Sometimes, I start shaking and can't stop."

He pulled back and she looked at him. "You all right?"

"It's just nerves. You know what I'm talking about."

The job. The pressure. The stress affected everyone, spouses more sometimes because they could do nothing, but wait.

"Call me when you're done." She disengaged herself and straightened her dress. "My brother will be disappointed."

But her mother wouldn't. Lizette pecked him on the lips and went out.

He went back into the library for his briefcase, thinking of their nice Saturday together and the sex that had followed. It was a nice day, a very nice day.

Now, he had work to do.

12:09 p.m. – Detective Bureau

"I don't know notin' about hittin' no old man."

Jasper Boykin didn't go to Parish Prison to visit Telrey. He went there to see a woman.

In the interview room, after LaStanza set up the video camera and read him his rights, Jasper said, "I didn't even know Telrey was in jail, man. What'd you bust him for?"

He was asking questions, which made LaStanza very happy.

"Armed robbery of Shoe Town, Carrollton and Claiborne."

Jasper looked around the interview room. "That what this is about?"

"Among other things."

"Like what?"

"Stolen car. Murder."

"Murder?" Jasper sat back, all surprised.

LaStanza took out the flyer, showed it to the camera and put it in front of Jasper. "Like y'all posed for them."

Jasper examined the flyer, then folded his arms. "What murder?"

"An old man."

"I don't know notin' about hittin' no old man."

LaStanza, who was taking notes, asked him to repeat that.

"I don't know noting about hitting no old man," spoken more carefully this time.

"What about the robbery? Shoe Town?"

"I didn't rob notin'. And ain't even seen any old man around there."

"How did you know the old man was around there?"

"You said it." Jasper looked flustered.

"No.

"You asked 'What murder' and I answered, 'An old man'. I didn't say where or when the murder occurred." And he certainly didn't say anything about hitting the old man. LaStanza pointed over his shoulder. "It's on the video tape."

Jasper looked at the camera and tilted his head to the side like Flash and Thompson did.

"Do you know Maurice "Mo" Zedimore?"

"Yeah, I know Mo. Ain't seen him in months."

"When was the last time you saw him?"

"Christmas. He come 'round to show off his new car. A blue Oldsmobile."

Putting it on Mo now. Only the blue Olds wasn't stolen back then.

"What did you do on Good Friday? That was Friday before last? March 28th?"

"Shit!" Jasper said. "I don't wanna talk no more. I want my lawyer."

LaStanza closed out the statement, turned the video tape off and booked Jasper Boykin at central lockup with armed robbery and first degree murder. Then he went back to Parish Prison to book Telrey with the murder of Grosetto Venetta.

He daydreamed about playing the videotape of Jasper's interview to the jury, then holding up the newspaper and explaining how everyone thought the old man was shot. Jasper had said it plainly, "I don't know notin' about hittin' no old man."

It wasn't a confession, exactly. But it might be just as good.

"I jus' remembered I hate Eye-talians worsen I hate spicks."

When he finished booking Telrey, LaStanza had the woman Jasper had tried to visit brought into an interview room. A prison matron brought in Georgia Turchin from the House of Detention, a black female, thirty-two, five-one, two-fifty.

Georgia wouldn't even sit down.

"What makes you think I wanna talk to your ass?"

"Actually," LaStanza said. "I wanted you to talk to my face."

"Well, you better think again, I don't talk to cops, 'specially spick cops."

"I'm not a spick. I'm a wop."

"Oh, no. Not that Eye-talian shit." Georgia leaned against the wall.

"I just wanted to ask about your boyfriend Jasper."

"Jasper Boykin? He ain't no boyfriend 'a mine. I wouldn't fuck that scruffy ass bastard. He gets me my shit sometimes, but I don't fuck him."

"Your shit?"

"There you go, asking about ma' biness'."

"All right. You've been in jail three months. Is this the first time Jasper came by?" That was according to jailhouse records.

"He came by?"

"We arrested him. He talk to you on the phone?"

"No. That's why he came by, I guess."

"You know anything about what he's been doing the last few weeks?"

"Besides stinking up the city. No." Georgia gave the matron a sneer.

"Do you know anyone else who he might have told what he was doing?"

Georgia told the matron she wanted out. "I jus' remembered I hate Eye-talians worsen I hate spicks."

2:25 p.m. – Detective Bureau

"He caught himself."

LaStanza finished his daily, put copies in Mark and Mason's baskets along with a copy of the arrest reports, then called Pauli Venetta across the lake to tell him they had Jasper and Telrey, before Mason released it to the media.

He stared with, "How's your mother?"

"She'll never be the same but at least she's eating. With her sister."

"We have both of the killers now."

"You caught the second one?"

"He caught himself." LaStanza told him how Jasper waltzed into Parish Prison to visit an inmate.

"I'll tell Lori," Pauli said. "She's up here this weekend."

LaStanza warned them it would be on the TV, with that old out-of-focus photo of his father again and new mugs shots of Telrey and Jasper. Before he got off the line, Pauli said Lori would see him next week to thank him personally.

Sitting at his desk, he thought *Personally? All I freakin' need.* But part of him wanted to see Lori again. He didn't like that part of him, but it was there.

He called the Estate for his wife and got her mother on the line. Her voice became instantly icy. "She already went home."

He called his house. No answer. On his way home, he called Jodie and Fel on the LFR, glad they didn't answer. They needed some time off.

3:30 p.m. – Exposition Boulevard

"And there'll be another one, then another and another."

Waiting for a street light, LaStanza looked out at the blue sky, at high billowy clouds. It was another pretty day, maybe even prettier than yesterday in Audubon Park. When the light changed, he proceeded and things started bouncing in his mind – the beauty of the park, the horror in Helen Collingwood's house, an image of

Dudley Rich coming out of that house with his tree trunk dripping blood, the greyhounds bounding along the grass, squirrels running away, Lizette walking in the park.

His felt the adrenaline rising and gunned the Maserati. They lived on the park and Dudley Rich was still out there and his wife wasn't home. He knew he was being paranoid, but still hurried home. As the automatic garage door opened and he saw the Range Rover inside, he felt a little better. Deactivating the alarm, he stepped into the kitchen and called out for her. No answer. And no dogs. ·

He went out front and the gate was open and he shielded his eyes as he looked out at the park. A quick movement to his right drew his attention and he spotted Thompson romping toward the lagoon and there was Lizette, walking slowly along the lagoon with Flash.

He stretched and went out the gate.

A movement to his left caused him to look that way as a white man walked at an angle that would intercept Lizette. He was about five-nine with a heavy build and brown hair. He fit Dudley Rich's description. LaStanza hurried.

Flash met him half way and he gave the greyhound a quick pet as the man closed in to Lizette, who was wearing a tee-shirt cut off so it wouldn't hang too far over her red shorts. LaStanza walked faster as the man passed Lizette and said something. She pointed across Exposition Boulevard and spotted her husband.

"Hey, Babe!" he called out.

The man turned to him and it wasn't Dudley Rich. LaStanza slowed his pace as the man moved away from his wife.

"What'd he want?"

"Asked which side of the park was Henry Clay Avenue?"

LaStanza gave the man a long stare but the man never looked back. Flash ran up to the man and sniffed around him. Lizette was already moving away, so he turned to keep up.

They walked next to the lagoon, Lizette looking down. Flash came up and LaStanza took of his muzzle. He called Thompson over and took off his muzzle too. A stranger might think twice going after a woman with two big dogs. Wouldn't deter a monster like Dudley but it might make him think twice.

"Why'd you take off their muzzles?"

"It's cruel and unusual punishment for dogs who've done nothing."

"I thought it was the law."

"Let 'em call a cop."

She gave him an uneasy look but he knew it wasn't about the hounds. He took her hand and she finally slowed down. A few more steps and he asked, "You wanna talk about it?"

She didn't.

"I've got them both in jail now."

"But that other guy isn't. The one y'all were looking for at the pool hall."

A full minute later, she squeezed his hand but didn't look at him as she said in a weary voice, "And there'll be another one, then another and another."

Monday, April 14, 1986

9:10 a.m. – Detective Bureau

"How'd he get a fan?"

Jodie had picked her partner up on the way to work and they walked into the office together, she in a black pants-suit, him in a black suit, white shirt and a silver and gray tie.

Snowood, in a gold cowboy shirt with fringe, gold denims, light brown boots, white Stetson on his desk, had pinned his gold star-and-crescent badge to his shirt yet again. He spotted them and called out, "I got y'alls things here."

"What things?" Jodie asked.

"Newspaper articles. Y'all all over the place."

LaStanza stepped up to Country-Ass and said, "Did you say you had 'y'alls' things?"

"Yep."

"Y'alls? Y'alls? Try English. Standard fuckin' English. *Your.* I've got your things here."

Snowood seemed surprised. "You suddenly ain't southern no more?"

"Y'all doesn't have a possessive form." LaStanza put his briefcase on his desk.

Snowood said, "You knew what I meant."

Problem was, he was right and Snowood picked up his phone to end the discussion. LaStanza looked at the neatly cut articles of the arrests of Telrey and Jasper and shook his head. He looked over at Jodie and she had neatly cut articles on her desk.

"Just peachy keeno," Jodie said as LaStanza's phone rang.

It was the desk sergeant out front. "A man's out here for Snowood. Says he wants to confess something."

LaStanza went to the coffee pot with his mug. Jodie joined him and by the time they returned, Snowood was just hanging up.

"Someone's out front for you."

"Who?"

"Somebody looking to confess something."

"The fuck. I ain't no priest." Snowood got up and went out just as Kelly and Glapier came in, each wearing black and LaStanza looked at Jodie who smiled and quipped, "We all knew you'd be wearing black today."

Mason stepped out of his office in black pants and tie and called out to LaStanza, "You coulda called me about Jasper."

"Why ruin your Sunday?"

Mason went back into his office as Fel came in with Stevens trailing and LaStanza laughed immediately. Both wore light blue suits. At least Fel's tie was also blue, while Stevens wore a brown tie with yellow and green stripes.

LaStanza was just explaining about Jasper to everyone when a pale-looking Snowood led in a tall, thin balding man with deep-set eyes. He took the man into an interview room and came out, asking LaStanza and Jodie, "Y'all know anything about the Sniper Case?"

"He's killed four politicians," Jodie said.

"Or is it five?" LaStanza.

Snowood nodded over his shoulder. "Fella in there say's he used a Mauser Model 68." Snowood went to Mason's office and for the first time in his career, left the others speechless.

Mason led Snowood back into the interview room, came out ten minutes later and told them, "Y'all better get outta here. The

Task Force is coming."

"And miss the cluster fuck?" LaStanza said.

Jodie scooped up the articles Country-Ass had put on her desk and announced it was time to search for Dudley. Again.

LaStanza bowed out. "I gotta get my preliminary report to the D.A. on the Senoré Case." He had two men in custody whose lawyer would file for a preliminary hearing as soon as possible and the D.A.'s Office might actually want to bring it before a Grand Jury before too long.

Jodie led the others out.

Stevens waited until they were alone to ask LaStanza what was up.

"Man came in to confess to the sniper killings. Your partner's in with him."

Stevens looked around as if he was the butt of another joke, even looking under his partner's desk. Snowood couldn't be far off. His Stetson was still there.

The Task Force arrived like the cavalry, rushing in, bouncing around, talking over each other. A smallish FBI guy, who made it clear he was in charge, told Mason he needed to see this man right away. Mason led him into the interview room, then led him out a minute later. The FBI guy was fuming, stomping off to huddle with the other feds away from LaStanza's desk as he sat typing his preliminary report on his Macintosh.

The FBI guy in charge passed a small envelope to another FBI agent who ran out of the office. LaStanza recognized him as the FBI agent who'd checked out his Maserati parked on the levee when Councilman Jacks was shot.

Mason huddled with several of the NOPD detectives assigned to the Task Force. Eventually Snowood came out and went to Mason. The FBI guy in charge came over and he and Mason and Snowood went into Mason's office for a short while. When Snowood came out, he carried an FBI issued note book, dark blue with a gold crest on it and a blank video tape. He looked at LaStanza and shrugged before going back into the interview room.

Stevens said, "I have a stupid question."

"There are no stupid questions," LaStanza answered. "Just stupid people."

Steven looked hurt.

"Not you." LaStanza nodded to the Feds who were whispering to each other as if the place was bugged by the K.G.B. "What's your question?"

"What's really going on?"

Thankfully Mason came over and told them. "His name is John Smith. Knows the details of each shooting, even the stuff we've kept out of the media. Even knows the secret code word. Says the murder weapon is a bolt action Mauser Model 68, 30-06, with a Zeiss scope. He brought a spent casing. The FBI guy who ran out of here took it to their office. They have a firearms expert there. They just called. It's a match."

LaStanza waited for the punch line because Mason was about to burst out laughing.

"Apparently," Mason said. "John Smith is a Paul Snowood fan. Seen him in the papers and on TV, the cowboy detective. Smith is from Texas and will only talk to Snowood."

LaStanza started laughing and couldn't stop.

"So we have to feed questions to Snowood, who doesn't know dick about the fuckin' case."

The FBI guy in charge slipped a sheet of paper under the door and LaStanza almost fell over as the guy leaned his ear against the door. Three FBI guys stood next to him taking notes. The other FBI guys glared at the laughing LaStanza.

Eventually LaStanza composed himself, but lost it again when Stevens said, "I don't have any fans. How'd he get a fan?"

By the time the U.S. Attorney and the D.A. himself came in, LaStanza got the fuck out, called Jodie on the radio and went to meet them for lunch at The Veranda.

2:05 p.m. – St. Andrew Street

"– where his soul will wander eternally."

They parked just off Tchoupitoulas on St. Andrew Street, everyone getting out to stretch after a nice lunch.

Glapier was just saying their luck might hold, the way they caught Zedimore, Telrey, Jasper and now the sniper. "Dudley may fall into our laps."

"What the fuck are we doing here?" Fel asked.

Jodie seemed irritated as she looked at her notes. "Dudley Rich was arrested here for burglary." She pointed to a small auto repair shop that occupied part of a long building that once was a warehouse. He looked up St. Andrew. "He was chased toward the projects but was caught by the Harbor Police."

Kelly pointed up the street to the brown brick buildings of the St. Thomas Housing Projects and asked LaStanza. "One of your old haunting grounds?"

Fel still couldn't believe about Snowood and the South Louisiana Sniper Case.

"It broke our string of weird names," LaStanza said.

"Huh?"

"Vada Ganoush, Piso Mojado, Prohibito Fumar, Boykin, Lamont Cranston, Herion, Ghostbusters Zedimore and Dana Barret, George Gershwin –"

"Cranston Lamont," Fel corrected him.

"Enough!" Jodie said, divvying up the assignments.

"Who put you in charge?" Fel said with a big smile.

Jodie sighed so LaStanza called for a vote and Jodie won, unanimously, even Fel voted for her. Shaking her head, she led Fel and Glapier toward the open garage of the repair shop while LaStanza and Kelly moved up St. Andrew Street.

The next two buildings were unoccupied. They managed to slip though a broken door of the second building and searched carefully. The third building had businesses on the first floor, a small import company and a smaller tire distributor. No one recognized Dudley's ugly face.

LaStanza asked what was upstairs. The building had three stories. It was vacant.

"If I can't go jogging today," he told Kelly as he led the way up the steep stairs, "I'll do stairs." For a moment he remembered running stadiums back in high school when he was on the track team. Going up and down stadium bleachers to build his legs and wind.

Reaching the top of the stairs, LaStanza slipped out his magnum and eased into a large room, a room occupying the entire second floor of the building. It was well lit, thankfully, by rows of windows with no curtains. It was completely empty, but divided by plywood walls that reached only half way up to the ceiling.

When Kelly started to go in another direction, LaStanza told him no. "Stick together. Never separate from your partner. Two guns are better than one." He was about to add that whatever happened to your partner, should happen to you when he heard a scraping behind them and two shots rang out striking Kelly in the back.

LaStanza wheeled to his right, ducking and firing at a man with a semi-automatic who fired back. LaStanza felt his side burning as his first three quick rounds struck the man in the torso, stumbling the man backward. LaStanza fired three more rounds, each striking the man, ascending up to the man's face. The man fell on his back.

LaStanza jumped behind a wall, dug out a speed loader and reloaded his magnum. Returning to his two-handed police grip, he listened for a moment and heard gurgling. He slid out from behind the wall, leveling his sights on the man whose left foot quivered. The man's hands were spread open, semi-automatic weapon on the floor now.

LaStanza stepped over quickly, kicked the gun away and looked at the dying face of Dudley Rich. Frothy blood spewed from the man's mouth. His right eye was gone.

He ran to Kelly lying face down. Holstering his weapon he turned Kelly over, reached in to clear his throat, cocked Kelly's head back and began mouth-to-mouth resuscitation and CPR. Pulling his LFR out with his left hand, he called Headquarters.

"3124 – Signal 108! Officer down. Ambulance Code Three. 525 St. Andrew. Second floor."

He dropped the radio and went back to mouth-to-mouth and CPR.

Headquarters responded and asked for more details, but LaStanza kept working on Kelly, blood on his hands now, pooling around his knees. He calmed himself, pushing the leopard away, keeping up the timing on the CPR, forcing air into Kelly's lungs.

Running footsteps on the stairs.

"Up here!" He shouted.

Fel stumbled in with Glapier.

He yelled at Fel, "Don't let Jodie up here!"

Fel looked from Kelly to Dudley and retreated. LaStanza breathed into Kelly's mouth, then told Glapier to go downstairs and flag down the ambulance. LaStanza heard Mason and Mark on the radio now, calling him. Fel answered, asking them to 10-3 – stop transmitting, and giving the location.

LaStanza concentrated on the CPR and mouth-to-mouth. Kelly's eyes were half open. He was gone but LaStanza continued. He was having trouble catching his own breath and tried to slow down, but couldn't. He couldn't focus and realized his eyes were wet. There were tears. He kept on going. He didn't hear them, but strong hands pulled him off Kelly and he realized two EMTees were there.

The same EMTees from the starved girl case. The big one taking over CPR, the smaller one slipping a tube down Kelly's throat, attaching a plastic ball and squeezing air into Kelly's lungs.

LaStanza sat back, wiping his eyes, trying to breathe.

The big EMT ripped Kelly's shirt and squirted salve from a tube, put paddles against Kelly's chest and said, "Clear."

Kelly's body lurched.

The big man looked at a small monitor then said, "Clear."

Kelly's body lurched again.

He tried a stethoscope and shook his head.

LaStanza looked at the door and Jodie was there, standing stiffly, watching. Fel stepped behind her. Two more EMTees squeezed in and went to Dudley and LaStanza smelled blood now and gunpowder and leaned over and retched, but only acid came up, burning as he spit it out.

Fel came over and knelt next to him. "You weren't hit, were you?"

LaStanza looked at his side at the brown burn mark on his shirt and shook his head. Fel checked him out anyway. LaStanza watched the men working on Kelly. The other EMTees didn't bother with Dudley.

Finally, the EMTees stopped and backed away from Kelly and Jodie came over on shaky legs, went down on her knees and pulled Kelly's head into her lap. Her head down, hair blocking her face,

LaStanza watched his partner's body shudder as she cried.

He found his voice and told Fel, "Nice keeping her out of here."

He couldn't see again and wiped his eyes. Then Mark bounded into the room, almost knocking over the four EMTees. He ran them out, then inched over to look down at Dudley Rich.

Mason came in, slumped against the doorway. John Raven Beau came in after him, glanced around and went straight to Jodie, kneeling next to her. He leaned close and started whispering in her ear.

Mark pointed Dudley's gun out to Mason, then pointed to all the bullet holes in the wall behind LaStanza.

"You sure he ain't hit?" Mark snapped at Fel who lifted LaStanza's arms and looked him over again, shaking his head.

"Musta shot a dozen rounds," Mark said. LaStanza hadn't heard them over the sound of his .357 magnum.

"Miracle he missed you," Fel said and LaStanza nodded to Kelly. "Some fuckin' miracle."

Mason came over and asked LaStanza if he could get up.

He got up slowly and Mason guided him aside with Mark.

"Talk to me," Mason said and LaStanza told him what he remembered, hearing a sound behind them and the shots, wheeling and firing and Dudley going down and trying to help Kelly.

Mason told Fel to walk LaStanza downstairs, leading the way himself. They brought LaStanza into a room on the first floor, part of the import company offices. Mason went out to grab Stan Smith, who just arrived, telling Smith to cordon off the area, keep the fuckin' media away.

Jodie couldn't stop the tears, didn't want to as she held Kelly, her lips pressed to his face. She heard a voice, a deep voice and knew it was Beau from his slight Cajun accent, but she didn't know what he was saying.

She was in a deep pit, holding on to Kelly, knowing when she let go, she'd never hold him again. She felt herself rocking. Then she felt strong hands pulling her up gently. She wiped her eyes and looked down at Kelly. She kissed his lips, then let them lift her.

It was Beau and she said, "This isn't even the Second District."

He nodded, holding on to her elbows and she realized he was keeping her up. She willed her legs to strengthen and they did, eventually, and Beau led her to the stairs.

When they reached the bottom, Mason was there.

"Where's Dino?" she asked and he opened a door and her partner stood with his back to a window, his arms folded and it was the first time she'd ever seen tears on his face.

"Were you hit?" she asked.

He shook his head.

Mark was suddenly there, telling Mason he would handle the scene. Mason said he'd get LaStanza out of there.

Mark nodded to Jodie, "Her too."

Mason decided to take Jodie and have Glapier drive LaStanza to the Bureau.

Fel Jones was upstairs, helping Mark with his notes when Beau came back up with a long knife in his hand. Looked like a hunting knife with a black blade.

"What are you doing?" Mark asked.

Beau went to Dudley, leaned over and sliced a swatch of the dead man's hair off before Mark could stop him.

"Thought you were gonna scalp him," Fel said as Beau came back to the door.

Beau held up the hair. "I'm sending his spirit to Wendigo, to the devil's underworld where his soul will wander eternally."

3:25 p.m. – Detective Bureau

"The Chief ain't gonna like this one bit."

As Mason led Jodie into his office, LaStanza picked up his phone and called Lizette, a little surprised when she answered.

"I'm OK," he told her.

"What happened?" her voice almost a whisper.

"Kelly's been shot. Dudley Rich is dead. I'm at the office with Jodie. I'll be home in a few hours."

"Anyone else get hurt?"

"No. But the news will say an officer's been shot and I wanted you to know."

She hung up without saying goodbye.

He called his parents and was surprised again when his father answered. Not surprisingly, the old man sounded half looped.

"I been meaning to call you," the old man said right away. "What's the big idea of paying for my car to be fixed? You think I don't have money?"

"Dad, there's been another police shooting. A friend of mine was killed."

"Anybody I know?"

"Edward Kelly, after your time."

"Now about the car –"

"Pop! I shot the guy who did it."

"Another one? The Chief ain't gonna like that one bit."

No fuckin' kiddin'!

"It's gonna be on the news. Better cushion Mom."

"Yeah. Guess I better. And you better start thinkin' about what you're gonna do after law enforcement. You all right?"

"Yeah, Dad. Just fine. Just do me one favor."

"What?"

"Enough about the car."

Mason came out to take his statement and LaStanza asked, "What happened to Country-Ass and the FBI guys?"

"Went to their office. Better coffee."

Mason took his statement in Mark's office. Gershwin came and swabbed his hands for a neutron activation test. The superintendent's hearing was set up for the next day. The grand jury would come later.

7:07 p.m. – Exposition Boulevard

"This is all too fast."

LaStanza wished Mason would have come in when he saw Jodie lying on one sofa, Lizette on another. At least Glapier was there, sitting at Lizette's desk and Beau stood by the fire place in the library, beneath the portrait of Lynette. Beau was in jeans and a tee-shirt now and stood sipping an Abita beer. Flash and Thompson were lying next to the French doors.

He met Glapier's eyes, then looked at Beau who nodded slightly. His wife and partner didn't look at him. Flash got up and moved to him and nuzzled his nose against LaStanza's leg. He realized it was Kelly's dried blood.

"I'm going take a shower."

Lizette and Jodie still didn't look but he knew it was for different reasons.

He took a long one, turning up the hot water until it slammed against him, letting it get very hot. After, drying himself, he felt a little better and went down with wet hair, in another tee-shirt and black running shorts. Flash nuzzled his bare leg and Lizette finally looked at him with a resigned look, a look similar to the one his mother used to give him when he did something that disappointed her.

He thought Jodie was asleep until she spoke, her voice gravelly. "Don't feel guilty."

"He was with me," LaStanza said.

"I was talking to Beau." She looked at Beau. "You put him in jail where he belonged. Not your fault he got out."

Beau looked at his shoes.

Jodie put her arm across her eyes. "You couldn't save Kelly," talking to LaStanza now. "It was an ambush. Bastard could have shot you instead of him." Her voice broke and she sat up.

"I have to feed my cats."

"I'll bring you," said Glapier.

The kitchen doorbell rang and LaStanza went and let Fel in.

"How is she?"

"In the living room."

Fel went through the dining room and foyer, stopping in the doorway to the library, turning to LaStanza as Jodie came toward them. He whispered to LaStanza, "I meant your wife."

"What?"

Jodie asked Fel, "How many times was Kelly shot?"

Fel put his hands in his pockets and said, "Twice. In the back."

"How many rounds did the ass-hole fire?"

"Twelve. Two at Kelly. Ten in LaStanza's direction."

Lizette was standing behind Jodie, gold-brown eyes staring wide-eyed at her husband.

323

Jodie to LaStanza now, "How many times did you fire?"

"Six."

"And hit six times," Fel said.

Jodie looked at the cut glass front door. Thompson nosed into the group and she petted his head and said, "He bought me a silver pin in Mississippi. Didn't want to wear it to work and lose it. The only thing he ever gave me."

Her eyes seemed clear suddenly, bright hazel now, wide cat eyes looking into her partner's light green eyes. "Too fast," she whispered. "This is all too fast."

"You sure you don't want something to help you sleep?" Lizette asked as Jodie started through the foyer.

Jodie shook her head and Glapier followed her out to the police cars parked on Garfield Street. LaStanza watched them pull away. Beau thanked Lizette for the beer, dropping the empty into the garbage can before heading to the door.

LaStanza caught his attention. "What did you tell her up there?"

"Just some lines from *Evangeline*." The big cop suddenly looked self-conscious, younger. "We Cajuns tend to go back to *Evangeline* when thing are bad. 'Then he beheld, in a dream, once more, the home of his childhood – As in the days of her youth, Evangeline rose in his vision – Vainly he strove to rise, and Evangeline, kneeling beside him, kissed his dying lips, and laid his head on her bosom'.

"I think I ran through the whole rest of the poem, all the sorrow, aching of the heart, the dull deep pain ending. They'd finally found each other."

He shrugged and thanked Lizette again and left.

It was Fel who explained to Lizette how Beau knelt next to Jodie when she was cradling Kelly and whispered to her.

"You gonna be all right?" Fel asked Lizette. He'd come to check on her, not Jodie, not LaStanza. She pulled her hair away from her face and nodded and Fel left.

LaStanza set the alarm, his arms so tired now, his legs aching as he followed his wife back through the dining room. Without looking back, she said, "I'm going to lie down here a while." She went to the sofa and curled up on it, her back to him.

He stopped in the doorway, then sat down, his back against the wall just within the library and watched her. Flash came over to lay next to him on the carpet while Thompson climbed up on the sofa by Lizette's feet.

LaStanza forced himself to think of nothing, nothing at all. He just watched his wife and when he saw her steady breathing, when he felt she was asleep, he turned off the lights and curled up on the other sofa and fell asleep.

11:50 p.m. – Exposition Boulevard

"I really don't know how much more of this I can take."

He thought it was the air conditioning that woke him. He sat up, shivering and looked at the other sofa. Thompson looked back at him but Lizette wasn't there. He realized her desk light was on behind him and turned and saw her sitting at her desk reading a book.

He got up, turned down the AC before going over to her. He could see the book's title, *The Poems of Henry Wadsworth Longfellow.*

"Haven't read this since grammar school," she said without looking up. He went around and leaned against the desk, looking over her shoulder at the lines. He'd read *Evangeline* a long time ago. Every kid who went to Catholic school in south Louisiana read it in grammar school.

Lizette read the lines softly, "All was ended now, the hope and the fear and the sorrow, all the aching of the heart, the restless, unsatisfied longing, all the dull, deep pain and constant anguish of patience! And, as she pressed once more the lifeless head to her bosom, meekly she bowed her own –"

Evangeline had finally found her lover. Separated when they were deported from Canada by the British, they searched their entire lives for one another to finally find each other as Gabriel lay on his death bed.

Lizette closed the book after reading the last line, stood up and turned to him. He looked back into her eyes, at the gold flecks in those topaz irises. The resigned look was gone and so was the fearful look. The look in her eyes was searching and he hoped what she was searching for what was still there in his eyes.

Lizette took his hand, reached back and flicked off the lamp and led him upstairs.

In the faint light streaming through the sheer curtains of their bedroom's French doors, they took off their clothes and climbed into bed, pulling the sheet up. Both lay on their backs, Lizette cradled in his left arm, head against his shoulder.

"I love you, Babe."

"I love you too."

After a long moment Lizette said, "I really don't know how much more of this I can take."

"I know." His heart racing again. "I know."

Tuesday, April 15, 1986

10:10 a.m. – Detective Bureau

" – and I'm a footnote."

The Superintendent's Hearing took less than twenty minutes, with Deputy Chief Jim Morris running the show. LaStanza's shooting of Dudley Rich was found to be justified. No mention was made of his previous shootings, but when the Chief of Police came back to town, everyone knew that would be addressed.

LaStanza waited outside the hearing room until Mason came out with the official memo.

"Go home," Mason said, "and don't come back until next Monday. That's the twenty-first."

"Am I suspended?"

"'Course not. Take some of those vacation days you've been hoarding."

They went down to the squad room.

"I'm going to wait for the autopsy results," LaStanza said, sitting at his desk.

Stevens was at his desk pecking away on an electric typewriter. Snowood, looking shell-shocked came in with a handful of the morning newspapers. LaStanza had already seen it, big photo of sniper John Smith being led into Parish Prison, along with pictures of his sniping victims.

"Only one time," Snowood fumed. "They put ma' name in *one* time and fuckin' misspelled it. How the fuck do you misspell Snowood?" The ever inaccurate morning paper had spelled it Snowoode.

"I broke the goddamn case. Took the longest fuckin' statement in the history of this department and I'm a footnote."

"They didn't put my quote in either," LaStanza said.

"What quote?" Snowood had either forgotten to wear western duds or everything he owned was in the cleaners. He was in a dress shirt and black slacks, dark blue tie.

"I told them what you said when the man came into confess. How you didn't want to talk to him. You said, 'The fuck. I ain't no priest'."

"Did I?"

LaStanza nodded and had to ask, "Why aren't you wearing one of your Tombstone get ups?"

Stevens answered for him, "'Cause that's why his picture wasn't in the paper. He looked like a refugee from a Hoot Gibson movie."

Mark and Fel came in and waved LaStanza into Mason's office.

Kelly had died instantly, or just about instantly. One bullet severed his aorta, the other perforated his left ventricle. A heart shot.

"Dudley was also shot through the heart," Mark explained. "And through both lungs, through the vena cava, through the right eye that blew up the medulla oblongata and once in the stomach."

Mark pointed at LaStanza. "How the fuck you shoot like that with a magnum kicking around while someone's shooting ten rounds at you I'll never know."

Snowood snapped, "That's cause you ain't Wyatt!"

5:25 p.m. – Exposition Boulevard

"I'd still like to know how to bomb a tent and not kill the guy inside."

Lizette had found the shirt LaStanza had thrown away and had it spread out on the kitchen counter, burn mark up. She came into the kitchen and stood in the doorway with her arms folded.

"Why didn't you tell me?"

He had no answer. She looked like she'd been crying, turned and went back through the dining room. He put his briefcase up on the counter and followed her into the library where she plopped on the sofa and turned on the TV in time for the CBS Evening News.

The screen was immediately filled with images of bombers and explosions. The U.S. bombed military targets in Libya and the home of Libyan leader Mohamar Khadafy.

LaStanza sat next to her and watched images of planes taking off from aircraft carriers, the *U.S.S. Coral Sea* and *U.S.S. America,* as Dan Rather explained how we also sank the entire Libyan navy, such as it was, sending it to the bottom of the Gulf of Sidra.

Film of F-111 Air Force bombers taking off from bases in England was shown as Rather reminded viewers of the heady days of World War II when American bombers lifted off from Britain to decimate the Nazis.

They had to fly around France, however, because the French wouldn't allow an over fly.

"My ancestors," Lizette said, "already forgot about two world wars and all those Americans buried at Normandy. Whatever happened to 'Lafayette, we are here.'?"

She was in history mode all right watching bombed out sites at Benghazi and Tripoli. "We've fought there before," she went on. "The Barbary War, 1803. The navy sailed in and blew up everything it could, only way to deal with the Barbary Pirates."

Then Rather explained how we tried to kill Khadafy, blowing up his tent, only we didn't get him.

LaStanza had to laugh. "How the fuck you blow up a tent and not kill the guy?"

"They shoulda sent you."

He looked at her but she wouldn't look back. Reagan came on, saying we did what we had to do.

"He's playing cowboy while the economy goes down the toilet," Lizette said.

They finally switched to another story, a bombing in Jerusalem.

The doorbell rang.

"That'll be the pizza guy," Lizette said. "We have to eat before we settle this."

"Settle?" He felt suddenly nervous.

"Why you didn't tell me you got shot."

He was going to correct her. *I didn't, my shirt got shot*, but knew better so he just said, "I'd still like to know how to bomb a tent and not kill the guy inside."

It was much later, in bed that she had her say, talking a good half hour about the fear in her heart. She even said she knew he was careful but Kelly was careful too.

He said nothing, but listened closely and told her, "I don't know what to do about it."

"That's the real problem. There's nothing either of us can do. We just have to live with it." She looked into his eyes finally. "I just want to you know how hard it is for me."

Wednesday, April 16, 1986

5:15 p.m. – Metairie Cemetery

"Sent shivers through us."

Family and friends were invited before the wake started at six.

They picked Jodie up on the way and Lizette parked the Ranger Rover in the side parking lot of the cemetery that was once a race course. Lizette wore a charcoal gray dress that reached mid-thigh, long for her, and black stockings and heels. Jodie wore her black pants-suit. LaStanza wore another of the black suits his wife bought for him, a black tie with cobalt blue specks to go with the cobalt blue dress shirt.

Edward Patrick Kelly's parents were young, still in their forties, both slim and tall with blue eyes dulled by pain, agony actually, right there for everyone to see. Mason stood next to them by the sign-in book.

Lieutenant Rob Mason, in his only black suit, white shirt and black tie, had gone to the Kellys with the police chaplain, had spent the time explaining to them exactly how their son died under his command. He looked tired, worn, cheeks sunken.

Mason introduced them. Mrs. Kelly seemed to realize who Jodie was but no one must have told them LaStanza was with her son in that goddamn building. After signing the book, they moved through a waiting room of empty chairs into the viewing parlor where Kelly's older sister sat on the sofa alongside the open casket and spoke to no one.

The police honor guard, standing in dress uniforms on either side of the casket, looked as if they'd come straight out of the police academy. Young, fresh faced, they looked determined and eager. Kelly was laid out in his NOPD uniform.

Jodie stepped up first and stood there motionless for a long time, staring at Kelly. Slowly her stiffness seemed to soften and she finally moved, brushing Kelly's cheek with her fingers. Lizette stepped next to her, made the sign of the cross and the women began whispering. LaStanza backed away, a headache starting from the sickly smell of roses. Too many police funerals made him hate that sweet scent of roses, carnations too.

When Jodie and Lizette moved away, arms interlocked, he went up to the casket and looked at Kelly whose hair, naturally wavy, lay flat on his head. LaStanza never understood people saying someone looked good in their coffin, that the mortician did a good job.

They looked dead.

Kelly, a handsome man in life, looked old and waxy, an impression of what he was like in life. LaStanza wanted to lean over Kelly and whisper, "I'm sorry." But Kelly wasn't there. Better if he just went out and said it to the oaks, said it loud so Kelly could hear him, wherever the hell he was, if he was anywhere.

He felt horrible as he held on the side of the coffin.

I was the senior man. I was responsible.

He found Jodie and Lizette outside the waiting room, Jodie sitting on a sofa, Lizette standing with Fel Jones who was with Donna Jamison, the A.D.A. from Zedimore's immunity. They were holding hands. Fel worked fast, especially on the female side of things.

"He in there?" Fel nodded to the parlor.

"No, Bela Lugosi's in there."

"Bela Lugosi's dead?"

LaStanza didn't feel like continuing the joke so he went around them and sat next to Jodie and took a closer looked at the silver seagull pin on her lapel. She noticed and patted it.

Belinda Collingwood was the first civilian to arrive. She was with a big guy in another black suit and LaStanza remembered her husband was an Airline pilot. He went over to them and Belinda smiled weakly and introduced her husband who had a firm handshake and said it was good to meet LaStanza.

"Understand you once tried to kiss Belinda." He winked.

They made small talk in low voices. Belinda remembered seeing Kelly with Jodie on one of their canvasses.

"Was he married?"

"No." LaStanza pointed out Kelly's parents and they eased over, fellow victims of sudden violence. He watched Belinda talking with Kelly's mother.

For a moment, LaStanza thought Danny Glover walked in but realized it was the man with the GTO from behind Uptown Square, Shelton Turner, III in a black suit. He went over to shake his hand.

"Where's your tux?" Turner asked.

He told Turner the car he'd seen driving the killer was a blue '77 Olds Cutlass and the driver had been black. Then he told him about Dudley Rich and how he'd killed again the following morning. Turner had put some of it together from the news but didn't realize the entire catastrophe.

"Damn," he said.

"Exactly. Nice of you to come."

"A boy like this dying. Like that young girl I saw die. Damn shame."

LaStanza pointed out Kelly's parents to Turner who went over to talk to them.

Steve Stevens came in a gray suit with a black tie and looked like the new kid in school, knowing no one, talking hesitantly. Paul Snowood also wore a black suit without a hint of western paraphernalia, not even cowboy boots. His wife, Carolyn, looked as if she'd lost weight, looking older and he realized it had been a while since he saw her. She looked angry.

LaStanza father came in with Fred Jersey. His father's belly was too large for him to button his black sport coat and Jersey wore a green polo shirt and jeans.

"I hate these things," Captain LaStanza said. He actually loved funerals and read the newspaper obits every day to see who he knew that had died, people he'd gone to school with, people he'd met on the job, drunks from the barrooms he frequented.

What he didn't like was Metairie Cemetery. Most cemeteries had a barroom across the street. This cemetery had the interstate across the street and was surrounded by residential areas.

Left Sider entered with several other officers, all in uniform. Stan Smith wore an immaculately pressed uniform with its shoulders taken in to mold to his muscles. He came up and hugged LaStanza and said, "Brother," all seriously. Then he looked around to see who was watching him as he moved to the viewing parlor.

LaStanza spotted Beau come in, holding the door for two elderly women. Beau wore a charcoal gray suit the same shade as Lizette's dress and a black tie, white shirt. He was the one who drew looks from people as he eased through the crowd. Lizette had told LaStanza that Beau didn't know how good looking he was, or was smart enough to keep it to himself. Lizette found him charming.

Beau came up and shook LaStanza's hands and said there was a traffic jam outside.

"Wait 'til tomorrow."

Deputy Chief Jim Morris came in with a host of ranking officers. The funeral home was filling quickly and LaStanza went to find his wife. He spotted Sheila Glapier wiping her eyes with a Kleenex as she sat with Jodie, Lizette standing next to the sofa.

Fred Jersey arrived as LaStanza moved up and put his arm around his wife's waist. Jersey said it was nice seeing her again. Very nice. He smirked and moved away.

"What's with him?" LaStanza.

"Weren't you the one who told me cops always have hard-ons?"

"Old fool hitting with my wife right in front of me."

Oh, brother, thought Lizette.

LaStanza spied Pauli and Gail Venetta heading his way and a hint of red hair behind them. Pauli shook LaStanza's hand as Lori Venetta came around from behind her father. Those large, dark brown eyes locking on LaStanza who turned and took Lizette's hand and introduced her. Lori turned that lingering stare to Lizette.

"We're so sorry about Officer Kelly," Gail said. "What a tragedy." She noticed Jodie move up and smiled sadly, then told Lizette how her husband and Jodie and that tall officer, indicating Beau in the background, came to their home and how LaStanza had told them, "You don't know me, but I always get them. *Always.* Sent shivers through us."

She looked at Jodie and her eyes filled with tears. Everyone had to take a step back to let people pass to the parlor.

Pauli spoke to Lizette now. "What my wife's trying to say is – how do we come up with people like your husband and Officer Kintyre and Beau and Kelly, how we keep coming up with people who do what they do is – a little amazing I guess."

Lizette's head nodded slightly, but she missed nothing, spotting the look in the pretty redhead's eyes as she stared at LaStanza. A woman knows that look. She glanced at her husband who pulled his eyes away from the redhead, gave Lizette a long, knowing look and squeezed her hand.

Lori sign languages her parents before reaching through the group to hand Jodie a note: *Didn't we see Officer Kelly with you at the Camellia Grill?*

"That was Kelly."

Lori looked away from Jodie's sad eyes, looked toward someone edging into their crowd. Paul Snowood said, "Well if ain't the perfect woman!" He reached his hand out and Lori had no choice but to shake it.

LaStanza made the introductions. "Gail, Pauli and Lori Venetta, this is Detective Paul Snowood. He works with us but not on the important cases."

Snowood looked hurt for a second before he said, "Yeah? I'm the guy who solved the Louisiana Sniper Case."

Lori wrote a note and it handed LaStanza. He held it so Lizette could read: *Why did he call me the perfect woman?*

Oh, no. Where was that Star Trek transporter machine when you really needed it?

Fel, now standing behind LaStanza, read the note and said, "Snowy thinks you're perfect because you're beautiful and you can't talk. A beautiful woman without all the yapping seems perfect to him."

Lori blanched and Snowood smiled at the recognition of his brilliance.

"That what you think?" A.D.A. Donna Jamison asked Fel.

"Not me!" Fel nodded toward Country-Ass. "He's our village idiot." Fel nosed toward Donna. "I like talking with women."

"Don't be offended," Jodie told Lori. "You meet his wife and you'll understand."

Snowood nodded, then looked around in case Carolyn was in range.

It was Mark who saved them, leaning in and asking where the coffee was. Fel and Donna led the way.

Lizette squeezed her husband's hand hard and pulled him close, whispered. "What's going on with the redhead?"

"Not a damn thing."

She stopped and looked into his eyes. He was going to try a joke about Fred Jersey but kept it serious, looking back at Lizette. He reached over and brushed a strand of her hair that was clinging to her bright red lipstick. Then he brushed his lips across those full lips.

If she can't see the love in my eyes –

But he could see she could and she sighed. Still holding his hand, Lizette turned to follow the others. Just before they stepped into the refreshments room, she said, "I don't like that woman." Lizette rarely said anything like that.

They were at two tables, Jodie sitting with Beau and Glapier on either side. Fel and Donna sat with them. Mark and now Mason moved to the adjacent table. Everyone already had coffee, Mark had a glazed and a chocolate doughnut.

"Glad we escaped," LaStanza said, "before Vada Ganoush showed up with Piso Mojado."

He went to the pot marked "Coffee-and-chicory" and fixed his wife and himself a cup.

Beau told him, "I just put in a transfer to Homicide."

"I knew you were cursed," LaStanza quipped.

Glapier said she did too.

"Thought you were smarter." LaStanza said with a wink, joining his wife, Mark and Mason.

Snowood stepped in and announced, "Didja' know a cougar'll turn on ya'?"

Everyone moaned.

Snowood wasn't discouraged. "Outta nowhere, Penelope tore up the sofa and trashed the entire livin' room."

"You call your mountain lion, Penelope?" It was Glapier. She still hadn't learned not to encourage him by talking to the village idiot.

"Yeah, she's a girl."

"She just trashed your living room without a reason?"

"She doesn't need a reason," LaStanza had to cut in. "It's cooped up in a freakin' house."

Lizette leaned close. "He's got a mountain lion?"

"Long story."

"Actually," Snowood said as he mixed his coffee, "it was the vacuum cleaner. The old lady cranked up the vacuum and Penelope went stone freakin' crazy. Sliced up the sofa, knocked over the TV."

Jodie rubbed her temples, eyes closed now. "Cats and vacuums don't mix. I have to put mine in the bathroom or they'll bounce off the walls. Why didn't Carolyn just turn it off?"

"She did, soon as Penelope started in on the sofa. When I got home and saw all the mess I didn't believe her, so I turned on the vacuum myself. That's when she knocked over the TV. Ever seen a mountain lion run around the walls? I mean runnin' sideways along the freakin' walls. Knocked every picture down."

Mark coughed up coffee through his nose. Lizette had tears in her eyes trying so hard not to laugh. Fel roared, slapping the table. Even Mason was laughing, quieter of course as the civilians in the room gave them a stern look.

Carolyn Snowood looked in, nodded to her husband and Snowood hurried out with his coffee.

"He needs to go back to dressing monkeys in a traveling

circus," LaStanza said when the laughing stopped.

"What?" – Lizette.

"We wouldn't be here if he hadn't said he was bored." LaStanza watched the recognition move from Jodie to Mark. "He started the Good Friday carnage with his goddamn big mouth."

A tall man shushed LaStanza. "Watch your language. We're Christians here."

"Christians?" LaStanza glared at the man. "As in the Spanish Inquisition? The Thirty Years War? Like Hitler and Goebbels and Goring? They were good goddamn Christians!"

The man left the room and Lizette tugged her husband's sleeve.

"What?" he turned to her. "You're the one told me about the Nazis being good Christians."

When they went back out, after finishing their coffee, LaStanza spotted a thoroughly uncomfortable looking Lori Venetta with Steve Stevens. She passed him a note and he looked at it, jotted something on the back and handed it back to her.

LaStanza pointed it out to Lizette. "Actually we have two village idiots. She can hear."

Thursday, April 17, 1986

6:20 a.m. – Milan Street

"Yow. Yow."

Cody climbed on Jodie and cried that kitty cry and she woke bemoaning how she'd taken them to be fixed too early so they'd never develop that deep male meow.

"Yow. Yow," went Cody, nuzzling around her neck until she pulled open the sheet and he could squirm under, then move around beneath the sheet until he aggravated her enough to get up or until Shane attacked the lump in the sheet and both would hiss and "Yow!"

Then it hit Jodie.

Kelly and the funeral. She looked at her clock, then closed her eyes.

A tear rolled down her cheek, then another. Shane jumped up on the bed and she felt his whiskers brush her face. She wiped the tears and Shane rubbed the side of his face against hers and began purring.

She had shocked them when she came home Monday night, lay face down on her bed and crying so loudly she thought she'd wake her parents next door. The cats have been following her around the place ever since, watching her, knowing she was suffering.

Cody poked his head from beneath the sheet and she noticed how much bigger it was than Shane's noggin. Cody had developed one of the over-sized tomcat heads, like a football with ears, probably because he was stockier. Shane as tall and thin with the elegant build of a mountain lion.

She smiled, envisioning Snowood with a vacuum and his cougar taking to the walls, ears pressed down, claws tearing at everything, trying its best to find a way out. She pulled both hands from under the sheet and petted her boys for a minute before climbing out of bed and going in to re-fill their food dish and start her coffee.

She had to go to her lover's funeral.

8:10 a.m. – Exposition Boulevard
"I couldn't pay for better press than that."

The South Louisiana Sniper case was demoted to page two as more articles about the bombing of Libya filled the front page, along with a report of three British hostages executed in retaliation in Beirut.

"And to think most people believe the Garden of Eden was in the Middle East." Lizette shook her head as she and her husband sat at their kitchen counter with their coffee and newspaper.

LaStanza had the metro section. Its front page featured another article about Dudley Rich, a fairly accurate article, by newspaper standards, with another picture of Kelly, not as big as the one in yesterday's paper.

An article below caught LaStanza's eye.

Cop is Judge and Jury, byline Dick Leeka.

LaStanza read the opening lines aloud, "The job of homicide detective, purported to be the most difficult in law enforcement, involves building meticulous cases against those who commit the ultimate crime – murder, unless you're NOPD Homicide Detective Dino LaStanza, who takes the short cut, often bypassing the judge and jury. A decorated twelve year veteran, LaStanza is the reigning champion, shooting more suspects than any other New Orleans cop, more than any other active officer in the U.S."

Lizette looked suddenly pale.

"Dick Licker," LaStanza snarled. "He's the one let go from two TV stations. Remember him describing an escaped prisoner from Parish Prison as 'extremely armed and dangerous'? How the fuck do you get extremely armed?"

"He the one who kept saying igernance instead of ignorance?"

"That's him. Outside a murder scene he said the bodies were found in the alleged kitchen. Kept calling the Ninth Ward, the Nynt. Bragging he's from the Nynt Ward. He's at the paper now. They have proofreaders, allegedly."

LaStanza read the rest of the article, seeing himself described as a man with "a penchant for extreme violence." Dick Licker described every police-involved shooting where the name LaStanza surfaced, even the ones where LaStanza never fired a shot, like the Dryades Street Shooting and the shootings of Jose Luis Garcia and Billy Boy Robbins.

Licker didn't bother mentioned Garcia was one of the men who killed LaStanza's brother and how Robbins killed Homicide Detective Millie Suzanne right in front of LaStanza. As an addendum, the article did acknowledge every shooting was found justifiable by the department and separate Grand Juries. Dick Licker added how the Gunfight at the O.K. Corral was found to be justified too but that left a town filled with bodies.

Jesus. The O.K. Corral. Just encourage Snowood, why don't you.

He and Lizette switched sections so she could read up on her husband while he read up on the murderers in the Middle East. When she put the paper down and said she was getting into the shower, he told her, "If I was in private practice, I couldn't pay for better press than that." He pointed to Leeka's article.

"What?"

"You hire a private investigator, you want someone a little dangerous, someone who could take care of business. Someone people would be reluctant to cross."

Lizette gave him a curious look.

10:35 a.m. – Metairie Cemetery

"Why is that woman laughing?"

It should have been raining, but the sun shined so brightly LaStanza had to squint behind his gangster glasses. Everyone wore sunglasses, even the priest. A sea of black-clad people surrounded by officers in various shades of blue, khaki, black and green uniforms stood between the concrete sepulchres and brick tombs as two men in kilts played the bagpipes.

The long, sad notes of *Amazing Grace* bounced off the tombs and Lizette, with her eyes closed, was reminded of the great battle downriver, all those young British soldiers bearing down on the well-fortified Americans. The bagpipes had a chilling effect on the rag-tag group of American regulars, Tennessee volunteers, free men of color, pirates and New Orleanians who had considered themselves Spaniards or Frenchmen until the British came. Field artillery, naval guns, squirrel rifles and muskets silenced the bagpipes in Chalmette that foggy January morning. The British suffered over 2,000 casualties, the Americans lost eight men.

When the pipes silenced in Metairie Cemetery, the priest prayed in the ensuing silence. The morning air, thick with the smell of flowers, was also thick with humidity. Fel wiped his brow for the third time as a uniformed NOPD officer played taps.

The crying could be heard now as Kelly's coffin was slid into the family sepulchre, a domed concrete house with multiple levels, some still vacant. The cemetery workers stood aside, waiting to seal up the tomb after everyone left.

LaStanza, Lizette and Jodie waited with the family, Fel and Donna, Mason and his quiet wife, Mark and his slim wife, Glapier and her daughter. The parents were escorted away by the priest. Slowly, the people moved away.

Jodie was the last person to leave.

"Meet you at the mansion," LaStanza told Fel and Donna as they separated for their cars.

Jodie didn't cry, not for the bagpipes, not even for the taps, until she spotted the billboard across I-10 with the laughing middle-aged blonde lady, raised hands open in glee, and the caption below, "We Celebrate Life at Metairie Cemetery!"

She heard Kelly's voice, "Why is that woman laughing?"

And she cried.

11:50 a.m. – Exposition Boulevard

"All this death."

Aunt Brulie was there in her white maids outfit, a small woman, rail thin with skin as dark as tree bark. In fact her arms look like tree branches, wiry muscles wrapped around gnarly bones.

She'd prepared a feast and Lizette had sent out for catered finger sandwiches and vegetable platters, mini-muffuletta sandwiches, boiled shrimp with cocktail and remoulade sauces available. Brulie prepared a huge pot of seafood filé gumbo with white rice, sausage jambalaya and homemade French bread.

Kelly's family said little and ate even less. Relatives who'd come from out of town huddled with them in one corner of the dining room while the others, mostly cops spread out along the first floor of the mansion.

Lizette looked shaky again. LaStanza watched her talking with Glapier and her tall daughter, who must have been eleven or twelve. Lizette wore a black skirt suit, slimming and short with black stockings. She'd curled her hair, which hung past her shoulders. When she stopped talking to listen, LaStanza could see her jitteriness. She only met his eyes in passing and for only a moment.

When Kelly's family left after only a short while, thanking Lizette on their way out, Lizette turned to her husband with another weary look and moved away. Donna Jamison eased over to LaStanza and said she'd overheard the Kellys talking. Someone read the paper. They'd just learned their son was with LaStanza.

It was later, when most had left, that Lizette looked him hard in the eyes and said, "All this death. I can't take it." And he knew, deep in his heart, he could lose her.

He couldn't imagine life without Lizette.

They loved each other fiercely.

But it was there, heavy in the air.

He could lose her.

Friday, April 18, 1986

9:45 a.m. – Constance Street

"It never ends good, does it?"

Fel took Glapier with him to explain to Monique Williams's parents what had happened. They lived in a small wood frame house on Constance just off Jackson Avenue. It was painted a light yellow with white trim, even a white picket fence out front.

Mr. Williams said little, Mrs. Williams even less as they sat in the tiny living room. They both looked smaller and older and worn. A window AC unit had the room cool enough, but Fel still had to wipe his face with his handkerchief as he told them about Dudley Rich and the '77 Olds and how the case was now over.

They nodded and thanked him for coming by but he knew the death of Dudley Rich did little for them. They now knew the bastard who had taken their child away was gone but Monique would never come through that door again.

Ever.

And that left a sick feeling in Felicity Jones' belly as he and Sheila Glapier waked back to their unmarked car.

"It never ends good, does it?" she asked.

"Not for them."

Fel decided it was better to think about his date tomorrow evening with Donna Jamison. Saturday night out on the town. Before leaving the Bureau with Glapier, he'd stopped by Snowood's desk and told him, if he even thought of the word *bored*, he and LaStanza would kidnap Country-Ass, shoot him and dump his body in the Bonnet Carré Spillway for the alligators to eat.

"And we fuckin' mean it."

Snowood chuckled but his heart wasn't in it.

10:20 a.m. – Exposition Boulevard

"All I know is this isn't over."

They'd gone to bed early and woke up late both feeling they'd slept too long. They remained in bed, neither ready to let the day begin.

Finally, it was Lizette who spoke first. "This isn't over.

He didn't know exactly what she meant so he didn't answer.

"Burying Kelly isn't the end of this."

He knew she wasn't talking about the trials, wasn't taking about the Easter Cases. She was talking about him going back to it Monday morning, talking about more deaths and more shootouts.

She said it before, how he lived in death. It was an old story, the job breaking up marriages. No, it wasn't the job. It was the cop who let the job break up the marriage.

"I don't know what to do about it," he admitted.

She rolled over and propped herself up on a elbow, hand holding her head and said, "I'm not talking about that. I'm saying, there's something else bad that's going to happen. I have a premonition. So does Jodie."

"Female intuition?"

"Something like that. All I know is this isn't over."

Jesus. What next?

LaStanza didn't even want to look at the newspaper but did as soon as he'd brought it in. On the front page was a story of another hostage, an American named Peter Kilburn, executed in Beirut.

Maybe this was Lizette's premonition? No. Couldn't be. They've been killing each other in the Middle East forever.

"So what's the plan for the weekend?" he asked his wife.

"I'm going shopping with Jodie today and we're hanging out with her Saturday too, going to the movies. Sunday you and I are having lunch at my parents' house and supper at your parents' house. Capiche?"

"What movie?"

"*Children of a Lesser God.*" Lizette looked at her husband and he crinkled his nose.

"Not a touchy-feely movie."

"OK." She was ready for this. "How about *Platoon?*"

"Saw enough of that shit in real life." LaStanza went to the movie section and spotted a compromise and smiled. "Paul Newman. Tom Cruise. Fast Eddie Felson is back!"

"What?"

"*The Color of Money.* Sequel to *The Hustler.*"

"I'll run it by Jodie."

Flash came in and rested his head on LaStanza's knee.

"Guess it's just you, me and your brother today. How about a run?"

Flash went immediately to the cupboard and for a moment LaStanza wondered if the hound could solve a murder. After all, Snowood solved the South Louisiana Sniper Case.

1:10 p.m. – Milan Street

"Yeah, they could solve murders."

Jodie had awakened early and put the morning to good use cleaning up her place. Now, as she waited for Lizette to pull up, she played with Shane and Cody. Sitting on her sofa with a pile of cat toys she'd picked up while cleaning, she waited until Shane wasn't looking and tossed a fluffy ball next to him. It bounced against him and he jumped, turned and attacked the ball. Satisfied he killed it, he shoved it around with his nose as Cody came over cautiously to make sure it was dead.

She tossed a fuzzy ball in a high arch and it came down between the cats. Both jumped out of the way, Cody immediately attacking the ball while Shane looked up at the ceiling, trying to figure out how the damn thing came down on them.

By the time Lizette came up the front steps there were twenty toys in the middle of the living room floor. Lizette rang the doorbell, which sent the cats scrambling, Cody running his big head into the door frame as they raced down the hall.

"Yeah, they could solve murders."

Lizette drove the Maserati, easier to park on the narrow streets of the French Quarter. She wore a red blouse that showed off her breasts nicely and tight jeans. Jodie was also in jeans and a white blouse. They went shopping, losing themselves among the shops along Royal and Chartres Streets.

They bought only a few things and didn't talk much until on the way home, when Lizette said she couldn't shake the jittery feeling she had.

"Me either," Jodie confessed. "I thought it was about Kelly, but you're right. It isn't that."

"What do you think it is?"

"Something not good."

"That's all I need to hear." And for a moment, Lizette didn't look like a teen-agers or even her proper twenty-five years. She looked older.

Monday, April 21, 1986

2:07 p.m. – Detective Bureau

"Well, it's over, Babe."

LaStanza opens his eyes and pulls his head away from the wall. The shock of the teletype had subsided, somewhat. He stands up and takes in a deep breath before asking the desk sergeant for a box.

"Box?"

"A cardboard box."

"Got an empty copy paper box here."

LaStanza steps around for the box, takes it into the Detective Bureau. Stopping a few steps into the wide squad room he watches Jodie at her desk with the Macintosh his wife brought in, when was that, three weeks ago?

Paul Snowood and Steve Stevens are at their desks engaged in an animated conversation that involves head bobbing. Felicity Jones stands by the coffee table with Sheila Glapier, mixing coffee and engaged in their own animated conversation with plenty of laughing.

LaStanza looks above them, at the emblem, the vulture perched atop a gold star-and-crescent badge and feels a pang in his heart. He takes in a deep breath, walks briskly across the room, straight to his desk and turns on his Macintosh and printer. As they warm up, he opens his desk and starting taking out everything that belongs to him.

Jodie slides a memo across to him, talking to him without looking away from her computer screen. "Crime Lab reports came."

He reads the report which confirmed blood matching the Senoré's extremely rare blood type B, genotype BB, Rh negative was found on the front seat of the '77 blue Olds, along with blood type matching Helen Collingwood's rare AB, Rh positive. Blood type matching Dudley Rich's type O, genotype OO, Rh negative was found on the carpet on the front passenger seat side of the car, along with more blood matching Collingwood's type. Fingerprints of Maurice "Mo" Zedimore, Dudley Rich and Jasper Boykin had been lifted from the interior of the car.

"That isn't all." Jodie holds up another crime lab report. "One of the jeans from the Boykin house had dried blood on it, type B, genotype BB, Rh negative."

LaStanza nods. "Grosetto Venetta's type, barely 1% of the population."

"I got California," Steven loudly announces. "Our women have more plastic than your average car!"

They are doing state license plates again.

"I got Kentucky." Snowood comes right back. "Five million people – Thirteen last names."

"That's West Virginia."

"Naw. West Virginia's is 'One big happy freakin' family – really!'."

"What are you doing?" Jodie asks LaStanza.

He doesn't answer as he stops packing and starts typing on his computer now. It doesn't take long before he pushes the print button, takes out a marks-a-lot and writes across the teletype before sliding it to Jodie. She reads it, looks up at him, reads it again before calling out, "Felicity! Can you come over here?"

Fel steps over with Glapier and Jodie points to the teletype on her desk. She pulls back from it as if it's contagious.

Fel reads it aloud:

TO: All Departments

FROM: Superintendent of Police

ATTENTION: Effective immediately, Detective D. F. LaStanza is transferred from Homicide Division to Records & Identification.

LaStanza had written across it in marks-a-lot, "Like Fuckin' Hell!"

The printer spits out two sheets. LaStanza signs the first, his fingers shaking, so he takes his time signing the second and brings that one into Mason's office, dropping it in front of his lieutenant, who reads it and looked up with a look of genuine pain.

LaStanza pulls out his ID folder and digs out his credentials, putting them on the desk.

"I'm keeping the badge. Keepsake. For a plaque on my wall." He walks back out to his desk and turns off the Macintosh and printer before continuing to pack.

Snowood and Stevens lean over the teletype, reading it now, neither touching it.

"I do not fuckin' believe this," says Country-Ass. Stevens looks at Jodie with those crooked eyes and LaStanza can read his mind. She'll be needing a new partner.

Mason comes out with LaStanza's letter of resignation and showed it to Fel, who sits down in Jodie's chair. Jodie's standing now against the next desk with her arms folded, looking like she's going to pass out.

"It's good Mark's off," she says with a strained voice. "He'd turn grizzly and destroy the place on his way up to maul the Chief."

LaStanza picks up his phone and called Lizette. When she answers he says, "Well, it's over, Babe."

"Over?" She sounded wary.

"Remember the other morning when you said this wasn't over? Well, it is now. I just got transferred to the record room, so I handed in my resignation. I'm coming home, Babe."

"Say that again?"

He does as he places his three mugs into the box, the one with *I'm One Of Those Bad Things That Happens To Good People,* the *Don't Piss Me Off! I'm Running Out Of Places To Hide The Bodies* mug and his old *Fuck This Shit!* mug.

"You're serious?" Lizette's voice is a whispers and he repeats himself.

He hears her breathing heavier now.

"We can have a nice long talk about my future after law enforcement. About our future."

"You bet, mister," – her voice deep with emotion. "You bet."

Fel comes over and leans against LaStanza's desk. He looked pale, skin looking gray. "J.F.C." he said. "J.F.C."

Jesus Fuckin' Christ.

"Don't blame him," LaStanza said with a smile. "He was a murder victim too, remember."

"We gotta do sometin' 'bout this!" Snowood declares.

LaStanza slips his gun into his briefcase and finally looks at Jodie who says, in a low voice, "You don't have to resign. You can work through this."

"They're not making a gelding out of me." He tries smiling. "Give me a lift home?"

Her eyes glisten as she stared at him and he feels a deep stab in his heart.

"We gotta do sometin' 'bout this!" Snowood starts bouncing around. "My God. Ya' can't just set Wyatt Earp out to pasture!"

Jodie turns her computer off and picks up her purse and briefcase. LaStanza puts his briefcase into the box and they started for the door.

"Wait," Fel calls out. "You just gonna leave like that?"

Over his shoulder, LaStanza says, "I'll be back around. I'm not leaving town. I have to talk with my wife right now, Capiche?" He turns around and faced Fel. "You can have the computer."

Snowood comes around and says, "Whoa? Where 'ya goin'? We gotta work this out."

LaStanza backs away with, "Sorry Doc, I don't work here anymore."

It sounds strange and feels stranger, turning away, feeling the heartache again as he heads for the POLICE ONLY elevator with Jodie. They have to wait, as usual and he can see she's breathing heavier.

She turns those cat eyes to him and says, "What are you going to do, really?"

He smiles at his favorite partner. "I'll think of something."

THE END

Note from the Publisher
BIG KISS PRODUCTIONS

If you found a typo or two in the book, please don't hold it against us. We are a small group of volunteers dedicated to presenting quality fiction from writers with genuine talent. We tried to make this book as perfect as possible, but we are human and make mistakes.

BIG KISS PRODUCTIONS and the author are proud to sell this book at as low a cost as possible. Even *great* fiction should be affordable.

For more information about the author go to
http://www.oneildenoux.net
•

"O'Neil De Noux ... No one writes New Orleans as well as he does." James Sallis

"… the author knows his stuff when it comes to the Big Easy." *Publisher's Weekly*, 3/13/06

O'Neil De Noux would like to hear from you. If you liked this book or have ANY comment, email him at
denoux3124@yahoo.com

Also by the Author
Novels
Grim Reaper
The Big Kiss
Blue Orleans
Crescent City Kills
The Big Show
Mafia Aphrodite
Slick Time
John Raven Beau
Battle Kiss
Enamored
Bourbon Street
Mistik
Short Story Collections
LaStanza: New Orleans Police Stories
New Orleans Confidential
New Orleans Prime Evil
New Orleans Nocturnal
New Orleans Mysteries
New Orleans Irresistible
Hollow Point & The Mystery of Rochelle Marais
Backwash of the Milky Way
Screenplay
Waiting for Alaina
Non-Fiction
A Short Guide to Writing and Selling Fiction
Specific Intent

LaStanza Books by O'Neil De Noux
http://www.oneildenoux.net/dx/LASTANZA.html

O'NEIL DE NOUX

GRIM REAPER

LaStanza
1

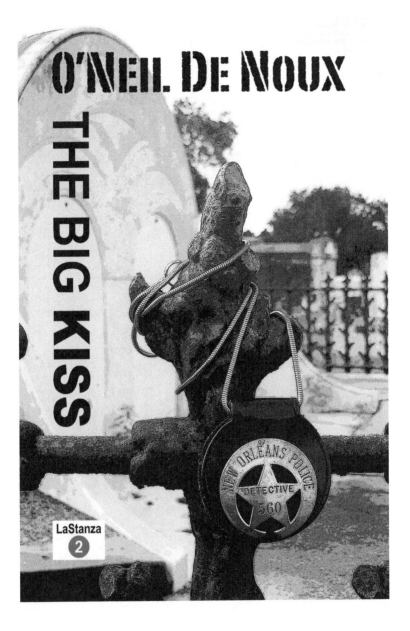

O'NEIL DE NOUX

THE BIG KISS

LaStanza
2

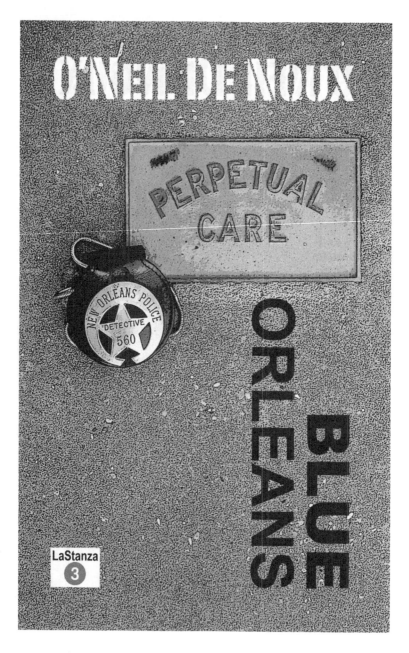

O'NEIL DE NOUX

PERPETUAL CARE

NEW ORLEANS POLICE
DETECTIVE
560

BLUE ORLEANS

LaStanza
3

CRESCENT
CITY
KILLS

O'NEIL DE NOUX

LaStanza
4

THE BIG
SHOW

LaStanza
5

O'NEIL DE NOUX

don't miss the short story collection which begins when
Dino LaStanza is a patrolman –

More LaStanza novels coming –

OTHER BOOKS by O'Neil De Noux
http://www.oneildenoux.net

CPSIA information can be obtained at www.ICGtesting.com
Printed in the USA
LVOW01s1604110114

369059LV00035B/1015/P